IMPERFECT

IMPERFECT

Claire Fraise

ISBN: 1511660740
ISBN 13: 9781511660747

To Papa, Mum and Tristan

Earth is a mess.

A genuine, freaking mess.

I'm not talking about the kind of mess you get after not cleaning your room for three months. That kind of mess is easily fixed by a long, painstaking cleanup while jamming out to the radio as you throw all your belongings into a massive heap in the hallway.

No. This kind of mess is the result of humans living on the earth for thousands upon thousands of years, changing and molding our society and the planet itself as if they were Play-Doh. It's the kind of mess that can be blamed solely on human nature and pure idiocy.

Honestly, I don't know how people managed to do it.

⋏   ⋏   ⋏

The air bites viciously at my nose as I walk down the streets of the demolished city. Icy rain is pouring down around me, melting the snow and making the road thick with slush. I pull my hood farther down over my head and breathe onto my hands in an attempt to protect them from the February chill.

In the Slump, the sky is always gray. Even in the early morning glow, the buildings around me look like something found in the oldest movies—the ones on the large, unwieldy tapes that no one has the archaic technology or the desire to play anymore. I don't know if the gray hue is a direct consequence of the bombings of the

Second Civil War—which tore up what was known as the United States prior to the Great Divide—but it's been that way for as long as I can remember.

I skulk through the jungle of ruined skyscrapers. They look as if they were once fed a steady diet of grenades. Some are simply ash, and the ones still standing look like they would collapse at the touch of a finger. It's hard to believe that this was ever a living city.

Yellow Pox wiped out more than half the population following the war. Most people blame the epidemic on a chemical used in the explosives. In the end, the land was split into seven regions—states, if you will—during the time known as the Great Divide. Each region is now ruled by a single, huge corporation, which in turn is controlled by its CEO. Making Perfect took over the region where I live and rebuilt it from the ashes.

Rebuilt it, that is, except for the Slump—the outermost ring of land, closest to the border fence, which acts as a buffer between Making Perfect's territories and those of its neighbors. After the plague, the remaining victims were sent here to die. Now, it is crawling with outcasts—the unemployed, orphans, and the elderly. This is where I have found refuge for myself, my two sisters, and our dog, Theo. I don't remember what the city was once called. Today, it is just the Slump, a city of ruins.

Every corporation performs a specific function that drives the economy. They trade with each other for the things they need. For instance, Knox, located down south, controls the distribution and production of food. Nova controls the national electric grid—it's a small region that is covered almost border-to-border with power plants. Both Spark and TERC (short for Technological Equipment and Relations Corporation) mass-produce all of the weaponry and technological gadgets used to protect and run the country. Sidra makes the clothing, and TT Water filters all the drinking water and designs the drainage. Then there's Making Perfect.

Making Perfect focuses primarily on genetic research—it creates various drugs and enhancements in order to improve and perfect the human race. Their research is highly classified, but some of the products they have released are mind-blowing: Limb regeneration for amputees. Cures for even the most serious ailments. Name anything, and Making Perfect is working on it.

My dad was one of their head scientists.

I spot movement from the corner of my eye and motion for Theo to stop. The graying shepherd sits promptly at my heels, his eyes trained on me. The street is so silent that I can hear my own breaths. Suddenly, a hooded figure springs out from behind a Dumpster and dashes across the street. It doesn't see me. Good. My hand slips into my jacket and closes around the slick handle of my pocketknife. It's not only useful for ripping open the market's garbage bags—it can also be used defensively. Having it close provides a wisp of comfort.

I know people who have died in brawls. Competition for resources in the Slump is no joke.

The figure vanishes around the corner and I pick up my pace to a jog, being careful not to slip on the icy road. The market is a decent walk from where I live—about forty-five minutes on a good day, half an hour if I sprint. It's right on the border between the Slump and the townhouse district, and it acts as a paltry source of food and supplies for most of the Slump's inhabitants. Theo brushes against my leg as we slip into an alley, letting out a thin whine. He is as desperate and hungry as I am.

My breaths heavy, I stop and lean against a wall. The pungent scent of spray paint lingers in the air, exacerbating the dull ache in my head. The graffiti opposite me looks fresh. I try to make out what the words say, but they swim in front of me. I brace my hands against my knees to keep myself from passing out.

I haven't been in an amazingly good mood this morning. Besides the fact that we have no food, I woke up to find my older sister, Tory, coughing blood into her pillow. By the time I cleaned up the mess and wrapped some extra blankets around her, I needed to get away. Our whole room is beginning to smell like death.

I really hoped that her sickness was pneumonia, but now I know that I was wrong. A plague-like illness has been traveling around the Slump all winter. People are calling it Red Pox. Like Yellow Pox, everyone who contracts the sickness starts coughing and ends up coughing out blood, hallucinating, and losing their ability to breathe. Nobody knows why this strain of the illness has suddenly flared up, but there doesn't seem to be a cure. Whoever contracts it usually has only a few days left.

But Tory doesn't need to know that.

Theo nuzzles my leg and I reach down to scratch his ear. Something catches my eye. I snatch up the small object before Theo can get to it. A smile crosses my face. I wipe the frost off the wrapper and realize what it is—a granola bar. Granola bars are hard to find, but I have discovered them to be among the best sustenance available. Finding one on the ground is the equivalent to winning the lottery. Somehow, its wrapper is still intact. I slip it into my pocket, still smiling.

The regions strictly control their borders—no one is allowed in or out unless on official business. I've heard that Making Perfect is particularly meticulous when it comes to this. A monstrous fence, topped with nasty coils of barbed wire and paralyzing electric cables, surrounds the region and prevents anyone without authorization from passing through.

So now one can add "brutal border control" to the list of reasons not to live here—right below Making Perfect's *impeccable* children's rights policies.

Every couple of months, company officials come into the Slump and collect as many children as they can, transporting them to various institutions—prisons—around the region. It is illegal for minors to live alone, even in the Slump. I've come to the conclusion that while Making Perfect doesn't really care about the kids' well-being, news that the company allows minors to live alone could severely jeopardize its relationships with the other corporations. It might even run the risk of being shut down.

So, Making Perfect's solution is this: put orphaned and abandoned minors in confinement until they reach the age of eighteen, then give them a job in the corporation and force them to work. Tory is over eighteen, but she doesn't have an ID to prove it. Nobody here does—if we're taken, we can't say anything in our own defense. It's a sick joke. Those who are taken never return, and they never see their families again.

Today is expected to be the company's collecting day. That's why I'm feeling on edge.

Like I said, this world is a mess.

I didn't want to leave Tory and Lily alone this morning, but I had no choice. We have no food. Yesterday, we had nothing to eat at all. I can't put this morning off any longer.

Theo and I move silently and steadily. A glance at my watch tells me that I've been traveling for about half an hour. I round the corner and am greeted by the shiny metal statue of a DNA double helix standing in the street. A large golden plaque at the bottom reads: MAKING PERFECT, INC. The company likes to decorate the Slump with statues and memorials that constantly remind us of its presence. I pass this one regularly on my food runs.

I glance up at the fence towering over me. On the other side of it, the TERC region begins. As far as I can see, the land near the fence is nothing but overgrown grasses and forest. Sometimes, on clear days, I think I can see the city that houses TERC—shiny, white skyscrapers that reach into the clouds. I wonder what it would be like to live outside the control of Making Perfect.

I wonder if their lives are better than mine.

"Summer?"

I spin around to see Tyler standing just a few feet behind me. His bright green eyes look at me from under his disheveled dark curls, which have a silver sheen in the fading moonlight. He's holding something in his hand, although I'm too far away to make out what it is.

"Hey," I say softly, taking a step toward him. Tyler is my best friend. We grew up together, took our first steps together, and were even dumped in the Slump together. Since he's a couple of months older than me, I literally have never known a world without him in it. He's the only person who can tolerate me for hours on end and who manages to keep me sane. Personality-wise, we're pretty much complete opposites, but that's probably the reason we're so close. We balance each other out.

Sometimes I wonder if anything hurts Tyler at all. He has always been better than me at hiding his pain. The exception was when his older brother, Sean, abandoned him and his younger siblings. Nobody knows whether he ran away or was taken by Making Perfect, but nobody has seen him since. After that, Tyler seemed to become empty for a while. He didn't eat or talk. It took me weeks to get him functioning again. I think having to look out for him helped me cope with everything. If I had been alone, I probably wouldn't still be here.

As for Tyler, I always thought he was slightly different after that. Slightly less trusting.

I guess it's called growing up.

"Did you eat?" I ask and he shakes his head.

"Not hungry."

Liar. You're always hungry when you live in the Slump. I narrow my eyes. "What's wrong?"

"Nothing. I'm fine." He shakes his head again, rubbing the sleep out of his eyes. "You look like you haven't slept in days."

"I haven't," I admit. I've found it impossible to sleep at all for the past week. I've spent my nights turning in bed, listening for any sign of officials barging into the hotel. If I sleep through the raid, it will mean definite capture for all of us. "If I'm not awake and they come in, what can I do?"

He's silent for a moment before replying. "Come over later so we can alternate watches. That way you can sleep and stop looking like a zombie."

Normally, I would laugh, but my eyelids are too droopy. I want to collapse on the road and never get back up. Ty reaches into his pocket and pulls out a piece of jerky, handing it to me. I look up at him, shaking my head.

"Eat it. You're going to pass out otherwise." He shoves the jerky into my hand. After a slight hesitation, I bite into it gratefully. "And I'm not kidding about coming over later. If you don't, I'm coming over there to carry your ass across the street myself."

"I'll be okay," I say. "Hopefully they'll come today, and we'll evade them." My tongue travels around my mouth, trying to pick up any leftover pieces of jerky that might be stuck in my teeth. This is the hardest part of not getting enough food—after eating what little you get, you constantly crave more. The hunger worsens for hours before it dies down.

At that moment, Tyler buckles inward, and a set of coughs rips through him. He clutches his chest roughly, like he's in pain, and turns away from me. I start toward him, but he stops coughing as quickly as he started.

"What was that? What's going on?" I turn him around to face me and gasp. Up close, he looks terrible. His face is as pale as the moon, and his eyes—which were already tired and dark—are completely bloodshot. My eyes widen in worry.

"It's not as bad as you think," Tyler spits out quickly.

I say exactly what he knows I'm about to say. "Why didn't you tell me it was this bad? Look at you!"

"I'm really okay. I promise. I—"

"Of course it's not okay. You look terrible," I snap, crossing my arms over my chest.

"I'm good; I swear. I'm just tired, and it's a little cold out. I'll be okay in a few days."

I glare at him. "And what if you're not? What's gonna happen then? I swear to God, if you—"

"Don't worry about me, okay? I'm *fine*." I wince at the sudden harshness in his voice, and I can see that he instantly regrets his tone. His expression softens, and he pulls me into his arms. I hold him tightly, resting my chin on his shoulder.

"Don't die on me, okay?" My voice is barely audible, but he hears it. I feel him take my trembling hand in his. He gives it three small squeezes—our special handshake from when we were kids.

"I'm not going anywhere. I promise. We've got to go, or we're gonna miss the truck."

I pull away from him and glance at my watch: 4:48 a.m. He's right—we only have ten minutes.

After checking that the granola bar and my knife are both still in my pocket, I call Theo over with a light pat on my thigh and start forward. I know Tyler is right behind me. He always is.

The market is right at the end of this street, so we're practically there. We have to arrive early, though, if we're going to get anything good.

Already, I can sense the presence of the other people in the shadows around the pile of plastic garbage bags. The truck hasn't come yet, but it will. Ten minutes.

We crouch behind a small pile of black bags to wait.

The "market" is what Slump dwellers call the giant pile of garbage bags on the border, where the townhouses' garbage is dumped. It provides the majority of our food, belongings, clothes, and supplies. Most people would turn their noses up at the things we find here, but when you've spent enough time living like this, you learn not to be picky.

The stench of garbage is overwhelming, but I've gotten used to it. I pull out my knife and clean it with the edge of my sweatshirt. I sharpen it frequently to make sure it will cut quickly through the plastic bags that the truck leaves behind. The daily haul depends on what the people in the townhouses throw out. Decent food is scarce; the haul is normally things like banana peels or empty yogurt containers. It's rare that you find anything edible. That's why everybody is so desperate.

My hand clasped around the knife, I glance back at Tyler, who's as tense as a spring. He goes to the market on behalf of his family as well. He has four siblings that he holds as close as I do mine: nineteen-year-old Sean, ten-year-old Michael, and six-year-old Riley. My parents were close friends with Tyler's parents. Like Dad, Ty's father was also an acclaimed Making Perfect scientist and had to commute to the facilities daily. I've always found it a little weird that both Tyler and I were left in the Slump at the same time, but I'm so thankful to have him with me that I don't think about it much.

Just recently, Riley got sick. Tyler rarely talks about it, but her symptoms resemble those of Red Pox. He has been working extra hard to find food and clothes for her, but because of her young age and already-weak immune system, we have no idea how much longer she's going to hold on. And now, he's beginning to show symptoms, too. I push back the fear fizzing up in my chest.

The earth rumbles under my feet, signaling the imminent arrival of the truck.

The large, cumbersome, vomit-colored garbage truck rumbles into view on my right. Nimble black shadows jump out of the way like fleas as the vehicle enters the square. Old, rotting bags are crushed under the giant wheels. Intense anticipation causes my body to feel like a rubber band being stretched. Both Tyler and I are ready to make a run for it as soon as the truck is out of sight. Fog comes out of my mouth like a dragon in the biting cold, and the thin sheet of ice beneath my fingers on the sidewalk sends the occasional chill through my body.

I hold my breath as the truck drives toward us. It rolls around to the far side of the garbage pile, where I can barely see it. Damn it! My haul strictly depends on the placement of the bags. I watch as the back of the truck opens and dumps a mountain of garbage bags onto the pile. I suck in a breath, ready for the sprint to the other side. Inside the truck, white-clad officials squint as they look around for any sign of trouble. They see none, and the truck loudly rumbles out of sight, leaving the air filled with exhaust.

If they only knew.

There's no chance to even take a breath before the square explodes with movement. People of all shapes and sizes spring out from hiding everywhere, brandishing knives and dashing for the black garbage bags. I don't have to think twice before I'm running, too. Theo is by my side. My lungs burn from the frigid air as I leap over scattered garbage and dodge other kids to reach the new pile of bags.

Most of the bags have already been torn open by the time I reach them. Various kids and teenagers swarm over the garbage like rats, grabbing anything they can. With a leap, I soar over their heads and land straight in the pile. Something tears through my pant leg, but I ignore it. I pull out my knife and start ripping open the bags that Theo indicates have food in them.

Nothing. There's absolutely nothing. I pull out plastic wrappers, moldy potatoes, banana peels, metal wires, and crumpled-up paper covered in some sort of brown juice. I can't find anything useful. I lift a handful of something putrid and crawling with maggots before quickly returning it to the bag. Already, most of the kids that were here have disappeared, and most of the bags are empty. I look around for Tyler, but he's also gone.

Ugh.

I shove my freezing, filthy, repulsive hands back into my pockets with a scowl. I can't believe it. Empty-handed and fuming, I run back to the alley where I was hiding with Ty. At least I still have the granola bar, though I have nothing else for Lily and Tory this morning. That isn't enough to feed two people for a whole day. No matter how much I try to reassure myself, I feel like I've let them down.

As I round the corner, I feel around for my pocketknife and let out a cry of frustration.

It's gone. I must've dropped it in the garbage.

"Uh oh," Tyler says when I run up to him, seeing the expression on my face. He is leaning against the DNA statue and is also empty-handed. "Nothing?" I nod. I need to find something for my sisters. They can't go another full day without food.

But neither can Tyler. He gives all of his food to Michael and Riley and probably hasn't eaten in days. I don't know if it's the sickness, lack of sleep, or lack of food, but this is probably the skinniest I've ever seen him. I clench my teeth to prevent them from chattering and hand him the granola bar from my pocket. He shakes his head.

"Please, take it," I say. "You look like a ghost. If you're not going to eat it, at least give it to Riley."

"What about you?"

"I'll be okay."

"I'm not taking this, Summer."

"Please?"

He shakes his head, pushing away from the statue. Something's off—I can see it in his eyes. He hands me back the bar, and I take it reluctantly. Turning to go, he says, "I can't walk back today. I have to go pick up something for Riley. Be safe today, okay? I'll drop by later."

I nod. "Tomorrow?"

"Tomorrow." And he's gone.

2

On my way home, I decide to stop at the convenience store. Because it's my backup source of food and my only supply of drinking water, it's a trip that I have to make often. There is a huge river not far from the hotel, but who knows if it's safe to drink from. It's most likely contaminated with chemicals or with the plague-ridden bodies of the dead. Though the market is essential to everyone in the Slump, anyone who doesn't have a Plan B has a one-way ticket to death. My Plan B sucks, but at least I have one.

Every few days, I risk the walk downtown. Three miles south of the hotel, there are a couple of old convenience stores. I discovered them a few months ago. Anybody who looks at them from the outside would think they're just more ruins. Glass and debris litter the sidewalk in front of them, and rubble is piled up high, blocking each entrance. There are ways in, though, if you know how to find them. Whenever I go, I load up on as much bottled water and canned food as I can fit into my backpack—which isn't much—and get back to the hotel as fast as I can. Dawn and dusk are the safest times to travel—it's dark enough to hide, but light enough to see easily.

I reach the street and make a sharp left to face the buildings. The sun is beginning to rise, casting a pale light across the landscape. The city is coming alive, and I can't help noticing all the people starting to come out. With a few precautionary glances, I dash across the street, slip into the alley, and climb into the store through the side window, being careful not to touch any of the menacing glass shards poking out of the sill.

But I'm not careful enough. I lose my footing and slip, crying out in pain and surprise as I feel one of the shards cut through my shin. I kick out instinctively, striking one of the piles of rubble that tower precariously just inside the window. As I touch down on the hard, tile floor, the rubble collapses, blocking the only way out.

"No!" My scream comes out as a whisper. I dart up, trying to ignore the searing pain in my leg, and place my hands in the slats of a pallet in the center of the pile. I start to push, hoping to move the rubble out of the way, but then I stop myself. Causing the crash was the equivalent of sending up a flare saying: Look at me! I'm right here! The noise required to move the pile will be even worse. If I leave before filling my pack, the risk will have been for nothing.

Theo barks once on the other side. This makes me cringe, but I reassure myself that Theo knows he should wait.

I slowly sit against the crumbling wall and roll up my pant leg, exposing a three-inch cut in my skin. The glass is still inside it. Gritting my teeth, I wipe my hands off on my pants and yank out the shard. The crimson-tipped glass clatters onto the floor beside me and I hiss in a pained breath. Blood starts to ooze more quickly out of the wound. I wish I had my pocketknife with me, or water, or anything to help me treat the gash. Reluctantly, I slide off one of my sneakers and pull off my sock. Tying it around my leg as tightly as I can, I pull my pant leg back down and hoist myself to a standing position. I'll finish treating the wound when I get home.

And that's when I feel it.

Something is off.

I glance around the room. Everything looks exactly like it did two days ago—the same overturned shelves, the walls so coated with ash that you can barely make out the graffiti behind it, and the floors strewn with cardboard boxes, shattered glass, old candy bars, and rat feces. Parts of the roof have collapsed, leaving hardly any space to stand up in. A broken, overturned cash register sits in the corner, and the front refrigerators have all been stripped of their liquid contents. It's the same corroding, filthy mess that I have been wading through every few days for the past few months.

But something is different.

Silence.

I take a careful step forward, shards of glass crunching softly beneath my feet. Soundlessly, I bend over, grab a long metal pole from the floor, and hold it tightly by my side. I don't want to make a sound—if there is something here, I'm trapped with it. Slowly, I take another step toward the back of the store, where the water and food are.

Before I can take another breath, a soft groan comes from behind the utility door. I freeze. My first instinct is to run, but it doesn't take long to realize that's not an option. Whoever is in there knows about my only supply of drinking water. No one but me can know. I have to do whatever it takes.

I value the lives of my sisters over the life of anyone else in this dump.

So I don't run away. I creep up to the door and push it open with such force that I'm afraid it'll come off its hinges. Darting around the corner toward the storage room, I suck in a breath and crouch down next to the opening. My shadow dances across the threshold.

It might be a trap.

But even if it is, I have to go in.

So I grit my teeth, ready myself for the attack, and slip around the corner.

3

She is crumpled against the wall about six feet away from me, her legs folded beneath her. She can't be much older than me. Eighteen, nineteen maybe, dressed in worn-down combat boots and a ragged, pink sweatshirt. Her left arm is clutching her stomach, and thick crimson blood is seeping through her fingers. She doesn't look armed, but her glossy eyes are glaring at me fiercely.

I instantly point the pole at her and freeze.

"Come to finish me off, have you?" she croaks, her darkly bruised face is contorted into a pained grimace. My jaw clenches. "Well go on, get it over with."

I don't reply and glance around at my surroundings. The whole place has been turned over, the water containers ripped open, and the shelves overturned. Most of the supplies seem to be gone, though I catch a glimpse of a single container of unopened water bottles.

The girl coughs, gritting her teeth to keep herself from screaming. "Don't just stand there; I know who sent you," she sputters, and I cringe.

I clamp my teeth over my tongue as she grins at me. Even her teeth are bloody.

Keep it together, Summer.

She looks like a Black Spider—a ruthless gang that stretches across the entire Slump. Instead of foraging for food, they steal it from others by raiding homes and attacking people on the street. I have even heard stories of them enslaving desperate little girls and boys in exchange for food. They're disgusting but deadly. Though I've always detested the Black Spiders and have avoided them at all costs, I have had occasional encounters with them. Near-death experiences.

But what's she doing here?

I don't say anything. I just grip the pole tighter.

"What's your problem? Kill me already!" Her voice is raspy when she speaks.

Sweat sticks my hair to my forehead. Kill her? I don't even know who she is.

I don't take my gaze off the girl's dark, almost black eyes as I lower the pole to the floor.

As the metal hits the ground, the girl throws her head back with a cry of agony. I stand there, motionless, as her body shakes. Her shoulders curl over and she clutches her chest. I can't tell what is wrong with her, exactly, but judging by the amount of blood gushing from her torso, I assume that whoever did this expected her to bleed out in this room.

She meets my gaze. "Listen," she spits out through gritted teeth. The flickering lights of the room are bouncing off her face. "I need help. It's obvious you didn't come on their behalf. So you can either help me, or you can take what you came for and kill me. At this point, I'd prefer the latter." My knees begin to shake. I don't know why I'm suddenly feeling so uncomfortable. "Stop looking at me like that! What do you think I'm going to do, hurt you?"

A moan escapes her lips, and her head hangs down, hair falling into her face. I watch the rapid rise and fall of her chest. She clearly doesn't have much time left.

I know I should try to help her, but I can't. I wouldn't know what to do anyway. Still, something about her keeps me frozen in place. She has so much hope in her eyes when she looks at me.

However, when I don't respond to her pleas, the hope is replaced by complete desperation.

"If you're not going to help me, the least you can do is finish me off quickly," she wails, almost screaming. Her hand slams down against one of the broken wooden crates, her knuckles turning white. Tears begin to stream down her face, and I take a step backward. My body begins to tremble as her hand stretches toward me. Panic flares in my chest. Before I can stop myself, I flinch away, stumbling backward over an empty water container.

"Please—" She shifts forward, reaching for me. I fight the urge to scream. Without another thought, I turn and run from the room as fast as I can. I hear her yelling behind me, words that I can't make out, but I try my best to ignore it as I desperately look for a way out of the building.

I soon find myself back out in the street. I don't remember tearing through the debris blocking the window. My feet pound hard against the gravel as I run back toward the hotel.

I'd like to say that I feel bad for what I did. But I don't. I've been handed my own boatload of suffering. Lily or Tory would have been on their knees to help that girl in a heartbeat. But not me. Of all the people who could have come across her today, it had to be me.

This kind of life can make you pretty hard.

My stomach is tied in knots. For the entire journey home, I'm unable to shake the girl's screams from my head.

4

TYLER

"Ty!"

Michael jumps into my arms instantly as I walk through the door. Even though he's only seven, his weight sends me staggering.

"Hey bud," I say, catching my balance against the wall. I set him down gently, and brush the dirty blond curls out of his face. His bright green eyes, identical to mine, shine with excitement.

"Did you get anything?" he asks. "I'm starving." I avert my eyes. Even though it wasn't my fault that the market haul was bad this morning, he still needs food. He frowns, knowing I didn't.

"How's your sister?" I glance behind him at the mound of blankets lying still on the bed. A clump of matted brown hair peeks out from underneath the blue fleece. I don't see any blood, which is a good sign. Michael shrugs.

"She's still sleeping." He bites on the end of his sweater, tugging on it with his teeth. "I'm hungry," he says again.

"I know." I rub my eyes. So am I. "Hold on, I'll get you something." I lean up from against the wall and shut the open door. Our apartment is small, and brutally simple. There's only one bed, a couch, and a small bathroom right off the kitchen. If it weren't for the running water and good insulation, it would be a pretty dismal place to live. It doesn't have windows, but at least we're not freezing to death.

Walking over to the sink, I reach up and grab a half-eaten box of crackers from the cabinet. Along with two cans of alphabet soup and three bottles of water, it's the only food we have left. I have to store our food reserves up high so neither Michael or Riley will eat them on impulse. I don't even bother to ration the box. I close the cabinet and hand the crackers to Michael. His face lights up.

"Don't eat them all at once," I warn, but he doesn't listen to me. He's already tearing into the box. My stomach lets out an audible groan, but I ignore it. I don't remember the last time I had food, but Summer wasn't wrong when she accused me of not eating in days. My head throbs painfully, and I resist the urge to go lie down on the couch as I walk over to the bed where Riley is sleeping. I sink to my knees and pull the fleece down off her face, finding it stained with thick yellow bile. Wrinkling my nose, I fold it over so the spoiled patch isn't touching her face. She stirs, blinking her eyes open as I set the blanket back down across her little frame.

"Hi, Ri." I try to make my voice sound as gentle as possible. "How are you feeling?"

She moans but doesn't say anything. When she grabs my hand, my mouth dries up. It's frigid. Before I left to meet for the market this morning, I layered all the blankets, towels, and sweatshirts that I could find over her. But it didn't seem to do any good.

"Do you want to eat something?" I ask her. She shakes her head, squeezing her eyes shut. Her lack of appetite worries me. If she's going to get better, she has to eat. I wish I could give her more antibiotics, but I already gave her this morning's dose and have to wait another six hours.

Two days ago, I traveled a few hours south to an old drugstore and managed to find a small bottle of antibiotics. There were only seven pills left, and the label was smudged so I couldn't make out the dosage. I've been cutting the little white tablets in half and giving them to her twice a day. It seems to be working, and I'm praying I'm not overdosing her, but I don't know what I'm going to do when the pills run out.

Riley traces her finger along the outline of the star on the inside of my left thumb. A faint smile forms on my lips. It looks more like a tattoo than a birthmark, but I've always had it. Summer has one too, except hers is right behind her ear. It's always been a joke between us—a sign that we were always destined to be friends. Still, it sometimes strikes me as a little weird that we both have them.

"Ty?" I hear Michael ask behind me, through a mouthful of cracker. Orange crumbs have gathered around his mouth. "Are there any more? I'm still hungry."

Pinching the bridge of my nose, I shake my head. My world swims. "I know. I'll go out and get more later."

Riley turns over again, heaving a sigh as she dozes off. I crawl over to the couch and collapse on my side. Even though I have to go out again later, just the thought of ever moving from this couch is enough to make my chest feel hollow. I'm in no shape to outrun the officials. Since this building doesn't have fire escapes, I have to run out to the street after hiding Michael and Riley in the cabinet behind the sink. I move fast, so I'm always able to evade them, but I don't know if I'll be able to do it today. I'm too tired and too sick.

Just as I'm about to drift off for a few minutes, Michael calls my name, jarring me out of my haze.

"Ty? You sure I can't have any more?"

I suck in a long breath and sit up, wiping my hands down my face. If I'm going to go out again, I should probably go now before the officials come. Telling Michael where I'm going and that I'll be back soon, I grab my pack from the floor and run out the door.

⋏ ⋏ ⋏

SUMMER

"Who is it?" My thirteen-year-old sister, Lily, calls out as I reach our threshold. I wipe my fingers over the dusty, silver plaque, uncovering the numbers *409* that label our door. The old hotel that my sisters and I live in is one of the most intact buildings remaining in the Slump, though the lights on its old sign have long since gone out. We lucked out in the housing department—it's nice to sleep without having to worry about the roof collapsing on your head.

I push the door open, cringing as the rusty hinges make a loud creak. Theo trots inside, and I follow him.

"Good, it's just you," Lily snaps. "What took you so long?" Her tone is curt, sounding more like criticism than a conversation-starter. She drops down from the escape ladder that leads up to the ceiling. Tory is waiting at the bottom of the ladder for her turn to climb up. I scowl. If this was any other situation, they would look funny, like they're part of a circus. But they were in plain sight when I opened the door, and these kinds of mistakes can be deadly.

"If I was an official, you'd have been taken."

"But you *aren't*, so we're still here," Lily retorts. She definitely takes after my mom in both looks and personality. Her deep-brown hair reaches just below her shoulders, and her ocean-blue eyes shine even under her giant, crooked, black-rimmed glasses. One of the hinges of her glasses broke recently. We did our best to tape them, but it didn't really work. "Nothing?" she says.

I shrug and pull the granola bar from my pocket.

"Is that all?" Lily asks, but she quickly grabs the bar from my hand. She breaks it in half and gives a piece to Tory. Tory looks at me before they eat. I nod to tell her that I've already eaten. It's a relief to watch them eat. Another weight off my shoulders—at least, until the next meal.

I take after Dad. From afar, one would assume my eyes to be blue-green, maybe, depending on what I'm wearing. But up close, they become a piercing, gunmetal tone. Messy golden hair falls onto my shoulders, and my face is completely covered in freckles.

Lily and Tory, however, look more closely related to each other than either of them does to me. Sometimes I doubt if I'm even their sister—maybe I'm the victim of some sort of baby swap. But, I must say, Tory's brown locks and fair features are much more complemented by her navy T-shirts than mine would be.

"How's Riley?" Tory asks, chewing vigorously.

"Hanging in there," I answer. "Tyler looks like he hasn't slept in years." I walk over to the ladder and tuck it back behind the dresser.

"He stopped by about half an hour ago," Lily remarks, finishing her piece of the bar. "Wanted to see if you were here. Said he needed to ask you something."

I rub my eyes. My muscles are becoming more tired by the second. "Do you think I should go over there?"

Lily shakes her head. "It didn't seem that important," she replies.

We jump as a fit of coughing racks Tory's body, sending her falling into one of her bedposts. Her chest caves inward, and she writhes and squirms like a snake.

"Tor!" I race to her side and hold her up firmly as she coughs. Her trembling subsides momentarily, and then the coughs take her again. This time, they're mixed with sobs. The sounds pain me, but I keep a steady face and hold her close until the episode is over. The raspy sound coming from her throat is like nails scraping across a blackboard.

Gently, I shift her body away from me and, with Lily's help, manage to lift her onto the bed. Her lips are gray, and her eyes are squeezed shut. Something resembling a croak escapes her lips, and I hush her. I grab the towel by the bedside and wipe sweat from her pale forehead.

"Are you okay?" I ask. She says nothing as she sinks back into the pillows. Her lips seem fused shut. Lily and I stare at each other blankly. I think Lily has realized what's wrong with Tory. But, like me, she doesn't want to say it.

It feels weird being the boss. I'm not used to being in charge. I have always been the one who handles the food, but Tory, as the eldest, has always been the head of the household. Now that she's sick, her chores and responsibilities have fallen on my shoulders. It's not fair, but nobody will catch me complaining. It has to be done.

After a few minutes, I stand up, walk to the sink, and wash my hands under the freezing water. Lily follows me and speaks in a near-whisper.

"What's going on? You look like you're going to pass out."

I brush it off. "I need coffee," I grumble, shutting off the water and drying my hands on my pants. A spark of pain shoots up my injured leg, and I lean my weight on the other leg in a sad attempt to lessen it. It's rare that I'm able to find intact packets of coffee, but when I do, it's all I drink for days. The smell of the black, oily French roast Mom made when I was little was pure magic. The coffee I make suffices, but I can never get it to smell as good as hers did. What I wouldn't give for a cup of that right now.

"I second that," Lily nods, walking past me and pulling out one of the water bottles that we keep under the sink. They're for emergencies, and we have them under strict rations in case I do what I did today and fail to bring anything home. "Want some?" she asks.

I shake my head and walk back over to my bed. Rolling up my pant leg, I wince in pain as I untie the sock and expose the nasty gash on my shin to the air. It's deep, cutting down to the bone. Since it's practically impossible to get a hold of antibiotics or medication, a bad infection is practically a death sentence. Lily sees the look on my face and walks over, sucking in a breath when she sees the gash.

"Geez, what did you do?" she exclaims, causing Tory sit up on her bed.

"What happened?" Tory asks, rubbing her eyes. When Lily doesn't acknowledge her, she pushes the blanket off herself weakly and comes to look over Lily's shoulder. Her eyes widen when she sees my cut.

"Summer, that's disgusting. How did you manage to do that?"

I shrug and push them back a little so I can look at it properly. Most of the blood has dried, but the flesh is open and hot. A little steam rises in the cold air around it. It's raw, and there are still a few little glass shards stuck inside the wound. Tory's right. It is disgusting. "I cut it on some glass by the convenience store."

Lily wrinkles her nose. "Do we have any sort of disinfectant? Anything at all?"

I shake my head. "You can check, but I doubt it." I press back the skin with my thumb and grit my teeth. "Really, Lil, I'm fine. I don't need it."

She ignores me. "Do you think Tyler would have some painkillers—because of Riley and all?" she asks Tory, who cocks her head to the side.

"Oh no," I say. "You're not going to ask Tyler. Riley needs those meds."

There's no way I'm going to let Lily ask him for anything. The other day, Tyler managed to get his hands on a bottle of antibiotics from a drugstore across town. He's been giving them to Riley, and she's been showing slight signs of improvement. Since any sort of medication is rare, the antibiotics were an amazing find. I'm not taking that away from him.

"So do you," Lily pushes, still not looking at me. "I'll run and ask him. Summer, don't hurt it."

I roll my eyes. "No, Lil, listen to me. I don't need it—I'm fine. Meds aren't going to help me anyways. I'll just clean it, and it'll be okay. I really don't want to make it a big deal." But she's already walking out the door. I swear under my breath, and Tory laughs.

"Trust us, Sum, you're going to be thankful for them later."

I shake my head. Sometimes, I really wish Mom and Dad were here. They brought us to the Slump almost four years ago. Dad worked for Making Perfect in their research facilities. He was a scientist—or, according to him, "a five-year-old who plays with fancy toys for a living." He would leave for work early every morning, decked out in his white lab coat, a thick cigar hanging awkwardly from the side of his mouth, and wearing goofy glasses remarkably too big for his face. Mom also worked for Making Perfect, but she worked in the public relations department. She commuted to a facility slightly closer to home, which meant that she didn't have to leave so early. Every morning, she helped the three of us get ready for school and made breakfast on the stove. Then she would go to work, and we would catch the bus. She was so elegant, the polar opposite of me. It was hard to picture her talking on the phone all day, but that's what she did.

We lived in the townhouse district then. Our lives were completely normal until my twelfth birthday. On that day, they brought us to the Slump and told us to hide. They didn't tell us anything about where they were going or why they were abandoning us. I've tried everything to find them, but they're simply gone. I've racked my mind for reasons as to why they'd leave us, and none of them make sense. Mom and Dad loved me…I *know* they did. So, why would they leave?

I sigh as I lie on the bed, cringing as the stinging in my leg intensifies. Tory sits on the edge her bed with her head in her hands. What if the officials come now? There'd be no chance that any of us would escape. I know the plan, but I couldn't carry it out with a raw, open leg.

Kylie, a friend of mine who lived with her little brother, Emmett, in the room opposite ours, discovered a trapdoor in her ceiling a few years ago. Exploring it, we discovered a network of passages through the walls, floors, and ceilings, connecting every part of the hotel. That's how we've managed to evade the officials in the past. We make it up to the roof so quickly that they're never able to catch us before we're out of the building. Though it hasn't worked for everyone, it's worked every time for us, so we stick with it.

But now, I barely have the energy to move, let alone to outrun a group of officials.

With another sigh, I turn over and close my eyes. It's an uneasy sleep. I have to be ready.

Making Perfect could barge into the hotel at any time.

5

Making Perfect is here.

I know it the second I open my eyes to Lily's incessant nudging. I jump out of bed, rubbing my eyes, and run over to the window to see the white vans parked in a line down the street. The doors are open. The officials are already inside.

They're here, I think to myself. *They're here!*

Before I know it, I'm running with energy I didn't think I had. My left leg is wrapped tightly in a towel. Lily and Tyler must've treated it while I was still sleeping. The bandage feels wobbly and unwieldy. I consider ripping it off. Theo is barking loudly, pacing in front of the door. I can feel the panic in the air. I look around the room, and my stomach jumps into my throat. Lily and Tory are already out of sight.

Good.

If they are going where they should, they'll be safe.

My heart pounding, I grab Theo by the scruff of his neck. I tie a hand towel around his nose to muffle his sounds and push him into the closet, locking it behind him.

Throwing open the door to the hallway, I dash out toward the stairs. I have to get up to the roof before the officials do, but before that, I have to buy Tory some time. It'll take longer for her and Lily to get there than it'll take me.

"Split up! Go search upstairs!" I hear one official yell. I ignore it and continue to plow upward. By the time I reach the sixth floor, I can hear pounding footsteps on the stairs below me. I throw open the door marked "Emergency Fire Exit" and step out into the hallway. Darting into the closest room, I almost run square into a slew of officials.

They are almost as shocked as I am. Before they have a chance to act, I'm gone. I spin around and run back toward the staircase. But when I push back through that door, more officials are there to welcome me.

So much for that.

I turn on my heel, but five of them from the room I left are blocking my path.

I'm trapped.

Slowly, as if stepping on eggshells, they close in around me. Fear builds up inside me. When one of them raises his gun, I leap over him and push through the ones blocking my way. Seven-foot jumps have never been a problem for me. I lose sight of them around a turn and duck into a spare room. The hole in its ceiling is where I expect it to be, and I jump up into the opening.

A burst of adrenaline pumps through my veins, and a devilish smile spreads across my lips. I can hear the muffled shouting of the officials. They have scattered, checking various rooms.

I crawl through the passages and up toward the roof. Lily and Tory should already be there—I've bought them enough time. But as I nearly reach the eighth floor, a wall of yellow smoke hits me. Tranquilizer smoke. They use it every time—people drop like flies if they inhale enough of it. I begin coughing and stumble backward away from the smoke. My muscles start to feel heavy, but I just move faster.

My luck doesn't last long, though. When I drop into the eleventh-floor hallway to get to the last passage leading to the roof, more officials are blocking my way. I want to run, but I'm trapped. Again. The smoke is filling the hallway behind me.

"Got one," one of the officials calls into his radio. As he raises his gun, I leap back into the smoke, holding my breath. A dart whizzes past my ear, followed by another.

The official swears loudly. I stumble toward the nearest trapdoor, which is in room 1199. This holds my last route to the roof. If I can get to the room first, then I should make it up to Tory before they do. If I can do that, we might have a chance.

But there are officials in this room, too. This time, I'm not fast enough. A yellow-tufted tranquilizer dart sinks into my shoulder. I quickly pull it out. The less of that stuff that's in me, the better.

I start to feel lightheaded as I slam the door in their faces and scramble down the hall. Some of the serum got in. I need to get into Kylie's room. There are ladders in there that go directly down to the street. Not the best way out, but I'm desperate. I don't know how much farther I can go. My world swims, and darkness is starting to pull me downward.

I swing open the first trapdoor that I reach and hoist myself up into it with a grunt. The officials hear my efforts from outside and barge in quickly, firing dart after dart in my direction. I feel at least two hit my leg. My head is throbbing, and my eyelids start to droop. Usually one dart is enough to knock a person unconscious. I'm lucky, I guess.

I just need to hold on long enough to escape the building.

But as I move, my limbs become so heavy I can hardly keep going. There's no way I can make it to the street. I have to try the roof again and hope the officials haven't beat me there. The old, black "I Heart New York" sweatshirt that I'm wearing might help to disguise me in the shadows. I feel my heart racing, and it's getting hard to breathe. More of the yellow gas is seeping into the walls, making my vision swim.

I climb up a small ladder. The officials are shouting outside the wall. I feel like a drunk as I stagger and stumble up the ladder, almost losing my grip on the railings. It's like all the energy has been sucked out of me. Part of me wants to find a place to lie down and wait until they leave. But they'll find me. At this point, they'll tear down the walls until they find me. My eyelids droop.

When I reach the eleventh-floor hallway again, there are no officials in sight. I glance around like a trapped animal as my legs begin to give out. I am so close to the roof—I just have to climb the last flight of stairs. I'm going to make it. I run as fast as I can, faster than I ever thought I could. I tear around the corner and up through the doors, bursting onto the roof and into the rain. The water creates a slippery layer on the concrete.

Tory and Lily are nowhere in sight.

Please, let them have gotten away.

I need to get to the fire escape. I start toward the edge of the building. Everything moves in slow motion. Two more yellow tufts sink into my leg and my side. The officials are on the roof. Harnessing all the energy I have, I throw myself off the edge.

In a moment of sheer weightlessness, I start to drop toward the street. My hands reach out to grasp an oncoming fire escape, but they fumble and I continue to fall.

Before I can fall any farther, hands grab me and hoist my body back onto the roof, slamming my head into the wet concrete. Thunder rumbles in the distance.

The last memory I have is of the rain running into my mouth and over my face, stifling my moans. The officials crowd over me. Then, the world goes black.

6

My eyes shoot open in a state of panic. I bolt upright and cry out in pain when my head slams against the side of the shaking van. I instantly collapse, pain pulsing through my head.

They took me.

The van has no windows and is completely dark. The cold, metal flooring is making my hands go numb. My screams pierce the darkness, but the van does not slow down. Nobody is coming to help.

My mind is racing. The terror is overwhelming. I shake like a leaf. The tears are almost a relief when they come. They are slow at first, but then, like a dam that breaks, they become unstoppable. I cry uncontrollably for what feels like hours but could really only be a few minutes. What about Tory and Lily? They got out. They had to have gotten out.

Tyler. Tyler will make sure that they're okay.

What about Theo?

I hope Lily knows where he is.

The van goes over a bump. I ache all over. The effects of the darts haven't fully worn off. I force myself onto my knees and lean against the van's inside. I need to get my bearings.

My sisters are going to be okay.

I will be, too.

But I don't believe it, and another wave of fear hits me. I want to cry, but I don't. I'm afraid that if I start crying again, I will never stop.

The van slows down and eventually comes to a stop. I have to find a way out of this. I push myself up and manage to stand, ignoring my aching muscles and pounding head. I brace myself. I hear voices and see the back doors begin to open. Instinct takes over.

The light hurts my eyes, but I spring forward with all the strength I can muster. I kick the door as hard as I can and it swings out, hitting one of the officials squarely in the face. He groans as he falls backward, and I jump out. I see the look of surprise on the face of the other official as my feet hit the asphalt and I begin to run. I look around desperately for cover.

The van is parked in front of a large warehouse. Numerous Air Transports (AirTrans) of various sizes are lined up on the side of a landing pad that stretches out to the horizon. Other white vans are parked near the AirTrans, and officials are loading both conscious and unconscious kids onto the aircrafts.

My heart sinks. Bare fields surround the airport. The only trees that I see are hundreds of yards away. I have no chance of escaping, but I try anyway, running as fast as I can. I brace for what I know will come next.

The dart hits me in the thigh. I try to keep moving, but I fall forward. I am completely immobile as an official roughly hoists me up over his shoulder. As the light fades, I see that I'm being carried toward one of the larger AirTrans.

I'm thrown into immeasurable darkness.

人　　人　　人

The next thing I know, I am strapped to a gurney that is bolted to the floor of an AirTran. The hum of the engines is all I hear. My body aches more violently than it did before. Metal cuffs around my wrists and ankles prevent any movement. A large metal bar like those found on roller coasters sits across my chest, and a bag of yellow fluid hangs to my right on a pole that is also bolted to the floor. The liquid flows down a tube connected to an IV in my arm. I see it disappearing into my vein.

I look around. Other gurneys line the floor and walls of the AirTran. Most of them have someone strapped in. It looks like we are on a ride at a twisted amusement park.

So many of us. They got so many of us.

The girl on my left hasn't woken up yet. The boy on my right is stirring. I stare at the girl. She looks like she would have beautiful brown hair if the majority hadn't been previously chopped off. The remainder reaches her shoulders and is streaked with a palette of different oranges and reds. She has large hoop earrings, and flame tattoos cover almost all of the bare skin on her arms and shoulders. There is so much makeup coating her face that it looks like she was attacked by sharpies. The piercings on her nose, eyebrows, and bottom lip look simply terrifying on a face that's contorted into a grimace. Her expression makes goose bumps rise on my arms.

The boy is tall and built like an ox, with light blond hair falling unevenly on his forehead. His giant arms are almost as big as my head and could snap my neck effortlessly. His mouth is moving, forming the same shape over and over again. He must be repeating a name.

I close my eyes.

After what feels like hours, an announcement comes over the cabin speaker.

A male voice says, "Officials, prepare for landing."

I wonder how they are going to get us off the transport. The answer comes quickly. A couple of officials walk down the aisle.

One stops at my row, reaches out, and turns a little nob on my IV. I feel my eyelids start to droop.

I don't have time to register anything else before I'm sucked under.

7

I wake drenched in sweat. My head throbs violently, and I place my fingers on my temples to steady the spinning room. I taste blood. I try to stand up, but my legs collapse under me. They don't seem to be working properly. There's something soft beneath my knees. I blink a few times to clear the haze.

The room is empty. Everything about it screams "hospital." A marble counter overflowing with medical supplies lines the edge of the room. The blue foam mat that I'm lying on is positioned in the corner opposite a large, reclining examination chair, and a menacing machine hooked with cables stands next to the chair.

A stinging sensation on my wrist causes me to look down. A black barcode has been tattooed on the top of my left hand along with the number *27441*. It hurts. A lot. The irritated skin around it indicate that it's permanent. It feels like a sharp piece of burning hot metal was digging into my skin.

A woman in a long, white lab coat walks in. I can just make out the logo on her chest pocket. She approaches me with a sullen determination.

"Relax, honey, I'm not going to hurt you." Her voice is warm, a strange contrast with her cold appearance. "My name is Dr. Nancy." I just stare at her. She asks, "How long has it been since you've had a shower?"

A shower?

She's offering me a *shower?*

I can only nod as she helps me to my feet and over to the curtain in the far corner. A basket overflowing with dirty clothes lies just to its side. My mouth gapes as she draws back the curtain and reveals a large, white-tiled shower. The various nobs have foreign settings. A large array of soaps and shampoos stand on a metal rack.

"Put your clothes in the bin. I'll get you a towel." She walks over to the cabinet and pulls out a thick, white towel. I slowly remove my sneakers, which are worn black with dirt, and toss them in the basket. I take off my socks and sweatshirt, and slowly walk past the curtain and onto the clean tile. She draws the curtain behind me. I strip off the rest of my clothes and toss them into the basket.

The woman hangs the white towel on the hook outside the shower. I hug my chest nervously as I stand there, naked. A chill cuts me to the bone as I study all the settings and eventually find the "on" switch. A steady spray of warm water jets out of the nozzle, and I walk under it cautiously.

I linger on every little moment: choosing the beautifully scented soaps, cleaning the grime out from under my fingernails, washing my hair until I'm cleaner than I've felt in my entire life. I don't worry about wasting water because I don't care. The woman waits outside patiently while I wash myself. Eventually, I have to force myself to shut off the comforting run of water and wrap myself in the soft, white towel. I emerge from the shower to find new clothes waiting for me on the chair.

It turns out to be a full-body, tight-fitting tracksuit. Gray-and-black highlights create a stark contrast with the white material. A long, embroidered, golden strand of DNA coils around the imprinted Making Perfect logo on the back, and small, colored cubes dance alongside. I run my fingers over the words, tracing each elaborate shape with care. I slowly pick up the tracksuit and slip it on over the clean underwear provided with it. The material hugs my body, making me feel deceivingly safe. I take the hard combat boots from the floor and slip them on my feet, tightening the laces so they hold them comfortably.

I feel so…clean. I haven't washed my body in a couple of weeks. All that grime was hard to scrub off. I smile involuntarily.

I'm drying my hair with the towel when the woman walks back into the room. She smiles warmly and walks over to the counter. She opens a drawer and pulls out something that resembles a staple gun.

"What is that?" I croak.

She explains that the device contains a tracking chip. It is a highly advanced piece of equipment that Making Perfect has used for years. Each pinhead-sized chip emits its own individual signal that notifies Making Perfect if we ever leave the premises. It's intended to keep track of us and ensure our safety, or so she tells me.

She walks over to me and asks me to sit. The smell of rubbing alcohol envelops me. She presses the gun to my wrist and injects the chip right into my skin. I feel a sharp sting as the needle plunges in. I grunt. Maybe I should've fought, but numbness is overwhelming my body, filling me with a gentle sense of calm that I've never felt before. I feel completely safe, able to push away the loud screaming of my brain, which is telling me to run and fight.

"The uniform looks great on you, sweetie."

With a smile, she ushers me to the examination chair. The paper on it crinkles when I sit.

I tense up as I watch her dart around the room in silence, fingering various tools with care. By the time she turns back to me, she has only one in her hand. I shy away when she approaches me.

"Relax. This is not going to hurt at all."

She takes my face in her hand and presses the cold metal to my forehead. My gaze doesn't waver from her eyes until the tool beeps and she pulls it away. I bite my lip and continue to stare forward. Neither of us say anything, and the silence is uncomfortable. I hear her mumble something under her breath as she marks on a clipboard. She walks back to me and uncaps a green marker. Before I can stop her, she marks my cheek with a quick line of green.

It doesn't hurt, but I cup my hand over it and flinch in surprise.

"Green signals healthy; red signals sick," she explains, the lines sounding rehearsed.

She's already gone back to the counter when I open my mouth. "What are you doing?" I growl at her.

"I just have to see what condition you're in. If you're sick, we need to help you. Don't worry, you're perfectly safe."

She shines a bright light in my eyes, which sends a kaleidoscope of vivid colors through my brain. She apparently decides that I'm fine and returns the device to the counter.

It doesn't take long before she turns back to face me, holding her clipboard.

"I'm going to have to ask you a few questions. It is for your own benefit that you answer truthfully. Okay?"

She doesn't wait for a reply—she just starts firing questions at me.

What is your name?
How old are you?
What are your parents' names?
Are they alive?
Do you have any siblings?
Are they alive?

"Where are they?" she coaxes finally.

I shrug. "I don't know." I am lying, as I did for most of the other questions.

She sighs and puts her clipboard down.

"Please don't lie to me, honey. This is to just keep them safe."

"I swear. I have no idea."

I meet her gaze innocently.

"Very well." She stands and returns the clipboard to the counter. She opens one of the cabinets above the counter and pulls out a small, wrapped object that I don't recognize. But when she hands it to me, I almost fall off the chair.

A granola bar.

My *own* granola bar.

I stare in awe as I hold the precious item in my hands.

"Well, go on, eat. You look starved," the woman prompts. I tear open the bar slowly, trying to savor each moment, but I quickly give up and shove half of it into my mouth. Rich flavor explodes across my tongue. I don't stop until it's finished, and the woman hands me another.

"Poor thing, you're skin and bones." She almost smiles when I finish the second bar. My stomach is screaming for more, but I don't dare ask for another. This is more food than I've had to myself in a great while.

The woman presses a red caller button on the wall. The door buzzes, and two intimidating, gray-clad guards instantly enter the room.

"Bring her to Alpha."

"What's Alpha?"

I look at her in confusion as the guards grab my arms. They pull me off the chair and out the door. We enter a whitewashed hallway lined with blinding lights. So many guards line the wall that I feel like if I breathe too heavily, I will be tackled by at least fifteen of them. I stiffen up, following the guards closely. I try to keep my gaze steady and in front of me, but I can't help but glare at them out of the corner of my eyes. Their faces are hidden behind their thick, black visors. I scowl when they push me around the corner and into an elevator.

Surprisingly, I don't see anyone but guards in the hallways. Where is the staff? Making Perfect must be bigger than I thought.

I stiffen as the elevator doors close. I've never been in a working elevator before, only a broken one. A few years ago, Tyler dared me to flip down one of the empty shafts in the hotel. I did, and it was fun, but the next time I went in, I got stuck for hours. I was so shaken by the time I squeezed my way out that I have been too paranoid to set foot in one since. But this one moves seamlessly.

With a bleep, the doors open and the guards usher me into a new hallway identical to the last. Heads of observers turn to look at me as I am pushed past them and through another door.

I stop in my tracks. The walls are made of glass, and strips of mirror are placed at regular intervals. The only object in the room is a white reclining chair with many colorful wires stretching from its headpiece to computers on the other side of the glass. Men and women in Making Perfect uniforms are stationed at the machines. All eyes are on me.

Guards push me onto the chair. They proceed to strap me in—metal straps around my wrists and ankles and a large leather strap across my chest. I shiver as the icy cuffs close around my skin. The doors slide open, and Dr. Nancy enters, followed by a man. His dark hair is slicked back, and small spectacles sit on the end of his nose.

My eyes lock onto Dr. Nancy as she picks up some wires from a table. She and the man work together, attaching electrodes to my head and chest. Her face is close to mine. I can smell the faint scent of her perfume.

The cold gel burns my skin. She sees me tense up. "Don't worry. None of this is going to hurt you."

In a voice that belies my anxiety, I whisper, "What's 'this'?"

Without answering, she backs away and steps behind the glass. She punches some commands into the monitor.

Her voice comes out of the speaker in the ceiling above my head. "Alpha is a program we developed after the Great Divide. It's quite effective and suits our purposes perfectly."

"What is it?"

All she says is, "It's a painless interrogation program." What the hell does that mean? A "painless interrogation program" could mean anything. "It allows us to see inside your head."

"See inside my head?" I ask again, frustration and fear dripping off my words.

Before she can reply, a male voice comes over the speakers. "Okay, here we go."

"No! Wait!" I shout, but Dr. Nancy ignores me. Feeling desperate, I ask, "What are you doing to me?"

"Don't struggle. The tenser you are, the more painful it will be," Dr. Nancy says, brushing aside my fears. I try to relax my body. She said it's painless, so it can't be that bad, right?

Before I have time to even form another thought, I am hit by wall of color. A myriad of images shoot through my head, spiraling around so quickly that it's impossible to make out any of them. Emotions stab me like knives. I want to close my eyes and make the spinning stop, but I'm completely helpless. The pictures spin around me with lightning speed, dizzying my senses.

When the scientists speak again, their voices are muffled as if I'm underwater.

"All right. Let's try this again. Do you have any siblings?"

I scream. The images stop spinning, a single vignette stopping in front of me. It's too blurry to tell what it is. Before I can even try to resist, I'm sucked into the picture.

Suddenly, it all comes into focus. I see a little girl, seven years old, holding Tory's hand as we walk home from school. I stare at her for a second before realizing she's me. We're talking about the cookies waiting for us at home. It's Lily's second birthday. Tory's wearing a blue and white bow in her hair. Fall breeze whips through our hair as we walk down the sidewalk.

As quickly as it started, I'm pulled out of that memory and back into the swirling color. The scientists are talking to me but it's as if their voices are coming from inside my head although it's hard to make out exactly what they're saying.

My senses are overloaded, and I strain forward in my seat, trying to force my eyes open. It doesn't work—Making Perfect has complete control over my body.

The fragments aren't coming to me in order. It's impossible to hang on to any image for longer than a few seconds.

The next question comes in. "Where are your sisters?"

Without warning, another memory stops in front of me and I'm thrust violently into it. They can't see this. I can't let them see this. I grip the edges of the chair, my voice raw as I shout for them to stop. Sharp pain cuts through my head, as I'm thrust into the next memory. We are in the hotel. It's three days after my twelfth birthday and Tory comes back with a squirming puppy. My eyes sparkle as she hands him to me. We wash him, and Lily names him Theo.

The next fragment hits me like a train. I spin around to see myself, barreling down a beaten Slump street toward a thirteen-year-old Tyler who's just been dumped in the Slump. As we embrace, utter joy and relief are written all over me.

The nonstop flow of memories is taking its toll. I fight for air, trying to stop this drowning feeling. My arms and legs strain against the straps as I lash out. A scream escapes my lips. The officials' voices are indistinguishable.

I see myself jumping off the dock and into the river with Kylie and riding my skateboard down the sidewalk in the summer. I watch Tyler finding me a candy bar for my fourteenth birthday, and the gorgeous view of the sunset off the roof of the hotel. I'm witnessing the most intimate parts of my life, watching it like a favorite childhood movie. It all flashes before my eyes, triggered by the officials' questions.

Everything.

"What are your parents' names?" This question is clear, cutting through the ringing in my ears.

No! I fight harder than ever. I can't let them into this one.

"Where did they go?"

And then it happens. The one I've buried so deep.

The Slump is eerily silent, a thin December frost coating the shadowed street. I'm twelve, following my parents as we run down the icy streets at full speed. Dad's face is tight with fear as he leads us around the corner, gripping my hand protectively. Tory is holding Lily, and Mom brings up the rear, her dark hair flowing behind her. The night gives us just enough protection to hide in as we slip around the corner. We make it a few more steps before a shout sounds from behind us.

Dad stiffens, worry written all over his face. Mom picks up Lily and pushes Tory in front of her. Dad scoops me onto his back as we run. We have to get farther into the city.

"They're coming. We have to hide them," Mom says, her voice barely audible as she whispers to Dad. I see him nod.

But Lily hears it. "Hide us? What do you mean?" I see Lily, tears flowing, choking on the words. Mom hushes her gently as we duck into the nearest building, shutting the door behind us. The neon lights of the hotel sign are slowly flickering out.

"Go upstairs and hide quietly. We'll be back." Mom gets down on her knees and smoothes the hair out of Lily's sobbing, red face, trying to quiet her down. Tory hugs Dad quickly before scooping Lily onto her back and darting up the emergency staircase. I turn to run after them, but Mom grabs my arm, pulling me into a quick embrace. She plants a quick kiss on my head, and I purse my lips. I can hear the shouts getting closer.

Dad looks behind his shoulder at the door to the hotel, his blue eyes growing wide. He turns quickly back to me. "Don't come downstairs no matter what, okay? We'll be back for you later. I promise."

No matter how hard I fight, I can't escape the memory's hold. I'm experiencing the night I've spent the most time hiding from.

Mom squeezes my hand again, and I race after Lily and Tory, tearing up the stairs as fast as I can. By the time I've reached the second flight, there's a loud popping sound from the Lobby. First one, then many more. Gunfire. The shots are loud and never seem to end. There are screams, some hoarse shouts, and then silence.

I promise.

I stop in my tracks. "Mom! Dad!" My voice breaks. I see Tory stop a few steps ahead of me, shaking her head swiftly.

Don't come downstairs no matter what.

Without hesitation, I dash down the stairs back toward the Lobby where I heard the gunshots. I am on the last flight when my foot misses a step and I tumble down the concrete stairs, smacking my head hard against the landing.

There are a few murmurs, and huge figures crowd around me. They look like huge lizards with big, sharp scales. My little body is lifted up into the air and held there for a second. One of the lizards throws a hard blow to my chest, and I am knocked back to the floor. I scream for my parents—I scream for them to help me—but it's no use. They're nowhere to be found. My fists and feet fly out, striking hard objects, but the shadows don't waver. A boot makes quick contact with my stomach, and I double over. There's a glimpse of silver and a butt of a gun whizzes toward my head. I roll and it misses me, coming in full contact with another official's shin. He screams in pain, and somehow I am on my feet.

I'm running now—running as fast as I can, back up the steps and onto the first floor. There I throw open a door and hide in the cabinet under the sink. I try to calm myself as tears stream down my face. There's a lot of shouting and footsteps pounding on the floor, but they don't find me. I taste blood in my mouth, and I will myself to stay quiet. I need Mom and Dad. I need them to come back. They promised they would.

But they don't. They never came for me.

I'm fighting even more vigorously against the restraints now, anger boiling up inside me. I will myself to break out of this terrible dream, but I can't. I am pulled farther and farther down, until I can't feel anything but emptiness.

8

'm drowning in a sea of nothingness. For the first time in my life, I feel absolutely empty.

A voice speaks into the darkness, and I latch onto it like a leech, using it as a lever to lift myself out of this never-ending abyss.

I break the surface, tears streaming down my face. My head is spinning so fast that I can't see straight. I look at my hands. They swim before my eyes until they finally come into focus. I grab the chair to keep myself from falling over. Dr. Nancy's face comes into view.

"Make this stop," I croak. My throat has dried up, and it burns. I feel almost weightless, like everything has been sucked out of me. "What are you doing to me?"

"We just needed to find out what exactly what you were hiding from us." Her voice is soothing. She gently unclips the electrodes from my face as another woman rubs a cold towel over my forehead, wiping up the sweat and tears.

I fight to focus. When she releases the leather strap, I almost fall over.

"It's finished, you're done." She hands me a paper cup. Without looking, I hold it up to my lips and drink it all.

Dr. Nancy talks to me in a soothing voice until I've had several more cups of water and my head is clear.

"Are you ready?"

"Where are you taking me?"

"To the rest of the group."

She helps me into a standing position, and I follow her to the door. Guards flank us as she leads me down to the elevator. I focus on moving my legs. I'm scared.

After what feels like an eternity, the elevator opens into a huge, concrete-walled room, like a warehouse. Its exits are heavily guarded, and its interior is dim and empty except for the people it contains. Scattered around me are kids of all ages, sitting and standing, both alone and in groups. I try to count them, but there are far too many—easily a few hundred. Everybody is dressed in the same uniform that I'm wearing.

I wonder if they all had to go through Alpha.

I wander into the mass of people without looking back at Dr. Nancy. Being careful not to step on any hands, I instinctively try to find familiar faces. Nothing. I wonder where all these kids are from. I find an empty spot on the wall, far away from the metal doors, and sit down against it. The doors close with a loud hiss as Dr. Nancy leaves.

I recognize the girl who was next to me on the AirTran sitting with others I don't know in a small group. They're not talking, just sitting. Making Perfect didn't do a great job of cleaning her up. Her hair, though it shines with a new sort of cleanliness, is still dyed. Her flame tattoos poke out from around her tracksuit. All of her piercings have been taken out, but in a way, she looks even more menacing with the barren holes. When I glance around the room, it looks like everybody has been similarly cleaned up.

I put my head in my hands and grit my teeth. I can't cry here. I have to keep it together. Slowly, over the course of what feels like forever, more kids are dropped off in the room. I look up every time, afraid that it will be someone I know. Thankfully, each time, it isn't.

I glance back down at my feet and get the feeling that someone is staring at me. The instant I raise my head, our eyes lock.

It's a boy.

And a really attractive boy at that.

His tousled hair, a mix between a dirty blond and auburn, is cut jaggedly. His skin is clear but not pale, with just enough tan to look healthy. The gray highlights in his tracksuit bring out his already-striking chestnut eyes. He has a lean, well-toned body and a light dusting of freckles. A bright green marker stripe runs down his left cheek.

His thin lips press up into a small smile, making me suddenly uncomfortable. I look away, biting my lip and clasping my hands together. The mischievous gleam in his eyes screams trouble. I can't stop myself from glancing up at him again, but when I do, he has slumped down with his face in his hands. The girl with the flame tattoos wraps her arm around him and whispers something in his ear. He looks up, and our eyes meet again for a second. I look away instantly.

Just then, the doors open and the guards bring someone else in. It is a tall, skinny boy who walks among the crowd, looking for a place to sit. I almost don't recognize him. His shaggy curls have been cut short so that they're no longer falling into his eyes. He looks uncomfortable in the uniform, though it doesn't hug his body like mine does.

No. Please no.

What about Lily and Tory? Who is going to look after them if he's here? What about Michael and Riley?

His bright eyes search the room, quickly meeting my gaze. Fear is plastered all over his face as he sees me—like he's just seen a ghost. He starts toward me, and before I can stop myself, I'm running to him. The second I reach Tyler, I stop in my tracks and bring my hand down hard against his cheek.

"That was for getting caught," I hiss. "Don't make promises you can't keep." I throw my arms around him and press my body tightly against his. I feel his arms slide around me, and I suddenly am glad he's here. I know it's selfish of me, but I can't help it.

"Damn it, Sum, what did you do?" he wearies, sighing heavily.

I don't reply. I don't think I can. I don't know how much longer I can hold it all in. Swallowing back the lump in my throat, I break away from him and notice the red mark on his face. I try to recall what Dr. Nancy told me about the marks, and my brow furrows. I'm about to ask him about it, but before I can say anything, a crackle comes over the loudspeaker.

"Attention," a raspy female voice blares across the room. "Please listen closely to the following instructions:

"Those marked with green are to stay where they are. Those with red marks are to go to the officials on the left side of the room, and those with yellow marks are to go to the officials on the right side of the room. They will take you from there. Those with green marks will stay put until given further instructions."

I look at Tyler and at the red mark on his face. He bites his lip.

"Ty," I say, my voice almost a whisper, "Did they say anything about the marks?"

"The officials? No, why?"

I shake my head. "I don't feel right about you leaving—"

"Red marks, keep it moving!" an official shouts from across the room. People around me are getting up and moving away. I notice that the yellow-marked kids all seem to be under the age of seven. They're tiny.

My stomach flies into my throat, and I wrap my arms around Tyler's neck. "Please be careful."

"I will. It's all good." He's lying. I can hear it in his voice, but I don't say anything. He lets go of me and starts to walk away. Everything in me is screaming to follow him, to not let him go, but my feet are glued to the floor. All of my hope disappears, and I'm filled with a deep, immeasurable hollowness.

My gaze follows Tyler as he vanishes out the door along with the others. It feels like my heart has been ripped out of my chest and there's a big, gaping hole where it used to be. I am so scared, so scared, so scared...

I almost fail to notice the hand grabbing my ankle.

"Hey there, sit down. You look terrible." The voice is soft and kind. I cast a glance down at the girl. Her light blond hair looks gray in the dim yellow lighting. She has a small frame but looks about my age, with fair skin and hazel eyes. A bright green mark has been drawn on the side of her face.

My heart is pounding so hard that it hurts. I do what I'm told. My head spins, and I place two fingers on my forehead to shake the queasiness from my body.

"Are you okay? You looked like you were about to pass out."

I force myself to nod and feel my face burn up.

She smiles. "You can talk, you know. I don't bite."

Something snaps back into place in my brain, and I shake my head clear. "Oh yeah. Sorry. I'm fine, just a little freaked out."

"I feel you." Her eyes shine. "I'm Ocean, by the way."

I can't smile back. "Summer."

She peers past me, and I realize that the loudspeaker has once again come to life. My ears focus on the voice coming out of it—a different male voice that is rapidly barking various orders.

"...numbers are called, report to the officials waiting for you at the front of the room. These people will be your group, and the officials will be your group leaders. If anyone doesn't report, we will find you.

"The groups, by number, are as follows. Group one is 23199, 23786, 23111, 23777, 23103, 23804…"

I study the large, black barcode on my wrist: 27441. The tension in the room is too much for me to bear. There's a slight movement beside me.

"You know, you can't hold your breath forever. Damn, Summer, you're turning purple," Ocean whispers in my ear, and I realize that I've been holding my breath.

I want to answer her, but the loudspeaker cuts me off.

"…27028, 27946, and 27441 will make up group six. Please be ready to leave with your escorts as your group is called. Pay attention, and do not ask questions. Failure to comply will have unpleasant consequences." The mic is turned off.

Group six.

My heart hammers rapidly in my chest, almost to the point of pain. My breathing gets heavy, the breaths coming out in short little puffs. Sweat is pouring out of me and soaking through my uniform. Some of the others looking around frantically, fear tattooed on their faces.

As if on cue, the guards step aside and six officials enter through the sliding doors. White, bulletproof scales cover their chests and thick pads protect their shoulders. One of them steps forward. He is decorated with golden stars, and the word *Official* is emblazoned on the front of the suit.

He calls out group one. About thirty kids stand up and walk over to him. About five minutes later, group two is called by another official. The guards, meanwhile, are completely unmoving and expressionless. I can hardly make out their faces through their black helmet visors. Though they are dressed completely in dark gray, their uniforms are otherwise the same as the officials'. A large black gun is strapped to each of their sides.

Group four. The tall and powerful boy who was next to me on the AirTran leaves.

When group six is announced, my heart jumps and I can barely move.

"Come on, I think that's us." My head turns to Ocean, who's already standing. I allow her to help me up. She looks so calm and collected. I don't understand how she's not freaking out.

I feel as if I'm about to explode.

Ocean and I walk over to the official. My nails dig into my palms until I can feel them breaking the skin.

Get a grip.

Most of the others in our group are already beside the official. I count twenty-nine.

"Listen up," the official spits out as soon as I reach her. "I am Official Banks. I was assigned to oversee this group." Her voice is sharp. She looks much older than the others, with deep wrinkles in her chocolate skin and dark, graying hair pulled back tightly in a bun. Her eyes are large and deeply set, with irises as black as charcoal. They make her look like the human version of a panther. "Keep your mouths shut and follow me. One murmur, and you're done."

She pulls a small remote device out of her pocket and pushes a button, causing the doors to slide open slowly. The guards, with their guns held at ready, step aside. We start to move forward. I don't want to be here, I don't want to be here—

My shoulder brushes against someone, and I look up to see the boy with the freckles. My stomach squirms, and I feel my face burn up. He doesn't notice me. I can't help but notice how much bigger he seemed sitting down. He is only a few inches taller than me— probably around six feet. He catches me looking and smiles, again.

How is it that everybody feels like smiling?

We turn a corner and walk into a dark, narrow tunnel. The walls slowly transition from concrete to sleek metal plates, looking less like a wall and more like the scales of a snake. I can make out my blurred reflection in the panels. As we move farther down the tunnel, the lights are grouped closer together, making the hallway brighter with every step. The light reflecting off the metal plates shines in my eyes, and I can't help but squint.

The boy walking in front of me stops abruptly, causing me to slam into him. My face smacks into his shoulder blade. I stumble backward, rubbing my crinkled nose. He doesn't look back.

The whole group has stopped, and Banks has her arms crossed. She doesn't say a word as another figure appears through the sliding glass doors. As it steps forward, I can see that it is a young man. His hair is cut short and slicked back with gel, and his dark, amber eyes shine in the light. He looks to be only a few years older than the boy with the freckles and seems oddly out of place in his uniform. He could be one of us.

"I am Captain Kace Foster," the man says. "I will be working with you and Official Banks as your secondary trainer and administrator."

I hate him already.

"Captain?" the girl with the flame tattoos asks, her voice raspy.

"Captain of the guard, captain of defense, take it however you'd like." He crosses his arms. "The door we are about to go through leads to the Lobby, which is where you will be kept for now. Do not wander. There are guards at each door with strict instructions not to let you out of their sight."

He steps aside as Official Banks pulls out her remote and presses a button. The doors open smoothly, and I step through behind a wall of people. I struggle to breathe.

The Lobby is perfectly named. The room is daunting, scary even, a warped version of a corporate lobby. It is huge and cavernous, illuminated by many white lights. Narrow staircases lead up to balconies that hug the white plaster walls. The rooms on the balconies are numbered with shiny metal plaques. On the ground floor, around the large gold statue of DNA, various couches, televisions, and foosball tables are randomly placed—the room seems like it could've once had a comfortable atmosphere but has become cold with the passage of time.

The ceiling is so far up that I can hardly see it. Observation decks stretch from one side of the Lobby to another at each level, rimmed with safety bars and covered with glass domes. Guards, officials, and various other people in suits mill around on the decks. Their eyes are trained on us.

I shift uncomfortably. People are everywhere. We must have been one of the last groups to arrive. Everyone in the Lobby is dressed in uniforms identical to ours. The cacophony of their discussions resonates against the stark white walls.

"Welcome to the Lobby," Kace says, snapping me back to attention. "If you look upward, you will see the various balconies, the doors off of which will be your living quarters. Group six is on the sixth balcony. Two of you have been assigned to each room. Your access to other rooms will be limited, and guards are always stationed around the perimeter. As I mentioned before, all of the guards have strict instructions to keep you in the Lobby, with the exceptions of meals and tests. For these, you will be allowed to walk down to the appropriate areas. You are under constant observation—any effort to escape will be quickly reported and will result in unpleasant consequences. You will be escorted to your tests and training exercises."

"Tests? I thought—" a girl at the front of the group cries. Kace stares at us coldly. He is enjoying this far too much.

"Making Perfect believes that humans have so much more potential than they currently show. Most people are weak and afraid. They lack direction and accomplish little. They are nothing more than sheep, going through life consuming much and producing little of real value. We can do better. It is in all of our power to improve ourselves, to perfect ourselves. But we choose not to." The obviously memorized speech rolls of Kace's tongue in a fast, monotonous voice.

"The reason for this is fear. Making Perfect wants to make you better, to make you perfect, but to do that, we need to push you. People have to learn that the changes they make to themselves will help them and their community to grow. This is where you come in. You will be the ones to show them, to teach them that with certain small alterations to our genetic codes, we can reach our full potential."

"What genetic alterations?" asks the frightened girl, sounding more desperate.

"All of you will undergo a procedure that will alter specific gene sequences. These alterations will let you access abilities that you can only dream of now." Kace picks at his cuticles, his disdain apparent. "Making Perfect will make you better and more powerful than you will ever become on your own." His eyes linger on me as he says this. "Since you are all minors, you belong to us. We have the right to test you, train you, and shape you in any way we choose." He pauses. "Your fate from here on will be determined by Making Perfect."

I feel a tingling sensation spreading through my body. The rumors from the Slump are lies. They don't bring you to the institutions. They aren't worried about enforcing the law. They want lab rats. Genetic mutations. Human testing.

I can't think.

I can't *breathe*.

"What happens if our enhancements backfire? Like, if they don't work?" the boy with the freckles queries, tension building in his voice.

"If that happens, our scientists will put you out of your misery," Kace explains indifferently.

"But that's insane!" the flame-tattoo girl cries, her voice almost a scream. Various heads turn to look at us from behind Kace and Official Banks. "You can't *do* that!"

"Then your enhancement had better work," Official Banks replies harshly.

I hear a gasp. My stomach drops.

And I snap.

So much anger, pulsing through every inch of my body. Disbelief, hurt, and rage make my bones feel like they are going to snap. They crack and bend, and I flare up into a blazing inferno. I've never felt this kind of power before. Now that it's found an outlet, I can't contain it. I need to do something. I need to *hurt* something. My eyes lock with Kace's. I feel a guard grab my arm. I don't know what my body is doing—I only know that it's tensing, and my knees are bending, and I am coiling up like a spring, and—

I lunge straight at Kace.

The guard collapses in a heap behind me but I'm only looking at Kace. With one effortless blow, I knock him aside. He slams into the wall, falling to the ground in a pathetic clump. Official Banks rushes for me. I have lost all control of my body. I am an animal. I thrust my leg out, my foot connects with her thigh, and I hear a loud crack. She falls to the floor, letting out a cry of agony.

My eyes dance wildly around the Lobby, looking for another target, when an immense force slams me into the wall, pressing my shoulders back so hard that I can't move. I am about to lash out again when I realize what I've done.

Oh my God.

My body goes slack, and I look down at Kace and Official Banks. Kace is sitting up slowly, blood tricking from his nose and lips, while Official Banks clutches her right leg tenderly as guards try to help her up.

Oh no, no, please, no.

I look up into the hard eyes of the man-boy, who has pinned me to the wall. They are narrowed into angry slits. I open my mouth to say something, but before I can speak, my offender drops me, letting me crumple to the floor. I am frozen, a broken mess on the ground. I watch him help Kace to his feet. I hardly have a moment to take a breath before two guards lift me up. One of them grabs me from behind and holds me in place, ignoring my struggles. When he jabs the barrel of his gun into my spine, I go still. Just imagining a bullet tearing into my kidneys makes me stiff as a plank.

The look that Kace is giving me makes me want to disappear.

"Captain, are you all right?" the boy asks him. I am instantly struck by how young he is. Though he is extremely official-like in his crisp, black suit and perfect posture, he looks Kace's age. His eyes are the sharpest and most piercing steel gray that I've ever seen. They tear through me, making me feel entirely naked each time that he looks at me. I feel like I've seen him before, though I can't remember where. His face is so familiar.

He looks beautifully peaceful on the outside. But if I found out that he shoots puppies in his free time, I wouldn't be surprised.

I rub my aching shoulder, and he turns to me. His muscles are quivering. "Are you finished?" I nod. "Because I am warning you in advance that any further displays like this will have extremely unpleasant consequences. You will not get another chance. Is that clear?"

I nod again. I don't know who he is, but he obviously has a lot of power or else the officials around us wouldn't be trembling like they are. A smile crosses his lips.

"What's your name?" he asks, and I bite my tongue.

"My name?"

"Yes, your name."

"Summer Greenwood."

Something flashes in front of his eyes, but he quickly pushes it away.

"You came from the Slump, yes?"

"As did everyone else here. There is no other place that you can mass-kidnap orphans and have no legal charges brought against you."

"Legal charges pressed against me?" He scoffs, clearly entertained. "I don't think you realize who I am." He exchanges a glance with Kace, who is still glaring at me. "Ian Cooper, head of Sector Forty-One and head of operations of this facility."

That's when I remember. Ian Cooper. He's the son of Michael Cooper—the CEO of Making Perfect. That's where I've seen him before—in the papers and on TV. Posing angelically for the camera alongside his twin sister, Elle. The last time I saw him, he was much younger, about fourteen years old. He's changed so much that I hardly recognize him.

"Pleasure," I say. My words barely come out through my tightly gritted teeth. I'm hoping he will notice my blatant sarcasm.

"Summer, let me give you a piece of advice. If you are to survive here, you must learn to take pity when it is offered, and try not to get into situations where you'll need it." He rubs the back of his neck casually. "Although, with your temperament I predict you will find that extremely difficult."

Arrogant asshole.

I meet his gaze and ignore his last comment. "I'll make sure to keep that in mind."

With a jerk of his head, he signals me to rejoin the group, and I do. I walk back over to the rest of my unit, who is frozen in horror and staring at me with wide eyes. I can't bear to look at their faces. Their expressions threaten to tear me apart.

When I turn back to look at Kace and Cooper, they are having a hushed conversation that ends with a terse nod from Kace. Cooper turns to the group.

"Captain Foster has agreed to let me explain the ground rules. I assume you already heard my introduction." He stands perfectly still with his hands behind his back.

I go as stiff as a plank, biting my bottom lip. He explains all the rules—a long list of them, with "no killing" at the top. After that come various instructions about meals, hygiene, and testing.

Why bother fattening us up if they're just going to kill us anyway? The thought makes me want to hurl.

"You are all now a part of something much bigger than you can imagine. If you wait until you're ready, you will be waiting forever. It is your turn to make a difference. It is your turn to seize the moment." He pauses. I can't stop staring at him. I know I should, but I can't. Seize the moment? He has to be joking.

"Dinner is in half an hour," Kace says. "If you are not in the dining hall at six o'clock exactly, there will be no dinner."

Cooper nods. "Starting tomorrow, you have a few weeks of mental and physical conditioning before you undergo the procedure. Afterward, you will go through testing to ensure the success of the enhancement." He grins, but not in a kind way. It's a grin that looks like it was etched out of stone.

Everybody is frozen in place. Kace's smirk widens.

"Just remember one thing," he says, staring directly into my eyes. "Stay compliant and you will stay alive."

9

TYLER

My eyes are trained on the floor. With so many people around me, I feel like I'm part of a herd of cows. The red mark feels like it's burning into my skin, though I know it's harmless. Seeing Summer back there was a slap in the face harder than the one she gave me. I swore I was going to take care of her, to keep her safe. I swore on my life, and then I broke that oath. I can hardly stand myself.

Guards flank us, their guns held to their chests. We are moving quickly through a maze of hallways. They must be trying to disorient us so that we can't escape. I would laugh if I could, but I have to admit it's working. All the hallways look the same, and in my mind, everything blends into a jumbled mess.

I try as hard as I can to calm myself, pushing all thoughts out of my head.

The people in front of me stop, and I keep my head down. Out of the corner of my eye, the guards pace up and down the line, occasionally pulling out troublemakers or prodding them with firearms. There is a voice shouting up ahead, but I can't make it out from here.

"Psst."

The sound is so faint that I assume I'm imagining it. It's not until I feel something nudging my forearm that I look down. A little girl—seven at the oldest—is poking me. The red mark on her face stretches from her temple down to the corner of her mouth.

Confused, I stare at her for a moment. I'm about to turn away, but then I feel her hand grab mine.

I am taken aback. I want to pull my hand away, but something about her makes me hold on. She looks so little, so out of place. Her big, brown eyes stare up at me, the golden flecks in her irises glimmering in the lamplight.

Someone shouts from behind us, and I feel a sharp pain in my shoulder. I glance back to see a guard glaring at me through narrowed slits. I look at the little girl, feeling suddenly protective of her. Tightening my grip on her little hand, I weave forward through the crowd. Eventually, I lift her up onto my back, allowing her to wrap her arms around my neck. The whole time, she doesn't say a word. I don't mind her presence—I guess she reminds me of Riley.

We stop again, this time for longer. Someone beside me coughs, and I wince as I feel spit land on the back of my neck. I touch it with my fingers, and they come back red.

Blood.

Grossed out, I walk a few steps to the side to get away from the cougher. I had just started coughing up blood the afternoon before the officials took me. On my way back from my food run, I ran into an alley and hung my head over a Dumpster. I felt so weak that I could hardly stand upright. I felt exactly like what Summer called me—a ghost. That's probably why I got taken. I was so discombobulated after hiding Michael and Riley in the back cupboard that I didn't have time to scramble out of the building myself. The officials shot a tranquilizer dart into my back, and I was out instantly.

I weave through people until I can get a clear view of the officials leading the group. We are stopped in front of a pair of large metal doors. Two officials talk in hushed tones. The little girl's grip around my neck tightens, and I lift her up a little higher as I feel her slipping. Judging by the official's expressions, whatever lies behind those doors isn't good.

What's going on? Aren't we supposed to be going to the institutions?

I feel a heavy shuffling of feet behind me and look over my shoulder. The guards are pointing their guns at us. They are lining up, trapping us between them and those doors.

I start to feel scared. It's not an unknown emotion to me, though as a typical sixteen-year-old boy, I would never show it. Especially not around Michael or Riley, or even Summer, for that matter. It wouldn't come across well—and now, with the little girl clutching me like a lifeline, I feel especially obligated to stay strong. Still, I can't help holding on to her a little tighter.

Then, in one steady, clockwork motion, the doors open and the guards at the back of the line begin to push us forward. I panic when I realize what's happening. I stop in my tracks, and my legs begin to quiver.

I get it now.

Green equals healthy; red equals sick. Sick equals useless; useless equals terminated.

Why would they want to spend money treating us when there are plenty of healthy subjects to take our places?

My whole body stiffens. The line narrows as the officials grab people's arms one by one, stab a serum into their bodies using syringes, and push them into the room beyond. More and more people walk to their deaths, completely clueless.

"Let's go!" a voice shouts, and the little girl lets out a cry as I stumble forward. The line of guards is coming up behind us relentlessly. I'm sure that, were I to stop right here, they would shoot me on the spot.

There's nothing I can do.

By the time I reach the doors, I can't take it anymore. I turn on my heel and throw a punch at the nearest guard. The girl clings to my back and wraps her legs around me, holding on for dear life. My fist meets air. I barely have time to recover before something slams into on my face and pain slices through my skull. I fall to my knees, clutching my head. An official stands over me as another pushes the little girl past the threshold. Someone hoists me up, and I feel the needle plunge into my shoulder before I'm thrown into the room. I hit the ground hard, and a moan escapes my lips. I feel the little girl come to cling to me, and I open my eyes a crack to see the doors sliding quickly shut.

No, no, no.

I can't move. My head spins, and I grasp the little girl's hand as the serum overtakes me. I sink into blackness.

10

SUMMER

The rooms are pretty easy to get to—just up the stairs and onto the sixth level of balconies. I am glad we got the higher rooms—the farther away from the guards I can be, the better.

My room is small and made of concrete, with two small cots against the back wall. White sheets are pulled tight on each cot, hugging the blue foam pad placed over the springs. The plastic covering makes a crinkling sound every time I shift my weight. Uneven sheets of metal have been bolted together to form the upper part of the wall; chipped white paint covers the concrete of the lower part, which ends about four feet from the ground. There's a small bathroom behind a wooden panel near the door, and a dresser sits between the two cots. A small, barred window lies in the top left corner of the far wall.

Everything is plain and cold.

The door opens, and Ocean walks in. I guess we're roommates.

She smiles at me, walks over to her cot, and pulls a sweatshirt over her head. "You made quite a display back there."

I flush red. "I'm not usually like that—"

"No, I get it. I was scared too."

I reach over to the drawer and put on a sweatshirt, sighing as the fabric surrounds me like a warm hug.

"Do you think they'll really kill us?" Ocean wonders aloud as I flop down on my bed, the springs creaking under me. If what they're saying is true, these little moments of comfort won't last long. I should enjoy this one while I can.

"I don't think Making Perfect backs down on their threats," I reply, staring at my bare feet. The boots I had on just moments ago are sitting in a clump by the door.

"But what about their promises?" Ocean asks.

The horrifying images circling through my head are too much to bear.

"I don't know." Squeezing my eyes shut, I try to forcefully put these thoughts back where they came from. I am worried about Tyler. Where did they take him? Is he going through the same thing we are? Dr. Nancy's voice pops into my head.

Green signals healthy; red signals sick.

I sit up.

Oh no. No, please, no.

"Summer, what's wrong?" Ocean asks, but I'm too distracted to reply.

Tyler was coughing that morning when we went to the market. He said it was no big deal, but I knew he was lying. He was showing symptoms of Red Pox. They marked him as sick. Does that mean he's useless? Is he going to be killed?

I shouldn't have let him go. I should have done something. I should have—

"Summer, calm down." I feel hands on my shoulders and realize that I have been lacing up my boots, muttering his name under my breath. I look up at Ocean and realize how crazy I must look to her. Putting on that display in the Lobby, then this—I would be afraid of me if I was her. "What's wrong?"

"They're going to kill them." The anger makes my voice shake. I sprint out the door and onto the balcony. Ocean grabs my arm.

"They're going to kill who?"

"*Them*. The red-marked ones." I feel helpless as I try to tug my arm out of her grasp. "Tyler is one of them. They're going to kill him. I need to help him—"

"Summer, listen to me." Her nails dig into my arms. "You can't do anything. You don't even know where he is."

"I don't care. I need to do something. I need to…" My voice trails off, and I give in to her. I collapse onto the balcony, my back against the railing, my face in my hands. She's right; there's nothing I can do. But not Tyler. Please, not Tyler. He can't be taken away from me like this.

Not Ty.

"What time is it?" My voice is a whisper.

Ocean sighs heavily and pulls one sleeve of her sweatshirt up, revealing an electronic touchpad on the fabric of her uniform. I look at my wrist and see that my sleeve is illuminated as well. My eyes brush over the time: 1751. It's 5:51 p.m.

"I'm going to dinner," she tells me, but I don't move.

I reply, "I'm not hungry."

"Yes, you are. You're coming." Her hand reaches down, and I weakly grab it. I allow her to pull me onto my feet.

⋏　⋏　⋏

All the tables are full by the time we reach the dining hall. It's full of people and the sounds of talking and clattering silverware. I assume that all the groups must eat here. Small, circular tables are scattered throughout the room, and a large buffet line stretches against the nearest wall. When I reach the counter with my tray, a woman hands me a bowl of some thick stew and a bread roll.

I break away from the line and look around the room for anyone I know. My eyes settle on a mostly empty table in the far corner. More people are entering the room, and I quickly find myself squished between Ocean and, a few seats away, a mousy-haired girl whom I don't know. In the center of the table there is a plate piled with a kind of sandwich I don't recognize. Between two crispy, golden pieces of bread is a stringy yellow goop. I pick one up and drop it to the table instantly. It's hot.

"It's just cheese," someone says. I look up to see the boy with the freckles sit down at the table directly across from me. My face flushes warm as I pick the sandwich up again and hold it in my hands. I nibble on its edge and quickly proceed to take a large bite. The flavor of warm cheese explodes in my mouth. It's the best thing I've ever tasted.

"You've never had a grilled cheese before?" the boy asks in disbelief as I finish the sandwich. I shake my head.

"Where I lived, it was hard to find anything to eat," I reply, taking another sandwich from the plate. "Everything came from cans or the trash."

He looks at me in such disbelief that I can't help but wonder: Did he even come from the Slump at all? How did he get here? The girl with the flame tattoo approaches us, her eyes on him. She slides onto the bench next to him, grabs a grilled cheese from the plate, and shoves it into her mouth.

"Oh, it's you," she says to me through a mouthful. A polite smile dances across her lips. "Summer, is it?"

"Back off, Gail," the boy says tersely, rubbing the back of his neck. She brushes him aside.

"What's wrong Blayze? I'm only trying to make conversation." *Blayze.* The boy with freckles has a name. The girl puts her half-eaten sandwich back on the pile. "I'm Flame."

She shoots a glare at Blayze before extending her hand to me from across the table. I shake it, noticing how delicate her hands are compared to mine. Blayze stares at her blankly, going back to his food within seconds. The tension between them is difficult to miss.

"Summer," I say, withdrawing my hand and going back to my food. I finish the last bite of my grilled cheese and grab a spoon from the jar in the center of the table. Pulling my bowl toward me, I taste the stew. It's better than it looks—meat and potatoes in a thick, brown sauce. I take another spoonful.

"I couldn't help but notice your little display back in the Lobby," Flame looks at me from under her carefully shaped eyebrows. "You were very brave, though I must add, quite foolish."

Relieved at this lighthearted conversation, I decide to go with it. "Well, I'm sure Official Foster didn't mind too much. No one was permanently injured." I think of his enraged face looking up at me. "Besides, I think it was the best entertainment he's had in weeks."

Blayze grimaces, but Flame doesn't skip a beat. "The best any of us have had, I'm sure." She glances at Blayze. "Wasn't it, Z?"

"Z?" I ask before I can stop myself.

"It's a nickname." He shrugs. Before he can say anything else, the dining hall doors open and a large group of guards and officials, who look between the ages of sixteen and twenty-five, enters the room. Silence falls as they grab trays and sit at various tables. I tense up as I see a few of them walking toward us. Kace is in the lead.

He sits down between me and the mousy-haired girl. On his other side is a bleached-blond guard. I cringe as I feel Kace's shoulder touch mine.

The blond guard mutters something under his breath and leans forward to eye me humorously. Now that he's closer, I can make out his features—lean and tall with high, angular cheekbones. One of his eyes is a bright, captivating green while the other is pale hazel. He runs his gloved hand over his hair, smoothing it into a gelled shine. "This is her?" he asks.

Kace nods, flushing slightly red, and I grin. They were talking about me. "Little small, yeah?" says the blond guard.

Ass.

"You might think twice about calling me small after I whip your ass." The words roll off my tongue like acid, though I keep my expression calm. I feel Ocean's elbow dig into my side. "Besides, I'm almost as tall as you." Which is true. The guard looks at Kace and then back at me.

"She's got a quick tongue, doesn't she?"

"I—" Kace begins.

"I hope you can keep up," I interject. "It really isn't fun bantering with someone who can't *walk the walk*, if you know what I mean." The guard flushes, and I try to stifle a grin of satisfaction.

"They're a pretty hopeless group," the guard says, trying to redeem himself. "I don't see them lasting long." I bite my tongue. Kace hasn't said a word this entire time.

"*Hopeless?*" I hiss angrily. "You're calling—"

"Yes," the guard sneers. Kace takes a sandwich from the center of the table and indulges messily. "Hopeless."

"She's right," Blayze pipes up. "Who are you calling hopeless?" I look at him, surprised, and he meets my gaze.

Kace turns to his friend. "If all goes well, I'll have better luck next time," he says through a mouthful. Gross.

I am fuming, but I bite my tongue.

"What are you going to do to us?" Ocean asks in a clear attempt to end the bickering.

"How many times do people have to ask that?" I mutter under my breath, and Ocean nudges me again with her elbow. I kick her under the table.

Kace looks up at the girl. "Haven't I already explained this?"

"Well, gee, thanks for—" I start.

"You're in a *charming* mood, aren't you, Summer?" Blayze remarks after swallowing.

I drop my eyes to my food.

"How many more threats is it going to take for you to shut up, Greenwood?" asks Kace as he returns his mocking gaze to me. I cross my arms over my chest. Words can't express how much I loathe this human.

"Way too many, so you might want to stay out of my way." I hold his gaze. The tension skyrockets like the fizz of a soda. Finally, I break the stare and push away from the table.

"I'm done," I say, rising from my seat. I'm tired. Not just sleepy tired, but tired of everything. With a loud sigh, I turn and dump my tray. Ocean follows me as I retreat to our room, trying to avoid everyone. When I reach it, I stumble over to my bed and fall face first onto the mattress.

Why is Making Perfect doing this? For fun? The world we live in has no place for this kind of entertainment. But why, then?

Damn it.

I wonder what Lily and Tory are doing right now. It's hard to believe I was with them only this morning. How are they going to get food? I have told Tory about the market before, but she's in such a fragile state that I doubt she'll be able to make it through the door. That leaves Lily. I shudder at the sight of Lily having to go to the market by herself. She washes every piece of food I give her three times just to make sure it's clean—she can't stomach the market.

And I didn't leave them with anything. If I had just grabbed more when I was at the convenience store, they would have something to eat for the next few days. Now they have nothing. I groan. If only I had run a little faster.

My head starts to hurt, and I suddenly feel exhausted.

My head falls down onto the rock-like pillow, and I close my eyes.

I think of Tyler.

The lights turn off by themselves.

11

TYLER

There's a faint hissing sound coming from my left. I shift slightly, an indecipherable groan escaping my lips. My head hurts, and the eye where the official hit me is swollen shut. A pungent smell is hanging in the air, and a cacophony of muffled voices is ringing through my ears.

What happened?

I turn over so that I'm facing up and try to steady my breathing. Something slips out of my hand and I turn my head, eyes shut in pain. When I sit up, my body screams in protest. With a loud groan, I fall back to the ground.

Suddenly, all noise stops. All the scratching, all the voices, everything. An eerie silence fills the room. Heart pounding, I force my good eye to open and look around the room. Guards are everywhere, frozen in place, staring at me like I'm a ghost. Horror engulfs me.

Bodies litter the floor. Crumpled inward, completely limp. Their faces are ashen gray, and their eyes stare straight ahead, lifeless. The guards have been stuffing them into body bags and carrying them out of the room.

I look down. The little girl's body is wedged against mine, her eyes squeezed shut. Her skin is gray like the others.

Fear, horror, disgust, and anger all fill me at once. I scramble away, tripping over the dead bodies of the red-marked kids. Why am I not dead? I should be. What's going on?

Why were all these kids killed?

This is *mass murder*.

Before I know it, guns are pulled on me and guards are pushing me into the corner. I try desperately to get away. My head is swimming, and my body wants to hurl. I try to swallow, to force it down, but my chest feels like it's going to explode. It all comes out at once, and I am sick all over the ground in front of me. My whole body is in a spasm and contracting, trying to eject all of my organs. Tears escape the corners of my eyes as acid burns the inside of my mouth.

I feel like I'm dying.

Whatever they used to kill everyone else didn't work on me. Hopefully they will shoot me now and get it over with.

But they don't. As I try to collapse, the guards pin me against the wall by the crooks of my arms. I go limp. What's happening to me? I make no effort to conceal my fear. The world around me is spinning so violently that I want to hurl again.

More officials rush into the room. I am helpless against them. My limbs start to quiver. I don't know what's happening to me. The official who seems to be in charge has a nasty grimace on his face as he turns me over, inspecting every bit of exposed skin. It's like he's looking for something. He jerks my left hand up and stops, running his finger over the star like Riley always used to do.

It's like I'm falling. Time seems to stop. My eyes are wide, and I stare at the official as he flicks his hand outward and signals the two guards holding me to take me away.

They waste no time. My head rolls back as they drag my helpless body out of the room and into the hallway, tripping over the remaining bodies littering the floor.

What's happening? I feel so confused as they force me into the light. I am lightheaded, and my knees are shaking uncontrollably.

Soon, I just can't take it anymore. I collapse to the floor, my head hitting the cold tiles. I welcome the darkness.

▲　▲　▲

When I come to, I find myself in a bed. I ache all over. My face is still swollen and probably bruised, judging by the throbbing pain shooting through my head. An IV has been inserted into my arm, connected to a large bag of fluid hanging above me. The tube is shiny, like it's made out of a substance that is not quite metal. I've never seen anything like it. I don't know what it's pumping into my arm, but I can't bring myself to rip it out. If they wanted to kill me, they would have done so already.

Shivers pulse through me, and I look around the room. I'm clearly in an infirmary, albeit one with more empty beds than full ones. Nurses mill around nonchalantly, sitting on stools or disappearing behind the curtain at the end of the room. I see no familiar faces.

One of the nurses notices that I'm awake. She gently dabs the drops of sweat off my forehead. When she starts to pull her hand away, I grab it. Judging by her cry, my grasp is more forceful than I meant it to be.

"What is happening?" I plead. "Why am I here?" My voice cracks, but I don't take my eyes off her. I think she sees the wild fright in my eyes because she gently lies me back down and squeezes my hand in a motherly fashion. I wonder if she knows what's happening to me—why I didn't die with the others, why they have brought me here, and why they're keeping me alive. If she does, she doesn't show it. She just holds my hand and wipes my forehead with a cold cloth.

"They will come to explain everything shortly," she says after a while. "In the meantime, we've got to get you feeling better."

"They? Who's they?" My voice cracks again, and she lays me down. I wish Summer was here.

"Shhh," she whispers, squeezing my arms. She stands to check the small meter connected to the fluid pumping into my vein. My eyes dart to the nametag on her blue scrubs. With a squint, I can just make it out. *Abby.* As I look at her more closely, she doesn't look much older than me—maybe even younger. She sits next to me, and I sigh deeply, ignoring the aching in my rib cage.

"What's wrong with me?" I eventually say, my eyes still closed. When she says nothing, I shake my head. "Please, I want to know."

"I don't know. You were really sick earlier—we thought you were going to die. The officials know what's going on. They're going to come in and tell you shortly."

"The officials? What offi—"

The doors on the other side of the room open with a loud hiss. A man dressed in a crisp, black suit and flanked by two heavily armed guards walks toward me. Abby's head turns quickly. She stands as still as a post by the monitors, watching the man approach my cot. His expression is cold as ice.

He stops by her and exchanges a few hushed words before walking over to me.

"Are you Tyler Evans?" His voice is strangely high, not a quality I would have pinned on him. I nod, and the man turns to Abby. "Unhook him."

"I apologize, Doctor, but he has not yet reached a stable condition. Unhooking him could result in—"

"Unhook him."

With a reluctant nod, Abby walks over to me and slowly pulls the tube out of my arm. It makes a small hissing noise as it retracts into its sheath. Guards grab my arms and help me into a sitting position. The corners of my vision go black, sending pangs of dizziness through my head. I cry out and grab the bed frame tightly, watching the world come back into focus. I swing my legs over the side of the bed and stand up with the guards' help. We walk toward the door on the heels of the black-suited man. I can almost feel Abby's gaze looking at me. I feel bad for never thanking her, but I'm out the door before I know it.

The hallways here are stark white, though they slowly fade back into concrete as we walk farther from the hospital. My head begins to clear as we walk, and I keep my focus on the man in front of me. He probably knows why I didn't die back there—why they kept me alive. We push through a set of glass double doors, exiting the medical wing, and reach an elevator. Once we arrive at the top floor, I'm pushed into the first door to the right by the barrel of a gun.

The office looks like something out a cartoon book. The mounted heads of various creatures hang on the walls, and the whole room is dauntingly messy, with papers strewn all along the dark bookcases. A desk sits in the middle of the room, and a short, fat, balding man in a disheveled gray suit sits behind it. The guards forcefully shove me into a chair across from him. He takes a few minutes to straighten his suit and get all of his papers into a neat stack.

He grins at me.

"Welcome, Tyler. We have an awful lot to talk about."

12

SUMMER

I wake drenched with sweat, breathing heavily. I'm clutching my pillow like a lifeline.

"It's okay. It was just a dream," says Ocean. I look over and see her sitting on her bed with her blanket wrapped around her shoulders.

My eyes wide, I look around the room, trying to comfort myself. It's okay. I'm in my room. Nobody's hurt. It was just a dream—just a dream.

I am sweating. The sweat feels exceptionally hot and sticky.

Like blood.

Nauseated, pained, and tired all at once, I wrap my arms around my stomach and rock forward slightly.

"Summer, it was just a dream," Ocean says again and walks over to my bed. I glance over to the little window and see that it's still dark out.

How long have we been sleeping?

"How long have you been awake?" I ask Ocean.

"Not long. You were screaming—you probably woke up the whole Lobby. It sounded like you were being murdered in your sleep."

"I was," I mutter under my breath. She gives me a shaky smile. "What time is it?"

"About an hour before breakfast. But I can't sleep." Ocean pushes the hair out of her face, rubbing her lips together. "God, I feel sick."

"Are you, like, *sick* sick?" I ask, and she shakes her head.

"I don't think so. I just don't want to start training." She sighs. "But I suppose we don't have a choice, do we?"

I frown and shake my head.

"You were pretty brave, standing up to them yesterday. I wish I could do that."

"No, you don't. I'm pretty much an idiot," I say, and a smile tugs at her lips.

"Maybe, but sometimes I wish I was more of an idiot." She looks at the floor.

"Count your blessings," I remark. "You have much bigger things to worry about."

I fall back to sleep. The next thing I know, Ocean is shoving me awake. My eyelids heavy, I slide out of bed and into the bathroom, where I get ready within a few minutes. Ocean and I are on our way toward the dining hall before the bell rings.

Kace addresses us with a stern nod as we walk to the nearest table, our trays piled high with food.

It's a new sensation to me, not having to ration out every piece of food I get.

"Aren't you just a ray of sunshine this morning?" I remark. Kace gives me an unmoving glare. I end up sitting between Blayze and Ocean. Flame isn't around. I catch Blayze looking at me, but I keep my eyes glued to my tray. I notice how sharp he looks this morning—his hair is still rumpled, but there's a new gleam in his eyes.

"Good morning," he says.

"Morning," I reply, not knowing what else to say.

"You sleep okay?" he asks, and I shrug.

"Yeah." He doesn't need to know. "You?"

"Relatively."

"Eat fast. We start training today," Kace cuts in before either of us can say anything else. I notice that the blond guard is missing. Why is Kace sitting with us? I ignore him while wolfing down my breakfast at an impressive rate. The oats have the texture of the slimy mud you'd find at the bottom of a pond. I'm done before I know it.

"Attention, groups one through six," the voice on the loudspeaker grumbles. "Your officials will be here to collect you soon. Eat quickly."

The doors slide open on the other side of the room, and three officials walk in, standing rigidly with their hands behind their backs. But Official Banks isn't there. Kace notices this too, and gets up to join the small cluster of white-clad officials. I watch as he talks to them, his face tightening in frustration. Everybody else seems to take this as a cue to leave, and I follow them, dumping the contents of my tray into the bin on the other side of the room. I follow Blayze over to our meeting point. He looks tense and nervous. After the whole group has arrived and is mumbling quietly to each other, Kace finally speaks.

"Banks won't be your head official anymore. I'm sure you all saw what befell her yesterday." I feel eyes on me, and I blush. "She is in no state to oversee your training. I will be in full control from now on."

To his clear surprise, nobody says anything in response. Not even me.

"I assure you, today will be a long day," he continues. I expect to see some sort of emotion in him, but his face is like a slate. "You will not complain. You will only do as I say."

The group exits the dining hall. I lose Blayze in the crowd. Flame seems to have reappeared out of nowhere, a few spaces to my right. There are only a few people between myself and Kace, who is at the front of the group. The hallways pass in a blur. A cool breeze whips through my hair as Kace quickens our pace to a brisk jog, causing us to sound like a stampede of animals tearing down the stairs. I feel goose bumps all over my skin, even through the sweatshirt. Would it kill them to heat this place in the winter?

This small branch of Making Perfect was built in 2365, seventy-six years ago. It took nine years to build. I remember writing a paper on it in second level. The assignment taught me all about the history of Making Perfect. This complex was built to be the center of the country's genetic testing. Though it's one of their smaller facilities, it is still larger than numerous football fields put together. It reaches far underground and houses numerous subway tracks, as well as runways on the perimeter of the property. There are so many hallways connecting the various parts of the building that it resembles a labyrinth. There's no way to navigate the place unless you have detailed directions or have memorized the floor plan. No doubt Kace has done the latter.

After many twists and turns, he stops us. He was right about us being out of shape—everyone around me is breathing heavily. He turns to face us and gives us strict instructions.

"This is the White Room. Once I let you in, sit in the chairs. Don't move, don't talk. Silence is key. You will be taken out individually once they're ready for you. Understood?"

We all nod, and the metal door slides open. People walk in silently. When I step past the threshold, I look around the room, eyes wide.

It isn't a particularly large space; it's about the size of our room in the hotel. But the similarities stop there. This room is completely white. *Everything* is white, from the chairs lining the walls, to the walls themselves, the floor, and the ceiling. Even the handcuffs on the chairs are white. The members of groups one through three have already been strapped to the chairs. The expressions on their faces are various mixtures of fear. A rubber flap on the other side of the room functions as a door, concealing whatever lies beyond.

Without a word, guards are instantly upon us. Escorting us to the white chairs, they use the cuffs to bolt our wrists to the wall so that they lie above our heads. The blood instantly rushes from my hands, making them throb and tingle. I struggle to pull my hands out of the cuffs, but they just get tighter. The seat that I'm strapped to is between Blayze and a girl with bright red curls that stick to her forehead in a shine of sweat. Her entire face is covered in freckles like a Raggedy Ann doll.

"Don't move. It gets worse if you do," I hear someone say.

I look up at the guard strapping me in, who meets my gaze. I don't know him, but his big brown eyes are soft and warm, and he is gentle. I smile gratefully, and he finishes locking me in, quickly returning to his post by the white door.

Listening to the stranger's advice, I go as stiff as the hardcover of one of Lily's books. The silence in the room is unnerving. Blayze is fidgeting next to me, turning his wrists around in the cuffs and rubbing his nose against his shoulder as if to scratch an itch. I can't help allowing my eyes to linger on him for a while. His tracksuit is hugging his chest, sticking to his torso because of the sweat poking through the fabric. Through the suit, I notice how defined his upper body is, and I focus on the rise and fall of his chest. As much as I want to, I can't seem to tear my eyes off him.

He notices and looks up at me.

"Stop staring at me," he mutters, his voice barely audible. He keeps his eyes trained in front of him. He's wearing a beaded necklace, which must be from home. How did he manage to keep that?

Don't they take all possessions away during screening? I feel my face grow warm when I hear him speak again. "It's distracting."

A laugh escapes my lips, and I quickly bite my tongue. Heads turn to look at me. I turn beet red. I can't bring myself to look at Blayze again—my whole face might melt off.

I hear a faint whimper and glance over at the girl on my other side. She is staring at her lap, hands slightly trembling with fright. She looks only slightly younger than me.

"Hey," I whisper to her discretely, searching for something to say that will comfort her. "If you relax your hands a little, it'll be a little less painful." The pressure that was previously on my wrists has been relieved slightly by holding still. The girl tries it, too, and a moment later her green eyes open and blink at me in thanks. They're soft green, like a mint leaf or spring dew on grass.

"I'm Sadie," she says. Her voice is distorted by a tense exhale that sounds like a moan.

"Summer," I reply, feeling just as anxious. Blayze notices my conversation and looks like he wants to say something, but decides against it.

I want to keep talking, but people are starting to notice our conversation, so Sadie and I fall quiet. I scan the room, spotting Ocean down the line on my right.

Sometime later, a woman walks into the room. She isn't particularly large—she looks to be about Ocean's height, though it's hard to tell from this far away. She is dressed in a version of an official's uniform that is somehow more feminine. Her brown hair is pulled back in a tight knot, making her look like a librarian from the TV that I watched as a kid.

"Two-six-five-five-nine-Foxx-fourteen," she calls out. Her voice is cold as steel, and she holds herself up straight, like a peg. By squinting, I can just read her nametag: Olivia Ross.

Sadie recoils at the sound of her name and number. When the guards unlock her wrists, she brings them down to her lap, flexing them in little circles. Then she is roughly brought to her feet and pushed toward the makeshift door.

Just before the threshold she stops, planting her feet firmly on the tiled floor. The guards try to move her, but she doesn't budge. I am impressed at her strength. I can see her tense up, readying herself for what's coming.

"No," she proclaims fiercely. She has decided to make her stand here. "Tell me what you're going to do to me, or I'm not going." Despite Sadie's strong display, or perhaps because of it, Olivia smiles at her in amusement.

"All right, we'll do this your way." Olivia snaps her fingers, and three more guards appear from behind the white door. I expect them to simply drag her away, but they don't. They carry her to the middle of the room, in front of everyone. When they turn her toward me, I can see the terror on her face.

Olivia's voice is sharp and painful, like nails grinding over the surface of a chalkboard. "Let what follows serve as a lesson to all of you. This is what happens when you don't do what you're told." She clearly relishes her power. A guard pulls out what looks like a shiny, black brick from his pocket and holds it up so we can see it. My fists clench in the cuffs, my body tensing up.

Everyone stares. There is nothing I can do. The guard squeezes the brick, and electricity sparks to life on its tip. I've seen such weapons before in school textbooks. It's called a "shocker." It automatically maps out your nervous system and adapts its charge to short circuit your neurological functions. If used properly, the customized electric shock can paralyze its victim for up to an hour, depending on how long it is applied to the body. I remember one of my teachers saying that he had been shocked once and describing how agonizing it had been. The scar that resulted from it ran from the back of his shoulder all the way up his spine and to his skull.

Sadie lets out a howl of anguish as the crackling blue and white sparks touch her skin. The guard presses it hard against the back of her skull, sending the shock all the way down her spine and through every nerve in her body. No blood comes from the wound—all the pain is internal.

I grit my teeth to prevent myself from crying out. My lip catches between my teeth, and I taste blood.

That's enough, I think. *If you continue for much longer, you're going to kill her.*

Maybe that's their intent.

Please, pass out.

After a few more agonizing seconds, the guard pulls the shocker away from Sadie's small frame. She crumples to the ground, lying awkwardly on the white-tiled floor.

"Did I say stop?" the woman asks, striding over to Sadie's crumpled body. The guards don't move—they just look at each other with a dumb expression on their faces. I wonder if they do something to their brains during their mutations to make them dumber. Taking Kace into consideration, it's always a possibility.

Eventually, one of them is brave enough to say something.

"But, Mrs. Ross, if we continue, she might die." I don't recognize the voice, but it sounds like the rumble of a train when you can feel it through the ground before you see it.

"Does it look like I care? She needs to be taught a lesson. Are you questioning my order?" she barks at him. When he shakes his head, she backs away, and he reluctantly brings life back to the shocker.

No. If they continue, Sadie will die.

Die.

The guard presses the shocker against Sadie's skin, causing her body to twitch uncontrollably.

She is going to die. I feel energy rippling through my veins. It causes my arms to harden with tension, like they always do when I get angry or I am preparing to do something physically challenging. I can feel a sheen of sweat forming droplets on my forehead and trickling down my temples.

My eyes stare fiercely at the shocker. That piece of pure power, crackling beneath someone's fingers, able to reach every nerve in another person's body—

It happens quickly. I throw my body forward, toward Sadie and that shocker as an enormous surge of adrenaline plows through my body. My cuffs rip off the wall, dangling around my wrists like bracelets. I throw myself between Sadie and the shocker, ignoring the looks of horror plastered on the faces of everyone in the room.

I yank the guard's hand away from Sadie's neck. He is so shocked that I don't meet much resistance.

"Stop!" I shout. "She's had enough."

I spin around to face Olivia defiantly. She is so surprised that her little spectacles have almost fallen off her crooked nose. My eyes bore into hers, my anger sending waves of power through my veins.

"Seize her!" she screams, her voice shaken. Two guards rush at me, and I leap toward the ceiling, praying that there will be something there for me to grab a hold of.

But my hands touch only smooth plaster. I fall to the concrete, my head snapping back against the hard surface. My world swims, and huge hands grab my arms and hold them behind me.

A stabbing pain cuts through my head. I toss my hair wildly out of my face as Olivia approaches me. Furious, she grabs the shocker that lies on the floor. "It wasn't supposed to be you, but as you wish," she says, her face contorted in anger. She is clearly not used to being challenged. "Hold her," she orders the guards. Then she moves behind me, and I brace myself for the blinding pain that I know is coming.

But it doesn't. "You're..." Her hand darts out and yanks a strand of hair from behind my ear. She gasps and turns me to face her. She points to my ear and shouts, "Where did you get that?" I stare at her blankly. Now it's my turn to be confused.

"My ear? I was sort of *born* with it—"

She glares. "Not your ear. The star." She points again.

"The star?"

I've always had the star, I think. *It's nothing special.*

"Yes."

"I've always had it." I fumble with my words, and she purses her lips, mumbling something under her breath.

"Are there any more of you?" Her voice quivers. Any more of us? What is she talking about?

"Uh..." My eyebrows furrow in confusion. "No?"

"Hold on to her, tight." Olivia walks toward the white door.

The guards relax as soon as Olivia's out of sight. Two of them lift Sadie's limp body off the ground and back into the chair. Her eyes have rolled back into her head, but her chest is still rising and falling.

At least she's alive.

I glance up, and the first person I see is Blayze. His expression holds something that I don't recognize. His brow is furrowed, and his hands are clenched tightly. I shift my gaze, but it isn't long before I'm looking at him again. This time, I see clear worry in his eyes.

Could he actually be worried about me?

He mouths to me, *you okay?* I force myself to ignore him, watching him purse his lips uneasily.

Olivia reenters the room, looking as white as a sheet.

"Cuff her," she says, letting out a shaky breath that rocks her entire body. "Miss Greenwood is in for a very special talk."

13

"**A**re you going to ignore me forever?" I ask Kace.

He turns his head slightly to glance at me, taking his eyes off the hallway in front of him. He hasn't said a word to me since he picked me up. He's in an even fouler mood than earlier.

We turn a corner, passing a group of people in white lab coats who are conversing quietly. I don't say anything else until we've reached the elevator.

"Where are you taking me?" I ask again for the fifth time.

He sighs through gritted teeth. "If I told you, would it make a difference?"

My heartbeat feels sluggish as we continue to move upward. "Why does this person want to see me?"

"He would like to speak with you," Kace finally snaps.

"That's a pretty vague answer." I pause for a moment as he presses the button. "How old are you?"

"Twenty-one. And you?"

"Fifteen," I reply, wiping the sweat from my brow. Kace still isn't looking at me, and I am growing frustrated. "Why do they call you 'captain'? Isn't that an old term? Why not just 'head official'?"

"I didn't invent the titles." The elevator doors slide open, and we walk inside. My jaw hangs slack. The elevator is lined completely with mirrors. It is a shock to look at hundreds of reflections of myself. I look like I just went through the washing machine. My hair is drenched with sweat and sticking up at all sorts of strange angles, and my tracksuit is ripped.

"Are you the head official? Or just the head of the guard?"

Kace doesn't reply.

After a while I break the silence again. "Neither?"

"Captain of the guard implies the latter, doesn't it?" he grumbles. I smile.

"Kace Foster, captain of the guard…It has a nice ring to it." I pause, fingering the hem of my sweatshirt nervously. I don't want to think about what in store for me. "Is Ian Cooper twenty-one years old as well?"

Kace shakes his head. "Nineteen."

"So he's younger than you. Are you close friends?"

Kace falls silent again. I roll my eyes.

"You really aren't very fun to talk to."

"In the future, I will make it my mission to come up with more stimulating answers to your irritating questions."

My smile turns into a smirk. "That would be much appreciated."

The elevator doors open, and he pushes me out. I stop in my tracks, completely awed. The hallway looks like a picture of a storybook palace, but with a darker twist. The walls are painted a warm, milky color, and gold trimmings enhance the dark mahogany doors. The carpet is thin and beige; it feels almost like a hard floor under my feet. The Making Perfect logo, identical to the symbol sewn into my tracksuit, and the company slogan are etched into the arched gold ceiling:

Making Perfect, Inc.: Improving the human race since 2341.

One hundred years.

I look at the letters along the ceiling in awe. I've never seen anything like this. It's beautiful. Kace walks me down to a door on the right that is identical to the others. The words

Commander Cooper are engraved into the plaque that hangs on it. My jaw clenches. I'm being taken to see Ian Cooper. Kace touches his remote to a sensor by the door, and I hear a muted buzzing inside the room.

"Come in." A smooth, perfect voice that I recognize as Cooper's speaks over the intercom. My stomach knots.

The door opens, and Kace gestures for me to enter. I hear him come in after me. The fairy tale feeling of the architecture continues into what seems to be a waiting room. There are two cream-colored armchairs and a large sofa. A little, ornate wooden table with golden feet rests in front of the sofa. It is covered in dark rings made by coffee cups. The sofa sinks under my weight as I take a seat. A crackling fire sends waves of heat toward me. I'm tempted to close my eyes and enjoy the warmth, but I don't dare.

"Thank you, Viktor," I hear Cooper say from inside the office. "You have already done enough. From what I've seen, this group looks excellent. Use them well."

The reply is too muffled for me to make out. Seconds later, the door opens and the man who must be Viktor exits.

I force myself to stay still, the fear building inside me. Viktor looks nothing like the scientist I had envisioned. Apart from his lab coat, he looks like he could be the leader of a drug-dealing street gang. His black hair is brushed back out of his face and swimming in hair gel. His dark eyes narrow when he walks out and sees me. His black clothing is tight underneath the lab coat, enhancing his muscles. Scoffing at me with disdain, he walks swiftly out the door. I sigh. I didn't realize I was holding my breath.

Cooper comes through the door, looking perfectly polished. He steps into the light, and I suck in a breath. He looks just as flawless as he did when I saw him in the lobby, only this time he's dressed in a more casual blue dress shirt and gray suit pants.

And he's smiling.

"Miss Greenwood," he addresses me, gesturing for me to come inside. He greets Kace with a nod. I hesitantly get up and follow him back into the office.

Inside his office, the walls are a pale green and the desk is pristine. Not one paper seems to be out of place, except for two yellow files in the middle of the desk. A black, leather chair sits behind it, along with two of the same facing it. The nearby cabinets must contain something important because they are under lock and key.

"Sit," he says, gesturing to the chairs in front of the desk. I take the seat closest to the door, gripping it tightly. Nervousness prickles my skin like bees. Kace sits rigidly on the chair next to me. "Long time no see, Summer," says Cooper.

His careful hands offer me a small ceramic plate. I take it and stare in awe at its contents.

Cookies.

"Take them," he says, and I sink my teeth into a beautifully decorated cookie. The flavor explodes in my mouth. "Nobody eats them around here. It's nice to know that somebody still likes them besides me." I continue to gulp down large bites of the sugary treat, only stopping to look up after I've eaten the whole thing. "You might want to slow down. I wouldn't want you to choke."

I look up at him. "Why did you want to see me?" I ask, licking my fingers clean of crumbs. Kace gives me a disgusted look. Because of the crumbs or the question, I can't tell.

Cooper and Kace exchange a glance, and Cooper grins. Kace is completely unamused.

"And why are you still here?" I ask Kace. He stares at me without emotion.

"I heard about your most recent display," says Cooper, leaning back in his chair and crossing his arms. The humor in his eyes

disappears for a moment before igniting again. He looks completely different than he did yesterday. "I wanted to ask you myself if
what I heard is true."

"The fact that members of your staff are inhumane and idiotic?
Yes, completely true. I don't need to be here if that's all you had to
figure out. But thanks for the cookies."

"I heard about how that girl was treated, and I will resolve the
issue." He looks down at the table, then back at me. "The rumored
star behind your ear—it's there, yes?"

"Um...yeah." I turn my head and push the hair out of the way
so that he can see it. Kace mumbles something to himself. Cooper
just nods.

"Seriously, why are you still here?" I ask Kace. "Don't you have
other people to annoy?"

"Why? Does it bother you, having me here?" Kace snaps back
and meets my gaze.

I don't say anything. Cooper raises his eyebrows at us. He
doesn't seem mad, just inquisitive. Our eyes lock. Maybe he can
see how scared I am, because his expression softens.

"You are perfectly safe, Summer. I'm not going to hurt you." He
takes a small cookie from the platter and bites into it, a few crumbs
falling onto his lap. I don't want to believe him. Why would he be
telling the truth, anyway? He and his associates have brought so
much pain and suffering to me and my loved ones. Why would he
stop being a conniving bastard now?

"Are you sure about that?" I say. "Because lots of people have
been going back on their promises to me lately." There is a cold
feeling of dread throughout my body. It feels as if water is being
poured into my bones and is freezing in place. Goose bumps rise
on my arms, causing me to shiver, and I bite down on my lip. He
rubs his shoulder.

"Don't worry; I have always been a man of my word."

"I hope so."

It's strange. Of all the ways I pictured Ian Cooper, this was not one of them. It's not fair. Evil lords aren't supposed to be this... well...honorable. Dignified. *Attractive.*

He clasps his hands together and rests his chin on top of them. "I only need a little bit of information from you, then I'll be glad to let you go."

I am so afraid. The anxiety building up in my body might tear it apart. "What is it?"

"Do you know where your parents went?"

I frown. Of all the things I expected him to ask, this was not one of them. What about the stereotypical interrogation questions, like, *How did you get here?* and, *Do you have any siblings at home?* Or even the expected ones, like, *How did you get that star?* I shake my head. "I have no idea."

"Are you sure?"

My patience is really thin. "Yes, I'm sure. How am I supposed to know? It's not like they *took me with them.*" I spit out the last part with icy hatred. I realize that I'm not even talking to Cooper anymore. I'm not stupid—I know my parents aren't going to hear me. But I want them to know. Know that I remember they abandoned me. Know that if I ever see them again, I won't hesitate to bloody their faces.

Cooper nods at me sadly. Kace's eyes soften a little. I want to knock their heads together. I *loathe* being looked at like that.

My eyes lock with Cooper's. "Why are you being nice to me?"

He almost does a double take. The surprise on his face is hard to miss.

"I care about you," he says simply.

"You *care* about me?" I feel my blood pressure rising, frustration cutting into me like a knife. "First of all, you hardly know me. Second, you kidnapped me, imprisoned me, then told me you want to use me as your personal lab rat and maybe kill me when you're done? How is that *caring* about me? Please, enlighten me." Without realizing it, I have stood up. I quickly sit, ignoring Cooper's amused expression.

"I didn't kidnap you—"

I cut him off. The anger that has been cooped up inside of me is pouring out onto him. It's probably an idiotic idea to lash out at him like this, but I can't hold it in. "This whole place is so messed up! I thought that the company takes so many of us from our homes, our *families*, because minors aren't allowed to live by themselves. But no, you bring us to this messed-up headquarters and torture us for 'the greater good.'" I lean back in my chair. "*Great*, that's fantastic. You should be so *proud* of yourselves for running this region so well—"

"Wow, Summer. Can you at least let me get a word in?" His eyes are like laser beams. I quiet down. "I am only trying to help you."

"Help—"

"Yes, *help* you, now." I stare at him accusingly, and he turns so that I can only see his profile. I can't help but notice how perfectly straight his nose is and that it is perfectly proportionate with the rest of his face. He clasps his hands, furrows his eyebrows, and looks back at me.

"You're a liar."

He considers this, touching his lips, and nods. The light above us flickers. "Most of the time, actually, yes. But for good reason. Are you?"

I bite my tongue. "I am a liar, but at least I'm honest about it."

The room grows so silent that I can hear the clock ticking in the corner. Cooper is looking at me, and I don't know what to do.

"What do you want from me?" I finally ask him. He stares at me, and I don't look away.

"I've already told you—"

"But I don't believe you. You would have already let me leave if that was it."

"I am a man of my word—"

"You just told me that you're a liar!" Frustration and confusion creep up inside me. His comments are nagging, chipping away a little of my self-control every time he opens his mouth. It's exhausting.

"Keeping one's promises has nothing to do with whether or not one tells the truth."

My mouth freezes. He's right. Very right. But there's no way I'm going to admit it.

I sigh, my hands clasping together tightly, my knuckles cracking. I listen to the sound of the ticking clock but don't dare to look up at it. Cooper's eyes don't waver from my face. Eventually, I find the courage to ask him the question that has been nagging me. "Why are you doing this?"

"Doing what?" He folds his arms over his chest.

"This. What's the point of all of these lives you are wasting?"

His mouth curves up into an exasperated smile. "As I've told you before, I'm not in charge. It's not my call to make."

"Oh, so you're the manipulator."

He pauses, lets out a slight chuckle, and looks up at the ceiling fan. "I prefer the term 'outcome engineer.'"

"But you support it, don't you? Killing for power?" It comes out as more of an accusation than a question, and Cooper looks at me blankly.

"So do you. You do more than support it. You perform it."

My jaw drops. "*Perform* it? Are you *kidding* me?"

"Lie to yourself all you want, but you are just as much of a practitioner of killing as I am, if not more so."

"I'm not lying!" My voice is almost a shout.

"Think about it. Whenever you feel threatened, you lash out. I've noticed that about you. You hurt people to make yourself feel secure. You can't tell me it isn't true." His voice isn't accusatory—simply factual. "Think about it."

I think of that girl in the convenience store. She was dying, slowly and painfully, and in no way wanted to hurt me. She just needed help. If I had stayed and helped her bind her wounds, maybe given her something to drink, she might have lived. I left her to *die*. Maybe I really am no different than they are.

Cooper watches me think and leans back in his chair. "You and I, we aren't as different as you think."

"We are *nothing* alike."

"And there you go, lashing out again. Just admit that I'm right."

My eyes rip into him. I open my mouth to say something, but a loud buzz comes from the door and Cooper looks past me. I watch as he pushes a thin, green button on his desk and speaks into a small microphone. "Just a moment." He props his elbows on the table. Kace has barely said a word this entire time. His gaze alternates between Cooper and me, and a smug look is plastered on his face.

"I really do apologize," he says, "but this is urgent. I expect to see you back soon. Please try to refrain from doing anything stupid."

"I will."

"You're lying. You have a tell."

Kace stands up, and I follow him. "I didn't pin you as being perceptive," I snap at Cooper, not bothering to look back at him.

His parting words barely register as I walk out the door: "As I mentioned before, we are very much alike."

14

COOPER

News that my father was in the building found its way to me far too late. He hardly ever comes to this facility. It's the most uneventful of the company's facilities. If it weren't for the fact that the test kids are being kept here, I'm sure he would never visit. Not that it would be a problem with me—in fact, I'd be all for moving them to a higher-end testing facility. Anyway, barely ten minutes after Kace and Summer left my office, I found myself sitting across from him, watching him sip his coffee while mine sits on my desk, steaming and untouched.

"I hear you have found two more." This is the first thing he says to me. I didn't expect more; this is a kind greeting. I haven't seen him in four months.

It's striking how different we look. If people didn't know we are related, they would not be able to tell. Unlike me, my sister Elle looks like a perfect cross between my mother and father. In most of my features, I take after my mother—except for my pale hair, which came out of nowhere. My eyes belong to my father.

I stare at him unblinkingly and nod. He continues. "Are they here?" His voice is cold and weathered. The gray is increasingly showing in his hairline.

"They are now, yes." He's talking about the test kids, of course. I don't know how the word about Summer and Tyler got to him so fast. That's the freakish thing about this place—how quickly word travels.

I almost couldn't believe it when Summer showed me her star. The so-called "test kids" are a project that Making Perfect has been working on for years. The later part of this time has been spent trying to find them and bring them back to the company after their families had released them into the Slump. It was an extremely bold move on the part of the children's families, who paid for it dearly.

The test kids were created during an experiment conducted on human fetuses while they were still in their mother's wombs. The goal was to create faster, stronger human beings. It worked—for a time. Only thirteen of the children were created before the scientist who devised the experiment betrayed the corporation and ran away with the formula.

It is crucial that we get all thirteen of the test kids together again. However, nobody has ever told me why—that information is kept under lock and key. All I know is that the corporation will stop at nothing to capture every one of them. My father has never informed me of his plan for the test kids once he finds them all. I almost don't want him to.

"Where are they now?"

"The majority of them are already in the lab, and the other two are currently residing in the main quarters with the most recent batch of children." I try to keep my voice as calm as possible as he stares at me. It's a good thing I am sitting in this chair—I don't know if I'd be steady on my feet.

"Do they know?"

I shake my head. I haven't told Summer about what she is. I wouldn't dare.

"Keep a close eye on them. I won't have them walking around freely, doing whatever they please. Keep them under strict supervision."

Gathering all the courage I can, I meet my father's gaze. "I don't think that will be necessary. Neither of them know what they're capable of, and both are watched closely enough as it is. They don't pose a threat."

"You watch your tongue, or you will find yourself in the labs."

"Then what? You'll give my position to Elle?" The words hurt me to say, but they don't even faze my father.

His expression tightens. "Remember who the CEO of this corporation is. Do not question me." I grind my teeth together, and his face softens slightly. "Mason has informed me that you've been doing a fine job taking care of the place."

"With someone like Mason watching me, I don't have the choice to do otherwise," I grumble, lowering my gaze to the stack of papers on my desk. "Father, what's going to happen to the test kids once you get them all together?"

He puts his coffee on the edge of the table. "This is confidential information. Word getting out about the procedure could mean—"

"Procedure? I thought—"

"Ian," he says, stopping me. I haven't heard him say my name in a long time. "The original experiment stemmed from the Star Formula." He pauses, taking another sip of his coffee. His condescending tone is difficult to miss. "The Star Formula, our military enhancement, was created to give us the power to create a soldier who was faster, stronger, and smarter than any ordinary human. But it involved an incredible amount of gene recombination, and the process indirectly altered much of the core DNA that humans need to survive. All of our early test subjects died." He leans back in his chair, and it creaks beneath his weight. "So our scientists divided the formula up into thirteen individual DNA enhancements that targeted the specific alleles corresponding to the traits we are trying to create. They were introduced into thirteen fetuses. As these children grew, their mutations matured with them. But we allowed them to escape. We have to reunite them in order to combine their specific DNA enhancements into a single one."

There is a long pause while this information sinks in. "Why would you collect stem cells? How can you extract that DNA?"

"The only way to ensure we have sufficient genetic material is to collect neural stem cells. The closer they are to the brain, the easier it will be to detect the little abnormalities and combine them into one—"

"But wouldn't that kill the subjects?"

For a second, I think he's about to laugh. "It doesn't matter. We'll have gotten all that we need from them." My stomach twists as he proceeds. "But we need all thirteen kids to be in one place before we perform the procedure because the specially enhanced cells cannot survive outside the host for very long."

I try to keep a straight face, but I am burning inside. Does he realize what he's saying? It's barbaric.

I don't say anything, so he continues.

"With our negotiations with TERC becoming increasingly difficult, we have enemies all around. I—"

I shake my head. "I wouldn't call them enemies yet, Father. The tense relations—"

"Don't question me. I've warned you before; you must watch your tongue." His face is flushed red, and I can see his patience growing thinner. "I will not have you ruining our hope of maintaining peaceful relationships with the neighboring regions. If word about the experiments gets out…" His voice trails off. I keep my eyes trained on the table. "I wouldn't want to be around when they begin filing cases."

Does he mean cases alleging child abuse? If so, I wouldn't blame them. In fact, I would support them. Kace has warned me about sticking my neck out with my father countless times before, but sometimes I just can't control myself. "This system is messed up. This region shouldn't be governed with such a threat-based culture."

"If it wasn't so, you would find yourself at the end of a rebel's gun within a few days."

It's the first time I've heard him explicitly mention the rebels. They're not a direct threat to us, but it's rumored that they're harboring some of the remaining test kids. I can hear the frustration in my father's voice when he mentions them—no matter how hard we try, no matter how often we overturn the Slump, we are never able to find them.

"It's a good thing you aren't CEO. You have a lot to learn," says the CEO of Making Perfect. He stands from his seat, walks over to the wall, pulls down a file from the cabinet, and opens it.

"Why are you so bent on keeping the test kids locked up?" I ask him.

"Nobody has any idea what they're capable of. We are going to run tests on them and study them in greater detail shortly. Besides, we can't perform the procedure until they're all here." He closes the folder and returns it to the shelf. "We just need to find the last three kids."

He pauses, then changes the subject. "That girl, Greenwood. Olivia Ross informed me of her skirmish this morning."

"They were torturing her friend." I don't want him to know how strictly I reprimanded both Olivia and those guards for what they did to Miss Foxx. Strongly.

"They were setting an example." He glares at me, his eyes pinning me to my seat.

"It was inhumane!" I raise my voice, and my father crosses right over to me, standing far too close for comfort.

"They were doing what *had to be done*."

I stand up. Anger builds inside me. "This isn't a game, Father. She—"

"Game?" He laughs softly. "Of course it's a game. Life is a game, Ian. Maybe if you were a little bit older, you'd understand that."

"If you could get off your pedestal for one moment, you'd realize—"

His hand comes down on the side of my face so fast that I don't even have time to flinch. I stumble backward, cup my cheek in my hand, and look at my father. Every ounce of defiance drains from me.

"You must be reminded of your place, Ian Cooper. I am your father, but I am also your superior." His look makes me want to melt into the floor.

I can't stand to be here any longer. Bowing my head to him respectfully, I slide out of the room, leaving my father and my office behind.

I glance down at my watch and suppress a groan. I barely lasted ten minutes.

▲   ▲   ▲

SUMMER

The whole rest of the day was spent in the White Room. After the display I put on that morning, everyone was a little more cautious around me. I had chains around my wrists and ankles along with large straps that went around my chest. It was impossible for me to move. Not to mention the flock of guards stationed at the doors—twice as many as before. When they finally released me, my wrists were practically rubbed raw.

It took forever for them to get through everybody—they never even reached me. I was the last one left. I don't understand. Blayze stayed behind the black curtain the longest out of everybody. When he was dragged back into the main room and strapped to his seat, he looked so confused that it was almost comical.

The next morning, I feel as if I've hardly slept. When I hear someone shouting my name, I open my eyes to the dimly lit room. Ocean is standing over me, dressed in her tracksuit, her hair pulled back tightly. I glance up at the window and see that it's just getting light.

"Wake up," she grumbles, throwing my tracksuit at my face. With a groan, I pull the blankets up over my head and turn over. I don't even want to know what time it is. I hear Ocean make an exasperated noise. "Seriously! Everyone's waiting for you."

"What?" I mumble from under the covers.

"Yes, *waiting for you*." Frustration is dripping off her words. The blankets are suddenly ripped off me. I curse loudly and glare at Ocean, a shiver running through my body.

"Give those back!" I reach for the covers, but she kicks them farther from my reach. I hug my knees to my chest, trying to keep myself warm.

"If you put that tracksuit on, you'll feel better."

"If you just let me sleep, I will—"

"Get up." Her arms crossed against her chest, she glares at me with her head cocked slightly to the side. My eyelids feel like weights. With a moan, I slide out of bed and scurry quickly to the bathroom on the ice-cold concrete floor. Only after I have changed into my tracksuit does she speak again.

"You completely missed breakfast. Kace is waiting for you in the Lobby."

I stiffen up. "What?"

"God, I've never seen you so out of it." Her lips curve up into a smile. I walk out of the bathroom looking completely disheveled, tying my hair back sloppily. She tosses me a shrink-wrapped muffin, and I waste no time in unwrapping it and gulping it down. It's so *soft*.

"Why are you so tired, anyway?" she asks as I swallow a large mouthful of breakfast.

"I couldn't sleep."

"Oh," she says simply and opens the door. The tracksuit does nothing to protect me from the cold air. I wish I had brought my sweatshirt.

We run down to the Lobby to rejoin the rest of the group. Except that the group isn't there. Kace is waiting by himself, and he's absolutely fuming. He is making a face like a bug has just flown up his nose.

"Good morning, Captain," I say in the sweetest tone possible. Considering the look he gives me, I'm lucky he didn't hit me right there.

"You took your time."

I shrug. "I was tired." Kace just scoffs. "Where's the rest of the group?"

"They're already outside. I had to come retrieve you when I realized you weren't with them."

It takes a few seconds for his words to sink in. "Wait, outside? What do you mean, outside?"

"We're running this morning. You all have to get into shape." He turns to go, and Ocean follows him. I don't move.

"Running? Seriously?" I mutter to myself. "Hell no."

"Move it, Greenwood. This is not optional," Kace snaps, and I grudgingly follow.

We rush through the twisting hallways, which are still absolutely freezing. We soon reach a large door that is teeming with guards. Kace moves through them with a nod, and they open the door, revealing a large gate. Its bars are so close together that my hand couldn't fit through. I am hit by another wall of incredibly cold air, and I cringe. Screw outside.

The "outside" that Kace was talking about is more like a prison courtyard than the scenic outdoors that I was hoping for. The space is at least twice the size of the Lobby. The ground is a mixture of dying grass and gravel with a few unhealthy-looking trees scattered around. A track rings the space, and guards mill around the perimeter. A lot of people are stuffed in here, some using the track and some quietly standing around. I am surprised so many people are choosing to run, but then I realize that various guards and officials are running alongside them, ensuring that they run and keep pace. The sun is rising, dotting the sky with a pallet of radiant hues. Ocean walks off almost immediately, joining the pack of runners.

I stand my ground. Annoyed, I turn to Kace. "You're not actually expecting me to run around a track. I'm not a dog."

He jerks his head to the pack of runners. I don't recognize anyone I know. "You're running."

"How many circuits?"

"Until we say stop."

Grumbling, I walk toward the group and quicken my pace to a jog. As I begin to move, I'm surprised at the speed the others are moving. It's fast. The cold doesn't help. After mere minutes of running around the large circuit, my hands are numb, my lungs are burning, and I can barely feel my legs. But I keep running. There's no way I'm going to stop while everybody seems to move so effortlessly. I didn't realize I was so out of shape. I just trudge onward, feeling like a hamster on a wheel.

After a while, heavy breathing and pained breaths surround me, mixing with my own. I keep my eyes trained on the ground and force my legs to keep moving. I don't see who's leading the pack, but it certainly isn't me. I catch a glimpse of Kace running with the group, ensuring that everyone stays in line. I feel his eyes tear into me, but I don't look at him.

How much longer? I pass the area that I started from. I don't dare look around to see if anyone has stopped. My breathing has become heavier, and my knees begin to shake. My heart beats so hard that I'm afraid it'll beat right out of my chest. I want to drop out of the line and stop running, but I can't. I gasp for breath as I feel a familiar presence beside me and turn my head.

"Enjoy your sleep-in?"

I am startled by the voice and spin around to find its owner. Blayze is running up beside me, his cheeks pink from the exercise.

"Good morning to you, too," I snap, the words barely coming out through my panting.

"I don't think I've ever formally introduced myself. I'm Blayze. You know, the one you stare at during training."

"I don't—"

He smiles, clearly knowing that I do. I play it off as casually as I can, but I can't hide the obvious redness in my face. "Can I run with you?" he asks.

"I can't stop you."

He chuckles. "That's true."

We round the bend, and I tighten my ponytail as strands begin to come loose. Just as my hands drop back down to my sides, my right foot kicks my left heel and I tumble forward. Crying out in surprise, my knees slam into the sharp stones.

Gritting my teeth, I pop back up as fast as I can. But before I can dust the little rocks from my shins, the plethora of runners slam into me, causing me to stumble again. My lips purse tightly as a hand grabs my arm.

"Woah. Easy there." I barely hear Blayze's voice under the clamor of grinding stone. With a glare, I shrug his hand off my arm. The runners are deliberately moving around us now, creating an air bubble in the sea of motion.

The grin grows on Blayze's face as he looks at me. I raise my eyebrows at him. He looks like he's about to burst out laughing.

"What?" I ask, suddenly defensive.

"Why did they take you away yesterday?" he answers, eyes glinting. I don't know if I want to tell him. Is it a secret? Neither Kace or Cooper told me to keep their meeting a secret. But even so, it feels like something I shouldn't be walking around advertising.

But he seems harmless enough.

I don't answer and start running again. He follows me. Clenching my teeth, I try to steady my breaths but quickly find that I need to open my mouth again. We pass the starting line once again, and I steal a glance at him. Both of us are silent for a while before I pipe up again.

"Commander Cooper's office," I eventually choke out.

Now it's his turn to be confused. "What?"

"You asked where they took me yesterday. Commander Cooper's office."

His eyes widen. "As in, Ian Cooper?" he queries, clearly shocked. I nod.

"Needed to talk to me; I have no idea why. They doubled my guard as well." I wipe the sweat off my forehead. My heart is beating so hard that it hurts. My breaths are choppy. I hate running.

Blayze smirks, shrugging his shoulders up to his ears. "Well, you do seem like the pain-in-the-ass type, with that little twinkle in your eye."

"Well, you seem like the remarkably haughty type, so we're even."

He lets out a mix between a laugh and a scoff, lowering his gaze to the ground in front of him. My face is so warm that I barely feel the cold anymore. The sun is slowly creeping up into the sky, and everything's growing brighter.

I am feeling like I'm about to fall over when Blayze puts his hand on my shoulder. "Come on. I'll race you." My eyes stretch wide. His pace quickens, and a spark of competitiveness flashes through me. Ignoring the burning in my lungs, I throw myself forward, matching Blayze's pace. He lets go of my shoulder, and we tear down the track. I watch his lips tighten as I threaten to over-take him. He runs faster, and so do I. Weaving through the others, we fly down the track at lightning speed. The wind whips through my hair, and I can't help but laugh.

When I finally can't go on any longer, I duck out of the group and lean against a tree, my chest rising and falling heavily. Blayze follows me, a goofy grin on his face. He's breathing just as hard as I am. He walks over to one of the water faucets that sticks out of the wall and starts drinking. I run up to the one next to him, greedily gulping down the water.

"Slow down, you're going to be sick," I hear him say, and I pull my mouth away from the nozzle. I think he notices the scowl on my face because his expression softens. "Oh, come on; it wasn't that bad. You didn't end up having to go to the medical wing." My mouth gapes slightly.

"Did you expect that I would?" I ask once I calm my breathing enough to get a word out.

He shrugs. "Well, I dunno…"

I shove him lightly on his arm. I feel a little lightheaded, but I'm smiling. Blayze's cheeks are flushed red, and his ruffled hair is sticking up at sharp angles. The dark circles under his eyes from yesterday have faded.

"At least we didn't come in last," he adds.

"That's where your bar is set? Not coming in last? I think you might want to lift that bar a little, Blayze," I say, taking another sip of the water.

"Depends who I'm running with," Blayze retorts. After a slight pause, he continues. "I've got to say, though, you surprised me. I didn't think you had that in you." He leans against the tree, sinking to a sitting position. I follow him, sighing as my legs melt into the ground. "Did you have to run a lot in the Slump?"

I shrug, sitting down next to him. "Yes and no. I took daily food runs, but I wouldn't run like this everywhere I went. It happened in spurts. Sometimes I would be moving a lot, and other times I'd sleep most of the day." I don't know why I am telling him this. "Where did you get taken from?"

"The Slump," he says.

"So, you lived there too?"

"Yeah, for a while, with Flame." He shrugs. "My mom and I escaped there when I was seven, after Dad and my older sister, Becca, left us. But four years ago, Mom got sick, and after that it was just me." He pauses, averting his eyes. Before I can say anything, he continues. "After that, I went to live with Flame and her brother. I was in the Slump for nine years. Our building was raided about a week ago, and Flame and I were taken here." A yawn escapes his lips, and he leans his head back against the trunk of the small tree. "How 'bout you? Do you have any siblings?"

"Two sisters," I say, suddenly wanting to yawn myself. "And a dog, Theo."

"That's a lot of people to take care of."

"We all pitched in." I change the subject, not wanting to talk about my sisters. "Did you sleep any better last night? Or was it worse for you, too?"

The truth is, I didn't get to sleep for the longest time last night. My mind just wouldn't shut down. I lay in bed, clutching my blanket so tightly you'd think my hands were made of stone. The conversation I had with Cooper yesterday was stuck in my head, his words replaying over and over like a skipping record.

"Definitely worse." Blayze perks up as a shrill bell sounds over the exercise yard and people begin walking back to the gates. He stands, offering his hand and helping me up. His fingers are ice cold.

"Next time, you'd better watch out," I warns once I'm on my feet. "I'm gonna beat you."

"Oh yeah?" He says. "That might depend on whether you can get out of bed before noon."

An easy smile dances across my lips as we walk back toward the iron gates.

⅄　⅄　⅄

Kace stops the group in front of a pair of heavy metal doors. He was waiting for us when we entered the building, and he has brought us straight here, not saying a word about what we are doing or where we are going. I am happy to see that I wasn't the only one winded from this morning's run. Some people look worse than I feel.

I tense up when Kace finally speaks. "Once you enter this room, you will begin what we call a limit test. It will assess your individual ability to withstand variables such as pain, stress, and so on, along with testing your problem-solving skills," he jibes.

He continues. I soak in every detail. All five groups will be thrown simultaneously into a maze. We will each have a dart gun filled with sedative. If someone is hit three times, he or she will fall unconscious and be collected (receiving a score of zero). Our goal is to find the way out of the maze. Making Perfect will activate the internal sensors in our tracksuits and connect them to monitors, measuring our motor control and neurological functions throughout the exercise. Everyone will encounter the same obstacles—it will be impossible to get out of the maze without encountering all of them.

"Understood?" says Kace, looking at us expectantly.

I have a thousand questions and open my mouth to say something, but Kace's stare makes me reconsider. I shake my head. He steps aside, and the doors open.

We enter a small, gray room. A large rack of black guns is against the left wall, and to the right of this are shelves filled with canisters of tranquilizers. Stored in a set of boxes are small plug-in chips that I assume will plug into our tracksuits. A few wooden benches line the walls, reminding me of a school locker room. On the far wall, in front of an intimidating metal door, three officials holding portable devices wait for us.

"Form three lines," one of the officials orders. I walk to the official in the middle, falling fourth in line. Blayze joins the line to my right. I wait as the officials use their devices to scan the barcodes on everybody's hands. After scanning each person, they plug the proper chip into the receptor on the forearm of his or her tracksuit and hand the person a gun filled with sedative. The line moves quickly, and before I know it, the two boys in front of me have already entered the maze.

I feel my heart racing as an official grabs my hand roughly and scans it. I turn to protest and notice that the official is a woman. This is one of the few female officials I have seen—other than Olivia and Banks. The woman's eyes are hard. She grabs a chip the size of an eraser and plugs it into my tracksuit. I feel the sensors in the suit come alive as the chip makes contact. She takes a strip of tape from her back pocket and secures the chip by taping its loose end to my arm. When she hands me the gun, I feel a strong desire to throw it away. I know it doesn't have bullets, but it's still a gun. I've never shot one before, nor do I want to. Guns have taken the lives of so many people that I've known.

But if I drop it, I'll just be forced to pick it up again.

A thin black holster is strapped to my waist and I take the weapon, walking tentatively to the door. My fists clench tightly around the gun. I take a deep breath. I can do this. I am the girl who is capable of doing triple back-flips down the shaft of an elevator. I can use a gun. But what happens if I'm knocked out? What if someone kills me? We weren't given any rules about hand-to-hand battles.

No. I can't think like that.

I grip the gun's handle so tightly that my knuckles turn white. I try to stop my hands from shaking. That is a sign of weakness. I am strong.

"Remember, nervous energy equals adrenaline. Use it," a voice hisses from behind me. I glance around, but I don't see who spoke.

Adrenaline starts to flow. The door is in front of me. The sooner I get into the maze, the sooner it'll be over.

Before I can panic and change my mind, I yank open the door and throw myself inside.

15

I can't see.

That's my first thought as I enter the maze. Everything is dark, and the air is musty and thick with humidity. It makes my face wet and enters my nose and lungs. Two black walls trap me on either side, making the atmosphere much more intimidating. I can't see how high they reach. My nerves bubble up like foam in a newly opened soda; now there is no going back.

The air is motionless. I had no idea what to expect, but I am surprised by the unnerving silence. I mean, shouldn't there be the sounds of fighting? Everybody else probably ran for it as soon as they entered. The kids behind me will be coming in soon. I have to get away from the door.

Breathe. In, out. Repeat.

I run forward into the fog. As I move, the gravel crunches loudly under my feet. The fog is disorienting—it feels as if I take two steps back for every step forward. My feet hammer the ground as I race, holding my gun at the ready in case someone jumps out of nowhere.

When the barrel of the gun slams into a black wall, I stop in my tracks. Left or right? I glance down both paths for a minute, but then I hear the door open behind me and someone stumbling into the maze. I'm not taking any chances. I make a random decision: left.

I run through the maze with surprising ease, choosing random paths. Eventually, I end up in a large, open space. Thinking of backtracking, I glance back at the path that I came from to see a girl approaching quickly.

When she sees me, she jumps back and scrambles for her gun. I recognize her as Flame's roommate. Her gaze meets mine, her eyes wide with fear and confusion—she's not like Flame. Her long brown hair, which is the same length as mine, is messed up, and judging by her clumsy and uneven gait, she's already been shot. As her fingers quiver on the trigger, I surprise myself and leap toward her.

I feel a rush of power, swinging the butt of my gun at her. I don't want to shoot it—not yet. Where is this aggression coming from? She brings hers up to knock mine away. Hand-to-hand combat has always been easier for me; I don't want to take my chances with my aim. She's shorter and not as strong as I am, so I hit her easily. The blow knocks her feet out from under her, and she falls to the ground, dropping her gun. I watch as she tries to find it, then I wait for her to get back on her feet before knocking her down again, viciously. I am surprised at how easy this is for me. I can feel myself anticipating what she is going to do next. When she rises again, however, she does so while hacking wildly. I step back and, in a flash, she's gone. Wow, she's fast. Not great at combat, but fast.

I don't bother following her. I turn and run in the other direction.

This part of the maze seems far too open to me—the walls are pretty far apart. If this is supposed to be an obstacle course, it's taking an awfully long time to find an obstacle.

And…I spoke too soon. I don't notice the pit until I almost run into it. It looks like a bomb blew a giant hole in the gravel at the center of the path, making the ground around it bumpy and full of potholes. The pit is too deep for me to see the bottom, and

I don't really want to. How am I supposed to get across? It's way too far to jump, even for me. I glance around and back up a few steps. That's it.

There, hidden by the fog, metal handles are positioned un-evenly on the wall along the pit. The first one is far enough that I can't just grab it—I'll have to jump for it. From there, I will have to jump from handle to handle, but that part should be pretty easy for me. I just hope that the handles go all the way to the other side be-cause once I make the jump, it will be impossible to get back. I am backing up to take a running start when I hear the gravel crunching right behind me. I spin around.

Flame is standing there, looking angry as ever. Her eyes shine as she recognizes me, and a cruel smile spreads across her face. I clench my fists around my gun. Part of me wants to fight. Instead, I tuck the gun into the canvas holster and, in a smooth motion, leap for the first handle on the right wall.

The handle is cold, and I grab it easily. As my body swings forward, I use the leverage to propel myself to the next one. I am barely aware of the pit below, and the possibility that I might miss a handle never enters my mind. However, I almost lose my grip when I hear a grunt of effort behind me. Flame has made the jump and is also using the handles to cross. She must want to save her ammunition. I turn to look for her and see that she is only two handles behind me. What she lacks in skill, she seems to be making up for in sheer determination and hatred. Her eyes fire daggers as she hurls herself to the next bar without any apparent fear. I focus on the next handle, catching it smoothly and, in one fluid motion, swing to the next one. This is easy, and it would be fun if I was not being chased by a mentally crazed girl who hates me for no reason. I reach the last handle and look down, hoping to see ground under my feet. My heart sinks, as all I see is the pit.

Damn. Please don't tell me that I will have to fight Flame like this. I try to see through the fog. I think I see the vague outline of the edge of the pit, but I am not sure. I have to take a chance—there is no going back anyway. Gathering all my strength, I prepare for the jump, which I should be able to make. Better to overreach than fall short.

Using my hips and every ounce of energy I can squeeze from my arms, I swing into the fog. My feet hit the ground well clear of the edge. Before I can enjoy the accomplishment, I hear a guttural scream and turn. Flame rolls awkwardly onto the ground a few feet from where I am standing. She quickly jumps up and raises her gun. Realizing that my gun has fallen to the ground nearby, I barely have time to duck before her dart whizzes past my head. Dizzy, she fires again, twice, and I dodge both. A look of frustration crosses her face. Raising her gun, sword-like, above her head, she leaps toward me like an angry lion.

I easily duck the first blow, but she swings again with surprising speed. I feel the sting as the gun hits my side. I cry out in surprise, and Flame bursts out laughing. Her gun comes up fast toward my face. I watch her hand squeeze the trigger, and a dart lodges itself at the base of my neck.

My world spins. This is not working. I jump over her, roll on the ground, and grab my gun. Then I fire a dart into her shoulder.

The sting of the dart, fired at such close range, brings a snarl of frustration out of Flame. She jumps on me, catching me off guard, and we both fall to the ground. She digs her knees into my shoulders, and I grimace in pain. She takes her gun in two hands, one hand on the barrel and the other on the butt, and pushes it hard against my throat. I try not to flinch, but the cold metal is making it hard for me to breathe. I try to struggle, but Flame is in the better position—not bigger or stronger, just luckier. I need to get out of this. Now.

I spit in her face. She squeals and leans back. Her weight shifts back, which allows me a little extra room to move my arms. Perfect.

Flame feels me moving and looks at me in shock, giving me just enough time to grab her shoulders. I throw myself up and come down on top of her.

She cries out in surprise, and I can't help smiling. I dig my knees into her shoulders and sit on her stomach. She can't move her hands, which are under my shins. I raise the butt of the gun to hit her. Flame has to come out of this unconscious. My first blow comes down hard on her collarbone, and she whimpers. I raise it again and bring it down on her jaw. She cries out in pain, and a gurgling sound comes from her throat as she tries to throw me off. She can only manage rolling me onto my side but still lands a knee in my stomach. Her hand shoots out and grabs her gun, raising it with lightning speed to strike my face.

I cry out in pain and surprise. My vision blurs, my eyes water uncontrollably, and I stumble backward, raising my hand to my nose. It comes back bloody. Behind me, I hear Flame stand up. I feel the stinging impact of another dart in my back. I fall to my knees and brace for another hit, but instead I hear a gasp and running footsteps, quickly getting fainter.

Discombobulated, humiliated, and angry, I raise my head and see him through the fog: Trout.

Since Trout got here, he has established himself as the "alpha male." He's the biggest of the boys by far, as I picked up on the AirTran, and extremely strong. He is a skilled fighter and a known member of the Black Spiders.

He is a killer, and he won't hesitate to snap our necks.

"Oh God," I hiss and struggle to stand up. Trying to make sense of my surroundings, I see what looks like a path through the fog. Without looking back, I make a beeline for it. My world whirls like a carousel as I run. The two darts that Flame hit me with are clearly taking effect, and my nose is aching and bleeding. I clearly underestimated her.

I keep running, hoping desperately that Trout took off after Flame instead of after me. I stop when I reach what must be the next obstacle: a climbing wall. Again? At least this one isn't that hard. Climbing is something I did on a regular basis in the Slump. I put my hands on the little stone knobs and begin scaling the wall. I am at the top in seconds—it's only ten feet tall. Then I jump off the other side and realize why the first one looked easy. Making Perfect never makes anything easy.

I face another wall that is about twice as tall as the last. I can barely see the top. I start climbing anyway, and when I am about halfway up, I hear someone behind me. I need to find someplace to hide: to assess the damage to my nose and get myself back in order. My stomach aches. I hate this feeling; as much as I like climbing, the sensation of my stomach trying to climb into my throat makes me want to cry out. Climbing faster, I reach the top and, without thinking, jump off the other side. I shriek on my way down, realizing what I have just done. I am flying through the air.

I brace myself for the impact, but instead, I land in a rope net. A sigh of relief escapes me, and I hurry out of the net, coming face-to-face with another wall. This one is so tall that I can't see the top.

There's a loud thud behind me and I start climbing again, faster than ever. Trout must have followed me. Being a Black Spider, he must be an excellent climber. His height probably doesn't hurt, either. I don't look down. Adrenaline runs through my veins, traveling to every inch of my body. I fly up the wall faster than I have ever moved before. I don't want to know who is coming up behind me. The little knobs fly past underneath me and, before I know it, I reach the top.

The fog conceals the ground almost entirely, but I can just make out the outline of a net.

Okay, time to jump.

Squeezing my eyes shut, I throw myself off the edge. I hold my stomach tight as it is starting to make me feel queasy. The net catching me feels good. It's over.

I climb out and stare ahead. There are three passages—three choices. Which way?

I want to get out of here. Now.

Gently, I take my sleeve and dab as much of the blood from my nose as I can. It's not bleeding much anymore, which is fortunate, but I must look like a mess. I don't realize that I've been standing there for a while until I feel a hand on my shoulder. Trout. With a grunt, I swing my gun around to hit him. There's an audible wince after the impact. I am raising my gun for my next blow when I see the person's face.

"What was that for?" Blayze growls, clutching his shoulder.

"I'm sorry! I thought you were…" I start, but a realization makes me stop. "Are you following me?"

"Why would I be following you?" he says, twirling his gun around his left hand. I rub my eyes. "What happened to your face?"

"Which part of my face are you talking about?"

The side of his mouth tugs up and he rubs the back of his neck. His knuckles are bloody. "Your nose."

"The butt of a gun," I say. "Flame clearly missed the whole 'no killing or maiming' part of the rules."

Blayze just nods. "I saw you fighting. You're good. Compared to your running, at least."

I scoff. "Thanks for helping."

"You were too far away," he says. "I couldn't get there in time. But I mean it, you're pretty good."

"I know, I'm fabulous, and I have the nose to prove it," I snap back. "How many times have you been hit?"

He doesn't seem to notice my aggravation. "Once. You?"

"Twice."

Before he can say anything, a loud thud sounds behind us. Trout has jumped down from the wall, his eyes gleaming. We dash down the left path. Trout is surely behind us. Blayze grabs my upper arm, and we make a sharp right, almost running into a wall. Dead end. Thankfully, we are able to take another route before Trout finds us. A dart whizzes past my ear. I can hardly see anything ahead, but it doesn't matter. I push harder. Blayze is right beside me.

By the time we reach the next obstacle, we seem to have lost Trout. Our eyes scan the area in front of us. A thin, wooden plank stretches over another dark pit. Even squinting, I can't see the bottom. It's completely dark. The little wooden plank looks quite unstable, like it will crumble if I set foot on it.

I turn to Blayze. "We need to get to the other side. One of us has to stay here to cover the other. If Trout gets onto the bridge at the same time as us, it'll collapse. I'll go first, to see if it's safe. Plus, I'm lighter." Not sure he's understood, I try to explain again. "Can you cover me? Once we're on the other side—"

"You think I'm really stupid, don't you?" Blayze says, wiping the nozzle of his gun on his pants and looking at me with amusement. His sarcastic troublemaker grin is forming on his lips, and I cross my arms.

"No," I reply. "Not *really* stupid."

He rolls his eyes.

"Let's go," I say. Before he can stop me, my muscles tighten and I spring into the air, landing on the balls of my feet in the middle of the plank. The wood creaks under my weight, making my stomach knot.

"WHAT ARE YOU DOING?" Blayze yells, clearly not taking the volume of his voice into consideration.

"I jumped," I remark, tentatively taking a step forward. The plank rocks back and forth, sending my stomach lurching. I want to jump again, but the downward force might break the bridge.

"I thought you were going to walk. Isn't that what you're supposed to do? What if it broke?"

"It didn't," I reply, wiping the sweat off my forehead with the back of my hand. Trying to steady my breathing, I take another step.

"You're an idiot," he replies, ignoring my comment. "What if you fall?"

It's my turn to ignore him. I take another step forward, my arms shooting out to help keep my balance. I can hear Blayze yelling at me, but I'm not listening. Before I know it, I've reached the other side.

My feet barely touch the gravel before something hits me in the back, knocking the wind out of me. I cry out in surprise and turn around, ready to hit back at my attacker. But there is no one there expect for my gun, which lies at my feet. I realize that I haven't had it since I was on the other side, with Blayze. I must have dropped it. But that means that Blayze threw it.

It's my turn to yell at him across the bridge. "WHY DID YOU THROW A FREAKING GUN AT ME? You could've *warned* me!"

"You could've listened! I was trying to tell you, but you were focused on dancing along the plank like a ballerina." He gets on his tiptoes and twirls around in a circle to prove his point. I plant my hands on my hips, annoyed. He smiles, and even from here, I can see his eyes light up.

"I'm not waiting for you, so if you're going to follow me, you'd better come quickly," I snap. Blayze bites his lower lip and starts forward. My fists clench. He's so built that I'm afraid he might fall right through the plank. After all, it creaked under my weight. As he steps onto the wood, I can see him tense up like he's about to spring.

No, no, bad idea, Blayze. If you jump, you'll fall right through.

Just because I did it doesn't mean he can.

"Don't—" I start toward the bridge to stop him, but it's too late. He takes off into a fast sprint across the board. The wood shakes violently under his feet, and my stomach jumps into my throat. But before it can fall completely, he makes it to the other side and tumbles face-first onto the gravel. The board snaps and falls into the pit. It hits the bottom with a loud clatter, and I cringe. That could have been one of us.

I watch him stand up, clearly in pain, and resist the urge to help.

"You waited," he remarks, spitting out gravel.

"You didn't give me much time to run."

He looks like he wants to say something else, but there's a crash to our left and I jump up. I take off into a sprint, tightening my grip on my gun. After going a few steps, I stop and look back at Blayze.

"You coming?" I ask. He nods, running to catch up. We move through the maze at a steady pace, shooting or scaring away the occasional kid. The dead ends seem to be multiplying. I can hardly find a path that isn't blocked. After a period of exasperated search- ing, I realize that I have lost track of Blayze. I collapse in exhaustion against a black wall in a corner, hoping that I'll be concealed by fog. This is pointless. Why does this need to be so hard? I wipe dirt and sweat off my forehead and smear it across my pants. It doesn't help—there is just too much dirt. Maybe if I hide for long enough, they'll come and take me out of this place.

But what if they don't? Or even worse, what if they do?

I straighten out my legs, heave a groan of exasperation, and bury my face in my hands. I have been there for what feels like far too long when I hear someone walk up to me. Fear zaps me like lightning. My eyes snap open, and I pull my arm back to throw a blow, but all I see is an extended hand. It's smooth, not callused like mine. Slowly, I raise my eyes to the face that the hand belongs to.

"Summer, get up. Let's go," says Blayze. In the distance, I hear screams and the ricochet of darts off the walls. Before long, those screams will be on top of us.

Reluctantly, I grab his hand and haul myself up.

As I turn to enter the fog again, Blayze grabs my arm. I spin around, and he quickly lets go. Turning warm, I stand up straight. "What?"

"I found something down there," he says, composing himself and gesturing to the passage on the left. "I came to get you. We have to get moving—people are starting to prowl around here like animals." I nod. There's a grunt behind us, and I spring into a run. Only when I'm well into the fog do I look over my shoulder at Blayze. He's right behind me.

"Don't stop!" he says, and I mentally kick myself. He passes me, his muscles tense as he plows forward. A dart nicks my ear, and a trickle of blood runs down my neck. I wipe it away and take off after Blayze.

"Here," he says, stopping unexpectedly and facing a wall. A dark rope ladder hangs in front of him, reaching up into the fog. Had he not pointed it out, I never would have seen it.

"Do you want to go first?" I ask him. After all, he was the one who found the rope. He declines with a swift shake of his head.

"Go ahead. I'm right behind you." I nod and walk over to the ladder, pulling down to test its strength. "Hurry, I can hear someone coming."

I hoist myself up the rope, climbing with my usual swiftness. The ladder is far longer than I expected. After a minute, I can feel it jerk under me and I know Blayze has started climbing. My hands clench the rope tighter with every rung. Eventually, the ladder stops and I come to a small platform built into the wall.

The second I let go of the rope, I scramble to press my back against the wall. This platform can't be bigger than a coffee table and I want to be as far away from the edge as possible. Leaning forward slightly, I peer down off the ledge and barely make out the maze through the fog. I swallow deeply.

High. I am very high.

The platform shakes under me and I jump back, clutching the wall. Blayze climbs up beside me. He glances over the edge of the platform and sucks in a breath. I stay perfectly still as he backs into the wall next to me.

"What now?" I ask, not looking at him. My heart is pounding.

Blayze's chest is rising and falling quickly. He screws up his eyes and peers forward for a second before glancing over at me. "We jump."

My jaw slacks and I gawk at him. "Are you *crazy?*"

"No, look." He reaches up and points straight out into the fog in front of us. My eyes follow his finger, and I realize what he's pointing at. Less than ten feet away, almost entirely concealed by fog, is a bridge. Made of the same black-painted wood as the maze, it's wide and protected by two thick railings on both sides. Because of the fog, anybody looking up at it from the maze wouldn't be able to see it. That must be the way out.

But I shake my head. "No way," I protest. "I'm not jumping."

Blayze's head snaps back to meet my gaze. "Why not?"

"Because this is ridiculous. What if we fall? There has to be another way."

He rubs his nose with the back of his hand. "Can you find one?" he argues. I glance around but don't see anything other than the fog. Reading my expression, Blayze continues, "Seriously, we have to jump. We don't have a choice. Besides, I'm sure they'll have something to catch us if we fall, the fog is just hiding it," he mumbles. I glower at him, but he's looking at the bridge, leaning precariously close to the edge. Suddenly, the platform begins to shake. I jump back, yanking Blayze back with me. With a glance down the ladder, I realize someone else has started climbing. It'll only be a minute before they reach the platform. We have to get out of here.

Reluctantly, I step toward the ledge. Blayze follows. There isn't even a place to take a running start. We have to take the leap virtually from a standstill.

"On three?" he asks, and I nod. The platform is shaking more violently now. "One…" I squeeze my eyes shut. "Two…" He grabs my hand, and I clutch it tightly. "Three!"

We throw ourselves off the side of the platform, and my stomach lurches into my throat. A scream pierces my ears, and it takes me a moment to realize it's mine. For a precariously long second, we're suspended in the fog. I suddenly think we underestimated the distance. Panic flares up in my throat, and my legs start kicking. When I collide with the bridge, my knees catch the edge of the wood and I'm knocked forward, my cheek scraping the railing.

We made it. Blayze hauls himself up over the edge of the bridge, breathing heavily as he leans against the railing. A smile stretches over my lips, and I ignore the stinging in my cheek and the dull ache in my knees.

"That was awesome!" I exclaim excitedly. "Did you see that?" I gesture back at the platform. "We didn't fall!"

"See? I told you. It wasn't so bad."

"Let's do it again!"

His glinting eyes widen, amused. When he gets up, he pulls me to my feet. "Come on, weirdo. Let's go."

We walk along the bridge for a while and eventually begin seeing the bright light emanating from the main building. Blayze was right. This is the way out. The wood of the bridge turns into sleek metal. When we reach the exit, officials are waiting for us.

"Dump your guns in the racks by the door," one of them says indifferently as the other removes the chip from my suit. They usher us through the door. "When you are finished, follow the hallway at the end to go back to the Lobby. You are dismissed for the evening."

The air is noticeably colder in here. Goose bumps rise on my arms, and I place my gun on the racks near a door that leads out of the maze. Blayze does the same.

We stand there for a second, staring awkwardly at each other, before he finally speaks. "I'm going to the Lobby," Blayze says. "I'll see you later." He turns to leave, but instead of walking through the exit, he walks right into the wrong door—the storage closet. I cross my arms over my chest and try to stifle a laugh. He exits seconds later, his face bright red, and disappears down the hallway.

"See you later," I call out, mostly to myself. I stand there chuckling for about a minute before exiting the room and making my way back to the Lobby.

16

The air around me is cold, chilling me through my tracksuit. The biting smell of cleaning solvents assails my nostrils. The old Making Perfect newscasts on the television drone on and on. But, I think, at least the sofa is comfortable.

This place reminds me of Tyler's apartment. Not the whole Lobby, of course, just this small slice of it. Since his building is mostly intact and had better insulation, Lil, Tory, and I would sleep there during the height of winter. Tyler and I would go out in the morning and gather loose, flammable items, carry them back, and put them in the old wood stove that he found and installed. It would heat up the air around it to an almost sweltering temperature. We would stay inside, playing games and reading books. Our campouts were always fun.

Whenever I got angry or just plain tired of life, I could always rely on Tyler to help me cope. He was my rock. He knew me inside and out, everything from my deepest fears and dreams to the fact that waffles are my favorite food. He was always there to hold my hand, make me laugh, and pick the raisins out of my salad because he knew how much I hated them.

Ty is the gentlest, most kind-hearted person one could ever hope to meet. The polar opposite of me. The Slump hardened him, sure, but not in the way it normally hardens people. He was compassionate, always putting the needs of others in front of his own.

I shift my weight on the sofa. I miss him. I miss him so much. Red equals sick. They probably killed them on the spot. They wouldn't have treated all the sick ones—they probably thought killing them was merciful.

I never got to even say good-bye. My face starts to feel puffy, and I swallow back the lump in my throat. I wish he was still here. Maybe if he was still here, I wouldn't feel like I am about to break in two.

I pull my knees to my chest, trying to focus on the television. But my mind can't focus. My vision swims in and out. They're playing an old newscast from a few years ago. The camera pans around, switching to a view of Making Perfect's CEO. I can't make out what he's saying because the volume is so low, and I don't bother trying very hard. Behind him is a thirteen-year-old version of Cooper. He is standing behind the wheelchair of his twin sister, Elle, his hands on the handles.

Elle's crippling illness is a well-known fact throughout the region. She was diagnosed with a terrible virus when she turned eleven. She lost the use of her legs, and the virus was quickly spreading to the rest of her body. At the time of her diagnosis, the doctors said that she would probably not live past the age of fifteen. The news had what seemed to be a crippling effect on her mother and brother.

I look harder at Cooper. He hadn't quite hit puberty when this video was taken, but he was beginning to look much taller and lankier. Completely different from the boy I saw earlier.

Except for his eyes.

"Hey," someone says. I spin around to see Ocean coming up beside me. She sits down on the couch. Her hair is wet, clumped together in pale blond dreadlocks. A large bruise is forming on her forehead.

"Hey," I reply, dabbing my nose with wet tissue from the bathroom. The bleeding has stopped, but I'm going to have one nasty bruise. At this second, I can't muster the energy to say anything else.

She makes an exasperated noise that sounds like the offspring of a walrus and a parrot. "Remind me *never* to engage in hand-to-hand combat with a boy." She looks up. "What happened to your face?"

"Look who's talking," I ask, not in the mood to joke. My nose is swollen, and my lips feel far too puffy and heavy—it's like a brick is resting on my face. Thankfully, Flame didn't get the chance to do much worse.

"I know what happened to my face. I was *there*," she laughs.

"Who was it?"

"One of Blockhead's crew. Kyle." I assume "Blockhead" is Trout. He's the only one with a thick enough skull to earn that name. Ocean tries to tame her matted hair by running her fingers through it.

"I'm surprised that he didn't break you in half."

"Shut up. God, he scares the hell out of me. It must be the violent gleam in his eyes. Or the fact he's built like an ox." She wrinkles her nose. "I swear he's deranged."

"Yeah," I say, rubbing my eyes. I squeeze the water out of the limp tissue, watching the drops of red-tinted water fall to the floor. Ocean notices.

"So, seriously, who did that to your face?"

"Flame," I reply. "She seems to find torturing me amusing."

"Let's add her to the deranged list."

I look at her again. "She won't leave me alone. I don't know what I did to hurt her, but she always goes out of her way to bother me." I flop backward on the couch, letting out a loud groan. "Can I just hide in this couch forever?"

"She hates you because Blayze is *totally* into you," says Ocean.

I groan. She leans over me, her long hair tickling my face. I try to push her off, groaning, but she is relentless. "Oh, come on; he is! He won't leave you alone! That's why she's totally jealous."

I look up at her for a second, meeting her amused glance. I open my mouth to tell her that Flame is practically Blayze's sister, but I know she won't listen.

She keeps teasing until I finally manage to get a word in. "Ocean, I *really* don't feel like talking about this right now."

She grins. "Okay, I'm going upstairs. See you."

I nod, slumping back on the couch as she leaves. She mutters something to me, but I don't catch it. I squeeze my eyes shut, lying there until the dinner bell finally gives me a reason to get up.

▲   ▲   ▲

I eat dinner alone that night. It's not because I don't have anyone to sit with—no, I just want to be alone. So naturally, when someone finally comes and puts their tray down next to mine, my jaw clenches.

"Can't you find somewhere else to sit? I'm really not—" I look up at the person and my stomach does a flip. No. No way. All the blood rushes from my face and I blink a few times, unable to believe my eyes.

Tyler.

What?

Tyler.

I get up from my chair, stumbling away from him. He can't actually be here. I must be going crazy.

"Summer, it's okay—" he says, coming up to me. I shake my head. This can't be him. He was taken away.

He looks like a zombie. Pale as paper, dressed in a ragged track-suit. The left side of his face is swollen, and an inflamed gash above his eye is just starting to recede. His eyes are full of pain. I thought I would never see him again. I must be seeing things. "It's okay; I'm not going to hurt you."

Is it really Tyler? Is he actually okay?

My eyes wide, I look at him again. My panic dies down and is replaced by utter relief.

Of course he's not going to hurt me. This is *Tyler*. He's okay. He's not dead.

I leap forward, wrapping my arms around him and pressing my body hard against his. My heart is pounding so hard I can hear it. I don't think I've ever held him this tight.

He's safe.

His hand cups the back of my head and pulls me close. I never want to let go of him. I can't let go of him. Last time I let go of him, he left. I can't let that happen again.

I bury my face in his shoulder.

"Oh my God, Ty," I say. "W-what happened? You were taken away with the red-marked kids. They were going to kill you. How did you get out?" He loosens his grip on me, and I look up at him. I'm just so glad to have him back. "Don't ever do that to me again, okay? You scared me half to death."

"I'll try to be more careful."

We both grin. When Tyler smiles, he doesn't just smile with his lips. He puts every ounce of his being into his smiles, lighting up the room. But this time, his smile doesn't reach his eyes.

I let go of him, but I don't take my hand away from his as we sit down.

He pulls his bowl toward him and starts to eat. "Are you okay? You look terrible," he says, glancing at me.

"I'm better now." I'm not hungry anymore. I just stare at him.

"What happened to your nose?" he asks. I shrug, not wanting to tell him how Flame bashed me up.

"A training exercise."

His forehead wrinkles in a mocking fashion. "A training exercise where you try to beat each other's brains out?"

"Something like that," I reply jokingly. I can't believe that I have Tyler with me. This is so strange, a novelty. "Where did they take you the other day? Where are the rest of the red-marked kids?"

Something flashes in his eyes. I have never been able to see what's going on in his head when he wants to hide it. He's pretty open most of the time, but he can be so well-guarded when he wants to be. There's no way he's letting me into his thoughts if he doesn't want me there.

"Nowhere. It was bad." I want more details, but I don't press him. I know that with Tyler, the way to get information is definitely by not pushing him. So I change the subject.

"What happened to *your* face?"

He runs his finger over the large welt on the side of his face, which is just beginning to turn blue. I shudder.

"An official," he says, shaking his head.

"I'm sorry."

"It's okay."

He pushes his bowl away. I glance down at my barely touched food. "I'm glad you're back."

"Didn't want you to have all the fun," he replies casually. I squeeze his hand.

ᛝ   ᛝ   ᛝ

Later that night, I am sitting in the Lobby watching the daily broadcast when I hear a familiar voice call out behind me. "Hey, Greenwood, are you up for a game of foosball?"

I turn around to see Blayze standing behind the couch that I'm sitting on. He is still wearing his tracksuit from earlier but is freshly showered. His hair is still wet, and a towel is wrapped around his neck.

"Is sneaking up on people your favorite post-shower activity?" I ask.

He shoves his hands into his pockets and repeats himself. "Can I interest you in a game of foosball?"

I burst out laughing. Foosball? Foosball is such an old game— it's surprising that Making Perfect has it at all. Couldn't they have chosen something a little more modern? I look around. The Lobby is basically empty, and as it's approaching ten o'clock, the lights are dimming. Almost everybody has retired to their rooms.

"Very funny." I look back up at him and realize that he's serious.

"I'm not kidding. I, Blayze Galloway, challenge you, Summer Greenwood, to a game of foosball." A few seconds of silence pass, and I look at him grudgingly. His puppy-dog eyes get wider. "Please?"

The corners of my mouth tug upward in a little smile. "Fine. But I suck at foosball." It's true—I've only played once before. Mom had taken me on one of her appointments. We visited an eccentric scientist that she worked with. He had a lot of old games for me to play around with while they talked.

"So do I," he says. "We'll be a fair match for each other."

I shake my head again, but he grabs my hands, pulling me onto my feet. My cry of surprise cuts through the silence of the Lobby as he drags me over to the nearest foosball table. The glossy little blue and white players are hanging in awkward positions, lying completely still. It looks like they haven't been used in years. Blayze stations himself opposite me, grabbing the two rods that control the white players and spinning them around. He reaches over, turns on the screen, and starts inputting information. I feel the table come to life in front of me. The sensors in the handles vibrate at my touch, and Blayze looks up at me with a fiery gleam in his eye—not a scary gleam, just an excited one.

I grab the two blue rods in the middle. Blayze leans against the side of the table, looking down at the players with a far-away expression. I can almost see the thoughts forming in his head, like in some sort of old movie.

"Is everything okay?" I ask. He snaps out of his haze, sliding right back into that easy smile that he was wearing before.

"Why wouldn't it be?" He presses a button, and an orange ball rolls out of one of the corners. Blayze grabs it. I tuck my hair behind me ears. "Be prepared to be crushed, Greenwood. I have a good feeling about this game."

"You must be pretty confident in your foosball abilities," I laugh.

"Just enough…I've been practicing."

"I thought you said you were terrible!"

"I am, but there's nothing else to do around here. I was going out of my mind." He tosses the ball onto the table, and I grab my rods so fast that I bump my knuckles on their ends. I spin my first rod around and hit the ball toward Blayze's goal. For a second I think it's about to go in, but he slides his goalie forward, knocking it out of the way. The little orange ball darts back and forth between our players at lightning speed. It's hard to keep track of. He hits it back toward me, and I spin the rod hard, hitting the ball with a whack and sending it straight into Blayze's goal before he can react.

"Ha!" I exclaim as the table lights up and a point is tallied on my side. It's hard not to laugh when the corny music starts playing.

"Beginners luck. Don't get cocky," Blayze remarks mockingly as the ball reappears in the corner. He releases it again.

The way we move our rods in unison, back and forth through the maze of little players, feels almost like dancing. Our laughs and shrieks are the music. I get lost in the movement, swinging the rods as hard as I can, darting quickly from rod to rod and defending my goal from Blayze's ruthless hammering. Part of me thinks this is stupid—that I should just stop playing—but my entire body is tingling and alive. By the time we're finished, I'm sweating.

"And *score!*" The table flashes in a kaleidoscope of different colors and sounds as I win my tenth point. I wipe the sweat from my forehead, pulling the hair out of my grinning face. His smile is as big as mine.

"Okay, okay! Fine, you win," he says, his breaths shallow. I watch as he walks around the foosball table and up to me. Our bodies are mere inches apart, and my heart is beating fast. "I guess my practice hasn't been doing me much good."

"You might want to step up your training regimen."

"Okay, smart-ass."

The shrill sound of a bell rings through the Lobby, and all the lights are shut off, leaving us in the dark. After a few seconds, the stair footlights are turned on, casting a faint, blue glow onto the concrete. My eyes slowly adjust until I can just make out Blayze's face.

"I think we've overstayed our welcome," I say. "Thanks for letting me kick your ass at foosball."

"It was fun."

Nodding my head in agreement, I look past him at the guards stationed by the doors. They are eyeing us strangely. "We should probably go before we get in trouble—I don't think they like people being out this late."

"What can they do about it?" says Blayze. "The worst they can do is sneer at us." I glance up at the people in the observation decks. They don't even seem to be paying attention.

That's not the worst they can do, I think. *They can definitely do a lot worse.*

My mouth stretches into a yawn. Blayze starts to say something, but he's cut off by a loud voice over the intercom. "All subjects need to return to their designated rooms for the remainder of the night. Testing begins at eight."

Blayze and I glance at each other. The lights in the observation decks have gone out, and the guards by the door are starting to move toward us.

"I think security has arrived," I remark, and he scoffs.

"I guess so."

I suppress a yawn. "Well, goodnight then," I say, getting up.

"I'm coming with you," he says. "My room is three doors down from yours."

My face is burning up, but I hope it's too dark to notice. "Oh, right. Sorry." Before the guards can get to us, we start up the stairs, taking two at a time. They don't follow us up. We reach the sixth floor and walk toward the end of the balcony. We stop in front of my room, and I put my hand on the knob. "Goodnight for real this time," I say, trying to keep myself together while cringing at how awkward I feel. If he notices how nervous I am, he doesn't show it.

"Goodnight, Summer," he replies, and I slip through my door and into my room, my lips spreading into a wide grin.

For the rest of the night, no matter how hard I try, I am unable to wipe that grin off my face.

17

I t's been a few weeks.
A few weeks of the same routine. Breakfast, testing, lunch, testing, dinner, testing, shower, sleep. The schedule has seeped into my blood. I'm surprised at how easily I'm adapting. I keep my mouth shut, mostly speaking to Tyler, Ocean, and Blayze. They're the only ones who can get words out of me.

The tests are strange—most are mental and physical in nature. Some of them are pretty scary. There are times when I don't think I'll make it out alive. Many of them are performed on an individual basis—they strap us into chairs and see how much electricity or heat we can endure. They inject us with various toxins, pushing us to the edge, testing our breaking points. They also regularly take samples of our blood for testing. They never tell us anything, but strangely enough, I've gotten used to that.

To my surprise, I haven't heard much from Cooper—I've only stumbled across him a few times during various tests. Yesterday, during the evening's physical conditioning session, I spotted him talking quietly with Kace. During their exchange, Kace started laughing, causing me to do a double take. I'd never seen Kace smile before. Cooper had a genuine grin on his face, too, which lightened up his features. He didn't speak to me, though. I didn't really expect him to. I suppose I'm just getting accustomed to his presence and slowly accepting the fact he's not going anywhere.

It's strange. He seems more human than I expected. After all these years of hearing about him and about all the terrible things that he and his father have done, I thought he was a monster. It doesn't feel right to see him talking and smiling. I have caught myself thinking that maybe he's not as bad as everybody says. Maybe he's not the one who did all those terrible things. Maybe he's just a kid, caught in a chaotic world, trying to make it through. Kind of like me.

But those thoughts doesn't make me loathe him less.

In the middle of all this chaos is Blayze. I've been watching him closely and talking to him frequently. He and Tyler have ended up as roommates. Blayze and I run together every morning, making it part of our daily routine. He seems to be adjusting as well as I am, though he didn't look too good in the beginning. Back then he would come to breakfast looking awfully pale and tired.

And he's nice to me.

It seems that everybody has gotten more and more comfortable as the days have gone by. People have found their groups of friends and stuck to them like glue. They seem to have forgotten the threat hanging over their heads—or maybe the never-ending testing has taken all their attention. But not me. I can't forget about the danger that waits for us. It's got an iron grip on my shoulders, pressing me into the floor every second of the day. I try to force it out of my head, but it feels bolted in place.

I'm scared.

But it's all going to be over soon.

Enhancements are scheduled to begin tonight.

There's no dinner. I don't know whether my stomach's incessant growls are from hunger or fear. We've been told to stay in our rooms, and they have doubled the guards.

Groups of officials are coming to the rooms and taking us away one by one. I am curled up on my bed, facing the wall. Ocean is pacing back and forth. Neither of us say a word. I don't even know what I would say. It might be the last time I see her.

But if there's one person who I think will make it through this, it's Ocean. She's one of the bravest people I know.

Running my fingers through my hair, I look up at the ceiling, trying to discern patterns in the uneven concrete. I'm so scared, yet I feel strangely calm. I just want to get this over with.

I catch a glimpse of snowflakes falling onto the window, decorating the glass in complicated little patterns. It's dark outside, and the white light hitting the snow crystals is casting small rainbows along the windowsill. They look as if they're dancing together, twisting inconsistently around each other. I can't take my eyes off them.

The doors open and an official calls out Ocean's name. I don't even look at her as she is taken out of the room. The door closes quickly behind her, and silence falls around me again. I should go see Tyler. I have to see him at least once before they take him away, assuming that he's still here. I don't want to say good-bye—God, I don't think I could survive another good-bye—but I need to talk to him. The guards might stop me, but it's worth a try.

I get up from my bed, push the door open, and look down the hallway. I'm going to have to time this right. The guard at the end of the hallway is alternating his attention between the two adjoining hallways. Good. Tyler's door is only three over from mine. If it's open, I may have a shot. Now.

Before the guard looks back, I've made it to the door. I don't bother knocking. I fall in and run straight into Blayze.

"What are you doing here?" I ask, the surprise evident in my face. "Where's Tyler?"

"We're roommates, remember?" he says. "And no. They came by to take him about ten minutes ago."

My heart sinks. "It's probably better that way," I mutter. I tried to say good-bye to Tyler this afternoon, but neither of us knew what to say. We quickly came to the conclusion that good-byes aren't our thing.

He nods. "So, I guess this is good-bye for us too, then?"

"I guess." After a moment of awkward silence, I look at the ground, not knowing what else to do. "Well, good luck with, you know…everything."

"Be careful, okay?" he says, and I look back up at him. After a moment's hesitation, I walk forward and wrap my arms around his chest, gluing his arms to his sides. I only stay there for a second, letting go before he can even hug me back. I feel redness creeping slowly into my cheeks.

"You too."

He smiles slightly. Just when I'm about to force myself to walk away, a squad of officials comes up behind us. My blood turns cold.

"Two-seven-zero-two-eight, Galloway," an official's voice grumbles. Ignoring the dread flaring up in my chest, I take a deep breath. I look into Blayze's eyes one last time before he swallows deeply and walks over to the officials. As I watch him go, I try to keep my breathing steady.

And they're gone.

My stomach is tied in knots. I barely make it halfway back to my room before I hear a voice behind me.

"Are you busy?" The voice is calm but has a hard edge. I spin around with a start. Cooper stands there, hands in his pockets, looking at me with a leering expression. I am suddenly unnerved. What is he doing here?

I look at him, and he laughs slightly to himself, shifting uncomfortably. "I realize that was a stupid question."

"What do you want? Are you here to insult me?" When he doesn't say anything, I continue, "If so, by all means, get it over with."

He shakes his head. I don't like the way he's looking at me...It's uncomfortable. "Nope."

My brow furrows, and I try to shake the tension from my shoulders. "Well, don't you have anything better to do?"

He laughs. "No. You looked miserable after they took your boyfriend away. I just want to tell you not to worry. You're one of the special ones."

"He's not—" I catch myself and stop. Why am I even bothering to explain myself? It's *Ian Cooper*. I don't owe him anything. "Special ones? What do you mean? And since when do you watch me?" I can't contain my irritation.

"It's my job to watch you," he explains without emotion. "I watch people. But not everyone—only the ones who I think need extra supervision." He pauses. "And you, my dear, are currently the center of my attention."

I am filled with discomfort. The center of this boy's attention is a *very* bad place to be.

I push his comment aside. "Just leave me alone." I try to sound unaffected.

He doesn't take his piercing eyes off me. "I'm sorry, darling, but I'm afraid you don't have a choice in the matter." His tone drips with sarcasm.

I narrow my eyes at him. He's right. I don't.

We look at each other for another moment before I feel it. That push-and-pull feeling. Like my stomach's turning over continuously as he looks at me. It's not a cute little "you give me butterflies" kind of feeling. No—this feeling makes me want to hurl.

I feel like he's taken a knife and skinned me alive, stripping the layers away to see what lies at my core. Nobody has ever made me feel this before, and I want it to stop. I'll do anything to make it stop. The longer he looks at me, the more intense the sensation gets.

Finally I tear my gaze away and look down at my hands.

After a while, he speaks. "Do you know what your problem is? You're far too pretty for your own good." He cocks his head slightly. "You are a very dangerous person, Miss Greenwood." He moves forward, and I instinctively recoil. He notices and grins.

"Greenwood." I hear my name being grumbled from behind me. Kace is standing with his arms crossed, surrounded by two helmeted guards, a tablet in one hand. His gaze darts questioningly between Cooper and me. "Time to go."

My stomach jumps, and I forget Cooper altogether. I ball my hands into fists to prevent them from shaking. I walk up to Kace, swallowing deeply. He gives me a nod.

It's time.

18

The examination room smells like alcohol and cleaning products. The room itself is about the size of my bedroom, with a large counter stacked with vials hugging the back wall. Four nurses dressed in stark, white uniforms stand by a metal examination chair. A couple of machines with long extension arms are positioned around it. My stomach jumps into my throat.

"Please, sit down," one of the nurses orders. I slowly sit on the thin padding and feel the chair recline beneath me. I know that even if I tried to run, I'd be right back in this position within seconds. The steel cuffs click into place around my wrists and ankles. I struggle against the straps as claustrophobia sets in. The nurses crowd around me, their hair tied back and masks covering the bottom halves of their faces. One of them injects me with something. I wince as I feel the large needle enter my neck.

"This is Summer Greenwood," one of the nurses says softly to another. "She and the boy are the ones we've been hearing about."

"What do you mean?" I ask, struggling to keep my words clear against the building drowsiness. My thoughts are beginning to swim together, merging into a giant, incoherent mess. A slew of arbitrary words and numbers float around in my head. The tips of my fingers begin to tingle, and my eyelids grow heavy.

The nurses don't acknowledge me. One wipes clean a spot on the back of my neck with an alcohol swab while another shaves away the hair above my ear and wipes it clean. The rest of my hair is neatly tucked into a surgical cap, leaving my neck completely bare. Suddenly, as if a switch has been unexpectedly turned off, my body slips away from me. I lose all control over my muscles. When the nurses see me relax, they slip another needle into my neck. I barely register the sharp sting.

I try to speak, but my mouth refuses to form the words that my brain is throwing at it. Is this what the enhancements are supposed to be like? A nurse slips a white cover over my body like a blanket. I hear the door slide open, but I can't see who just entered the room. The last thing I see is their faces looming over me, the bright white hospital lights blinding me as I slip away into unconsciousness.

19

I sit up with a start, my hands flying out to either side of me and hitting something hard. My breaths are raspy. When I try to open my eyes, the blinding white light makes me instantly squeeze them shut again. Where am I?

Slowly squinting my eyes open, I run my hands along the sleek glass underneath me. When I try to stand, I bang my head. Fear setting in, I crawl forward until I quickly reach another wall that feels as smooth as the floor under me. My eyes are slowly adjusting. I see light and move toward it, pressing my nose against the glass. A faint gasp escapes my lips.

I'm in a tank.

I'm in a lab.

My hands press against the front of the glass enclosure, trying to push it open. It doesn't move. What's wrong with me? My hands form fists as I try to punch through the glass, but it doesn't budge. It must be modified. I look around. The tank is small, equipped with nothing except for a small cot and a metal drain on the floor. Sheets of metal behind the glass obstruct my view to either side. In the back of the tanks is a metal panel that appears to be some sort of portal. I try pushing through it, but like everything else, it doesn't yield.

I have tubes coming out of both arms and my neck. Sensors are attached to my chest and head. They all pass through a small, gray panel in the ceiling and connect to monitors in the lab.

"Get me out of here!" I scream, so loud that my throat hurts. Nobody replies. I can see doctors and scientists outside my cell, milling around nonchalantly, not noticing my panicked expression. They are talking, but I can't hear anything. A tablet is strapped to the door. I can read it from here.

Test #27441. Greenwood, Summer.

I pound my hands against the glass so hard that they begin to burn. When I pull them away, sores have appeared on my skin. The glass must be coated with something. I sit back on my heels and look around the lab. My heart pounds when I see what lies on the other side.

People in tanks similar to mine are submerged in liquid, with so many tubes coming out of them that I can barely see their skin. They appear unconscious, but their faces are contorted into such horrific expressions that I don't want to think about what kind of images they're seeing or what Making Perfect is doing to them.

I feel sick.

Is Tyler here, too? I look closely at the faces of the kids in the tanks opposite me and don't see anyone I recognize. With a whimper, I retreat to the back of my cell, tucking my legs into my chest. No. This can't be happening. What are they doing to us? My mind is unraveling, and I start to scream. My screams are so hard and so guttural that they strip my throat raw. Eventually, my vocal chords give out altogether. But nobody can hear me. Nobody can hear anything at all.

I am silent for a while before, finally, two scientists walk up to the glass.

Bright white light burns into my eyes, and I cover my face with my hands. There's a faint hissing sound as the front of the tank opens and slides up into a recess in the ceiling. They walk in, accompanied by two guards. Before I can react, hands grab me underneath my arms, yanking me upward. I struggle.

"No! Please, stop!" I scream, thrashing with a terror-driven strength. It takes four of them to subdue me. "Not again!" Before I know it, I am hauled to the door of the cell, where one of the scientists punches a combination into the touchpad on the door. I only catch the first two digits: *14*.

They drag me out onto the slick, white tile. People in white lab coats crowd around me, and I fight harder than ever to get free. One of my legs kicks out violently, and I hear a wince from one of the officials. Then I feel a sharp pain on the side of my face.

A realization strikes me: the door. I look up and see the large EXIT sign above the doorway. If I can reach the threshold, I can get out of here. But before I can do anything else, I feel a needle slide into my neck. My body goes limp against the hard tile.

▲　▲　▲

My eyes blink open. All I see is a fuzzy, bright light. Once my eyes adjust, I see that I am in a different room. Long aluminum examination tables line the wall. My head feels heavy. I shake it, but it gets no clearer.

I flex my wrists and find that they are bound tightly to the table's sides. I shift my weight and feel the other restraints close around my chest, ankles, and hips.

"What's happening?" My voice is a hoarse whisper.

It'll be okay, I reassure myself. *They're not going to hurt me.*

I glance at the exam table next to mine. There is a person strapped to it. I freeze as he turns his head to look at me. His shaggy, overgrown white hair falls into his face as he moves. I recognize him as one of the boys from the tanks. One of his eyes is cloudy and half shut, and a long scar runs across his forehead and down to his jaw. His body lies limp in his restraints. Judging by his face, he is much older than Kace. His hard, gray eye falls on me.

"Welcome," he says. "I'm one-seven-one-five-five. My name is Sterling." He looks back up to the ceiling, not expecting an answer.

"Summer," I reply through gritted teeth.

"What's your number?" he asks indifferently.

"Two-seven-four-four-one."

"They use numbers here, not names." Sterling closes his eyes and sighs. "Your head?" I give him a confused look, and he adds, "What happened to your head?"

"What do you mean? What's wrong with my head?" A cold chill runs down my spine. What did they do to me? My arms strain against the restraints as I try to reach up.

He chuckles. "Relax, you're just bruised up." I don't say anything. "Did you try to escape?"

I stay silent, which he takes as confirmation.

"Well, that was a terrible idea." He turns his head to look at me again. "Do you have anger issues?"

This aggravates me. "I don't have anger issues. This is just a messed-up place."

He smiles smugly, keeping his eyes shut. I look at him, puzzled. What's wrong with this guy?

"What's going to happen to me?" I ask him, and his eye opens.

"The same thing that's going to happen to me, love," he replies. "And to all of us."

Before he can finish this thought, two scientists walk into the room and wheel his table past the curtain and glass separator. I hear something click into place, and muffled voices sound from behind the curtain. I lie still, gripping the edge of the exam table nervously.

The silence is soon broken by the sound of screams. Raw, guttural screams that send a chill down my spine. There are pauses, but only brief ones—enough time for Sterling to catch his breath before he begins screaming again. My heart aches for him, and I try to block the sound out. Eventually, I can't take it anymore. I bang my head against the back of the table in a failed attempt to make myself black out. When the sound finally stops half an hour later, there's complete silence.

Did they kill him? I get my answer as two guards slowly roll his body back into the lab. I can barely see him—his body is completely covered in a blue tarp. But as he rolls past, I catch the rise and fall of his chest. He's alive. His hand hangs limply out from under the covering, swinging from side to side as he's rolled out of sight.

What did they do to him?

Waves of terror wash over me. Two scientists come up to my exam table and roll me toward the curtain. I struggle, trying to escape my restraints, fear for my life kicking in. The restraints just get tighter and tighter until I can't move at all. I freeze as they roll me into the glass examination room.

The room is empty expect for the black cabinets lining one wall and a man, dressed in a white lab coat, who is washing his hands in the sink. There are countless large monitors and machines set up in all parts of the room, hugging almost every inch of walking space. I feel the table underneath me lock into place, and I watch as the man shuts the water off before turning to face me. It's hard to tell from behind his mask, but he looks relatively young compared to the other doctors I've seen here. He is probably in his late twenties. His eyes are so dark that they seem to be black. "This is two-seven-four-four-one?" he asks.

"Yes, sir," one of the guards replies, stepping back from the table.

I struggle against the straps as the doctor walks over to me, running his eyes up and down my body. "She's one of the new ones?" The guard nods. "Thank you, gentlemen," the doctor says, dismissing the two scientists with a nod. I hear them murmuring under their breath as they walk out of the lab through the thick glass doors. The doctor's eyes lock with mine. "I understand that you must be a bit frightened, but don't worry. I'm not going to kill you."

I spit at him. He takes a step back. I don't know where this bravery is coming from, but I like it. On second thought, it might not be smart.

The doctor's voice is colder when he speaks next. "Do that again, and I'll gag you." He walks over to the side of the room near the cabinets and pulls out a thick, metal apparatus from the wall. It extends over to my body, whirring to life with a soft buzzing sound. A pale light turns on as he runs it over my body, scanning me.

"What are you looking for?"

He doesn't answer. The scanner reaches my feet and gives a little beep. He grabs a tablet from behind him and jots down a few things. Then he finally speaks. "Normally, all of you come to me in functional condition—I just needed to double check before we begin testing."

The sharp stench of alcohol bites my nostrils as he cleans a site right below my elbow. I watch him rip open a needle from its package and insert it into my arm, taping the little IV in place quickly before retracting the needle. I try to stay calm, though I feel my heart pounding hard in my chest. "Testing" must be what Sterling just endured…I *hope* that's not what's in store for me.

The doctor walks back toward me with another needle, this one filled with a bright blue liquid, and squeezes it into the IV. The second the drug enters my bloodstream, I relax, a faint numbing sensation coming over me. I don't even ask what he's putting into me—whatever it is, it feels good. He moves out of sight, and after a moment I feel his hands touching my head. He traces his finger over my forehead, and I tense slightly.

"Hold still, this might hurt a bit." I feel a sharp object cut into the skin below my hairline, and I let out a surprised cry. A trickle of warm blood runs down my temple. I suck in a breath. What's he doing? My eyes strain to see as he grabs a large needle from the table.

"This next one always stings like a bitch," he says with a smirk. I hate him.

He slips the needle into the incision and injects its cold contents into it. I let out a cry of pain, and my hands ball into fists. I have no idea what he's doing, but I want him to stop, now. When he closes the small wound, I heave a sigh of relief.

"What are you doing to me?" I hiss as he washes his hands at the counter. He opens up a container filled with small metal chips about the size of grains of rice.

"I'm setting you up to begin testing."

"Begin? I've been tested since I got here," I say.

"Not this kind of testing. Only a few get this treatment—only ten of you. I need to figure out which of those ten you are."

Ten of us? I watch him load one of the little metal chips into the needle and position the needle behind my ear. I tense up, bracing myself for the pain. The chip shoots into my skin, and I bite my lip. He injects one on the other side, too, and another right at the base of my skull. After what feels like an eternity, he gathers his equipment in his tray by the sink and pulls off his gloves and mask.

"That's enough for today. We'll start the real testing tomorrow." All I can think of is Sterling's broken body being wheeled away. A shudder runs through me. Will that be me tomorrow?

"But are you going to test our enhancements?" I ask, and I hear him chuckle.

"You didn't get any enhancements," he explains, not looking at me. I absorb his words, feeling like I've just been hit in the head with a brick. "Believe me, the ten of you are enhanced enough as it is."

20

I need to get answers.

I have given up trying to put together all the pieces of the puzzle. Screw the pieces. I need real answers, and I'm tired of people lying to me.

I don't know where I'll get the answers, but it has to be in one of these labs.

First, though, I've got to get out of this tank. This lab doesn't have a night watch, only guards outside the doors, which makes my task *way* easier. The others around me are so silent that you could hear a pin drop. I don't know if that's because the tanks are soundproof or because everybody's sleeping, but I don't really care.

I need to get this door open. But in order to do that, I need to punch in the right code. I remember that it started with *14*—what are the other three numbers?

I look around the tank. I remember that when I was younger, my dad taught me a trick to decipher the code on a touchpad. You use a handful of flour, blowing on it carefully until a thin layer forms on the numbers that make up the code. The powder will stick to the oil from people's fingers. He told me that the only way to keep a passcode safe is to wipe the screen after every entry—but nobody does that.

The problem is, I have no powder. There is absolutely nothing in this cell.

My eyes travel over the cot, and it hits me.

Dust.

Powder.

I reach under the cot and run my fingers along its frame. A thin coat of dust appears on my fingertips. Perfect. Using both hands, I wipe the entire frame clean and gather all of the dust into my palms. I hope it will be enough.

I walk over to the keypad, bring my hand up to the numbers, and gently blow the little particles onto the screen. With two small blows, my hands are clean. I look at the keypad. It looks the same.

I groan silently. Dad made it look so easy. I lean in closer to the screen and narrow my eyes, noticing specks on some of the keys. One, four, two, seven. That's only four. Where's the last one?

I try typing in the four digits, racking my brain to figure out the fifth one. The number has to have some sort of significance. There is something familiar to the pattern, and I arbitrarily arrange the numbers in my head until, finally, it comes to me.

Why didn't I think of it before?

It's just the numbers of my barcode, reversed.

Stupid.

I punch in the sequence, and the pad flashes green. The door unlocks.

I sigh in relief as I step onto the smooth tile. Nobody heard me. Nobody even stirs as I walk past their tanks to reach the door. I try not to look at their slack faces—I don't want to think about whether they're sleeping or something worse.

It takes an eternity to reach the door. It makes a soft scraping sound when I push it open, and my breath gets caught in my throat, but the guards don't move. Their faces are completely blank. When I look closer, I realize that they are asleep. Some guards.

Glancing over my shoulder, I slink down the hallway as quickly as I can, ducking behind the nearest corner for cover. I'm sure there are security cameras covering every inch of this place. Great. Great planning, Summer. But I've come this far, so I may as well follow through.

But where am I going? Cooper would know where to find this information, but why on earth would he tell me? I'll just play it by ear. I begin jogging, praying that everybody's sleeping and that the alarm won't sound. I make random turns, hoping that by some chance I'll end up near the lab.

No such luck. Instead, I have to duck into a branching hallway when I hear the sound of thumping feet. My stomach jumps into my throat, and I cover my mouth with my hand to keep quiet. Five guards walk casually down the hallway, helmets off, talking among themselves. They are all men, ranging in age from eighteen to thirty—the night shift, apparently. Some of them are laughing, though I can't hear what they're saying.

There's a crackling sound, and one of them stops in his tracks right next to my hallway. I stop breathing. Please don't turn around. A few murmurs pass between them, and a voice comes over one of their walkie-talkies. I bite into my palm.

"Shift one-one-five, report to Lab Eighteen," the voice snaps. One of the guards curses softly and mutters a few indistinguishable words to his companions. My heart is beating so hard that I can hear it. Lab 18…As good a choice as any. I peek my head around the corner and see the group of guards disappearing down the hallway, pulling their helmets on. As discretely as I can, I follow them.

Somehow, I am able to follow them all the way to the lab. I am grateful that we didn't have to go down any elevators to get there— I'd be caught before I could take another breath. I look down at my trembling hands and bite my lip. The guards go in, and I wait outside. I can't hear anything they're saying, but their visit to the room seems to take forever.

A loud bell rings, and I flinch. Is it an alarm? Have they found me? I don't think so. I hide as the scientists silently leave the lab, carrying their belongings with them. Where are they going? Are they going to leave the lab unattended all night? Hopefully they won't. If they do, this whole endeavor has been futile.

Luckily, the guards accompany the last of the scientists out the door and down the hallway. When they round the corner, I slip through the door just before it shuts.

The lab is enormous. Since the lights are off, it's difficult for me to make out anything. My eyes take a moment to adjust to the dim night-lights. Small tables are scattered throughout the room, each of which is equipped with computers. There are huge screens everywhere, displaying undecipherable formulas in faint blue light. Hundreds of folders are stacked on the tables, and the smell of new printer paper makes my nose wrinkle.

How am I supposed to find anything in here?

I walk over to the nearest table.

Maybe it'll have some information about me. Maybe my parents. What about the enhancements?

The files are old, worn-down pieces of yellowed paper with stains and scribbles all over them. I can hardly understand anything that's written, especially in the dim light.

I look at the random files scattering the table and start to flip through them. One catches my eye, and I stop there. It looks like a statistics chart:

Formula 4.8 #S49IOp5q - 28% success rate
Formula 7.0 #I29OU05b - 70% success rate
Formula 55.84 #U85REh4f - 54% success rate

The list goes on and on for page after page. This is useless. There's no way I'm going to scour the entire lab to find out what these numbers mean, and the odds are that they have nothing to do with me anyway. I back up and accidentally bump into a table covered with test tubes filled with different-colored serums. Once it stops shaking, I realize that I've been holding my breath and exhale in relief.

Just as I relax, a small tube filled with green, glow-in-the-dark liquid tips over and spills on the tabletop. The thick substance oozes across the papers, turning them bright green.

No! I run over and try to stand the tube upright. All of the papers under it are soaked and glowing. This is hopeless—I can't mop it up. They're going to know that I've been here.

I gather all the green papers. Might as well throw them out. I carry them around the room, but I can't find any place to dispose of them. Where is the garbage? This is a science lab; don't they have a trash can?

"Hell," I mutter under my breath and lean back against the wall. As I glance around the room, my gaze falls on a terminal placed apart from the others. Clusters of wires connect to a bay of servers on the far wall. I walk over and sit on the metal stool in front of it. I set aside the glowing folders and wipe remnants of the serum off my hands.

I move the mouse, trying to bring the screen to life. I hear a whirring sound, and a number of servers light up. The Making Perfect logo appears on the screen with a box prompting me for the password.

Wonderful.

Hmmm. Maybe I can guess it.

I try the most obvious one first: "makingperfect."

Access Denied.

"perfect"

Access Denied.
"imperfect"
Access Denied.
I start to get frustrated.
"scientistsarestupid"
Access Denied.
Screw this. I push away from the computer, and the screen turns black. The passcode warning disappears, and a new window pops up to take its place. I lean in to read it.
Place your finger on the pad below.
I look down and see a small pad slide out of the computer. Hesitantly, I place my finger on it. I feel a sharp sting and pull my finger away, staring wide-eyed at the little drop of blood pooling on the pad.

They took a blood sample? Oh God. I get up, ready to bolt as soon as the alarm sounds, but there is none. Instead, the computer unlocks. I'm in.

Another screen pops up, and my forehead wrinkles as I read it.
Welcome, Mr. Greenwood.
Mr. Greenwood? I rub my eyes.
Dad.

It thinks I'm Dad? That's weird, but I don't have time to linger on it. I click on the documents folder. I haven't used a computer in a long time, and this one is much more sophisticated than anything I've used before.

A seemingly endless list of folders pops up. I scroll down until I find one that catches my eye. It's labeled, "The Fetus Project." It sticks out only because it's the only title that isn't labeled something like, "Document #r679Jui5lO."

My stomach knots when I start reading.

The Fetus Project - February 2, 2427
The fetus project is an experiment developed by scientists Dr.
Rodger Mason and Dr. Robert Greenwood.

I stop, my breaths becoming shaky. Robert Greenwood…Dad. But who's Mason? I've heard that name before, but I don't remember where. I continue reading, too fast for the information to sink in.

Its goal is to determine if an enhancement can be performed
on a fetus in its mother's womb with the result that the baby
is born already enhanced. It stemmed from the Star Formula
(see #h6888ryTj).

My eyes skip over whole paragraphs filled with detailed descriptions of genetic recombination and other scientific jargon that I don't understand. My heart is pounding so loudly that I can hear it.

The first test was done on Evelyn Mason on November
29, 2423. It resulted in the successful birth of a baby with
exceptional strength, sight, hearing, sense of smell, resilience,
and speed. After the birth of the first baby, each subsequent test
subject was born with a specific ability slightly differentiated
from the others. Each baby was born in the Making Perfect
facility, then quickly transferred back to its original parents or
to a foster family.

I shake my head. The room is spinning. I take a deep breath and keep reading.

Each child belonging to the fetus project is marked by a star
tattoo applied at birth. In the beginning stages of this project,

*85 percent of mothers died during childbirth. But as the process
was improved, the survival rate of mothers grew. For unknown
reasons, the project was stopped three years after the first test.
Its end was due to unknown causes. Thirteen "test kids" were
made, and their future is yet to be determined.*

At the end of the document, other relevant folders are listed by
reference numbers and file names.

I feel weightless. I keep staring at the screen, trying to make
sense of it.

This has to be a mistake. This is absurd.

But the star.

The more I think about it, the more that star explains everything. It explains my star birthmark, why I didn't get an enhancement, and why Cooper had me come to his office. It explains why
I've always been stronger, faster, and had better reflexes and stami-
na than any other kid I know—aside from Tyler.

Tyler. Oh my God. He has a star, too. Does that mean he's part
of the experiment, too? I think so.

What about my parents? It said that 85 percent of initial test
mothers died in childbirth. Mom didn't. And what about my dad?
He *created* this project. Did he experiment on Mom? Why?

Is that why Mom and Dad were killed? Because of me?

My stomach is twisting as I run to the door. It can't be true.
This is so wrong. The test kids' future was "to be determined."
What is that supposed to mean? One thing is for sure: they're never
letting me out of here.

I don't even bother to shut down the computer. I push through
the door and dash down the hallway, getting away from the lab as
fast as I can.

21

My feet pound against the floor as I run through another hallway. I don't know where I'm going. I'm just running. I reach a set of stairs and take them two at a time. Throat burning and legs throbbing, I reach the top. My breaths are fast and shallow. I feel dizzy, but I keep running.

I reach an intersection and stop in my tracks. This is definitely not the way I came. Three hallways branch off, all of them so dark that I can't see where they lead. Frustrated, I swallow tears and choose the middle hallway.

My pace slows to a jog. The farther I move down the hallway, the brighter it gets. Lights begin to dot the ceiling at regular intervals. I still have no idea where I am. The hallway's dark gray walls become narrower. Up ahead, the hallway ends in a T-junction.

I hear voices coming from around the corner on the right. Careful not to make too much noise, I move closer to the sound. They must be guards. Their voices get clearer as I approach the corner—if I round the corner, they'll see me. Backtracking isn't an option—I'm not going back there. Maybe this time I'll be lucky and they'll just move on.

"Eddie! What's wrong with you?" I hear someone say. The voice is older, deep, and rumbling. "I'm tired of saving your ass. You've got to take this seriously. You know what happens if they turn on you."

"You think I give a damn? I am so sick and tired of being put on the godforsaken night shift. Compared to this, whatever they do to me would be a blessing." This one—Eddie—sounds young, maybe even my age.

I can hear a few other voices in the background. They all seem as annoyed as the older one.

"You arrogant fool. You're lucky to be here. Would you prefer to still be in the institution?" The older one cannot hide his contempt.

"Shut up, Glenn!" Eddie snarls. "You think I asked for this? I don't know if I can take any more of this shit."

I want to look, but I'm too scared that they'll see me. My throat feels closed up.

"See you guys," one of them says. "My shift's over." Oh no. I hear footsteps getting closer, and I press my back against the wall. There are no doors, no places to hide. It's just me and the wall. The footsteps grow louder. My heart is beating so fast it hurts. Three guards walk straight past me into the hallway on the left, their helmets held in the crooks of their arms. Oh, please don't see me—

The guard who's the farthest away from me—that's who sees me first. Our eyes lock, and I mentally beg him not to say anything. But it's too late. The other guard catches him staring and turns around.

I am frozen. I can't breathe. I can't move.

For one, peaceful moment, the only sound is that of our breaths. One beautiful, weightless moment.

But what goes up must come down.

Crashing and burning down.

There's a shout, and the nearest guard reaches out to grab me. My legs kick into gear, and I take off the way I came. I run as fast as I can, shaking the green-streaked hair out of my face. I can hear them barking at each other, and I don't have to look back to know that they're following me.

Adrenaline pumps through my veins as I see the end of the hallway. I am almost there.

A loud pop goes off behind me, and something nicks my ear. I touch my hand to it, and it comes back red. They're using real guns. I spin around, and a streak of gray that is a man's body slams into me like a train. It throws me against the wall, knocking the wind out of me.

The guard looks about forty, with a hole through his nose and a large, golden tooth in the front of his mouth. His grin is cruel. The other guards flank him, cutting off any hope of escape. I open my mouth to scream, but before any sound can come out, a fist collides with my mouth.

"It's just a little runaway lab rat," one of them says. Pain explodes through my jaw and into my head. "We've gotten no alerts. I think we can have a little fun, no?"

No! I feel a sharp blow to my stomach, and I drop to my knees. It is mere seconds before the guard picks me up again. His face is so close. His putrid breath stings my nose. "She's a feisty one. This is going to be fun."

I throw out my leg, trying to hit my offender, but it finds only air. Laughter cuts through the hallway. I elbow someone in the chest, and there's a loud crack. The guard loosens his grip on me, but before I can get away, another one grabs me and lifts me up to press me face-first against the wall. My whole body is screaming in agony. "Stop!" I yell out, trying to cover my face. I can taste blood in my mouth. Gold Tooth sneers at me, and I feel the back of my tracksuit begin to unzip.

Horrified, I scream. I lash out again.

"Oh, stop screaming," one of the guards growls, delivering a blow to my nose. My head spins, and my body throbs.

Suddenly, someone rips the guards off me, and I fall to the ground. My body shivers as my bare skin hits the floor.

There's a lot of shouting, but I can't make out much. I pick up some words: *Hell, girl, rat, came out of nowhere.* My head throbs, and I curl up into a fetal position. I hurt; I hurt; I hurt.

The cold floor is welcoming, pressing up against my cheek and soothing the burn. My hands clutch my stomach, and I press my body into the wall. Maybe I can disappear. Maybe, just maybe.

Hands touch my side, and I flinch away. But these hands are different. Gentle. They try again, scooping my limp body up and into their arms. I crack my eye open and catch a glimpse of red. Burying my face in my rescuer's shirt, I allow myself to relax into the gentle sway of walking.

22

When I wake up, I hurt everywhere. I can't bring myself to open my eyes. My face feels heavy, and I want to pull the covers farther over my head. I open one eye and look around hesitantly. The small bedside lamp casts a dim glow around the room. I wipe a few strands of hair out of my eyes and notice that they're not green anymore. I try to sit up, but sharp stabs of pain tell me not to.

Where am I? How long have I been here?

I glance around the room. It isn't big—about the size of my hotel room. A small kitchen is on the far side, equipped with a stove and a refrigerator. A white sofa sits behind a shiny glass coffee table. The carefully laid floorboards heighten the warmth from the light, making the room feel cozy. The Making Perfect logo is printed boldly on the wall, right above a large window overlooking the surrounding landscape.

I glance down at the bed. It's big and square, with a thick comforter pulled tightly over the mattress. The pillows are fluffy. This is by far the most luxurious bed I've ever been in.

Something shifts beside me, and I turn around. My eyes widen in shock. Cooper is lying on the other side of the bed, over the covers, completely asleep. He's facing me, but all of his facial muscles are slack. He looks younger. Less scary. He's casually dressed in a plain black T-shirt and gray slacks. His hair is short and newly trimmed. Sweat has soaked through his shirt and is coating his forehead in a thin shine. He looks like a boy—not as intimidating as I remembered.

"Oh my God," I hiss, my voice not sounding like my own. His eyes fly open, and I sit up, ignoring the throbbing in my body. He jumps up, running a hand over his face to shake the sleep off.

"How are you feeling? Are you all right?" he asks me. Dark circles are now evident under his eyes.

"What—" I start. Was he the one who saved me last night? Is that why I'm in his room?

Was it even last night?

I don't realize that I'm trying to get up until he puts a hand on my shoulder. "You don't want to do that; you're not in good shape. I promise you—" I struggle against him, kicking the covers off my body. I gasp at what I see.

My body looks like hell. My joints are swollen, and I am covered in cuts and bruises that are turning various shades of yellow and green. The rags that used to be my tracksuit are nowhere to be seen. Instead, a red T-shirt a few sizes too big for me hangs over my underwear.

He *undressed* me?

"Now, don't panic. It's okay—" he starts, but I cut him off.

"What do you mean, it's okay? This is most definitely *not* okay!" He reaches out to touch my arm, but I slap him away. My arms go to wrap around my stomach, but even that is painful. Alarms are firing in my head, telling me to run, to get away. But I can't move.

"What's not okay?"

I glare at him. We're sitting mere inches apart. I suddenly feel nauseous and cover my mouth with the crook of my arm. The room is spinning. My stomach is twisting and turning, compounding my anguish. I just want it to stop.

I feel his arms shoot out to steady me, and I don't have the energy to stop him.

"You have to let me out of here," I demand.

"Don't worry. I promise you're safe—"

"Safe? What are you talking about? I'm not safe! This place should be put next to the *definition* of *unsafe*. I…" I swallow hard. "They touched me, and hurt me, and—"

"I know they did, and they're not going to get away with it." Something scary flashes in his eyes. "I know you're scared, but I'm not going to hurt you."

Maybe he's not going to hurt me, I think. But what about everybody else down in the labs getting *knives stuck through their eyes?*

"How am I supposed to believe that? How do you expect me to trust you?" He seems to take this into consideration. He closes his eyes, leans back, and bites his lip. I continue, "You told me before that you support killing for power. You're a liar and a manipulator. By the way, why haven't you killed me yet?"

Now he looks angry. He sits up and looks me straight in the eye. "I'm not going to argue with you. It is true. I do bad things, but that doesn't mean I'm a bad person. And the answer to your question is that you can trust me because I brought you back here last night. I washed the serum out of your hair, cleaned your cuts, held you *all night* while you coughed and puked your guts out. If I didn't care about you, I would have just taken you back to the lab. If that doesn't deserve a little bit of trust, I don't know what does."

I realize that I've been biting my lip. It feels as if claws are ripping through my gut. The vulnerability in his eyes almost hurts me. I want to hate him for all the terrible things he's done, for all the people he's hurt. But it's becoming harder and harder to hate the boy who saved me from the guards last night. He hasn't done anything to make me question his intentions on this.

But, ugh, I'm trying so hard to hate him.

My mind is being pulled in so many different directions.

He runs his hand over his hair and looks at me. "Is there anything else bothering you, other than the fact that you think I'm a monster?" I press my lips into a thin line. When I don't say anything, he asks another question. "You visited the research labs, didn't you?"

I open my mouth to say something, but again no words come out. He nods. "I figured as much, after seeing all the serum on your hands and face. Why did you go down there?"

I hesitate to tell him, but the words spill out of my mouth before I can stop them. "There were questions that I needed answers to."

"So you risked everything to search a giant room for information?" I don't reply, and he continues. "You could have asked me."

I scoff. "What do you mean?"

"I could have given you the information you were searching for." He shifts his weight, and his thigh brushes against my knee. "It was the test kids, right? You were looking for information about Mason's experiment?"

I nod reluctantly. He merely shrugs. "Next time, just come to me. It'll save us both a lot of trouble."

"Are you going to report this?" I blurt out.

He looks at me for a second before replying. "No. I don't want to have to explain to the officials how you broke into the labs without getting caught and yet are still allowed to roam around the facility. They would probably want to lock you up for good." I flop back down onto the pillows, relief rushing over me. "*But*, if you ever try to do this again, I'm going to lock you up myself."

"Because I broke into the lab?"

"Because you could've been killed last night." I look up at him, and he meets my gaze. "If you'd seen yourself, you'd know what I'm talking about."

"It was that bad?"

He nods. "Worse. On top of what the guards did, that green serum entered your system, and you didn't react well to it. You got *sick*. You spent half the night with your head in a basin."

Wow. "Last thing I remember, you were carrying me away. I must have been out cold."

He nods. "You're not going back to the test center yet. They've got enough from you for now. Remember, I run this place. They won't come for you here." He means it—I can see it in his eyes. "They suspect you, you know," he says.

I tense up, crossing my arms over my chest. "Who's 'they'? Suspect me of what?"

"Of breaking into the labs. Kace, the guards, everybody. You have to be careful. If they catch you trying anything else, they'll kill you."

"Wow, I really made a mess, didn't I?"

"There was a lot of serum." He sighs deeply, and I notice how tired he looks. He must have just barely fallen asleep when I woke up. I see his eyelids drooping, and he slumps back down on the bed.

"Cooper?" I say as he turns away from me.

"Mmhm?" His reply is barely audible.

"Thank you."

He mumbles and is asleep almost immediately, his chest rising and falling steadily. I close my eyes, letting myself drift away as well, feeling a little safer.

23

When I wake up, Cooper is gone. The bed is cold—he must've left a while ago.

I sit up, pulling the blanket over my shoulders. It's raining. Big, full droplets fall onto the snow below, turning everything to slush. Everything seems to be slower today—the AirTrans aren't taking off, delivery trucks aren't going out. The whole place seems to have been put on hold. I don't know why. It's just a little rain.

Sliding off the bed, I rub the sleep out of my eyes. What time is it? I look around the room for a clock and find one above the door. It's after noon. No wonder Cooper's gone. My stomach groans, and I realize how hungry I am. It's been a whole day since I've eaten—actually, I don't remember when my last meal was. They haven't been feeding me in the labs. They must have been sustaining me through the IV.

I groan when I open the refrigerator. Since Cooper never eats at the dining hall, I expected his refrigerator to be packed. Instead, it has only a few apples, three sandwiches wrapped in plastic, and some milk cartons. It's actually sad how empty it is, given all the resources he has. He must have some sort of private dining hall, or maybe he has his meals delivered to him. Probably the latter, I decide.

I pull out one of the apples and wash it in his sink. The water is cold. Nice. I splash my face and wipe my wet hands on my neck. As I turn to grab the towel, I notice a clean tracksuit hanging on the chair. Cooper must've left it for me. I pull it on, tossing the red

T-shirt into the corner. Deciding to make the most of having so much space, I go over to the sofa and kick my feet up on the table. I don't think an apple has ever tasted so good.

Excitement builds in my chest when I see the TV mounted on the wall. Sinking my teeth into the apple, I walk over to it and pull the remote off the receptor. My finger hovers over the *on* button. I'm almost afraid to push it.

Screw it. I push the button, and the screen flickers to life. Returning to the sofa, I crank up the volume so I can hear it. A woman's face pops up on the screen. She is the anchor of the mainstream news, which is played to the entire region. There are only three channels available on TV: news, adults, and kids. This TV is switched to news. I would've expected as much of Cooper.

I watch as the screen moves away from the woman's face to show footage from a fancy-looking city that definitely doesn't belong in Making Perfect. All the buildings are white, shiny, and of various shapes and sizes. The camera pans across the landscape, and I admire the immaculate conditions the city has been kept in. People are walking around with a set determination and purpose. Looking at them from afar, they look like ants in a colony—all with their own specific jobs.

The lens zooms in to the sign on the tallest building in the city. The TERC logo—large, blue-and-silver brushstrokes next to the company's name—is branded across the facade, the only distinguishable colors in a sea of white.

It's hard to know what, exactly, the reporters are talking about since I missed the beginning, but whatever it is, they don't seem happy about it. As another segment begins, I hear the door open.

But it's not Cooper.

"Miss Greenwood, Dr. Mason would like to see you in his office," the guard says. He stands tentatively in the doorway, as if he's afraid to come any further into his commander's room.

Mason?

"Now?" I ask.

The guard nods. I sigh and switch off the TV. After pulling my hair up into a ponytail, I walk out the door and find the guard waiting patiently for me. Without a word, he walks me down the hallway and around the corner.

Questions start firing in my head.

Mason? As in, the co-creator of the fetus experiment? He knew my dad!

I catch a glimpse of the door to Cooper's office. We walk past a few more doors before the guard stops me. The placard on the door reads: DR. RODGER MASON.

I tense up when the guard knocks on the door. Almost instantly, it swings open and a little balding man is standing in front of me.

My brow furrows. What? I look at him with a confused expression on my face. He is at least a head shorter than me and looks to be about fifty. He is dressed in a gray shirt with the top three buttons opened and dress pants that are too long for his legs. A large magnifying glass hangs from a chain around his neck.

This is the guy responsible for the test kids? For what happened to my dad? Is this a joke? This guy looks like a janitor.

"Welcome, Miss Greenwood," he greets me. Turning to the guard, he says, "Thank you. You may go." The guard nods and resumes his post at the end of the hallway. Mason retreats back into his office and, hesitantly, I follow him.

I freeze. This place is unsettling. The stuffed heads of strange creatures line the walls. Tall bookcases are filled with old books of varying colors, the binders of which are peeling off. The large desk in the middle of the room has disappeared under piles of file folders, open notebooks, and a large microscope that teeters precariously on its edge. Something screeches at me, and I spin around, locking eyes with what looks like an angry, overgrown canary. Along the wall behind the cage are shelves displaying what appear to be body parts in different-sized jars. There are eyeballs, brains, feet, and even a swollen hand. But not a human hand—it's got scales.

I recoil. What is this place? Why would this man keep body parts in jars?

"Make yourself at home," Mason says, breaking the silence. He walks to his desk and gestures to a large, purple chair that I somehow didn't notice before.

"Why are there body parts on the wall?" I spit out, hoping my voice won't betray my disgust. The screeches of the bird are like nails on a blackboard. Mason ignores me, leaning back in his spinning chair.

"Please allow me to introduce myself. I am Dr. Rodger Mason, scientist and overseer of special projects here at Making Perfect."

"I would introduce myself, but you already know who I am," I snap, walking over and sitting on the edge of the purple chair. This guy is creepy, and I'm ready to bolt.

"I sure do. Welcome to my humble office, Miss Greenwood. You are an exceptional child. Really, simply amazing." He walks over and pulls a book off one of his shelves. The title reads: GENETIC MODIFICATION: RECOMBINANT DNA AND CLONING. After flipping through a few pages, he pulls out a hidden file and returns the book to its shelf. He scribbles something on a piece of notepaper and slips it into the file. All of a sudden, he seems to notice that I'm still here and appears startled.

"Oh, hello, Miss Greenwood. I didn't see you there."

Yes, obviously not.

"What do you need to talk to me about?" I ask. Mason doesn't really seem to hear me. He has started searching through the mound of papers on his desk. Eventually, he pulls out a little piece of notepaper and smiles brightly, like he just won the lottery.

"Talk to you? Oh yes. Yes, of course. Yes, yes, yes…" What's wrong with this guy? You would think that one of Making Perfect's top scientists would be more…normal.

Slowly, so as not to make a sound, I stand up and make my way over to the door, hoping to get out of here before he notices that I'm leaving. I'm about to turn the handle when something moves in my peripheral vision. I scream, jumping back to see that the "canary" has flown free of its cage and swooped up to rest on one of the shelves. A cloud of dust is raised as it touches down on the wood.

"Don't mind him; I just wanted to let him stretch his wings," Mason says, returning to his seat. He gestures for me to return to the chair, and I reluctantly do.

"Now, Summer. You are really exceptional. One of my prize creations. After recombining much of your DNA, we made you a fully fledged superhuman. A great accomplishment, if I do say so myself." I don't dare say anything. He's actually finishing his sentences! "And the fact that it was done so early, really…truly amazing. Your parents would be proud."

Resentment courses through me. *They would still be here if it wasn't for you.* "My parents?" I ask. "You knew them?"

"Of course I knew them. Your father was a good friend of mine." And now he's back to being his distracted self. He gasps in surprise and grabs a book from the floor. After flipping a few pages, he frowns and returns it to the pile. If I squint, I can just catch some of the titles. *Mutants: Genetic Variety and the Human Body. The 2201 Official Guide to Human Anatomy. Mapping Man. The Basics of Cloning.*

All of the titles look the same to me.

"Now, Summer, I assume that everything has been going well." It's more of a statement than a question. I nod, folding my hands in my lap. I need to get out of here.

"Yes, thank you," I say, looking at the floor. Why did he even call me here?

"Nobody's treating you terribly, I hope."

I don't say anything. It wasn't really a question.

He nods, leaning back in his chair. He looks much more focused now. An almost scary gleam has taken up residence in his eyes. "As you probably don't know, our relationship with TERC has become quite...*tense.*" He takes a sip out of a cracked white mug hidden behind a wall of papers.

"What do you mean by 'tense'?" I ask, clasping my hands together.

He ignores my question and changes the subject. "Now, Summer. When I ask you this, you have to promise me something. It is *critically* important that you give me a truthful answer." He pauses, leaning in toward me. His expression has grown severe. "Where are Robert and Virginia Greenwood?"

I shake my head. "You took them away from me. They tried to protect us, and you took them away."

"Please don't lie to me. This is just wasting both of our time."

"I'm not. Why don't you check my Alpha profile?"

He sighs. "Ms. Greenwood—"

"What do you want me to say? I'm telling you, *I have no idea!*" I end up shouting the last part so loud that he flinches.

"All right," Mason sighs. "I didn't want to have to do this."

He leans forward and presses a button. I tense up, rising from my chair. The gleam in his eye is scaring me—I need to get out of here.

Before I can get to the door, four guards enter and block my exit. They are quick, but I'm hoping my years of experience will trump theirs. I slip through their grasp, throwing out my leg and sweeping the first guard's feet from under him. I hit the next on the side of the face and reach forward to grab the door handle. But before I can reach it, something hard and cold slams into my jaw.

The world spins, and the barrel of a gun clicks against my head.

"Don't move," one of them—a female—growls. I suck in a breath. The other one grabs my wrists and shoves me against the wall, twisting my arms behind my back. My head throbs, and my vision swims.

"I'm afraid you're hiding something from me." Mason's voice sounds vicious, completely different from a few minutes ago. He is walking toward me.

"You are *insane!*" I spit out. "I am telling the truth. Hook me up to whatever machines you want, but I'm not lying. They left us in the Slump without telling us where they were going, and they never came back. That's it."

"I really want to believe you, trust me, but I don't," he says. The male guard raises his arm, and Mason continues. "I'm going to give you one more chance. *Where did they go?*"

"Damn you," I growl. I feel the back of my tracksuit being sliced open, exposing the bare skin of my back. I don't have time to take another breath before something sharp and hot slams into my skin. A powerful wave of electricity surges through me, and I scream involuntarily. The sound of the rod whipping through the air a second time gets to me a split second before the actual rod does. I grit my teeth. This time, I'm not giving them the satisfaction of hearing my agony. It's like a burning fire being etched into my flesh, spreading the length of my back. The next one is even harder.

I arch my back, and a small whimper squeezes though my tightly closed lips. The lashes stop for a moment. It's enough for me to catch my breath, which is coming out in short, sharp puffs. I open my eyes and stare right into Mason's.

"One more chance. Where are they?"

Silence.

"Have it your way. I'm sure we can get someone who knew them just as well as you did. Someone a little less stubborn."

Lily and Tory.

"No!" I scream, feeling a surge of power explode inside me. With strength I didn't know I had, I lash out and throw the guards off me. They buckle inward and collapse on the ground. Colors dance before my eyes, and everything slows down. I know what to do without even thinking about it. I see one guard coming from the left, and my leg shoots out to meet his gut. I hear a cracking sound, and he crumples to the ground. I duck under the hands of another guard and rush to the door. In one motion, I slam into it and burst through into the hallway.

I run straight ahead, not looking back at the commotion I left behind. The elevator doors are closing at the end of the hallway. Somehow I make it and jump through, just as the doors close behind me. My heart is pounding so hard I can hear it. The burning in my back is so painful that I have to grip the side of the elevator to keep from blacking out.

"What happened?"

I jump and turn around, coming face-to-face with an official. He just stands there as I stare, showing no aggression. I'm filled with relief when he pulls off his helmet.

Kace looks at me through narrowed eyes. "What happened?"

"Nothing," I lie. Even breathing hurts right now.

"Show me," he says, and I shake my head. "Do it."

"No," I retort. I tighten my grip on the gold railing to steady myself.

"Just turn around."

Slowly, I turn around. Kace sucks in a breath. I cringe every time the fabric of my tracksuit touches the blistering wound.

"You need to see Aaron."

"Who's Aaron?" I ask him as he unlocks the control box and pushes a few buttons. The elevator stops, then changes direction. My legs start to give out. Kace grabs me by the shoulders and props me up. I am grateful—it feels like my strength is being sucked out by a vacuum.

The elevator stops. Kace pulls a key from his pocket and closes and locks the control box.

"Where are we?" my voice is hardly a whisper as the doors open. An immediate wave of bitter cold hits me, and bright light fills my eyes. The icy wind bites at my bare arms and raw skin, accentuating my pain.

We're on the roof. Large vent openings and small domes the size of large potted plants fill the space, and a black railing surrounds the entire perimeter. Small puddles of water dot the floor. Kace helps me over to the railing along its edge. Below, I see officials and guards filling up large, white delivery trucks with notebook-sized boxes. A multilane road stretches into the horizon through the wetlands that surround the facility. I can see for miles. There are hardly any trees—they must've all been cut down.

"There are no cameras up here. We are free to talk," Kace explains as I sit down on one of the domes.

"Who's Aaron?" I ask again, squinting in the sunlight.

"Aaron is the leader of Troop Five." Kace walks over to the railing, placing his hands on the bone-chilling surface. "The largest resistance group in the region."

My mouth gapes. The rebels are real? All my life, I have thought they are a myth—are they real? All my life, I hated them because they didn't come to help us. If they are real, why have we never seen them?

"Does the boy, Tyler, trust you?" Kace asks, staring out into the distance.

"Yes," I reply quickly. "Why? What does he have to do with this?"

He walks over and squats in front of me, resting his elbows on his knees like he's about to lecture a small child. He lowers his voice to almost a whisper.

"I'm going to take you to meet Troop Five."

24

I stand on the roof, gripping the railing. Wind whips through my hair and blows it out behind me. It's almost midnight. It's colder than it was earlier, but I'm warmer in the clothes Kace has given me. Below, guards and officials are still loading and unloading trucks. This place never stops. Tyler is standing beside me, his hands in his pockets. He just arrived, and he looks exceptionally tired. I was so relieved to see that he was okay.

"Are we just going to stand here until he arrives?" he pipes up. Some officials on the ground start shouting about something, and he crouches down behind the railing so as not to be seen.

"Don't worry, they can't see us," I say, and he stands back up.

I haven't told him yet about what happened in Mason's office. Maybe I never will. It'll save him the worry. But the pain in my back has been agonizing all afternoon, threatening to make me pass out almost every time I move.

After we left the roof, Kace brought me back to the officials' quarters and let me clean my wounds. By then, my lower back was covered in dark blisters and had completely stiffened up. I tried washing it off in the shower, but eventually I couldn't take the pain and shut the water off. Kace and his roommate, Brian, helped me disinfect it and wrap it so I could move a little easier. I changed out of my tattered tracksuit into one of Brian's old uniforms and crashed on their couch for the remainder of the evening. It wasn't long before Brian woke me and brought me back to the roof, giving me food while we rode in the elevator. Kace wasn't there.

Neither of them gave me any details about Aaron or about what was going to happen. They didn't even answer any of my questions about the test kids or about what Tyler had to do with any of this. They kept reassuring me that I'd be filled in soon enough.

"Are we gonna run?" Tyler asks, sensing my unease.

I meet his gaze. "We can't leave everybody behind."

I wouldn't be able to live with myself if we ran. But part of me really wants to. To get out of here, get my sisters, and never look back.

"You're right." He is silent for a moment. "I just don't know how much more I can take, you know? All the stuff they do here. I…" He looks down. I can see him searching his brain for the right words. He bites his lip. "I need to get out of here." He sighs and hangs his head.

"I hate Making Perfect," I say.

"Me too."

Before either of us can say anything else, the elevator doors open. Kace has finally arrived, and with him are Brian and another guard I don't recognize. Two bulging, brown sacks are slung over Kace's shoulders, and he tosses them to us.

"Put those on. If you walk around in white, you'll be too easily spotted."

We open the bags. I hold up baggy black pants and a long shirt, obviously meant for a grown man. A pair of heavy boots are in the sack as well. Judging by the smell, they have been used many times before. I quickly put the clothes on over the ones I'm wearing. I slip the boots onto my feet, tying the laces as tightly as I can. Tyler does the same.

"Brian," Kace prompts, and Brian starts to unbuckle the straps on the front of his body armor. The other official does the same. They remove pieces of the shell-like armor until they're dressed in simple, black clothes identical to ours. Kace gathers the armor and hands it to me.

"Put it on," he says curtly, and I give him a confused look. "How else did you expect us to get out of here?" He looks at Tyler, who is already shrugging on the shoulder plate and buckling it into place. His nametag reads: LEE.

I quickly lift the heavy armor and place it on my shoulders. I wince as the hard scales press against the wounds on my back. After Tyler has secured his, he comes over to help me. I wave him away. In less than a minute, I'm ready. My nametag reads: KRULL.

Brian and the other official grab the sacks and leave without another word. The wind whips through my hair, bites at my nose, and makes me smile. I can't believe we're getting out.

Kace walks up to us. His eyes are unflinching.

"You will follow my orders at all costs. One mistake, and we're all dead. You have to be back by six, or people are going to notice. There is a supply truck leaving in twenty minutes for the town-house district. You'll be on it. When you get near the fence, you have to make sure you jump off. Ridge will be waiting for you near the train tracks. He's going to bring you to Aaron. He'll give you instructions for the way back. I'll make sure you get back in safely."

"Wait, you're not coming with us?" Tyler asks, trying to conceal his obvious nervousness. Kace shakes his head.

"No, if I come with you, it would be far too suspicious." He pauses, taking time to run his eyes over Tyler's body. "Tyler, come here." Tyler slowly walks over to him. I tense up, wanting to grab his arm, but I don't. I can't. "Give me your arm." I watch, confused, as Tyler rolls up the sleeve of his guard uniform. Before either of us can do anything, Kace plunges a needle into Tyler's arm. He flinches, pulling his arm away in shock and quickly pulling down the sleeve. Kace slips the needle back into his pocket.

"What was that?" I growl, running up to Tyler. "What did you just do?"

"It's a security measure," Kace says, tossing each of us a pair of gloves.

"What security measure?"

"I just injected him with a toxin," says Kace. "He will be fine, but in a few hours, he'll start weakening. Within a day, he'll be dead. I have the antitoxin here, and he'll get it once you come back. But he won't if you decide to take off."

"Why do you care if we take off?" I snap.

"Because if you don't show, and they realize you're gone, it could be traced back to me. And that will be the end of me." Kace shrugs. "But as long as you both come back, it'll be like you never left."

"But…this is not going to work," I say. "They're going to know we're not in the lab. Mason is probably still looking for me."

"Let me worry about that. Just get back here on time."

I scowl but don't say anything. Suddenly, a strong gust of wind blows over the roof, tipping me backward. I catch myself, but as I do, a stabbing pain shoots through my back.

"Will you make it?" Kace asks, and I glare at him.

Tyler looks at me, his brow furrowed. "Why wouldn't you make it? Are you okay?" he asks.

"I'm fine," I say, still glaring at Kace. Tyler's worried expression cuts into me.

"You didn't tell him?" Kace raises his eyebrows. Then, seeing my expression, he stops. "All right, we've got to go." He turns to go, but stops, seeming to remember something.

"Oh, these are for you." He pulls two large knives out of his leather sack and hands them to us. I stare at the weapon. The moonlight reflects off the blade, making it glisten. These knives aren't anything like the pocket knives we had in the Slump. These knives are weapons. The blades are lightweight and thin, and they balance out the handles beautifully. Perfect for war. Built to kill.

I slip the knife into its sheath and look at Kace expectantly. He turns back toward the elevator. I place the helmet on my head and fold my hair under it. Without another thought, Tyler and I follow.

Kace once again controls the elevator panel, preventing us from stopping at any floor on the way down. I watch the numbers get smaller as we descend, eventually stopping at three. We follow him down a narrow hallway, empty except for the occasional passing guard. I am amazed at how the guards don't even acknowledge each other—not even a nod.

I train my eyes on my feet and count my steps to keep focused. Tyler's shoulder is only a few inches from mine. We hurry forward until Kace reaches a thick metal door. The little light bulbs that illuminate the hallway are flickering. My stomach clenches as Kace opens the door with a touch of his remote. Stairs.

He glances over his shoulder, checking to see if I'm okay. I force myself to nod and start to follow him down the stairs. With every step, I get more and more of the strength sucked out of me. The lack of sleep doesn't help. How can I possibly make it all the way to the border if I can barely get down the stairs?

Thankfully, I'm able to get all the way down without fainting. I try to ignore the pain. We quickly walk down the last hallway and through a large door. Bright lights illuminate the loading docks.

Hold on.

The crowd of guards and officials is thicker than it looked from the roof. The docks are bustling with activity. A cacophony of sounds ring out as people shout orders and whirring machinery helps to load boxes onto the trucks. As we walk, I try to block everything out.

White light stabs at the back of my eyes. I feel all the blood rush out of my face, and before I can stop myself, I stagger forward, grabbing on to Tyler to prevent myself from collapsing onto the asphalt. My ears are ringing. I can hardly hear anything else. A couple of nearby guards and officials turn their heads to look at me.

"What's wrong?" Tyler hisses at me. One of his arms wraps around my waist and gently steadies me. I tell myself to focus on Tyler.

Breathe. Try not to fall. If you do, we're all dead.

"Is there a problem here, soldier?"

A tall, white-clad official stands in front of us, his arms crossed like he's inspecting a piece of art in a gallery. If I squint, I can just read his nametag: HANK.

Kace steps in front of us, blocking us partly from Hank's view. I can't hear what they're saying—it takes all the energy I have to stay upright.

"What's going on?" Tyler whispers. "And don't tell me you're fine, because, clearly, you're not."

"I'll tell you later."

"No, I want to know now." Before I can answer, Kace yanks me forward by my armor plate.

"Official Krull!" a voice shouts from near the back of a nearby truck. "In the truck!"

I nod at Hank and make my way over to the truck. The official who called for me introduces herself as Pierce and ushers me and Tyler into the back. There is hardly any room among the boxes, but we manage to tuck ourselves in between two columns of large crates. Pierce closes the sliding metal door, and near darkness covers us, leaving the two of us alone. I hear the truck rumble to life. We pull off our helmets and put them on the floor beside us. After the truck is in motion, Tyler speaks again.

"Don't think you're getting off that easy. What happened back there?" he asks, his irritation evident. When I open my mouth to reply, he cuts me off. "And don't even think about lying to me. I know it wasn't just lack of sleep."

"Mason wanted to know where my parents went. When I didn't tell him, he hurt me." I avoid his gaze and lean backward so the armor doesn't rub against my back.

"He hurt you?"

"He hit me."

"Summer—"

"He shocked me, okay?" My voice cracks a little as I say this. "He took an electric metal rod and had guards beat me with it."

He pauses. "I—"

"Just don't, okay? I'm fine."

"Obviously not, after what just happened back there!" he hisses at me. As my eyes adjust, I can make out his face.

I sigh. "Tyler…"

We sit in silence for a while, hearing only the truck rumbling under us and our own heavy breathing. Droplets of sweat form on my forehead, and I close my eyes. I try to force myself to stay awake. If I fall asleep here and we miss the jump-off spot, Tyler and I are pretty much dead. Plus, since Kace is going to all this trouble to allow us to meet the rebels, he obviously thinks it's important that we do so.

"You don't have to do this, you know?" Tyler mumbles, so softly that I can hardly make out what he is saying.

"Do what?"

"Just go to sleep. I'll keep watch."

"No, it's okay. I'm all right," I reply, blowing a rebellious strand of hair out of my face.

He closes his eyes. "I'm really glad you're okay, you know. I was worried that I would never see you again."

"So was I." I look at the floor. "What did they do to you?" I rub the grogginess out of my eyes and lean my head against the truck door. The cold metal presses against my forehead, sending a dull ache through my head each time we hit a pothole.

"It wasn't fun," he says, brushing it off. "You should probably get that uniform off. It's doing more harm than good." He leans over to me, careful not to lose his balance in the shaky truck. With his help, we manage to get the armor shell over my head. I can tell the skin on my back has fused to the back of my cotton shirt. Still, it's not as painful without the shell over it.

The truck goes over a deep pothole, and I'm thrown off balance. I cry out in surprise as I slam right into Tyler and both of us are sent flying into the vehicle's side. When the truck rights itself, I find myself completely on top of him. I glance up, and he meets my gaze. After a few seconds, he bursts out laughing. I can't help myself—I join him. Laughter contorts our faces, and the sound that comes out pierces the stillness of the truck. We keep laughing until our throats run dry, until our chests begin to ache. It's been a while since I last laughed. It feels so good.

Then it dawns on me. How are we supposed to know when to jump? The idea snaps me back into focus, and I sit up with a start.

"What's wrong?" Tyler asks, running his fingers through his hair.

"How will we know when to jump?" I ask, creases forming on my forehead. To my surprise, Tyler softly chuckles. "What is it?"

"Nothing," he says. "I'll check."

He crawls to the door and smoothly pulls it up. I am hit with a wall of wind. To my surprise, no alarms go off.

I can hardly see anything past the bright taillights of the truck. The road has gotten wider, but the land on either side of us is still wetland. If we jumped now, we would land in the middle of nowhere.

I remember learning about the layout of the region in school. The testing facilities are isolated from the cities, located in more easily protected areas. Making Perfect's districts are isolated like the layers of an onion: the testing facilities are at the region's core, then the mansions (where the executives and other important people live), then the townhouses, and finally the Slump, which extends all the way to the border. To get to the Slump from the facilities, Tyler and I will need to travel through both the mansion and townhouse districts.

It is dawning on me that we will have only hours to cover a huge distance. When Kace originally put us in the truck, he made it seem like it was a short ride. What if Kace's toxin kicks in too quickly and Tyler won't be able to make it out of the truck? We'll be stuck.

Tyler closes the door, casting darkness upon us once again. "I'll be fine, Sum," he says, reading my worried look. "Don't worry about me. I'll be okay." When I try to protest, he shuts me up. "You're the one who looks like hell. Get some sleep. I swear I'm going to kill Mason."

"Not if I beat you to it." I smile weakly. There's no point in fighting him. I know he's right. If I try to tough it out, I'll be useless within the hour. Without a sound, I crawl over to him and lean against his shoulder. He slouches down slightly and leans his head on mine. My body warms with familiarity. The tires beat loudly against the pavement, drowning out my thoughts.

I hope this ride will be over soon.

25

My eyes snap open, and for a moment I don't remember where I am.

"Relax. It's okay," Tyler says, and then I remember. I notice that he has not moved from my side. The pain in my back has subsided a bit.

"Where are we?"

"I was just about to check." He crawls to the door and opens it a crack. He drops to his stomach and looks out into the night. After a few seconds, he says, "Sum, you might want to come see this."

Excitement building, I move to the door, carefully dropping to my stomach and peeking out. I've heard about the mansions—that they were huge compounds with enough floor space to fit five townhouses in just the bottom floor. They provide the largest, most heavily protected living spaces in the entire region. But it didn't hit me until just now how imposing the buildings actually are.

The road we're driving on isn't particularly wide, but it is extremely smooth and well paved. No potholes. Manicured lawns stretch between the buildings as far as I can see. The actual mansions look more like fortresses. The exteriors are steel gray, and a slew of armed guards patrol the perimeter of each. Despite the late hour, many lights are still on. I catch a glimpse of some potted plants in one of the upper-floor windows. I wonder who they belong to—only the most important and wealthy people are permitted to live in the mansions. People like Cooper's family.

A light turns on in one of the bottom windows. I catch a glimpse of a woman's silhouette. She seems to be talking to a young child. She scoops it up and cradles it in her arms, laughing. The child wiggles out of the woman's embrace and dashes away from the window.

Longing bubbles up inside me, quickly turning into pure hatred. How can they live like this, so happy and protected, without a care in the world, not even acknowledging the suffering taking place so close to them?

"Those bastards," I hiss, not taking my eyes off the mansions, which don't seem to be getting any smaller even as we drive away from them. The crisp air fills my lungs, and the scent of asphalt and freshly mowed grass hang around us. "How can they just ignore us when they have all that?"

Tyler opens his mouth to speak, but the slowing truck stops him. I push the door up a little higher and glance around the side and see it. The fence. The fence between the mansions and the townhouses—between the lucky and the rest. Nobody even counts the Slump.

I dart back into the truck, and Tyler pulls down the door. I haven't been to the townhouses since I was twelve, when my parents took us away. I never had any intention of coming back; I didn't want to hold on to the hope that my parents might still be there. Tyler hurriedly closes the door and presses himself against the wall as the truck comes to a complete stop.

There are muffled voices outside as the driver goes through the process of authorization to cross the fence. Tyler and I move deeper into the truck in case they decide to lift the door to check the cargo. They don't, however, and within minutes, we drive through the gate. I don't dare to open the door now. Nor do I want to go to sleep. I just sit, staring at the crates.

"Can you take next watch? I'm exhausted," he says, and I nod. He leans against the side of a box and is instantly out cold. The truck rumbles on, and the road once again becomes bumpy, occasionally throwing me off balance. I fight the urge to open the door.

The townhouse district isn't wide, but it's long. I spot the large sign displaying the name of the community: CHARLOTTE. Two communities away from where I used to live. I observe the identical little gray houses, all lined up in rows with variously shaped blocks of grass in front of them. The yellow light from the street lamps reflects off the thin coat of water from the recent rain shower, casting a peaceful glow onto the street. We pass a large food warehouse to my right, and I catch a glimpse of the elementary school on the other side of the street. It's long past curfew, so everybody is already inside. They'd be stupid if they weren't. That's something I definitely don't miss about the townhouses—the strict curfew. If you are out after curfew, you run the risk of arrest and prosecution. The cameras set up on every street corner keep a close eye on the residents. One step out of line, and they will find you.

I could get to the Slump from here—I want to jump out of the truck and make a run for it. But with one glance at Tyler, I realize how selfish that would be. I wouldn't be able to live with myself, knowing he had died because of me. So I just sit there, waiting, for what must be hours, picking the label off one of the boxes and reattaching it. By the time the truck finally begins to slow, multiple boxes carry the evidence of my twiddling.

"Hey!" I hiss, throwing a crumpled label at Tyler. "Get up, we're slowing down." His eyes are open in an instant. We both pull on our helmets and secure the rest of our armor. When the truck slows to just above a jogging pace, Tyler grabs the handle of the truck door.

"We have to go," he whispers. I just stare at him, dumbfounded. "Summer! We have to move!"

"Wait—what do we do? What's the plan?"

"Just follow me."

Tyler slides the door up. I look around. We're almost in the Slump. With a quick glance around, I realize that we've exited the housing district and are driving through the heavy woods that hide the townhouses from the Slump. All the trees look like skeletons—completely barren of leaves except for the occasional evergreen. The truck, though it has slowed, is still traveling steadily.

"We've got to jump," Tyler whispers, grabbing one of the brown bags and looking at me with a worried expression. I nod through gritted teeth and grab the other.

Tyler jumps off, hits the pavement, rolls, and is on his feet in one smooth motion. Before I can think twice, I follow. The impact on the pavement sends a shooting pain up my back, but I roll and quickly come to a stop. I get up slowly. Tyler makes his way over to me.

"Are you okay?"

"I'm fine. We have to get into the woods," I blurt out. "We have a lot of ground to cover."

"Okay," he replies. We hurry off the road and into the dark, meager cover that the forest provides us. After we have put a decent distance between us and the road, we stop to get our bearings.

"How do we get to the train tracks?"

"I think it's this way," Tyler says. "But someone should be here to meet us."

"Let's just keep going. Maybe they'll meet us at the fence." We make our way through the dark, careful not to trip on fallen branches or rocks. Our progress is slow. The soggy, fallen leaves conceal the forest floor and make it hard to see where we're stepping.

Where is our contact? If we don't get there soon, I'm afraid we won't get back in time to save Tyler. When is the truck going back to the facility? Kace never said anything about how we're supposed to go back.

Just when I start to get frustrated, I hear voices and see the flicker of flashlights deep in the trees. Quietly, Tyler ducks behind an evergreen, pulling me with him.

"We're not supposed to go over the fence, right?" I whisper.

"I don't think so," he replies. "You lived here for longer. Do you remember there being any sort of train system in the townhouses?"

I nod. "Yes. The transport trains." The trains are set up to link the communities together. All the employees of Making Perfect use them to go back and forth to their respective facilities. The train schedule coincides with the work shifts and runs day and night. They move people to and from the Making Perfect laboratories, institutions, storage units, and other facilities in the center of the region. I remember walking with Mom to the train every morning on my way to school. I used to watch it until it was out of sight. "The tracks cut a straight line from the fence to the heart of the region. There's one on the border of Charlotte and Howard."

"Let's go there first," he says. Suddenly, his knees buckle under him and he winces in pain. One of his arms flies to his chest, and he grabs on to the tree for support.

"Ty, what's wrong?" I ask, helping him into a sitting position against the tree. His face is contorted into a pained grimace, and all the blood runs out of it. "Tyler!" I shake his shoulders. He twists to the side, vomiting up the meager portion of food that we ate for dinner.

The toxin must be pretty fast-acting if he's already throwing up.

"Hey, it's okay," I say, trying to comfort him as I reach into the bag to look for anything that might help. "Try to keep your stomach in your body until we get back into the truck." I find a small cloth, pour some water onto it, and use it to wipe his face down. I hand him the bottle of water, and he takes a few sips before returning it to me. His breaths are shallow, like he's desperate for air, but the color in his face is slowly returning.

"You okay?" I ask as he reaches up to take the cloth from me.

"Yeah," he replies. "It's just the toxin."

"Well, make sure you don't hurl all over me," I reply with a smirk, gently helping him up. I ignore the stabbing pain in my back as he clears his head and picks up his sack from the ground.

When he looks back up, he's grinning weakly. "I'll be sure to keep that in mind."

I can't help but smile too.

"You sure you're okay?" I ask as he slings the sack over his shoulder.

"I think the drug attacks in spurts. I feel fine now," he replies. "Let's keep moving."

I nod, and we walk parallel to the fence, staying just inside the tree line so we won't be seen by the officials patrolling the border. I tuck my hands into the pockets of my oversized black pants. My breaths come out in puffs of fog, and the cold eats away at my fingers until I can't feel them at all.

We walk like this for a while, until I hear a bullet click into the barrel of a gun. I don't have time to do anything else before I feel cold metal press against the back of my neck.

"Don't move," a deep voice growls venomously. "One more step, and the girl dies."

Tyler's grip on me tightens. "Who are you?"

Before the man can say anything, I instinctively spin to my right and grab hold of his wrist, twisting it back painfully until the gun drops to the ground. I hear him cry out in pain as Tyler picks up the gun and points it at him.

I turn to face him, watching him clutch his wrist in pain, his eyes wide with surprise. As I'm expecting to see an official, this man catches me off guard. He isn't one. He is young, probably in his late teens. His hair is dark, shining in the moonlight, and a large scar stretches from across the corner of his left eye to his ear lobe. His skin is almost stark white.

"Don't shoot; I'm on your side." His voice is strong and clear, with a slight melodic drawl that I've never heard before.

"And which side is that?" I ask, glancing at Tyler.

"I'm with Aaron. I am here to bring you to them."

I sigh with relief. He's with the rebels.

"Sorry about your wrist," I say, looking at his arm.

"It'll be fine in a second."

I open my mouth to ask what he means by that, but he cuts me off. "My name is Ridge O'Brien. I'm going to take you to the others." He studies our faces for a minute. "You don't look so good. Luckily it's not that far. Follow me." Ridge turns on his heel and heads deeper into the woods. We follow him, moving further and further away from the towering fence.

26

We only have to walk about fifteen minutes before we reach the tracks. It's so dark this far into the woods that it's hard to see anything. My feet are so cold that I can't feel them except for where they rub against the oversized boots.

As soon as the tracks come into view, Ridge stops. At first glance, they seem just as abandoned as any other part of the woods. But when Ridge raises two fingers to his lips and whistles—a sound so soft that one could mistake it for wind—dark figures begin creeping out of the shadows. They come out from behind trees, rocks, and bushes. My mouth gapes. Every single one of them is clad in the same gray uniform that Ridge wears. Some of them wear skullcaps of various colors. As they get closer, the moonlight reveals their faces. Most of them appear to be in their teens or early twenties.

A red-haired girl gracefully walks up to Ridge and whispers something in his ear. My eyes dart down to the patch on her uniform: *Troop 5.*

A boy, who looks to be about twenty, confidently walks up to us.

"You're Summer and Tyler?" he asks, and I nod. He is only slightly taller than me, but he's clearly well-built, even under his uniform. He has a square jaw and short-cropped brown hair. His hands are in the pockets of his jacket, and a long, black gun is slung casually across his shoulders. "Welcome, both of you. Please be assured, you are safe. We aren't going to hurt you. I am Aaron

Steele, and this," he gestures to the people around him, "is some of Troop Five. You'll get to know them in time, but let's get you out of the cold."

He starts into the woods away from the tracks and glances back to see if we're following. Nervously, I do. We walk for a minute through the woods before stumbling into a clearing where two Making Perfect delivery trucks are parked. I stiffen, fear rising in my chest, and I look at Aaron, but he's completely relaxed. The weight falls off my shoulders when I see some of the other rebels enter the trucks. This must be how they manage to get in and out. Tyler looks as tense as a tightly wound cord.

Aaron holds up the back door of one of the trucks and gestures for us to get in. The second I enter it, my eyes widen. Instead of boxes, this truck is stacked with supplies, medical equipment, and weapons. Folding benches line each side, some of them used as shelves and others as cots. One boy, who looks my age and bears an uncanny resemblance to Ridge, is sitting on one of them and eating from a metal bowl. A thin, black ring pierces the side of his lip. When he sees Aaron, he cocks his head to the side.

"Do you want me to go?" he asks, and Aaron shakes his head. The second he opens his mouth and reveals his accent, I realize why he looks so much like Ridge. They must be brothers.

"You can stay," Aaron tells him. Then he glances back at us. "This is Xander. He's one of our best navigators."

Xander scoffs. "Yeah right. It's not hard to earn that title when you're the only one willing to take the job." But there's humor in his voice.

Aaron smiles. I notice the rest of the rebels milling about outside the trucks, keeping watch and softly conversing with one another. I wonder if they're listening. I bet they are.

I sit down on the edge of one of the benches closest to the door. The back of the truck is still open so the rest of the rebels can jump in quickly if needed. Aaron grabs three plastic water canteens from a box behind Xander, tossing one each to me and Tyler before sitting down opposite us. He unscrews the top of his and takes a few gulps.

"Why are we here?" I finally say. They're the first words that I've spoken to Aaron.

"We needed a safe place to talk. Besides, it's really hard for us to get into Making Perfect...It's much easier to get you out. I just need to ask you a few questions." Based on the way Kace talked about him, I pictured Aaron being older. On second thought, I thought they would all be older. It's slightly unnerving, yet comforting. Ridge climbs into the trailer and sits down next to Aaron.

"Why should we trust you?" I ask. Aaron smiles.

"We hate Making Perfect as much as you do. Believe me." He turns his head toward Ridge, who nods in agreement. "We're just a group of former thieves, orphans, and test subjects. Troop Five has taken us all in. We're not a rebel group so much as a refuge." I see Xander nod through his food. Aaron places his bottle on the floor. "And the truth is, we need your help."

My brow furrows. What does he mean? "I don't understand. Why do you need us?"

Ridge runs his hand over his hair, and another soldier hops into the van. It's the same red-haired girl from before. Aaron purses his lips, looking at her with worry. "Anything wrong?"

"No. Did Kace say what time they need to be back?" She doesn't even acknowledge us.

"They have to catch the same truck back," he says, then looks at us. "Did Kace use the toxin?" I glance at Tyler, who nods. He looks weaker. Beads of sweat dot his forehead and upper lip. Aaron smirks apologetically. "Only Kace. He's brilliant, but *man* is he stubborn. Callie would know." He gestures at the red-haired girl, who now has a name. "Anyway, that gives us, what…twenty minutes?"

Callie nods, slipping out of the van and back into the night. Aaron looks back at us.

"I just want to talk to you. I need you to trust me."

I stiffen. "I'm not good at that."

He smiles. "I'm not going to harm you, none of us are. We need your help."

"Our help? For what?"

"Have you ever heard of the Fetus Project?" I nod, remembering what I read in the labs. Tyler also nods, and I wonder how he knows. Surely he didn't break into the labs as well…did he? Aaron continues, "The experiment was stopped after ten years, when Mason's own wife, Evelyn, died giving birth to her third test kid. Since the Star Formula was only divided into thirteen parts, only thirteen test kids were created in total. This makes them extremely important to Making Perfect. In order to recreate the Star Formula, they need to collect stem cells from each—"

"What?" Tyler asks, and I look at him. "What's the Star Formula?"

Aaron sighs and explains. As he talks, my arms and legs begin to tingle, and time slows down. Everything I read in the lab was true. I have been trying to convince myself that it couldn't be, but Aaron's words shred any remaining doubt. My heart is racing, and my feet feel bolted to the floor. I am a test kid. So is Tyler. That's why we're here. Making Perfect needs all thirteen of us to complete the formula. They need our neural stem cells. Once they have them, they'll build an army capable of conquering all the other regions. Nothing will stop them. Not TERC, not Spark, none of them. The rising tension between Making Perfect and the other regions will act as a catalyst for them to launch an all-out assault with an army trained in their military facilities. They now have ten of us. The rebels are harboring three. That's why Making Perfect is so desperate to find them.

Tyler looks like he's been hit by a train. All the blood has drained from his face, and his hands are shaking as he rubs the back of his neck.

My stomach is in so many knots, it's painful. "But how would they collect the stem cells without…" My voice trails off as it hits me.

Oh my God.

They're going to kill us.

Everything suddenly clicks into place. My breathing gets heavy. We can't go back there. They only need three more. Once they find those three, we're finished. Then nothing will stop Making Perfect. Tyler looks at me, and I know he's thinking the same thing. I try to compose myself.

"That's why Making Perfect needs to find us so badly. It's because we're preventing them from completing the procedure," Aaron explains.

"But what about our enhancements?" I ask, rubbing my eyes. The truck has become freezing cold, and my breath is coming out in visible puffs.

"We never got them," I hear Tyler remark and turn to stare at him wide-eyed.

"What do you mean we never got them?" I gape. "Of course we got them."

"We never got them," he repeats, turning to Aaron. "After the 'enhancements,' Mason called me back into his office to discuss a few things. When I asked what my enhancement was, he told me that we were not given one. We're test kids, so we are already enhanced. We already had our special abilities and didn't need any more." When I stare at him, he adds, "Remember Protocol? The whole 'if test kids get enhancements, it'll mess up their whole system' thing?" I shake my head. He looks at Aaron for help. As Aaron begins to say something, I cut him off.

"So, we've had these abilities since we were little?" I ask. Tyler nods. "Then what's yours?"

He shrugs. "I haven't found it yet."

I sigh. This feels so unreal.

"But what about my mom and dad?" I ask Aaron. "Did they know about this?" My voice becomes terse and thick. I am *not* going to cry.

Aaron nods. "Robert was the one who started the experiment. He wanted to find a way to protect children from the new diseases stemming from Yellow Pox. He knew all the ins and outs of the procedure but knew nothing of Mason's plan to create soldiers. When the test kids were born, they were taken from their biological mothers and given to trusted foster families. When your mother became pregnant with you, she got sick. So sick that they didn't know if she would survive the pregnancy. Desperate to protect both of you, your father decided to use the experiment on your mother. It worked. She got better, you were born, and they raised you as they raised their other daughters. Later, when he learned about Mason's plans for the test kids, your father wanted nothing to do with it. He got into an argument with Mason, who wanted to bring all the test kids back to the facility and contain them until they were mature enough to perform the final procedure. Robert knew that the only way to keep his family safe was to escape to TERC. They tried to run away with you and your sisters, but Making Perfect caught up to them in the Slump before they could get over the border."

I swallow hard. For years, the only emotion I have had toward my parents is a simmering hatred. I hated them for abandoning us. I hated them for leaving without telling us anything. I blamed them for all the hardships and all the pain I experienced. I needed to hate them to make sense of the world I was in. Now, as Aaron speaks, that world is turned upside down. I am overcome with a flood of emotions I've never felt before. It's like a balloon has suddenly popped in my chest.

They did love us. They did want to protect us. They didn't want to abandon us. Waves of regret, sadness, and anger, but also of joy, relief, and gratitude wash over me. My stomach flutters. My vision blurs. I bite my knuckle, but tears well up in my eyes anyway. I wipe them away as they run down my cheeks, but I can taste the salt in my mouth. When I try to speak, all that comes out is, "How do you know all this? How do I know you're not lying?"

Aaron shrugs. "You can't. You just have to trust me." I look at the floor, trying to pull myself together. He continues, "The point is, with you and the others, Making Perfect has a weapon with power that no one can even imagine yet. We need to do everything we can to keep all of you out of their hands." Tyler rocks slowly back and forth. He knows what's coming next. "We need you to join Troop Five." Aaron's stare is penetrating. "If you are with us, you will be safe, and Making Perfect's plan will fail."

My stomach aches. Tyler crosses his arms over his chest, a shiver running through his body. He is clenching and unclenching his fists. I notice he's gotten even paler. The toxin is beginning to take its toll.

Suddenly, the sound of helicopter rotors resonates through the quiet woods. Columns of bright lights are nearing our position.

"Let's move!" Callie pops her head back into the truck, and both Ridge and Aaron are out in seconds. Tyler and I follow. The rebels are filing into the vehicles, closing the doors, and starting the engines. Ridge runs over to the other truck, disappearing from sight. The first gunshot is heard as we follow Aaron into the woods.

"We have to get out of here. It's probably the border officials picking up your tracks. The rest of my soldiers will leave in the trucks, but Ridge and Callie are going to stay. They're going to get you and Tyler back to the road to catch the truck to the facility. You'll have to be quick."

The shouting is getting louder. Ridge and Callie run over to us,

"Get them to the road quickly," Aaron orders, and they nod. He turns to me. "Tell Kace I'll be in touch. Best of luck to you two." He nods at Ridge and Callie and takes off into the dark, blending completely into the shadows. I don't have time to linger before Ridge ushers me forward. We cross the train tracks and run in the opposite direction of the fence, deeper into the woods and away from the sound of the shouting. I can see Tyler trying his best to keep it together, but the running is really taking its toll. He can hardly move his feet anymore. Ridge and Callie practically have to carry him.

There is the sound of a gunshot not too far behind us. Through the woods up ahead, I can see the road.

"Where's your armor?" Ridge asks, holding Tyler upright.

"We buried them in the leaves. I don't remember where. It was near the road."

Ridge curses. "You need to find where you jumped off, it should be around here. Go!"

I race out alongside the road, looking frantically for the two piles of leaves covering the armor. Thankfully, I find them, and I gesture for the others. I slip the painfully cold chest plate over my head and flinch as it comes in contact with my back. I pull the helmet over my head. Ridge and Callie help Tyler put on his as tremors run through his body. I support him as best I can, anger at Kace building inside me.

There are two more gunshots. Closer this time.

The lights of a truck appear around the bend. Callie grabs my arm. "Help him, get him into the truck. They think you're with them. Good luck." With that, they disappear back into the woods.

The lights of the truck catch us. Tyler does his best to walk straight. The truck slows and pulls up beside us.

The driver pulls down his window and stares at us. "Do you need a ride, soldiers?" The young man doesn't have his helmet on. Two other officials look at us, somewhat amused. I nod, and the driver simply says, "You can ride in the back."

My head swims, but I manage to get the door open and help Tyler into the truck. It's empty, except for a few large bags and two crates. Tyler collapses against the side, and I roll the door back down.

I can feel the truck shift into gear, and it starts moving. I prop Tyler up into a semi sitting position and keep my eyes trained on his chest. He dozes off to sleep, but I stay awake, staring at the truck door the whole way back.

27

It's five o'clock when Kace finally locks Tyler and me back into our cells. I instantly collapse from exhaustion. When I wake up a few hours later, tubes are pumping medicine into my forearm. I sit up and immediately notice that my back doesn't hurt. I reach back and touch the skin, finding it completely healed. Whatever they gave me obviously worked.

Tyler felt much better after getting the antitoxin. He has ended up in the cell next to mine. My mind has been replaying the conversation with Aaron and the rebels ever since we got back, going through it over and over until, now, I feel like I could recite it in my sleep.

When we arrived, Tyler could hardly breathe. Luckily, Kace was waiting for us. He pulled us aside and managed to slip the antitoxin into Tyler's neck without making a scene. I remember feeling Tyler relax beside me, after which he went so limp that it was impossible to drag him up the stairs. It got so bad that Kace and I had to slip him into a supply closet so the antidote could take effect. The second he was settled, I turned on Kace.

"Now, before you freak out—" Kace started, but I couldn't contain my anger. My fist collided with his nose. There was a crack, and he swore loudly, pulling his arm up to shield himself.

"That was for making us go alone." I punched him again, this time in the stomach, and he stumbled backward. "That was for the toxin." I tried to punch him again, but he grabbed my wrist and twisted it hard. I winced and grabbed it in pain. Before I could lunge at him again, he put up his hands. A small trickle of blood was running from his nose into his parted lips.

"Stop! I did what I had to do, okay? Now, I've got to get you back into your cells before the next shift comes on."

We had to wait until Tyler was well enough to walk before we made our way back to the labs. I didn't want to go in, but I had no choice.

I'm almost asleep again when someone opens the door to my cell. I raise my head. Please, no more tests.

It is a scientist, and he is pointing the barrel of a gun at me. I freeze in shock as two guards enter and hold me down while the scientist removes the tube from my forearm. They pull me through the door and out into the lab. The bright light hurts my eyes.

"What's going on?" I ask, frazzled.

"Two-seven-four-four-one transfer commencing now," a guard says into his remote. Their big hands push me forward as we make our way out of the lab. As we walk, I see all of the other test subjects being pulled out of their cells. What's happening? Are they finally taking us out of here? Where's Tyler? When I try to look over my shoulder at his cell, I can't see him.

The guards lead me away from the lab. Large white tiles line the floor hallway, and the walls are painted gray. Multiple glass doors line the wall, leading to various smaller labs and examination rooms. Before I know it, we've already turned a corner and reached a large supply elevator. We wait there with two other kids that I haven't seen before, who look as confused as I am. When the doors open, the guards push us in.

I lean against the wall of the elevator for support. My body is so exhausted that I just want to go back to sleep.

The elevator stops, and the door opens. I stop in my tracks when I see where we are: the Lobby.

I feel like laughing, screaming, and crying all at once. What is happening? Did they decide that they were done with us and that we will be moved back to the Lobby? I sure hope so. But nobody stops. The guards just keep moving us forward, toward the dining hall. After we've walked down the familiar hallway and entered through the sliding doors, all I can do is look at the scenery in confusion. What is going on?

Not including the guards, there is only a handful of people in the room, all around my age. I don't recognize anyone.

"Get breakfast. Instructions on how to proceed will come over the loudspeaker shortly," one of the guards snarls, and they all turn on their heels and walk back out the door. The three of us who came together stand there hesitantly. Finally, one girl breaks the tension.

"I guess we should do what they say, right?" she asks, sounding unsure. "I'm sorry, but this is really weird. I haven't been here in ages."

"I have no idea," the other, a boy, says. "But I'm going to make the most of it while it lasts." He breaks away from the group and heads for the breakfast counter.

I shrug. "Instructions on how to proceed will come over the loudspeaker shortly." Proceed with what? I give in and follow the boy. When I reach the counter, I scoop a small portion of mush into a little bowl. I'm about to go find a table when I hear a vaguely familiar voice.

"You look lost, love. Are you looking for someplace to sit?"

I spin around and come face-to-face with Sterling. His once-shaggy gray hair has been cut so that it no longer falls into his eyes. His half-open, foggy eye looks even creepier than I remember. Not knowing what to say, I nod, and he beckons for me to follow him. We find a place at an empty table by the wall with another girl Sterling picks up on the way over, who introduces herself as Maggie. Her matted, blond hair is cut short, and her eyes are a dull brown. She has a large scar through her eyebrow, but a large, bubbly smile is plastered on her face.

"What's going on, Ster?" she asks, shoveling a large spoonful of mush into her mouth. "Why are we here?"

"I don't know, Mags. I haven't been out of that lab for years. This is a luxury, and I'm completely clueless." Sterling takes a bite of his breakfast and sighs, his lips turning up into a lopsided smile.

I swish my spoon around my bowl, nervously. I am the opposite of hungry—I don't think I could muster one bite. Where is everybody? Where's Tyler? My eyes are trained on the door.

"So, Summer, are you a test kid?" Maggie asks, and I snap my head around to look at her. She looks a little taken aback. "Oh, I'm sorry. I didn't mean it in an accusatory way. Just…look." She pulls up her sleeve to expose a large, black star on her wrist. "I am. So is Ster." She jerks her thumb at Sterling. "That's how we met. We were in the same unit before we got taken to the tests. He's like my brother now. I just—"

"Yeah," I say. "I am. A test kid, I mean." Then it clicks in my head. I look around the room and count eight of us. Aaron said there were thirteen test kids in total. Three are with the rebels. Tyler's not here. All of the rest together would be ten.

Oh my God.

"Oh…cool!" Maggie says enthusiastically. She doesn't seem the least bit nervous.

Do they not understand what's going on?

"Do you know any others?" Maggie continues. "I'd love to introduce myself. I know being a test kid is weird, and it's ten times as weird if you don't know anyone else who is one. Heck, I didn't even know what a test kid was until I arrived and was taken to see Mason. He explained it all to me."

"Yes, I know another test kid. His name is Tyler." I glance around the room. "But I don't know where he is." I pause. "Wait, you sound like you've been here for a while. How—"

"A few years at least, right, Sterling?" Maggie asks, and Sterling nods.

"Probably around there," Sterling says turning to me. "Don't worry, love. Whoever you're waiting for will probably be here soon. You don't have to train your eyes on the door." I look at him blankly, and Maggie giggles.

"Loosen up, Summer. It'll be fine." She smiles at me, and I can't help but give her a weak grin in return. Just as Sterling opens his mouth to say something, the doors to the dining hall open and Tyler enters, escorted by two guards. When he sees me, he heads over to the table without bothering to get breakfast.

"Hey," Tyler says, sitting down beside me. He looks better this morning, though the dark circles under his eyes betray that our excursion last night wasn't a dream. "What's going on?"

Before I can say anything, Maggie cuts in. "I don't know, but I'm sure we'll find out soon." She is practically bouncing up and down in her seat. "I'm Maggie, by the way."

"Tyler," he replies, nodding his head at her. Her eyes widen.

"Ooh! You're the other test kid that Summer knows! I'm a test kid too, and so is Sterling. So are all the others here." She looks around at the rest of the kids in the dining hall. "You get to know each other after spending years in the cages together. Oh boy! If all of us are here, we must be getting out!" Maggie exclaims, grabbing on to Sterling's shoulder excitedly. "Ster! We're actually leaving!"

I would hate to ruin her excitement, so I keep quiet. Whatever they've planned for us can't be good. It's probably just as bad as this facility. "Summer! We're leaving!" Maggie grabs my hand from across the table, smiling at me as if we've known each other all our lives. I can feel her pulse racing she's so happy.

I force a smile. Maybe she's right. Maybe wherever they're taking us is better than this. Maybe I should try taking on some of Maggie's optimism.

"Is everything all right?" Sterling asks me, and I snap back into focus.

"Yeah," I reply. "Sorry. Everything's fine." Sterling glances at the floor.

"All right, whatever you say." He takes another bite, and I look at the door. Just then, it opens. A dozen officials file into the room and position themselves at the exits.

A booming female voice rings through the dining hall over the loudspeakers. "All test subjects, please line up against the back wall. You will be scanned and logged in before being escorted to the AirTran." Hushed whispers break out all around me as everybody stands up and gets in line. Maggie bounces up like a little kid in a candy store and grabs Sterling, pulling him over to the line. He looks at me apologetically. I put my bowl down and follow them, my eyes scanning the room.

I get in between Sterling and Tyler, my shoulders brushing against each. Most in the line seem almost as confused and worried as I am. Some fidget, some stand still. Others are practically jumping up and down, relieved to be out of their cells. I get it. I was only in there for a day or two, but it felt like an eternity. If I had been in there for as long as they were, I'd be elated to be out too. Heck, I'd be ecstatic to jump off a bridge.

Officials go down the line, scanning the barcodes on each person's left hand. Just in front of Sterling, I see Maggie's hand shoot out willingly. My eyes are still trained on the door. When the official finally reaches me, I don't even realize she is standing there. She has to grab my hand. The red light reads the black code on my wrist, and she moves on to the next person. I glance over at Sterling, who is staring straight ahead. His foggy eye is facing me. It feels unnerving, and I have to look away.

Suddenly, the officials guarding the doors draw their weapons and move toward us, stopping a few feet from our line. I glance around, eyes growing wide. They've completely trapped us. Just then, I hear a cry of surprise coming from my left. My head snaps around, and see a girl falling limp against the nearest official, who is gripping her arm. Two officials grab her and carry her out of the room. My mouth hangs open in shock. The official who caught the girl begins to move down the line, injecting the next boy with the same thick liquid. Almost immediately, he's down too, and they carry him away.

The guards step closer, their weapons pointed at our heads. I briefly consider rushing them, hoping that they won't shoot and that I'll be able to escape, but the risk is too great.

A guard grabs my arm, and I push him away instinctively. I try not to look at the barrels of the guns, which are only a few feet away. Two more guards approach me, holding me still as the needle is stabbed into my arm. Immediately, my vision becomes blurry, and I feel myself slipping into darkness.

I don't know why, but my last thought is of Maggie and her annoying optimism. I wonder what she's thinking right now.

I'm sorry, Mags. Hope is a bitch.

Everything goes dark.

28

A cry of surprise escapes my lips when the AirTran lands, jolting me awake. Looking around groggily, I try to clear my swimming vision. Eventually, everything clicks into focus. I am sitting in a hard canvas seat, shoulder straps keeping me from sliding down. Thick, red netting along the side of the plane provides some cushion for my back. I glance over my right shoulder and see Maggie, who's still sleeping, two seats down from mine. On her right, a boy I don't know is leaning forward, looking at me. Across from me, on the other side of the plane, Sterling and Tyler are just waking up. Next to them are the other six test kids from the dining hall. Two guards are sitting on both ends of the rows of seats.

A shiver runs through me. The air around me is cold, and I shove my hands in my pockets.

Where are we?

The AirTran's engines slow to a stop, but all the doors stay shut.

What's going on?

The door on the other side of the aircraft finally opens with a hiss.

"Stay in your seats."

Two officials walk up the ramp and through the door. Two guards stand on each side of them as they walk down the middle of the plane. My eyes are trained on them as one official stops at the front of each row. I try to get up, but the guards push me back down.

"Not so fast, princess," one of them grumbles. They hold me down while the nearest official turns on a device the size of a fist by pressing a button on the side. A little green light appears, and he pushes my head down, exposing my neck. I try to push him off.

"What are you doing?" I hiss at him.

"We have to inject you with the chip. It's protocol," one guard says with unflinching indifference.

"What chip?" I try to lift my head, but the weight on my neck prevents any movement.

"Well, aren't you feisty?" Before I can do anything, I feel a sharp sting right at the base of my skull. A cry escapes my throat. The guards let go, and I snap my head back, my hand cupping protectively over the sore injection site.

"What was that?" I scream, but they've already moved on to Maggie.

"It's a vaccine chip," says a voice in one of the seats across from me. It belongs to a girl I don't know. She is rubbing the back of her neck achingly—she must've just gotten the injection too. "It's to protect us from Red Pox."

"What?" Red Pox is here? I thought it was confined to the Slump. "How do you know?"

She shrugs. "I've seen them before. Besides, it makes sense."

I look at my feet. I guess it does make sense. I mean, I'm not complaining. The last thing I want is to get sick. It doesn't take long before the officials have injected all of us, and they exit the AirTran.

"Get up. Follow the line of officials out of the aircraft and into the building."

I stand up. My head spins, and blue dots dance in front of my eyes. A few officials stand at the entrance, waiting for us to make our way to the door. The guards flank us as we move down the ramp and into the open.

Chilling wind washes over me like a wave. I rub my nose as my boots crunch against the gravel. It's the peak of day, and the sun is out and shining beautifully. The compound is huge but very different than the one we just came from. A massive Making Perfect logo adorns the slanted wall of the building closest to us, reflecting the light and stinging my eyes as I look at it. The rest of the interconnected buildings have battered blue walls and long, tinted windows that line the bottom floors. A few large AirTrans are parked in front of a cream-colored hangar. Lots of guards and officials trot around hurriedly, unloading boxes and escorting people through the heavy, metal doors of the first building. The smell of burning fuel and rubber hangs in the air. Heavily armed soldiers patrol the fences surrounding the compound. Coils of barbed wire sit menacingly on top of the fences, and large satellite dishes are scattered along the perimeter.

This place looks impenetrable.

The guards walk us straight toward the doors. Nervous sweat is tickling my brow, and I bite my lip. As we get closer, the doors open automatically, letting us inside. Warm air washes over my face. A senior official, flanked by two heavily armed guards, is waiting for us. He doesn't waste a moment.

"You are now in the Making Perfect military headquarters. This building used to be known as the Burlington Airport but has since been converted into a state of the art military facility. We train all of our soldiers here. This is the most secure compound in the entire region. Now, if you follow the terminal to the left, officials will be there to scan you in and point you to the barracks." With that, he spins around and walks away.

The guards on either side of me start moving, and we merge into a sea of people. Hundreds of soldiers and kids move through the terminal, making it difficult to push our way through. I quickly lose sight of Tyler and the others as I try to make my way to the far wall. The tile that lines the floor is grimy and caked with dirt, a stark contrast to the clean labs we just came from. Every once in a while, I catch a glimpse of someone I know. People bump into me, and I stumble forward, trying to keep my head together.

I push my way through the horde of people, frustration gnawing at me, desperate to see where the rest of my group has gone. Suddenly, I hear a familiar voice shout my name. My heart stops. I scan the crowd. Our eyes lock. It's the first time I've seen him since before the enhancements. His hair is tousled, his eyes wide.

Blayze.

I rush toward him, weaving through the crowd. He takes a step forward, and I throw myself onto him. His arms slip around me and I hear him mutter my name.

When I pull away from him and look into his eyes, I notice the new strength in his expression. Short stubble covers his cheeks, and he has a new scar above his right eyebrow. He's lost most of the muscle he had when I first met him. He looks older, different from the boy I left behind in the Lobby.

I don't know what to say. "You're alive."

"I am," he replies. He looks tense. "I've missed you."

"You too," I say, pulling my mouth into a tentative smile. He smiles back. Someone calls his name, and he looks over his shoulder. The second his eyes leaves mine, I feel cold.

"I've got to go, but I'll see you soon," Blayze says, and my focus snaps back to him. He looks suddenly flustered. I just nod and watch him disappear into the crowd, my chest deflating.

Someone slams into me, and I stumble. I spin around, fire in my eyes, coming face-to-face with a guard.

"Keep it moving!" he shouts, and I stagger on, quickening my pace. When I round the corner, long lines of people are moving slowly toward a row of officials standing behind computer terminals. They scan barcodes and let people through the large doors one at a time. I don't know what lies on the other side, but there's no other place to go. The lines move forward, and I slowly make my way to the front.

While I wait, I go over our situation in my head. Making Perfect Military Headquarters…Why are we here?

But I already know the answer. Aaron told me last night.

They're building an army.

They're training soldiers.

Way too much contact with human bodies later, my arm is grabbed by an official, who scans my code and shoves a dark beige tracksuit into my hands. Before I know it, I'm being pushed through the door.

The next hour is spent wandering around terminals, aimlessly trying to find the others. I guess the officials thought that once we were signed in, we'd know where to go. The result is confusion. Everybody else is just wandering like I am. After I while, I give up and find a place in a corner next to a window. I slump down to the floor and put my face in my hands.

We're never going to get out of here.

29

finally hear my number called out. Feeling totally lost, I make my way to the front of the terminal where, to my surprise, the rest of my unit is waiting. The same official who greeted us earlier is also there, his arms crossed tightly over his chest. He is scowling at me.

Shivers run down my spine. I walk up to Tyler as the official introduces himself to the group. His name is Winston.

"I will be overseeing your unit until further notice," he says. "The ten of you are now my responsibility. You will follow the rules, stay out of trouble, and not ask questions. Do, and we'll get along. Don't, and your stay will be a lot less comfortable. Now, come with me." Heavy industrial doors open behind him. A gust of cool air washes over us as we're ushered outside.

We're led down the muddy paths away from the converted terminal building. Different noises assault us—the roar of the AirTrans landing, the hum of electricity coursing through the fence, the shouts of the soldiers conducting training routines. My eyes linger on the soldiers as we walk by, watching them perform their tasks as the officials call out orders. I notice how powerful they look dressed in their sleek black uniforms. I wonder if that's going to be us.

We approach a large, imposing building far closer to the fence than the others. Connected to the surrounding hangars by above-ground tunnels, it is heavily guarded and teeming with soldiers. I force myself to keep moving. I know once I enter this building, I'll lose all hope of getting out. Winston stops, turning back to us. Our two escorts tighten their grips on their guns.

"We are about to enter the main barracks," Winston explains. "Follow closely. It's very crowded."

As soon as we enter the doors, I stiffen. He was right. It is crowded.

The entire place is packed with soldiers dressed either in their black armor or the same beige tracksuits we all hold in our hands. We've entered into what seems to be the common room, which is really just a room with numerous wooden benches, a few squares of thick burlap carpet, and three oversized brown leather couches against the far wall. Soldiers are everywhere. They slouch on the couches, sit on the floor, or simply stand and talk, interacting with each other in a relaxed, open fashion. The noise is overwhelming. The Making Perfect logo boldly covers the back wall, looking down on us ominously.

The soldiers push us through the crowd and a doorway marked BARRACKS. We walk through the relatively empty hallway. Winston stops in front of the last door. A gold star hangs next to a plaque with the number one.

Winston quickly covers all the ground rules, but I'm not listening—everything he says goes in one ear and out the other. That's been the case more and more lately.

"You are to stay in your room until further notice," he continues. "Nobody is allowed to leave the building unless specifically instructed and accompanied."

When he stops talking for a moment, I look up. Winston turns on a small black device and looks at the screen. He calls out numbers and names and scans our individual barcodes before letting us into the room. Tyler is first. Then Maggie. Then Sterling. I watch the other kids closely as they are called: Jackson Samuels, a shaggy, dark-haired boy a few inches shorter than me with an empty hole through his left earlobe; Bas West, who has an aquiline nose and messy, dirty blond hair that makes his pale skin seem even paler; Bella Jones, whose complexion and evil grin remind me of Flame; Jasper and Jess Sanchez, fraternal twins who nevertheless look identical; and Hailey Brown, a smiley, tiny, dark-haired girl with warm, chocolate skin who doesn't look like she could be a soldier until I see how muscular her scarred arms are.

I recognize Jess from the labs. She had the cell next to mine. Recognition flashes in her eyes when she sees me, and she offers a slight smile.

Wow. They are all test kids? They all seem so...normal.

I'm the last one in. As I step through the door, Winston closes it behind me.

The room is brutally simple, with seven thin, metal bunks lined against the walls. Plain white sheets are pulled tightly over the mattresses. A thin pillow and small, folded gray blanket are at the foot of each bed. The floor is concrete, and walls are gray tile, with three small windows and a dark metal door leading to the hallway. Long strips of fluorescent lights line the ceiling. Everybody splits up to claim a bunk. I'm not quick enough to get one at the back, and instead I end up with the one above Maggie, closest to the door. Each bunk has a locker on both sides. I don't understand what those are for—none of us have any personal belongings. Making Perfect has made sure of that.

I climb up to my bunk and collapse. After what feels like hours, Tyler walks up to me.

"Sum, we should go get food. Everybody else already left."

Did they? I didn't even notice. I shrug. "I thought we couldn't leave. And anyway, I'm not hungry."

"Winston said we can leave for dinner. Sometimes, listening helps." He smiles, and I roll my eyes. "You have to eat."

"No, I don't. I'm not hungry," I grumble, and Tyler shrugs.

"Fine." He walks out the door, and I listen to his footsteps growing fainter as he makes his way down the hall. I pull the blanket up and wrap it around my body, curling up on the wrinkly old mattress.

Tyler comes back about an hour later with a sandwich for me. I take it but can't bring myself to eat it. It sits on my lap for a good fifteen minutes before I slip it into my locker, putting the sad-looking metal container to some use. I stare at it for a while before closing the door. My feet dangling over the edge of the bed, I lean forward against my elbows, wondering what tomorrow has in store for us.

🔺 🔺 🔺

I can't sleep. I haven't been able to sleep all night. There's no particular reason, I just haven't been able to keep my eyes shut for more than a few seconds. I can't seem to get my sisters out of my head. I wonder if they're okay, if they managed to pull through. Guilt tears at me for leaving them behind. Anything that happens to them will be my fault.

I groan and turn over again. My headache has grown since this afternoon, and it's now threatening to tear my skull apart. Eventually, I can't take it anymore, and I decide to go shower. Maybe getting clean will help clear my head. As quietly as I can, careful not to wake up Maggie, I lower myself to the ground and slip out the door.

I glance down at my watch. It's 2:09 a.m.

Exhaustion weighs me down, and I wish I could just go to sleep. My bare feet don't make a sound on the concrete. Goose bumps rise on my arms from the cold. I am surprised at how quiet it is. Just a few hours ago, this place was bustling with activity. But now, it could be mistaken for abandoned.

The bathroom is empty. I feel around for the light switch by the door and flip it up. The bright light strips flicker to life, casting a cold sheen on the tile. Glancing around, I walk over to the nearest available shower, turning on the hot water with a flick of my wrist. I grab a towel from the rack and hang it on the hook right outside my stall. Quickly, before anybody else comes in, I slip behind the curtain and strip out of my tracksuit. Hot water pours all over me as I step under the spray. I grab a recently used bar of soap on the little ledge and lather it in my hands. The steam of the hot shower fills my lungs. It feels magical, wonderful. I massage the soap into my hair, closing my eyes. I'm just starting to rinse it all out when the water shuts off unexpectedly.

"You've got to be kidding…" I mutter angrily. I turn the faucets, but no water comes out. I hear a soft chuckle from outside the shower and freeze. Oh no. I didn't even hear the door open.

"How 'bout you get out and let someone else have a go, huh?" A deep, mocking voice breaks the silence.

"Well, this one's taken," I grumble, hugging my chest. I can hear people muttering to each other.

"I know, but you see, that shower's my favorite, and unfortunately, I can't use any of the others," the voice sneers, and others snicker. I roll my eyes and reach outside the curtain for my towel, but my hand just finds air. There are laughs from outside.

"Need your towel, princess? Come get it." I poke my head out from around the corner of the shower curtain and see a group of five boys and girls sneering at me, arms crossed over their chests. The middle boy is holding up my towel in one hand, and my tracksuit in the other. My forehead wrinkles. Those assholes!

"This princess is going to kick your ass." I know it won't work, but I try anyway.

"You have five seconds," the boy with my towel gibes; he looks around eighteen, "before we tear the curtain down."

"Five...four..." They all start counting down in unison, and I bite my lip. There's no way out other than through the curtain. What am I going to do? My eyes flick up to the curtain, and I get an idea. "Three..." Before they can grab the curtain, I rip it out of its rings and wrap it around my body. When I turn back to the group, they are all frozen with surprise. Idiots. I slip through them and yank my towel from the boy's hand, punching his face in the process. He tumbles backward, grabbing his nose.

"Get out of here!" I scream, anger rising. I wrap the curtain tighter around my body. They all close in around me. "Go waste your time bothering someone else." One of the boys tries to grab the curtain, and I knock his hand away. "What do you · want?"

"Nothing, princess, just a little show," says a brown-haired boy with angular features who is cupping his bloody nose. Under normal circumstances, I'd be able to fight them off, but I don't know what I can do without dropping the curtain. One of the boys takes a swing for the fabric and latches on to it, trying to yank it free. I hold on tightly and raise my fist to hit him when a harsh voice calls out behind me.

"Noah! Hey! What are you doing?" I turn around to see Blayze heading toward us, looking at the dark-haired boy with fire in his eyes.

"Nothing, man, just having a little fun. This doesn't concern you." The brown-haired boy, who must be Noah, looks at his peers for support, and they all snicker.

"Get away from her, you hear me?" Blayze warns. "Now." He gets between Noah and me, staring him down. They glare at each other for a long moment before Noah buckles.

"Fine, man," he says, throwing his arms up. "You win. Count yourself lucky, princess. If *he* hadn't shown up…" He laughs and walks out of the bathroom, his pack following him.

"You okay?" Blayze asks, turning to me. I hug my stomach with my free arm.

"Fine," I face him. "I didn't need your help, by the way. I had that situation completely under control."

"I know, but he was being an ass," Blayze says, running his fingers through his hair. Why is he even up this late? Why are *any* of these people up this late?

"Yeah. Well, thanks." My chest tightens, and I brush the strands of hair out of my red-hot face. "What are you doing here, anyway?"

"Couldn't sleep." He shrugs. "You?"

"Same." After a few seconds of silence, I turn to go. I only get a couple of steps before he stops me, his voice pinning me in place.

"Summer?" I can hear the humor in his voice. "You might want to lose the curtain." I glance back at him. His eyes are twinkling with mischief. I look down, realizing that I'm still in the shower curtain. Burning up, I can only stutter.

"Oh. I…Um—" I look around and see no cover. Stepping behind the towel rack out of Blayze's direct line of vision, I wrap my towel around both me and the curtain and drop the curtain so it falls to my ankles. Making sure the towel is secure, I pick up the curtain and walk over to the shower, trying to hang it back up. Blayze is laughing as he comes over to help. Together, we manage to get it hanging again. I really wish it was dark so he wouldn't notice the burning heat in my cheeks as he stands so close to me.

"Well, as fun as this has been, I've got to go back to my bunk," I say, backing up away from him and grabbing my tracksuit off the floor.

"Okay. You sure you don't need an escort back to your room? You don't know what could be prowling around these hallways, and that towel doesn't provide much protection." He asks, and I rub my eyes tiredly.

"I think I'm good."

"Okay, then walk fast."

"Goodnight, Blayze. And thanks."

He shrugs. I walk out of the door, not running into anyone on the way back to my bunk.

30

I wake up with a start. Rubbing my stinging temple, I glare at my pillow. On it sits a paper airplane.

"What the hell?" I mutter groggily, and someone laughs loudly from across the room. I look up to see Jackson, two bunks across from mine, cackling with laughter. Crumpled pieces of notebook paper litter the mattress around him. I throw the plane right back at him. He ducks before it can hit his face.

"What was that for?" I snap at him, and he shrugs. About half of the room seems to be awake. Jess, who's giggling on the bunk under him, pipes up.

"I bet him the plane wouldn't fly, so we had to test it." She's laughing too. "Turns out it did, but sorta crooked."

I rub my eyes, propping myself up on one elbow. It must be really early. Bright streaks of light illuminate the room even though the ceiling lights are turned off. "What time is it?"

Jess glances down at her watch. "One."

"One?" My brow furrows. "You're not serious." She shrugs, pulls off her watch, and throws it to me. I catch it and turn it over in my fingers. One.

I slept until one.

I never sleep until one.

What's going on?

I throw Jess her watch back and slide off my bunk. Below me, Maggie is still asleep. I walk over to the other side of the room and up to Tyler, who's sleeping soundly. Dropping to my knees, I nudge him awake. He blinks slowly.

"Sum," he groans. "What is it?" He closes his eyes again.

"It's one. In the afternoon. They let us sleep until one. Something's not right," I say, and he shrugs.

"Maybe we've got the morning off. We're probably starting everything tonight." He pulls the blanket higher onto his torso. "I wouldn't worry too much. Enjoy it while it lasts."

He turns away from me, pulling the blanket farther over his head. I can't shake this weird feeling in my gut. Something is definitely off. I purse my lips and walk toward the door, pulling my hair back as I go.

"Summer, where are you going?" Jess asks as I open the door.

"I'm going to go find out what's happening," I reply, and I walk out.

I wander around the barracks for ages, trying to find anyone to talk to other than the guards. But there's nobody. Where is everybody? I make my way to the common room, but it's also deserted. Absolutely no one. But just as I start to get worried, I run into Official Winston.

"Where are you going, Miss Greenwood?" he asks me. "You aren't permitted to leave your bunks until further notice."

I cross my arms defensively. "I came to find out what's going on. Where are all the other units?"

"You will receive further information shortly. Return to your bunk, and go to the mess hall at eighteen hundred for dinner."

"But...I—" I sputter indignantly. He shuts me up, pointing back to the barracks. Anger rising in me, I turn back toward our room. I feel his eyes on me until I turn the corner.

What are they hiding from us? I don't understand. Why did they bring us here if they're not going to use us? I throw open the door of the room in bitter frustration and collide with the person coming out. I trip backward but quickly catch myself. I look up. It's Kace.

My eyes widen, and I blink at him. "What…"

He steps out of the doorway, a disheveled Tyler directly on his heels. He pulls me forward, dragging me a few feet before letting me go. He waves us in front of him and into one of the adjoining rooms. Its layout is practically the same as ours, except there are many more bunks crowded into the small space, making it feel ten times as crammed as ours. The unit it belongs to made themselves completely at home—the place is littered with towels, boots, and extra clothing. Kace closes the door, looking around nervously.

I put my hands on my hips. The last time I saw him, I was ready to tear him to pieces for what he did to Tyler. "What's going on?" He ignores me and walks around the room, checking every corner. What's he looking for? "Kace!" I try to get his attention.

He turns back to us, lowering his voice. "We can't stay here long. Hopefully we're far enough away from the cameras that they won't pick up our voices."

"Cameras? What cameras?" I ask.

"You didn't think they weren't watching, did you?" Kace retorts.

"What's wrong?" Tyler asks, sounding much more concerned than I am.

Kace explains everything: about our sudden transfer, about why we were allowed to sleep past noon. My mouth hangs open. I can hardly believe what he's saying.

Making Perfect decided to bring all of the test kids here because it's the most impenetrable facility under their control. There have been increased reports of rebel activity in the region, so they decided to move us. They have no intention of training us or of doing anything but keep us as prisoners until they're ready to perform the procedure.

I feel a sharp twinge of dread.

"Then we have to get out of here," I hiss. "The security will only become more intense the longer we wait."

Kace swiftly shakes his head. "No. We can't. Not yet."

"Not yet?" asks Tyler. When Kace doesn't respond, he sighs, spins around, and uncharacteristically slams his fists against the wall. "Damn it, Kace! She's right. We can't just wait around until they come for us!"

"And we won't." He looks at us with a hard-set determination. I furrow my brow. "We're going to get out. I know how, we just can't yet. You have to trust me."

He knows how? What does he mean? I don't get a chance to speak, because Tyler beats me to it.

"Trust you?" he chortles. "The last time I did, I almost died." He pauses, then continues. "I say we leave now. We need to leave now!"

"We can't. The time isn't right."

"What does that mean? Why isn't the time right, Kace?" Tyler spits. I'm shocked. I've hardly ever seen him like this. "We have *families* who are dying. Hell, they might already be dead. We can't just sit around waiting because 'the time isn't right.' Do you know what my little sister said to me the night I got taken? She asked me if I was going to leave them. When I told her no, she said how sad she was that everybody else she loved had left her and that she was glad I was going to stay. If we can get out now—"

"Tyler!" Kace stops him. "We are not leaving now, and that's final. Trust me or don't. Either way, you will follow my directions or face consequences. Is that understood?"

Tyler's jaw is clenched. For a minute, I fear he's going to lash out again. But finally, he nods, averting his eyes. I know the only reason he wants to leave now is to get to Michael and Riley. But Kace is unflinching, and we can't go without him.

"Sit tight for a few weeks," Kace continues, curtly. "Be ready. I'll come and get you when it's time to go. Don't tell anyone else about this—I can only get you two out."

And with that, he's gone. As soon as the door closes behind him, Tyler curses under his breath and leans his against the closest bunk, covering his face with his hands. We stand in silence.

"Did Riley really say that?" I finally ask. He shrugs.

"Yeah. Right after I gave her the medicine. She just came out with it." He shuffles his feet. "It breaks my heart, you know? I think about her all the time. I just want to get back to them. I can't stand knowing they're out there fighting to survive while I'm cooped up in here doing nothing."

I nod. I feel the same way. I hope Lily and Tory managed to survive the winter. I don't know how they could have, with Tory sick and Lily all by herself, but a part of me still hopes.

"Yeah," I reply, my voice barely audible.

There's a long pause before he speaks again. "Do you think it's possible that Michael and Ri made it through?"

I bite my lip. If I lie to him, he's going to know I'm lying, which would just make things worse. But seeing his pained expression, I'd be willing to tell all the lies in the world for him to stop feeling so guilty.

"I don't know," is all I come out with.

We return to the bunk shortly afterward, and I try to go back to sleep, but it's futile. My stomach is aching. I can't remember when I last ate, and dinner's not for another four hours.

I think I finally manage to fall asleep because the next thing I know, Maggie is tugging on my arm, forcing me awake.

"Summer!" Maggie exclaims. I shake my head in an attempt to clear it. "Come on! Come eat with us! Sterling found a table in the mess hall big enough for all of us, and I'm *not* letting you skip dinner."

I don't protest. I'm so hungry that I feel lightheaded. Excitedly, she pulls me down from my bunk and drags me through the door. I can hear the ruckus of the mess hall from here. We turn the corner and pass through the common room. I force myself to pick up my feet. I'm still groggy from sleep. All I want to do is go back to my bunk and have Tyler bring me dinner. The noise continues to grow as we move farther down the tunnel.

The overwhelming sound of laughter and shouting surrounds me the second I walk into the mess hall. It's much larger than the testing facility's dining hall, and the thick canvas of the tent doesn't provide much insulation from the chill. Long, plastic folding tables occupy the entire space. People are crammed around each one, eating and talking. Goose bumps rise on my arms under the tracksuit.

Maggie urges me toward the food counter. Following her example, I grab a tray, snake through the horde of people, and grab one of the prefilled, heated aluminum packages. It burns my hands. Grabbing a fork and some napkins, I rejoin Maggie—who's waiting for me at the end of the line—and start walking toward the back of the room.

I spot our group almost instantly, all the way in the corner. I work my way through the rows of tables. As we get closer, I notice Blayze sitting at a table near the wall. He's facing away from me, his hand resting on the back of the chair next to him. The two girls beside him seem to be hanging onto his every word. He is laughing and gesturing broadly as he talks. The girl closest to him smiles and puts her hand on his arm. My grip tightens on my tray.

"Summer!" Jess shouts as we approach. Maggie sits down at the end, and I take the spot between her and Jackson. "It lives!"

I place my food on the table, and someone shoves my shoulder. I look over and see Jackson snickering at me. "We placed bets on Maggie's ability to get you here," he explains, nodding at Bella, who is immersed in a deep conversation with Bas. "The majority of us thought no."

"The *majority* of you had no faith in me," Maggie peels open the top of her meal, waving away the steam that immediately billows up.

I smile. It's weird—back in the labs, being a test kid was treated as a secret. But here, it's practically tattooed on my face, and nobody seems to care. Even though we're being kept as prisoners, this place has an aura of safety to it that I haven't felt in a long time. Regardless of the circumstances, it's nice to feel completely protected.

"So, how long did you guys live in the townhouses?" Jess asks, taking a bite of her food. Maggie shrugs.

"Until I was in sixth grade. Then Making Perfect pulled me out of school and brought me to the labs." Maggie replies, eating as well.

"*Sixth grade?*" Jess's eyes widen. "Geez, you were there for a long time."

"Yeah, but it's okay. I'm out now." Maggie shrugs. "And anyway, my townhouse community wasn't very strict about schooling, so they let me out pretty easily. Besides, nobody argues with Making Perfect."

"Which community?" Jasper asks. I think it's the first time I've heard him speak.

Maggie tries to respond through her mouthful of food, but Sterling stops her, answering for her. "Austin."

A familiar figure walks into view and I look up, my heart almost leaping into my chest. Ocean walks with a group that must be her unit. I hadn't thought about her since arriving yesterday—I almost forgot that I hadn't seen her. She sits down at a table at the front of the room, tucking her hair behind her ears. It's longer than I remember it, but she doesn't look all that different.

She's okay. Ocean's okay.

I am so relieved that I guffaw.

"Summer?" Maggie waves her hand in front of my face. "You there? Thought we lost you for a second."

"What?" I ask. I hear Tyler laugh.

"Don't worry, Maggie. She's just aloof by nature."

"I'm not aloof!" I protest, crumpling up my napkin and throwing it at Tyler. He catches it and wipes his mouth with it.

He grins. "It's okay. You can stay aloof. We don't judge."

I realize that I'm laughing. It feels good. "I'm totally not aloof."

Hailey slaps Tyler's shoulder playfully. "Don't be mean to her. It's a new place and a little scary. It's normal for her to be a bit aloof."

"But I'm not—"

"Sure," Maggie teases, and through my grin, my face flushes pink.

Finally, I muster up the courage to take a bite of the food lying in front of me. After opening the top of the package, I poke my fork into the concoction of potatoes, carrots, green beans, and meat. Surprisingly, the warm food melts in my mouth, and it takes all my self-control not to eat the whole meal all at once.

I am so preoccupied with my food that I don't follow any of the conversation until I'm finished. I am folding the container in half when Hailey catches my attention.

"So, how do you guys know each other?" Hailey asks Tyler, nodding her head in my direction. I look up. He looks at me.

"I dunno." He shrugs. "Our parents were friends. I've known her ever since I can remember."

Maggie's smile stretches from ear to ear. I try not to grimace. "Aw, that's cute. It's kind of a crazy coincidence that you both ended up here at the same time."

Tyler and I exchange a gaze.

"Yeah, so crazy."

31

The next few days feel endless. I'm so bored that I'm going out of my mind. There is absolutely nothing to do. Somehow, the other kids in my unit manage to find things to fill the hours. I envy their ability to keep themselves occupied, though their activities are primarily stuff like playing cards, making paper airplanes, sleeping, talking, reading, or drawing. I sometimes join them, but other than sleeping, none of these activities hold my attention for very long.

I don't know how I'll be able to wait weeks for Kace to be ready. If he doesn't get us out soon, I'm going to go crazy.

I only get to see Blayze and Ocean during meals, and even then, I can't talk to them. They're always with their unit, and the guards keep a close eye on us. One night after dinner, I'm finally able to corner Ocean on the way back to the barracks. We sit down on one of the big brown couches in the common room while everybody else retreats back to their bunks and spend a good hour talking through what happened in the labs.

I skip the parts about meeting Aaron and about the test kids. I don't know why, I just don't really feel like explaining those things.

It's almost ten, and practically everybody has retired back to their rooms, when Ocean's expression turns mischievous.

"By the way, I know that you and Blayze aren't at all into each other, but he doesn't seem able to take his eyes off you."

When I don't say anything, she giggles. "He looked absolutely pathetic today during training. You're messing him up hardcore."

Ocean, Flame, and Blayze are in the same training group. From what I've heard, their regimen is really intense. They focus mainly on building strength and endurance, but they also spend hours working with guns and other weapons. There are many outdoor training facilities and shooting ranges around the base.

I haven't seen Blayze since earlier today, when I stopped him on his way back from training. We only talked for a minute because he had to go back to his bunk to change, but he looked pretty shaken. I wanted to know what happened during training, but the way he looked, I could tell it wasn't the right time.

I flush. "No, I'm not."

"Poor guy. As I told you before, he's absolutely crazy about you." She pauses for a moment. "Do you like him?"

"As I told you before, I don't want to talk about this," I protest, trying to shut her up. I try to ignore the butterflies welling up in my stomach. "What did you guys do in training today?"

She cocks her head. "Nothing special." She shrugs. "Why?"

"No reason," I say. Maybe she doesn't know. But something must've happened for Blayze to have looked like that. Her gaze doesn't waver, so it's hard to doubt her.

"I mean, we only went through our normal training routine," she says. "It wasn't…" I catch a glimpse of movement behind her. I lean forward, looking past her, at the figure creeping along the back wall. It stops at the hallway leading to the training room and slips past the cameras. My stomach clenches. Judging by the figure's muscular build and the endearingly awkward way it walks, it has to be Blayze. Questions pop into my head, but I brush them away. "Summer! You still there?" Ocean's voice trails off when she sees the far-away expression on my face. She sighs, leaning back into the couch.

Imperfect

"Sorry." I mutter without taking my eyes off the back wall. She glances over her shoulder, following my gaze. Blayze has already disappeared around the corner, so there's nothing there. Looking back at me, and realizing I'm probably not going to be very talkative for the rest of the night, she gets up.

"I'm going back to the bunk," she yawns. "I'm really tired. Hey, do you think the kitchen can spare a bottle of hot sauce? I want to pour it in Flame's mouth while she's sleeping."

"Okay," I laugh. "Let me know if you need help."

"Will do. You coming?" She raises her eyebrows, and I shake my head.

"No. I'm going to hang around here for a little."

"Okay." She shrugs. "See you tomorrow."

"See you."

I wait for her to round the corner before standing up and quickly making my way to the hallway that Blayze disappeared into. I try to keep my steps quiet. The hallway is dimly lit, and I'm careful not to trip over myself in my hurry. As I near the end of the hallway, I slow down and slip through the already-open doors as quickly and quietly as I can.

I suck in a breath. I'm struck by how big, how clean, and how organized the room is. I expected it to be grungy, smelly, and completely uninviting. This is the opposite. The air smells like a crisp mixture of paint and rubber. Three octagonal fighting cages on raised cinderblock platforms occupy the center of the room. The ceilings are stripped bare, with cleanly painted rafters and pipes casting shadows onto the floor and equipment below. The main lights are off. Only a handful of ghost lights cast a warm, yellow blanket over the room. The wall to my left is lined with dozens of thick canvas punching bags and lifelike rubber manikins drilled

239

into the floor. The wall to my right is covered with rows of weights, gloves, mock weapons, and other training equipment. The back wall has been turned into a huge climbing wall dotted with jet-black handholds.

To my surprise, there's no one here but Blayze and I. He is crouching to my right, fastening black training gloves onto his hands. I duck behind one of the pillars by the door. He walks over to one of the punching bags, opening and closing his fists. When he reaches the bag, he stares at it for a few seconds before raising his hands in front of his face.

Like a spring, he leaps into action, throwing blows at the thick canvas. His punches, though not perfectly executed, cause the bag to swing back and forth so violently that the sensors have trouble righting it. My eyes widen. He's good.

I watch him in awe. He moves powerfully and with a controlled swiftness that I've never seen before. After he stops and the bag locks back into place, Blayze just stands there, sweaty and breathing heavily. He leans against the bag, pressing his forehead into the cloth.

There is a long silence before he speaks.

"You," he says between breaths, "are a terrible spy." I slowly stand up, shoving my hands into my pockets.

"And you're not terribly stealthy," I counter, walking over to him. "Isn't this place off limits after training's over?"

He shrugs. "They never said we weren't allowed to use it. Besides, I was bored."

"Yeah," I stop a few feet away from him. "Can I join you?" He stares at me blankly.

"What?"

"If you haven't noticed, they don't let my unit out much. I'm dying of boredom. Besides, I'm the perfect fight partner and it would be good for you to get some real-life practice. It's a win for both of us."

He rubs the back of his neck, shaking his head. His eyes betray his unease. "You're asking me to fight you?"

I nod. "Oh, come on." I smile. "Let's do it. I promise to go easy on you." He smiles faintly. I continue to push. "Enhancements included. Please?"

The moment it slips through my lips, I realize that I have no idea what Blayze's enhancement is. He realizes this too, and it's his turn to smile.

"Yours is actually useful?" he asks.

"No," I say. I don't want to tell him I never got one. Not yet. "What's yours?"

Instead of replying, he takes my hand in his. I instinctively tense up in surprise until I realize what he's doing. Gradually, I feel my skin growing warmer and warmer until the heat coming off Blayze's hand is too hot to bear. White-hot heat. I yank my hand away, rubbing it to ease the burning sensation. My eyes widen in realization. He can regulate his body temperature.

"See?" He shoves his hands into the pockets of his uniform. "I told you. It's completely useless."

"Unless you're trapped in an Ice Age," I tease. "Is it just heat?"

He nods. "Yeah. It's weird—at first, I had no control over it, and I would suddenly go from being normal, to burning up, then back to normal. The whole thing's really pointless. I mean, really, when am I ever going to use it?"

"Never," I agree. There's an awkward moment of silence, and I force myself to ask him the question that's been bugging me all afternoon. "What happened during training today? You looked pretty shaken earlier."

He purses his lips. Hesitation builds in his eyes like a wall, and I suddenly regret asking. "They put us through a slightly different routine today," he finally says, his voice flat. "After lunch, we were taken to the other side of the compound, to a big facility that has all of the simulations and large-scale obstacles. When my group was climbing across the nets, the guy next to me slipped. I tried to catch him, but I couldn't, and he fell down onto the concrete. We were pretty high up, so it wasn't good. He was still alive, though, until the officials did away with him. Right in front of everybody. Then we were forced to finish the exercise. I guess I was just still in shock when you saw me."

My eyes widen as he speaks. "Oh my God," I mutter. "They just killed him? Right there?"

"Right there." He sighs and quickly shakes his head to clear it. "But on a brighter note, this morning, we were using the punching bags, and I broke one."

The side of my mouth tugs up slightly. "Broke it? How did you…" He jerks his head over to a crumpled bag in the corner of the room. The cables are snapped, and it's completely caved inward, huge clusters of wires poking out the bottom. I stare at it for a second, then look back at Blayze, who's smiling proudly.

"I didn't even hit it that hard," he boasts playfully. "I just swung at it, and the cables completely snapped." Looking at the expression on his face, I can't help but burst out laughing. He crosses his arms over his chest, fighting the smile tugging on his lips. "What?"

"You're such an idiot," I say, shaking my head. He grins.

"Okay, let's start." He walks over to a crate in the corner behind the bags and tosses me a pair of training gloves. I catch them and slip them onto my hands, feeling the thick fabric tighten as I pull the straps. When I look up, Blayze has already opened the door to the fight cage and is backing into the middle. I follow him, closing the door behind me.

"Don't you dare go easy on me," I say, stepping up to face him.

"Thirty seconds, as many hits as you can," he states, and I nod to confirm. He flips open the control panel in the concrete underneath a thin, wooden floor. He flips a few switches, turning on the lights and activating the sensors. The timer starts. I clench my fists. The gloves start glowing.

Before he can take another breath, I lunge at him, landing a blow to his jaw. It's light, and Blayze knows it. I try to slip in another but he blocks my fist, throwing my arm to the side and trapping me in an arm lock. I wiggle free, dodging his punch, and hit him square in the chest. This blow is a little harder. We continue like this, fighting as hard as we can until the timer signals us to stop. My lungs are burning, and sweat is forming in tiny droplets all over my body. Adrenaline is pumping vigorously through my veins. I love it. Blayze is beaming.

"Whoa," Blayze says, grabbing a water bottle lying near the door. He tosses another to me. "You're relentless."

A smile tugs at my mouth. I feel like a little kid. "Can we go again?"

He nods, and we do. We fight about a dozen more times, taking occasional breaks in between for him to teach me how to both throw and block certain punches and kicks on the punching bags. Sometime around our second to last fight, Blayze does a sloppy job at blocking one of my blows and my hand slips through his defense, hitting his eye. I feel terrible, but he reassures me that he's fine. By the time we decide to stop, it's swollen almost shut.

I press the cold water bottle to my forehead as we walk over to the wall near the door. I collapse against it, sinking down into a sitting position. Blayze does the same. My lungs are fighting for breath. Blayze holds his water bottle to his eye to soothe the pain. We are both breathing so heavily that we can't talk. Blayze leans his head back against the wall.

"We should do this again," he says when he can finally get a word out. "You're right. It is nice to have a real fight partner."

"It was fun," I remark, a yawn stretching over my lips. I glance up at the clock on the wall above us. It's one thirty. No wonder I'm so tired. I've been here for hours.

Blayze looks down at his feet.

"I dunno Summer," he says. His eyes scan the room as he searches for the right words. "This whole thing doesn't feel right."

"What do you mean?"

"This whole military training thing." He looks at the broken bag in the corner. "I just don't understand why they're putting us through this if they have no need for an army." My brow furrows. "The regions haven't really fought since the Great Divide."

"Maybe they're accumulating a force for future use," I suggest, wringing my hands in my lap. "Any of the regions would have enough forces to attack each other if they had allies. If Making Perfect teamed up with Spark, the whole country would be doomed."

"But they have no way of making us fight for them. We all still have free will." He looks at me. I scoff.

"I'm sure they've already figured that out."

He nods. "Yeah, I guess." The expression on his face suddenly changes, and he averts his eyes. "Summer, what's up with you and the rest of your unit?" he asks. My gut twists. "Why do you guys never show up for training? And please, don't say you do," he quickly adds. "I know you don't."

I look at my boots and pick nervously at my cuticles. I think of what Aaron told me about the Star Formula. Something tells me he wouldn't want me sharing that information.

But this is Blayze. If I can't trust him, I can't trust anyone.

So I tell him everything. From the test kids, to the Star Formula, to the fact that the rebels exist and are harboring the remaining three that Making Perfect needs. I explain I'm part of the experiment, so are all of the others in my unit, and that we're being kept here as prisoners instead of soldiers. I tell him what Making Perfect will do when they get their hands on the rest of us, and what it might mean for all the regions.

He stays calm as I ramble on, but it doesn't take long before my tone becomes accusatory and I realize I'm yelling at Making Perfect instead of talking to him. Not just for the Star Formula, but for everything. Everything they did to me. Everything they did to my sisters. Everything they did to all of the kids under their control. It all pours out of me as if on a rapidly moving conveyor belt. I yell until my voice is dry and I'm just too exhausted to go on. I slump back against the wall, hiding my face in my hands.

He doesn't say anything until I'm done. It doesn't matter. There's nothing either of us could say that would fix anything.

An eternity passes before I finally speak again.

"This world is a mess," I groan in defeat, stretching my legs out in front of me. Blayze smiles weakly, nodding in agreement.

"A record-breaking one," he smiles, and I sigh. "How long have you known about all this?"

"Since the labs. That's when Kace took us out to meet the rebels. They told us everything." I swallow hard. "But it's fine, we'll be out of here soon. Kace has a plan to get us out, and I want you to come."

It slips out of my mouth before I have time to think. Of course I meant to tell him, but not yet. Not when I still don't have any idea when it's going to happen and Kace hasn't given me a concrete plan. Blayze stares at me for a second as my words settle in his head.

The silence is so loud it's unnerving. But just as I'm about to break it, Blayze opens his mouth.

"I can't."

My chest tightens. He can't? Why not? My heart is pounding, and I grip the hem of my tracksuit. Of all the ways I thought he'd respond, this was definitely not one of them.

"What do you mean, you can't?" Disbelief edges my voice. He looks up, and his eyes meet mine.

"There are people who I can't leave behind."

Oh. He means Flame. Of course he wouldn't want to leave her behind. Frustration pulls at me fiercely.

"You'd prefer to be stuck in here for the rest of your life?" I can't believe it. "You'd sacrifice your future for her?"

"Yes, I would." He sits up straighter. "I can't walk out of here and leave her behind. As obnoxious as she can be, she's my family, and I—"

Anger prickles up in my gut, though I try to push it down. "Family? You can't possibly consider *her* to be family."

He knits his eyebrows together. "I do. Her and her brother took me in when no one else would. We made a *promise*." There's bitterness in his voice now. "If that's not family, I don't know what is."

This sends me over the edge. "God, you're so stubborn!" I exclaim. "Making Perfect's going to kill you, don't you see that? Did it ever occur to you that your actions affect people other than Flame?"

"Summer—"

I brush him aside. My eyes start to well up. "Maybe if you stopped being such a coward—"

"Hey!" His eyes narrow, full of hurt. "That's not fair!"

"The world doesn't revolve around you, Blayze Galloway!"

Our noses are only a few inches apart. I chomp down on my tongue to stop myself from crying. Frustration and hurt are ripping me apart. We stare at each other for a long moment, and when he finally speaks, his voice is flat.

"If it were Tyler, you wouldn't either."

My words stop in my throat. He's right. If it were Tyler, I'd be reacting the exact same way. I chomp down on my tongue and sit frozen, my back hovering mere inches off the wall. The fact that I can't come up with a suitable comeback is killing me.

But I realize, now, just how much I want him to come. No, need him to come. This entire time I've been subconsciously picturing the escape in my mind, he's been there. I don't know why, but I don't see how I'll be able to leave him behind any more than he can leave Flame behind.

I draw my knees to my chest and clutch them tightly as I sit there. I don't look at him, and I don't say anything. He shifts next to me.

"We still have time before anything happens," he sighs. "Let's not worry about it all now, okay?"

"Yeah," I mumble, not raising my head. My face feels so hot that I'm afraid it's going to melt off. I hear him laugh softly.

"Hey, no pouting." He grabs my hands and pulls me up onto my feet. I yelp in surprise as we stumble backward, and I grip his hands tightly to keep myself from falling over. He opens his mouth to say something but just laughs instead.

A faint grin tugs at my mouth. "What?" I ask.

He tries to straighten his face. "Nothing." He starts laughing again.

"*What?*" Even though I don't know what he's laughing about, it's getting harder to keep a straight face. I pull one off one of my training gloves and throw it at him.

"Oh, you're on." He picks the glove off the ground and pegs it right back at me. I try to dodge it, but I stumble over my own feet and it hits my stomach. It doesn't hurt, but a flare of competitiveness ignites in me. I pull off my other glove and aim for his torso. But before I can hit him, he turns and runs back toward the door.

"I didn't peg you as a quitter!" I holler, placing my hands on my hips. He ducks behind a pillar and disappears from sight. I scoff. There's a soft rumbling sound, but I still can't see anything. "Dramatic much?"

The rolling gets louder, and Blayze comes out from behind the pillar rolling a big black crate in front of him. His eyes are twinkling with excitement.

"Prepare," he says as he gets closer, "to taste leather, Greenwood!"

He reaches into the crate and pulls out two bulging handfuls of gloves. He starts chucking them at me. I laugh, bending down and picking them off the floor and pitching them back at him. We keep going, back and forth, and he starts inching closer until we're mere feet apart. I throw a handful of gloves at his face, and he hoists the crate up over his shoulder, dumping its entire contents over my head. I squeal in surprise as the gloves fall around me, briefly enveloping me in a curtain of black fabric. Blayze is practically cackling when I look up. He holds his stomach as he tries to get a breath in.

"You are so dead," I mutter and run up to him, trying to rub the sweaty gloves in his face. He turns his head away and grabs my wrists, pushing them away from his face.

"Okay, okay, truce!" he exclaims, and I loosen my grip on the gloves. I grin widely and look up at him, my breaths heavy. It's suddenly so quiet, the only thing I can hear is the faint buzz of the electricity. We lock eyes for a second, and my breath gets caught in my throat. After a moment, he softly lets go of my wrists. It's hard to tell, but I think I see a hint of redness in his cheeks.

"We should go back," he says, shoving his hands in his pockets.

"Shouldn't we clean up?" I ask, and he shrugs.

"I don't think it matters."

"Okay."

We clean up anyway. It only takes us minutes to retrieve all the gloves and for Blayze to wheel the crate back behind the pillars. Together, we toss our empty water bottles in the bin and walk back up to the bunks.

It takes me ages to fall asleep. Scattered thoughts circle my mind, refusing to leave. Star Formula, stem cells, abilities, enhancements, civil war. It's like a huge raincloud in my brain. I groan, turning over, my head throbbing painfully. Eventually, I give up and stare at the ceiling for hours, exhaustion tearing away at my body. Out of everything, one sentence seems to be superglued to the forefront of my mind: *We need you to join Troop 5.*

32

I flop backward on the long leather couch, sinking deep into the pillows. It's been four days since Blayze and I trained together, and still nothing from Kace. Another holler echoes from the training room. I groan. All the units were called in there hours ago, and the noise is becoming harder and harder to ignore.

Eventually, I can't take it any longer. I stand up from the sofa, shove my hands in my pockets, and walk to the training room.

I can barely recognize it. It's bustling with activity. Officials are clustered near the central fight cage, talking in hurried voices. The others are standing in tightly knit groups, watching the officials from the corner of their eyes. The smell of sweat pierces my nostrils. Nervous energy pulses through the air.

What's happening?

My shoulders tensing, I squeeze through the mass of bodies toward the center of the room. Maybe I can find someone I know and figure out what's going on. The cages are turned on, but nobody's inside. I spot Kace in the crowd, and I push through to him.

"What's going on?" I hiss, coming up right behind him. He glances back at me.

"You're not supposed to be here. Go back to the bunks."

"No. Nobody stopped me from coming in." I cross my arms. "Tell me what's going on."

"It's fight day. One-on-one combat," he grumbles. "All the schedules were merged."

I furrow my brow. "Really? Why?"

He shrugs and doesn't reply.

One-on-one fights? For real?

An official steps into the center cage and silence falls over the room. All eyes are glued to him.

"Listen up!" he calls. "This is how it's going to work. The matches will come up on the screen, and you will meet your fight partner in the assigned cage. Each fight is scored out of three. One point every time your opponent hits the floor. Feel free to use any tool or skill in your arsenal—but no weapons."

Excitement sparks in my chest. Murmurs explode across the crowd, but the trainers quickly shut them down. I lean toward Kace.

"I want in."

He spins around angrily. "No."

"I'm going crazy cooped up in that room all day. It's not going to hurt anyone. Put me on the list."

He pauses for a second as if he's actually considering it, but then he shakes his head again. "I can't. If word gets back that I let you fight, it wouldn't be good for either of us and could screw everything up."

"Get back to whom? Cooper?" I press. I want to do this so badly. "Have a little faith. Nothing's going to happen. Please, Kace."

He grits his teeth and looks back out at the cage. "You are such a pain in the ass." I grin.

He walks over to the officials standing right at the front of the control panel. The large screen above them flickers to life, displaying the matches. My eyes travel down the list, scanning for anyone I know.

Blayze is paired off against someone named James. Ocean isn't on the list. There are a few other familiar names, but none that stands out. Someone steps in front of me, blocking my view of the ring. I stand up on my toes to see if Kace is still talking to the official, but he's already back.

"So?" I ask, and he nods.

"They'll throw you in somewhere." He rubs his eyes. "I swear to God, if you screw up and we get reported…"

"I won't. I promise." I don't know why I'm so bubbly. "Thanks."

He grumbles. I squeeze between him and the person in front of me so I can see the cages. The official standing in the middle shouts, and the room falls quiet again.

The remaining rules are explained curtly. I'm only half listening. My eyes are scanning the crowd, wondering who I'm going to be paired against. As the official rambles on, I see Blayze. We lock eyes for a second, and he raises his eyebrows, worry flashing across his face. I want to go over and talk to him, but the official's words stop me.

"Let's begin. Fight one, in the box. You—"

Another official steps into the square, cutting him off. She mutters some hushed words, and they go back and forth for a few seconds before the first official nods and turns back to us.

"There has been a slight change in plan. Summer Greenwood and Abigail Steele, please step into cage one. The others will proceed as follows: Owen Glynn and Jack Anderson, cage two. Brad Dung and Emma Schmidt, cage three."

I freeze. Steele. Where have I heard that name before?

Then I see her, walking up to the cage with confidence. My stomach twists.

Oh no. Please, no.

What are they thinking?

As I step forward, I immediately lock gazes with her. Flame is standing on the opposite side of the cage, eyes gleaming. She looks *completely* different from when I saw her last. Her hair is almost as short as Tyler's used to be, tapering off right below her ears. It looks like she just took a knife and chopped it all off. There are new scars on her arms, but the scariest part about her is the newfound darkness in her eyes. Her arms are crossed over her chest as she looks at me, a leering grin on her face.

I wonder what her enhancement is.

The officials step out of the ring without a word. I walk up the steps and through the door, hearing it slide shut behind me. My hands feel bare without the fight gloves on. The official at cageside raises his arm.

"Five seconds!" he calls out. Flame and I step toward each other. "Go!"

My arms are up in a guard instantly. Flame slinks toward me like a cat. She is smirking. I hate it.

In a split second, she closes the distance. She's so fast that I barely register her movements. Her leg kicks out, sending mine flying out from under me. A stab of pain shoots up my back as I hit the wood with a thwack. A buzzer sounds. First point.

What? That can't be one point. I look at Kace, and he just shrugs at me.

That little *bitch!*

"You ready this time, Greenwood? I'm pretty sure the fight starts when they say go," Flame gibes as I stand up. She got me down within seconds of the set starting. That was *pathetic.* Anger bubbles inside me. When the round starts again, I waste no time moving in toward her and throwing a blow at her face. She manages to sidestep it and send a kick flying toward my side, which I also manage to block. I duck her next blow, wiggling around her and elbowing her back. She cries out in surprise, and I duck down, kicking her knee so hard that she buckles.

But she doesn't hit the floor. Before she can touch it, she swings to the side and leaps back up again. A sharp pain shoots through my head, and I stumble backward, cupping my hands over my nose. It only takes one more well-placed blow before I'm crumpled on the floor again. My head is screaming in agony, and when I open my eyes, Flame is crouched on top of me, pinning me down. There is an almost inhuman ferocity about her.

Fear rises in my chest. The rounds are supposed to be over once I hit the floor. She chuckles as she digs her nails into my shoulder and jams her knee into my gut. She looks ready to rip my head off. I try to push her off, but she doesn't budge. I feel water well up in my eyes, frustration and anger oozing out of my body.

"You can cry, Greenwood. It's okay. I don't judge. But you are done." Her eyes are cold. Lifeless. She raises her fist, and I struggle harder than ever. But before she can deliver the blow, two officials rush toward us, pulling her off.

Flame is thrown backward and blocked from my view. I sit up, and my world violently shifts. I have to grip the floor to keep myself from passing out. When I look up, Kace is squatting in front of me, his elbows resting on his knees.

"I'm going to pull you out," he asserts, and I shake my head.

"No way. I can't let her win."

He looks more irritated than I've ever seen him. He starts to speak, but an official cuts him off. "Greenwood! Ready?"

I nod and force myself to stand up. Kace, biting his lip and glaring at me, gets up and backs out of the cage. I stumble forward, barely finding my balance. When I look back at Flame, my face turns bright red. One more point, and she wins.

I can't let her win.

My breaths heavy, I face her. She paces in a circle. The officials retreat outside the cage, and the middle one gives us the go signal. I narrow my eyes. There is something very wrong. Something must have backfired in her enhancement.

Or what if this is her enhancement? This animal-like violence?

By the time the official lowers his arm, she's already moving toward me. I try to duck, but she's too fast, and the punch reverberates through my nose. My vision blurs. But instead of crumpling, I feel rage bubbling up inside me. The pain in my body is receding, and my fists are clenching and unclenching as I glare at her closing in for the kill. As if in slow motion, I see her body twist and her fist pulling back, energy rippling through her skin.

But as her skin comes in contact with mine, something strange happens. Instead of hurting, all the energy and adrenaline coursing through her body is sucked out of her and pushed into me, filling me up to the brim with energy and power. I don't know where it comes from, this power. It's more than I've ever felt. I see Flame collapse on the ground in a heap, completely limp. But I don't care—all this energy is tearing through me, threatening to rip me apart. I can do anything, break *anything*.

Then, like a light switch, it flips. The pressure is building in my body. I feel like I'm going to explode. It needs to go somewhere, the energy. It needs to get out of my body, or it will consume me. But how do I release it? I look around, my vision completely blurred. I am suddenly overcome by this incredible fear. I need to find a place to send the power.

With a cry I drop to my knees, plunging my forearms into the *concrete floor*.

33

The whole floor is ripped apart.

The second my fists come into contact with the ground, it's a mixture of excruciating pain and utter relief as the power drains from my body. I stay there for a split second, looking at my arms in horror, before I collapse completely onto the broken floor. All the energy is gone from my body, and all I can do is lie there. The thought of ever moving again makes me want to hurl.

I feel hands on me, gently lifting me and pulling my shattered arms out of the floor. I hear someone whispering into my ear, but I can't understand what they're saying. My hands burn as soon as they touch the open air. I can't move them—I wonder if they're broken. They sting so badly.

I can't open my eyes. It's as if they're completely fused shut. My lungs are fighting for air. Someone scoops me into their arms, and I press my body against them tightly. It's Blayze—I can just tell by the smell of his armor and his gentle callused hands. I cry in pain and bite down on my tongue until I taste blood. I want my hands to stop burning.

I sink into Blayze's arms, my head throbbing so hard that I fear it's going to explode.

⋏   ⋏   ⋏

KACE

I've never seen anger like this before.

Everything seems to happen at once. Summer drops to her knees and slams her fists into the floor. Like an earthquake, I feel the ground shift powerfully beneath my feet, and I stumble back into the crowd. Everyone is looking at Summer in complete and utter surprise.

When the shockwave dissipates, Summer slumps limp on the ground. Her forearms are buried in broken concrete in the middle of a large crater in the floor. Flame sits up with a start, the energy that Summer took returning to her body. She looks around, wildly, and the officials crowd in around her.

By the time I can push through the crowd toward Summer, Blayze is already there. He is cradling her gently in his arms, talking softly into her ear. As soon as I reach them, I drop to my knees, pressing my fingers to her neck to check for a pulse.

It's scary how tiny she looks. She's surprisingly tall when she's awake, standing just slightly below eye level with me. But seeing her limp and lying like this in Blayze's arms, she looks frail.

I feel the faint heartbeat and know she's alive.

"Kace!" Blayze snaps me back to attention, his voice raw. There is utter terror on his face. "Is she...?" I shake my head. He sighs in relief. Together, we manage to lift her chest up and pull her arms out of the ground. As she collapses back into him, a faint whimper escapes her lips. He is talking to her, trying to calm her. Meanwhile, my eyes are fixated on her hands.

They are mangled. Her bone structure seems mostly intact, but her knuckles are so raw and bloody that some of the bone is poking out from the folds of skin that have been pulled back. There are long, deep gashes on her forearms, and little pieces of rock are embedded under her skin. When Blayze looks down at them, he turns white.

My heart wrenches for her.

"Get her to the infirmary, *now*. I'll meet you there," I snap at Blayze, who looks up at me with a stupefied expression on his face. I watch as he gently lifts her, pushes through the crowd, and carries her down the hallway to the infirmary.

☇   ☇   ☇

SUMMER

When I finally wake up, my hands are wrapped tightly in thick, white bandages. My eyes are foggy, and I groan, not wanting to move. My head hurts.

I squint and look around the room. It's empty. Where is everybody?

Then I remember.

Oh God.

What happened? Looking back on it now, it feels like a dream, but the bandages on my hands tell me otherwise. I touch my nose with my shoulder and feel the bumpy canvas tape stretching across it. I must've been hurt worse than I thought.

I almost killed Flame. *Killed* her. Not that I didn't want her dead, but I never wanted to be the one to do it. I hope she's okay.

What was her enhancement? What did they do to her? They turned her into a monster!

I punched through concrete.

I *punched* through *concrete*.

I didn't know that was possible.

I must have an enhancement of my own, right? The test kids aren't supposed to have received enhancements, but no normal person could do what I did back there.

I'm not normal.

But I'm hungry.

I glance down at my wrist to check the time, but my watch has been removed. I squint at the clock on the wall and see that it's five fifteen. Everybody should be almost finished with training by now. But where's my unit? Don't tell me they were brought out of the barracks for the first time and I missed it.

I try to sit up, but my vision jerks to the side and I grab the edge of the cot for support. A wave of nausea washes over me. Eventually, I'm able to reach the floor, but my stomach lurches and I stumble over to Tyler's bunk to lie down. They must have me on a pretty strong drug.

My hands ache. I'm really scared to see what sort of mutilated mess lies under that wrap.

It's almost five forty-five when I finally make it out of the room. I push through the door and slowly walk down the hallway. Maybe there'll be some food out early, so I can eat before everybody gets here. But I don't make it there. Instead, I collapse onto one of the couches in the common room, all of the energy suddenly sucked out of me.

What's wrong with me?

I'm not that hungry anymore; I just want to go back to the bunk. The last thing I want is to be here when everybody gets back. But as I have that thought, I hear the footsteps coming down the hall. As the first person comes in, I slouch farther back into the couch in hopes of disappearing completely. Like a waterfall, everybody barges into the common room, their uniforms completely drenched. They walk right past the couch I'm sitting on, some pushing through the door leading to the bunks. I catch a glimpse of Ocean walking to the dining hall with a large group. She doesn't see me, but I watch her until she's completely out of sight.

My eyes search the crowd for any signs of my unit, but they're nowhere to be found.

Where were they taken? I need Tyler to come back.

The number of people passing through is endless. I want to be back in my bed. The crowd begins to thin, and I'm about to make a run for it when I see Blayze walk through the door. The second he sees me, he rushes over.

"How are you feeling? You shouldn't be out here," he says, worriedly. Like the others, he is completely soaked. His hair is stuck to his forehead, and his sleeves are dripping. I stand up, and he steadies me. "As soon as we got to the infirmary, they kicked me out and sent me back to training. I tried to stay, but they…" He stops, flustered, his voice trailing off when he sees the heavy bandages on my hands. His face tightens into a grimace. I bite my lip.

"They're that bad, huh?" I ask, and he looks back up at me.

"Let's go get dinner."

Despite my now-nonexistent appetite, we slowly make our way down to the mess hall, taking occasional breaks as the drugs threaten to pull me under. Clearly, I'm not supposed to be out of bed. Although the tent is completely packed, we are able to maneuver through the crowd, get food, and find a place to sit at one of the corner tables. It feels so good to sit down again. I hardly notice the hushed whispers and side glances cast in my direction.

After we sit down, he rustles his hair to try and get rid of some of the water.

"So…what happened back there?" he asks, peeling back the top of his dinner. It's cold today, and it looks fairly unappetizing. I'm not touching mine.

"I—I don't know," I admit. It is such a lame answer, but it's all I think to say. "I really don't."

"Okay. Why were you there in the first place? You told me that you guys aren't here to train."

"We aren't," I poke at the bread roll on the side of my plate. "I was bored, so I snuck in and convinced Kace to let me fight."

"And he agreed?"

"Grudgingly," I make sure to keep my voice low. Blayze shakes his head. "I convinced him to let me, and I promised not to screw up and get reported."

"How'd that go?" he smirks. "Damn, he's such an idiot."

"Hey, I didn't know I'd be paired against Flame. Really. Could you think of a worse match for me?"

"Kace must've been confident that you could beat her," he remarks, taking a sip of water.

"I don't think he was the one that made the pairings." I purse my lips, looking up at him. "Blayze, what is her enhancement? What did they do to her?"

He sighs, swirling his fork around in the food. You'd have to be really hungry to eat that. "I'm not entirely sure. When we were transferred here and I saw her again, she was completely different. She remembered who I was, but it was like all emotional connection was severed." He doesn't look at me. I can hear the pain in his voice. "And that continued into everything she did, especially fighting. All of her compassion, her humanity, is gone. I think that's her enhancement. If you can't feel emotion, you can't feel fear. That's probably what they were going for."

"Last thing I remember, she was collapsing. Is she okay?"

"I think so. She doesn't talk to me much, so it's hard to tell."

There's a slight pause. I don't really know what to say. All of this is obviously much harder on Blayze than he's letting on. He and Flame grew up together, like Tyler and I did. I try to imagine what it would be like if they did that to Tyler. But I have to stop—it just makes me angry.

I finally muster up the courage to nibble at the bread roll. It takes all of my concentration to get it in my hands, but when I try to take a bite out of the bottom, it falls right back onto the table. Blayze looks over at me, and a little smile is etched on his face.

"You good?" he asks. I nod, but he leans over anyway, lifting up the roll and holding it up to my hands. I scowl at him, but I'm on the verge of laughing.

"You are not feeding me," I say to him. "I am not *that* handicapped."

He grins and puts the roll down. The look he gives me fills my body with warmth. I pick the roll up again, and this time I'm able to take a substantial bite. The food tastes strange in my mouth, and I put it back down.

My vision starts to spot, and pain shoots through my head. I wince, and my hands shoot up to my forehead to steady myself.

"Summer?" Blayze asks. "You okay? You're really pale."

"I'm okay," I protest, but it's clear that I'm not. He reaches over and grabs my plate, slipping his arm around my waist and lifting me to my feet. My legs are shaky under me as we make our way back to the common room. I keep my eyes on the floor in front of me as we walk. When I just can't go on anymore, he lifts me up. I rest my head on his shoulder and sigh, allowing my eyes to fall closed. Before I know it, we've reached my bunk, and he's laying me onto my bed. I turn over so that I'm facing him, my head sinking deep into the pillow.

I want to stay awake, but it's like someone has crazy-glued my eyes shut. When I try to thank him, it comes out a garbled mess. He says something to me, but I can't make out what it is. I'm already too far gone.

34

'm sitting in the middle of the fight cage when Kace finds me.
I don't really know why I came. I guess I just wanted to see it. It's
been three days since my fight with Flame, and this is the first time
I've come back to the training room. Making Perfect's wasted no
time in filling the hole I made, laying noticeably glossier new wood
over the concrete.

From his point of view, I must look pretty strange. All the lights
are off except for the ghost light. I don't know how he found me.
Everybody went to sleep hours ago.

He walks through the open cage door.

"So, this is how you solve your problems?" he asks, looking
down at me. His arms are crossed. I don't look at him. "You come
in here and sulk?"

I try to ignore him in hopes that he'll go away. I just want to
be alone. No matter how hard I try, I can't stop thinking about
my conversation with Tyler from a few nights ago. The rest of my
unit came back a few hours after Blayze left me in my bunk. Tyler
nudged me awake as soon as he came in. After he saw that I was all
right, he calmed down. According to him, the unit had been taken
out to the green for "recreational activities." Judging by his descrip-
tion, I'm glad I got to sit that one out.

"Sum!" Tyler exclaimed when he woke me. I blinked at him,
and he laughed faintly. "This is so cool! You've found your ability."

"Yeah, some ability." I grumbled, and he rolled his eyes.

"No, seriously. You know that every test kid has an ability. Sterling is a genius; Bas is an ox; Maggie has an endless supply of energy; Hailey has groundbreaking endurance. We all bring a slightly different thing to our unit, and this is yours."

"This can't be mine," I sighed. "What a rip-off."

"Rip-off? You're joking, right? You can punch through concrete. That's cooler than all of our abilities put together. You're like our very own personal Superman."

I smiled a little. "If all of us have one, then what's yours?"

He shrugged. "I haven't found it yet."

We all went to bed pretty quickly after that, but the conversation has been circling my mind for days now.

I glare at Kace. "I am so not in the mood for joking right now."

"Who says I'm joking?" He crouches down in front of me with his elbows resting on his knees. Now that he's here, I just want to go back to my bunk. "Are you still upset about the fight?" he asks.

I give him just about the nastiest glare I can muster. "I'm not *upset.*" I grit my teeth continuously while he looks at me. I can almost *feel* the judgment.

He brushes me off. "Yeah, about that—you can never do it again. You're lucky they're still letting us stay here. They weren't very happy when they found out." I don't say anything. "Do you suddenly have a problem with cinderblocks?"

"Do you want something?" I snap, turning toward him. He doesn't say anything, and I give up. Apparently, he's not going anywhere. "How did you find me here, anyway?"

He replies to this one. "I had a sense." I wrinkle my nose at him, turning away again. "You know, there's been something nagging me since your fight." He lies down next to me on the floor, propping himself up on one elbow. "In any other circumstance, I would think that you have an enhancement—there's no way one could possess that kind of power without one. But there's no way one you could've have gotten an enhancement. It was your ability, wasn't it? The whole 'punching through the floor' thing?"

I scoff. "Gee, I wonder how long it took for you to figure that one out." He ignores this.

"That's a beast of an ability. It makes the others pale in comparison. But you're going to have to learn to control it, or it's going to be a mighty pain in the ass." There's a brief pause. "I think it's an energy thing—you can only use your strength if you take it from someone else. Like an energy transfer. That's why Flame collapsed the way she did. But there has to be a trigger—something that causes you to tap into that energy. Does that sound right?"

I shrug, studying the laces on my boots. "I guess."

"So what do you think this trigger is? What did you feel when you did that?" he asks, and I stifle a laugh.

"Geez, you're starting to sound like a therapist."

"Be serious. Please."

"Okay, fine." I stop to think. "Well, I was just angry. Flame made me really, really angry. And also scared. I didn't know what she was going to do to me since her mind is messed up. When it happened, I got so much energy. It bubbled up inside me, turning my body into a condensed spring. There was so much tension, and I guess it just needed to pour out of me. Like an outlet." I shake my head. "I don't know, Kace. I haven't figured it all out yet." I exhale loudly and flop backward onto the wood, looking up at the ceiling. He scratches his nose.

"So, what you're saying, more or less, is you have to get super pissed in order to take the energy?" I nod. "Like the Hulk?" He looks for a reaction. Doesn't get one.

"I'm not even going to pretend like I know what that is," I sit back up, crossing my legs under me. "All I remember is that when it happened, I could literally *feel* her energy pour into and through my body. It felt pretty spectacular. I felt so powerful. Like I could do *anything*. But I could only hold it for a few seconds before it needed some place to go. Like a game of hot potato." He nods. "What?" I ask.

He glances up at me. "You know, when I first got my enhancement and was transferred here, it took me about four days to actually leave my bunk," he remarks, running his fingers through his hair. "Something happened during my procedure that made my enhancement backfire. It altered my brain in a way that caused me to get these terrible hallucinations. Terrible ones. For the longest time, I couldn't tell what was real and what was imaginary. It got to the point where they were going to terminate me if I didn't turn myself around. If it wasn't for Cooper, I don't think I would have made it."

"What did he do?"

"Nothing. He just befriended me." He sighs. "Since the enhancement didn't take, I had to train just to get myself back to a normal level of functioning. That took a lot of work." He sits up and meets my wide-eyed gaze. "The point—er—what I mean is, once I was able to get in touch with my energy, it became a lot easier to control my mind and body. It made me grounded. Do you know what I mean?"

"No."

He sighs. "Well, maybe if you were able to find which part of you this feeling of anger resonates from, it'll be easier to find the source of the enhancement. If you just focus—"

"It's not that easy!" I snap, suddenly annoyed. "Stop with all of this 'you just need to focus' crap because it doesn't help at all. I just need to somehow keep myself from punching my goddamn fists through the floor."

"I know, and I'm just saying that—"

"Shut up, Kace!" I exclaim, and the air around us gets suddenly cold. I hope it's too dark for him to notice how red my face has gotten. He's right. Of course he's right. I know I need to focus, but I don't know how. I'm just so done. We sit there in silence for a minute before he finally stands up. I'm entirely convinced that he's leaving when he stops, reaching his hand down to me. I look up at him with a furrowed brow.

"Get up. You and I have work to do," he says, his voice softer than before. I grab his calloused hand and hoist myself up. All the blood quickly rushes out of my head, and I place a hand on my forehead to steady myself.

"What are we doing?"

"I am going to make you angry," he explains.

"That doesn't seem very hard for you."

"We are going to find that trigger, even if I have to shove those angry thoughts into your head myself. You obviously have some crazy abilities here, and we need to learn to harness them." I knit my brow, and he steps toward me, grabbing my wrists. I try not to think about the aching in my hands. Thankfully, I'm still pretty high on painkillers. "Okay," his brow knits together, "so what makes you angry?"

"You're asking me?"

"Never mind," he says, noticeably peppier. "I want you to take my energy."

I wrench my wrists from him. "No way."

"Yes, but let's try a calmer approach." He grabs my wrists again. "Visualize your energy coursing through your body. White-hot, crackling energy. All of the power you possess, running through your fingertips. You can do anything, break anything. You can crush anything with the tips of your fingers. But you are in control.

Not your body. Not me. Not anyone else. It is your energy, your power. You—"

And I feel it. That bubbling-over feeling. Before I even have time to register the fear, it overtakes me, pulling every inch of my body into its merciless clutches. Kace cries out under my grip, but my head isn't even there anymore. My heart is pounding so hard that I can hear it in my ears.

With a gasp, I pull my fists back toward my chest and slam my feet into the ground, sending myself flying back across the cage and slamming into its side. Pain shoots through my body, and all of the wind is knocked out of me as I collapse on the floor. My head is spinning so violently, I can barely see straight. When my vision rights itself, I can just make out Kace sitting up slowly, wiping his forehead with the back of his hand. I think I hear him laughing. When he sees me, he rubs his neck and collapses back down onto the ground in exhaustion. I can almost hear his thoughts from here.

We've got a lot of work to do.

35

COOPER

"I an!" Elle squeals into the phone, and I laugh. There's a scraping sound of wood on wood, and I can almost see her pushing her chair away from the kitchen table. The house is still vivid in my mind—everything from the tables, the chairs, and the dark, gloomy atmosphere that you can only achieve by living a long way underground. "You're gross."

"That's what I'm here for." I squeeze the phone between my ear and my shoulder as I move some files back into the cabinet. Being closed up in an office all day drives me crazy. I almost wish I was training with the rest of them. Then at least I'd have something to do. My sister seems to have the same problem—I find her calling me a lot. I'm grateful for the calls, though honestly I'm frustrated at my parents for not letting her get out more. Ever since she was diagnosed with the virus, my parents have kept her locked in the house. It's been far too long since she's seen sunlight. She doesn't talk about it much, but I know how fed up with it she is.

"Hey, have you heard anything from Father?" she asks. A pile of papers goes flying out of my hands and falls all over the ground. I curse under my breath and crouch down to pick them up.

"No, why?" I fan through the pages and scoop them up into a pile.

"Ian?" Elle says into the phone, and I snap back to attention, sitting down in one of the dark blue armchairs facing the front of my desk. "You there?"

"Huh?" I run my fingers over the worn edge of my desk.

She sighs. "I was just saying that I'm leaving."

At this, I perk up. "What?"

"I'm leaving home. I'm heading back to Sutton."

I instantly freeze. Sutton is the region's top medical facility, where we handle all the most difficult medical research and treatment. Elle was originally sent there when she was young to be treated for her virus, but she moved home when she started taking her medication. For her to be going back there must mean that something's not right.

"Elle, what's wrong? Why are you going back to Sutton?"

The other line goes silent for a minute. "Elle, are you there?" My voice cracks loudly, and I shut my eyes tightly.

"Yeah." Something's strange in her tone. I'm suddenly worried.

"What's going on?" My voice rises. "Why are you going back to Sutton?"

"I had a visit with Dr. Gray yesterday." Her voice is soft. I am on the verge of panic. "She said the virus has spread."

I shake my head, my voice becoming thick. "What? No that's impossible, they contained it—"

"They're gonna cut my meds. They say they're no longer working, and I only have a few months left." I am frozen, my mouth slightly ajar. "Two, maybe three if I'm lucky."

"No. Remember? They said that years ago. They said you wouldn't live to see your fifteenth birthday—"

"I know, but this time it's for real."

I don't know what to do. It's not possible, Elle can't be dying. Not for real. She will be okay...She has to be okay! "I'll call you tomorrow, okay? Bye, Ian."

"No, wait. Elle, listen to me!" I shout into the phone. "It's going to be okay! Just—"

The line goes dead. I throw the phone across the room and put my head in my hands, rocking back and forth slowly to the sound of the ticking clock.

▲   ▲   ▲

SUMMER

I smell muffins.

That's my first conscious thought when I wake up.

As I walk down the hallway, my stomach growls loudly at the smell of breakfast. The effects of the more powerful drugs have worn off, and my appetite is back. My pace quickens as I get closer to the mess hall, but just as I'm about to enter the common room, I feel a hand over my mouth and I'm jerked backward.

I'm pulled into the corner of an adjacent hallway. I scream, but it's muffled by the hand. I throw my elbow back. I feel a wince from behind me and twist my body so hard that I am yanked out of my attacker's grasp. When I spin around, anger contorting my face, I freeze.

Blayze?

He glances over his shoulder, wringing his hands together. Regaining the ability to move, I storm up to him.

"What was that, moron? You—" I start, but he holds a finger to his lips. I lower my voice to a whisper. "What's wrong?"

"I know what the chip is for."

I cross my arms. "What are you talking about?" I've rarely seen him this spooked. "Blayze, what's going on?"

"The chip."

"What?"

He rubs his neck. "The chip. Remember? The one they injected us with when we arrived? On the plane?" Our faces are only inches apart. The intensity in his eyes is starting to scare me.

"Are you okay?" I ask. His gaze softens.

"Remember the other night when we were talking about combat training?" he says, and I nod. "You said they've probably already figured out how to control our allegiance. You were right!"

"You're not making any sense," I say, trying to reassure him. He looks so freaked out. "The chip is supposed to protect us against Red Pox."

He shakes his head again, laughing nervously. "There's no way they care that much about our health." My eyes widen. "The whole thing's been bugging me for a while. Then yesterday, during training, they turned it on for the first time, and it hit me. It's the chip. The chip doesn't protect us from Red Pox, it links us to each other. Not all the time, just when they want it to. Making Perfect can just flip the switch and somehow link us to all the other soldiers in our unit. When it was turned on, I suddenly knew what all the others were about to do before they did it and where they were at all times…like a big digital map in my brain. It was like we all morphed into one being." He pauses for a second. "Don't get me wrong, I was still able to control what I did, but it was weird—my commander's instructions were transmitted directly into my head. It's not like I heard their voices or anything, but I knew what they wanted me to do. And the weirdest part was, I actually wanted to do it. I wanted to carry out the tasks they were giving me because… because I didn't want to let my unit down."

I swallow hard. He takes a shaky breath but smiles softly.

"Being connected to other people like that—my world became *huge*," he continues. "I felt like I was part of something bigger than myself, you know? I was stronger than I've ever felt before. For the first time in ages, I felt like I belonged. Like everything wasn't resting on my shoulders. Like others were there for me. If I did my part, everything would be okay. I was almost sad when they turned the chip off. My world became small again."

I shake my head. No. What he's saying can't be true. But one look into his eyes, and I know that it is. "Blayze, you know this is a bad thing...right? Making Perfect—"

He cuts me off. "Of course it's a bad thing!" He shoves his hands into his pockets and sucks in a breath. "It's a terrible thing. Don't you see? This is how they control their soldiers. They link them to each other and feed them orders through the control center. But the really scary thing is that they can make us want that sense of belonging. *Crave* it. They're taking kids that have come from the Slump and spent their lives alone, always looking over their shoulders, and putting them in an environment where they feel like they belong and have a purpose far bigger than themselves. They're playing on human nature, turning around our allegiances without any fancy mind control. When we go into combat, they'll just flip the switch and we'll become these unflinchingly loyal, brutal...killing machines."

Goose bumps rise on my arms. Preying on human nature... it's so much more twisted and efficient than mind control. That feeling of safety, belonging, and purpose is a Slump kid's deepest desire. Give it to them...and they'd probably do anything to keep it.

That must be why all of Making Perfect's guards and officials are so loyal. They were probably put through this system as teenagers. It's so wrong that it makes me want to hurl.

Making Perfect is wickedly smart.

"But...can't you fight it?" I struggle to keep my voice steady, but it's only half working. I have a fearful pain in my chest, like a giant claw is ripping out my innards. "Since you can still control your actions, it won't affect you, right?"

Blayze bites his lip. "Technically, no. I'm still in control. But it feels like I'm being ripped in two. I don't want to fight it when it's on. It feels so good, Summer. I haven't felt this complete in a long time."

I chomp down on my tongue, and my nose tingles. I rub it with the side of my hand. "But they're manipulating you!" My voice cracks. There's a hollow feeling in my chest. "You have to—" The bell cuts me off, signaling the end of breakfast.

The urgency in Blayze's eyes heightens. "I know. I'll think of something." I pinch the bridge of my nose, my head spinning. "I have to go."

He turns to leave, but I grab his arm. "Does everyone know about this?"

He shakes his head. "Just you." The bell rings a second time. "I'll see you later."

"Blayze, wait—"

But he runs off.

I stay in the storage closet for a while before going to get breakfast. By the time I finally make it over to the mess hall, everything's either been eaten or taken away. On my way back to my room, I run into a scrambling pack of girls who are clearly late for training. They whiz right past me, one of them knocking into my shoulder so forcefully that she almost sends me into the wall.

The rest of the morning is uneventful, but I can't tear my mind away from my conversation with Blayze. I try to keep myself occupied—even taking part in one of Sterling's incredibly complicated card games and making paper airplanes with Jackson. My theory is that if I'm doing something, my thoughts won't have time to wander. But it doesn't work. I think Tyler notices that something's wrong, but he doesn't say anything. Every time I look at him, the thought of the chip pops right back into my head. Will they turn it on for our unit too? Will his allegiance be switched over? I've always been the more hot-headed of the two of us…I know I would never succumb to it, no matter how wonderful it feels. But I'm scared that it might work on Tyler—other than me, he's had nobody to lean on these past few years. Maybe having that sense of security will make him feel safe again. He might forget all the times we've spent together, or worse, not even care.

No. I can't let that happen. I have to tell him. We have to solve this.

As I unfold my paper creation for the eleventh time, he catches me staring and flashes me a reassuring grin.

I try to find Blayze at lunch but can't. Apparently, his unit was taken to a facility outside the compound and hasn't come back yet. I am forced to go back to my bunk to wait. Every minute of that afternoon is agonizing. By the time the units come back at six o'clock, I'm ready to tear my eyes out. I take off toward the common room the second I hear the doors open. People stampede around me, and I frantically look around, but can't find him.

Frustrated, I grab a roll from the mess hall and take off through the barracks. I pop my head into the door of his room.

"Hey, Summer," Ocean greets me when she catches me in the door. "What's up?"

"Nothing," I answer between breaths, squeezing my roll. "Have you seen Blayze?"

She shakes her head. "No, not since training, sorry."

I wonder if the chip has been used on her, too. Probably, since she's in Blayze's unit. If I think about it too much, it's going to drive me crazy.

"Thanks." I run back into the common room, but still, I can't find him.

Where is he?

Then I see him: he's standing by the door to the mess hall in a tight group of other boys whom I don't recognize. A weight lifts off my shoulders. I run up to him, tugging on his arm urgently. He turns around, the lighthearted grin instantly disappearing from his face.

"What—"

I lean up toward him and drop my voice to a whisper. "I need to talk to you."

He nods. He grabs my arm gently, and we walk out of earshot of the group. I can see them glancing at us.

"What's wrong?" he asks. There's dirt smeared on his face. "Are you okay?"

My instinctual nod slowly turns into a head shake. I grit my teeth. I need to keep it together. "No, I'm not okay. We need to get out of here. Right now. As long as that chip stays in our brains, we're completely at their mercy! And I know you think it feels good, but you're an idiot because you can't just let them manipulate you and accept it. We need to get out of here so we can get rid of them before…before…" My voice trails off, but the panic builds almost to a point of hysteria. I look over his shoulder at the door leading outside. If only we could just sneak out…

"Summer." His voice snaps me back to attention. "I know what I told you this morning was a little crazy. I'm sorry for dumping this on you—" He tries to calm me down, but I shake him off.

"We're going to be killing machines." My voice starts to shake. "One day, I could just wake up and everyone around me will be gone. And Tyler—I need to tell him. He needs to know, I can't lose him too." I stop and wipe my hands down my face, forcing myself not to cry. Anger boils up inside of me to the point of pain. "I'm so tired of losing everybody!" I can't hold it together any longer.

When Blayze opens his arms, I walk straight into them. He tenses up initially but slowly relaxes as he holds me. I press my face into his shoulder and start to cry. My chest feels like it's being ripped apart. All of the sadness and fear that has been brewing inside of me for months is finally pouring out and leaving me a crumbling mess.

"H-hey," Blayze says gently, pressing his head into my hair. "It's okay. We'll...we'll figure something out." I can feel his hands trembling on my back.

I let out a deep sigh, focusing on the humming of the vents above our heads. I listen to it until I can't think of anything else but that dull, rumbling sound and Blayze's arms around me.

36

COOPER

I hold the phone in place with my shoulder as I sort through the files scattered all over my office floor. It is less than fifteen minutes since I hung up with Elle, and the panic still hasn't diminished.

If anything, it's grown.

My father's secretary picks up the phone. "Michael Cooper's office—"

"Felicia, it's Ian," I snap. "I need to speak with my father."

"Let me check his availability," she murmurs, and I groan as I hear her put down the phone. She is back within seconds. "Sorry, Ian. He's busy. I'm afraid—"

"No. I need to speak with him now."

"That's not possible. You know the policy—"

I slam my fist against the desk. "Goddamn it! Get my father on the phone right now, or else I swear to God I'm flying over there to do it myself."

There's a long pause before she replies, her voice quavering. "I'll transfer you."

"Thank you." I lift a stack of files into the box on my right and pull another from the shelf. Opening it, I scan down the page and close it quickly when I realize it's not what I'm looking for. The phone rings five times before Father picks up.

"Michael Cooper," his husky voice growls into the receiver. This would normally send chills down my spine, but now I couldn't care less.

"You are putting Elle back on her meds."

He laughs. Resentment prickles over every inch of my skin. "I take it she told you."

I scoff. "Yeah. Not only did she tell me, but I could barely believe my ears when she told me you ordered the doctors to cut her meds." I grab another file, slamming it onto the ground. "Are you out of your mind?"

"Calm yourself, Ian. You wouldn't want to do anything rash."

"Rash? You're joking." I rub my eyes. "You want her dead, don't you? That's what you've always wanted, isn't it? She was the sick one, and not worth your time. But isn't that what Making Perfect was created to do? To find cures for this kind of thing? There has to be something you're not telling me because I know there is a cure somewhere in here. Somewhere in these stupid *files!*" I throw a stack of folders onto the floor and slam my fist on the desk. I feel tears well up in my eyes and loathe myself for crying.

The line is dead silent for a long time before my father speaks. "There isn't anything, Ian. Your sister has been dying since she was born. You have always known that. You just need to accept that this is her time and enjoy her while she's still here."

"Of course it's not her time yet. It's nobody's time at nineteen!" My voice is thick. "If you just put her back on her meds, everything will be okay."

In my fury, I grab a file and rip it open, tearing it at the hinges. When I pull out the first piece of paper and look it over, something catches my eye. Excitement rising slightly, I place the paper back down on the ground and run my fingers over the words. My eyes widen in realization.

That's it.

"Ian, there isn't anything we can do. You need to accept it and move on." My father's tone is sharp and condescending, but I'm not even listening to him. When I don't say anything, I hear him sigh and hang up the phone with a loud click.

Star Formula...

I grit my teeth.

...will create a being that is stronger, smarter, and stealthier than any human.

My mouth tugs into a vicious grin. Father is a liar. He always has been a liar. He doesn't care about Elle. He doesn't care about me, either. He is intransigent, ruthless, and self-centered.

The phone slips out of my hand and clatters onto the floor.

I'm going to have to save Elle myself.

Maybe there's a way we can speed up that process.

We just need those three remaining test kids, and I know where they are.

I grab the folder and walk out the door.

▲ ▲ ▲

KACE

I stand at the back of the room, my arms crossed against my chest. It has been twenty minutes since I got here, and the meeting still hasn't begun. The dreary conference room is dimly lit; no outside light is allowed in by the concrete walls. It's late, and I swallow back a yawn.

The number of officials crammed into this room is slightly unnerving. These are all of Making Perfect's top officials and trusted military advisors. The information discussed in these meetings is strictly confidential—sharing it is considered treason.

I watch them as they mingle, conversing softly. It all seems so fake...all the fake conversation and the fake politeness. I want to bang all of their heads together.

It's almost a relief when the large screen on the wall flickers to life and Ian's face appears.

"Good evening," he greets us. I immediately notice the unnaturally heavy bags under his eyes. "Thank you for joining me tonight." The camera adjusts itself slightly, zooming in closer to his face. "It is widely known that there have occurrences of rebel activity lately, and I would like to inform you that the border guard has now been doubled and that all travel into and out of the Slump is regulated and documented." I tense slightly at the mention of the rebels. Since Summer and Tyler's visit, Making Perfect has been extremely vigilant. They came so close to catching Callie and Ridge that night. I don't know what I would have done if they did.

"As you know, Making Perfect has been trying to hunt down the rebels for years," he says. "But now we are running out of time." I twist my wrists nervously. Ian hardly ever calls into meetings. Whatever this is, it must be bad. "As most of you know, our relationship with TERC has been in turmoil for the past few months. Recently, they have cut off all relations with us, going to the other corporations to get their necessities. It's only a matter of time before they reveal our practices. If the situation is not handled properly, we could be heading toward a nationwide civil war." There are a few murmurs in the crowd. Ian quiets them with a wave of his hand. "Our defense is not strong enough. If a coordinated attack took place now, the other corporations could take us out. We need to strengthen our defenses. We need to complete the Star Formula."

What? Is he crazy?

"Pardon me for asking, Commander," Official Forest asks, "but how do you plan to do this? We have been trying to complete the formula for years, but we simply don't have all thirteen."

The gleam in Ian's eyes is scary. Something's very wrong. "We know that the remaining three are in the Slump—most likely taking refuge with the resistance. We have been trying to find the rebels for this reason, but we need to expedite the search." He takes a sip from the cup sitting on his desk. "We will go to the Slump and weed out every single resident—resistance members included—capture them, and bring them back to our facilities. Through our intake process, we will collect the three remaining test kids and complete the procedure, attaining the formula and implementing it on our currently existing soldiers. Any surviving rebels will be imprisoned, interrogated, and terminated. We will do this, and then we will be invincible. No more war or rebellion will be possible."

It feels like someone has just pushed me off the top of a building. I am completely speechless.

Ian wants us to attack the Slump? There is no way to find everybody without burning the entire city down. But one look at his face, and I know that this is exactly what he is planning to do.

What is wrong with him? The Ian I know would never have suggested this.

I know for a fact that the rebels have the three remaining test kids. I will do *anything* to ensure that Making Perfect never gets their hands on them.

His words take a while to sink in and the room falls silent. As emotionless as most of these people are, the idea of going in and killing all of the Slump kids seems to have stunned them just as much as it has me.

Ian takes advantage of this silence, a malicious sneer forming on his lips. "The attack will happen tomorrow night. Bring as many soldiers and firearms as it takes. Flip the switches on all the soldiers as they board the transports. I want all thirteen test kids here, and I want the leaders of the resistance and the rest of the Slump…eliminated."

He ends the call.

The officials in the room break out into rapid conversation. But I don't care. This plan is ridiculous. He can't burn down the Slump—there's no way he could propose this if he has thought through the repercussions.

Rage is pouring out of every inch of my body. It takes all of my self-control not to storm out and slam the door behind me.

37

call Ian as soon as I exit the meeting. I am fuming.

"What the hell are you thinking?" I almost scream into the phone. "You can't just break into the Slump and kill all those kids! This is not you!"

"Yes, we can," he sneers. "We will find those remaining three if we have to burn down the whole damn city."

Fury rises in my chest, threatening to overwhelm me. I try to push it down. "Ian. Listen to me. Don't make any rash decisions. If you stick to protocol, you will be able to find all of them without completely eliminating your only source of more subjects. What if any of the three die during the attack? You'll never complete the formula. Everything will be lost."

"I trust that they have better survival instincts than that," he says. "We'll burn the edges and push them all into the center, trapping them and leaving them defenseless. It won't be difficult. Nobody wants to be burned."

"Listen to yourself. You want to burn down the only place you are able to take your test subjects from? Where are you going to put them all once you have them? Are you going to kill them?"

For a second, I think I have gotten to him. The line is silent—all I can hear is the faint whir of the ventilation system. I stop pacing and press my forehead against the wall of the hallway. He finally speaks again. "I don't have a choice."

I shake my head. "I can't believe this. Why the sudden rush? What's preventing you from continuing the way we have been? You're going to find them eventually."

"We've run out of time. We need them now," he snaps.

I lose it. "Ian, if you were ever my friend, listen to me now. This is a terrible—"

"I give the orders around here, Kace." His voice is unusually sharp. It sounds like his father's.

"I'm sorry, but this is ridiculous. I can't let you do this—"

"You don't have to let me do anything, Foster," he says, and I grit my teeth. "It's already done."

I shout his name. He hangs up the phone. I throw the phone against the wall.

We need to get out of here.

Get out of here before Ian turns the Slump into an inferno.

38

I sit on the edge of my bed, turning a little steel washer around in my fingers. It was only last night that Kace pulled Tyler and I out of our bunks to tell us his escape plan. Even though it's only a few hours away, I still can't believe it's actually happening.

We're actually getting out.

I keep running through Kace's plan in my head. After everyone's asleep, we're going to meet in the hallway behind the common room, and he's going to take us through the barracks' main entrance. We'll all be wearing soldier uniforms; since Kace is an official, this hopefully won't arouse any suspicion. We'll get under the fence through an old network of tunnels that stretch underneath the compound, catch the cargo train heading to the townhouses from one of the storage facilities, and cross the fence over to the Slump. Then, we will split up—some to find our families and others to warn the rebels—and get out of the region before Making Perfect can set foot in the rubble. Kace didn't tell us where we're going after that, but I didn't ask.

If all goes to plan, the trip shouldn't take longer than a few hours. It's about ten o'clock now, and my unit is just getting ready for bed. Tyler, who's a much better actor than I am, pretends convincingly that nothing is different, with his nonchalant appearance and a towel slung casually over his neck. I, on the other hand, am stiff with anticipation and barely able to tear my eyes away from my cold locker door where my stolen soldier uniform waits for midnight.

The washer drops from my fingers, clattering onto the concrete floor. Maggie walks by and picks it up.

"Summer, are you okay?" She hands me back the washer. "You've been playing with that thing for almost an hour."

I try to rub some of the rust off with my thumb. Has it really been that long? "Yeah, I'm fine. Just tired, that's all."

She narrows her eyes at me slightly, but doesn't drop the never-fading smile from her face. "Okay, if you say so. Just holler if you need anything."

She walks off, and guilt prickles my chest. In just a few hours, I'm going to be leaving every one of these people behind. All but Tyler. I didn't think it would bother me, but I've grown to care about them more than I expected.

As soon as I found out, I went to wake up Blayze. Despite the way he reacted to the initial idea in the training room that night, I needed to tell him anyway. When I found him in his bunk, he was asleep, the blanket kicked completely off his body. His face was scrunched up against his upper arm, a small bubble forming between his lips. I had to stifle a laugh. He was so deeply asleep that it was almost comical. I woke him up as quietly as I could, and we slowly made our way out into the hallway, being careful not to trip on any of the equipment lazily strewn across the floor.

The words tumbled out of me faster than I had planned. He took it in calmly, running his fingers through his disheveled hair. It was easy to see how tired he was, and I felt bad about waking him up, but this couldn't wait. After I finished, I stood there frozen, my heart almost beating out of my chest. There was only a momentary pause before he told me he was in. Relief washed over me like a wave, and a wide grin stretched across my lips. He didn't mention anything about Flame, but at that point, I wouldn't have cared if he did.

I hardly slept at all the rest of that night. I forced myself to wait until the next morning to tell Ocean, but when I stopped her on the way to breakfast, her reaction was not what I expected.

"I can't go," she said, shaking her head. "I'm sorry, Summer, but I can't go with you."

I furrowed my brow and looked at her in disbelief. "What are you talking about? You have to come."

"No, I can't." Her voice stays calm, but her eyes betray her sadness. "I don't have anyone left there. All my family and friends back home are gone. I don't want to move out of the region and live with a bunch of strangers. I have friends—a family—here. I belong with them, and I can't leave that behind."

I pleaded with her for over an hour, but she was unyielding. It was the chip. My face felt puffy even though I hadn't been crying. Although it was hard to accept her decision, I knew there was nothing I could do to change it. Still, I was losing a friend—one that I'd probably never see again—and I couldn't shake the sadness from my chest.

I hugged her tightly.

Jackson turns off the lights. It's just past eleven o'clock. Every minute that goes by feels like an eternity. I force myself to stay still, my hands still fidgeting with the washer, which has now become slippery with the oil from my fingers. I need to wait for Tyler's signal before we can go, but first, the whole unit has to be asleep.

After half an hour, he still hasn't given me the signal, and I start to worry that he's fallen asleep. But at exactly five minutes to twelve, he raises his hand, and I quietly slip out from under my covers. I slide open my locker door, careful not to wake Maggie up, and strap the uniform onto my body. The thick armor plates feel good tightened against my body. I tuck my hair into the helmet.

With Tyler beside me, I slip the little washer into my pocket and walk out of the barracks for the last time, not glancing back once.

▲   ▲   ▲

Ten minutes.

We've been waiting here ten minutes, and still nobody has shown up. Not even Kace. I'm desperately trying to keep calm, expecting the night patrol to round the corner any minute. Tyler is pacing up and down the closed door as I lean against the wall, rocking back and forth slowly. Both of us are too wound up to say a word to each other.

"Where are they?" I mutter the question under my breath for the fifth or sixth time. My eyes are glued to the door. He couldn't have forgotten, could he? I don't see how he could. Was he held up? Maybe Making Perfect found out about the plan and—

The door flies open, and Kace storms through, Sterling and Maggie right on his tail. His face is tight with annoyance. Sterling and Maggie look like they've just been jolted out of a very deep sleep, their uniforms hanging sloppily on their frames. Their hair is sticking out of their helmets at strange angles, and their eyes are wide with fear. This must be what took Kace so long.

What are they doing here?

I push back from the wall and place my hands on my hips. Kace walks over to us, trying to keep calm. He doesn't acknowledge his lateness.

"Have you already cut out your trackers?" he asks us. I shake my head. He pulls out a short, silver knife from his belt and wipes it on his pants. He extends his palm to me. "Give me your wrist."

I do, and he rolls up the sleeve, sliding the knife cleanly into my wrist. I try not to flinch, but the stinging intensifies as he moves the blade deeper. I bite my tongue. He seems to know exactly where the tracker is because he's dug it out within seconds. As soon as the knife exits my arm, I press my thumb onto the incision to stop the blood. The little rice-sized electronic pellet looks even smaller in his fingers as he kneels down and slips it into the air vent.

"Shouldn't we put those in our rooms? I doubt they'll believe all four of us spent the night in the ventilation system," Tyler pipes up, and Kace shakes his head, walking over to him.

"It doesn't matter," he says, cutting into Tyler's arm. "As long as you're in the building and not in the Slump, they won't see the difference."

I glance down nervously at the watch built into my uniform. Where is Blayze? Worry builds in my chest. Has something happened? I've got to go find him. There's no way I'm leaving without him, but if he doesn't get here soon, I'm going to kill him.

"There is no guarantee we'll get out," Kace's voice is clear. He slides the last of our trackers down the vent. "One mistake will mean recapture. This is the most difficult facility to break out of in the entire region. If they take us again, fight hard. The consequences are much worse for traitors than prisoners, even for test kids, and you don't want to be caught alive. Do exactly as I say. My orders are law. Understood?" There are nods all around. My stomach knots. He made it sound so easy at first. But it's too late to back out now. I have to take the chance. "Good. We'll give the other two a few more minutes."

The door opens again, and a huge weight is lifted off my shoulders as Blayze hurries through. That weight is quickly restored when I see Flame walk in behind him, biting her lip. Something flares in my gut, and I look at my feet. I glance up at Kace, expecting to find anger, but he simply nods at them. Blayze comes up next to me and squeezes my hand.

"All right, let's move. Keep close," says Kace. With a last glance at all of us, he turns and pushes through the doors.

I'm going to see my sisters again. I wonder how they're going to react. I was gone a long time.

The second we get in the open, the butterflies in my stomach kick up a notch. I hardly even notice the slight temperature change. The breeze is gentle and far warmer than the last time I walked through these doors. I feel strangely out of place in the armor strapped to my back. It looks so natural on Blayze, yet fits all the test kids in strange ways. I wish I could rip it off, but if I did, the cameras would pick us up right away.

We start down the dry dirt path toward the terminal building. Kace quickly maneuvers us away from the large hangars, which are bustling with activity. Officials, guards, and mechanics are busily milling around the AirTrans, attaching large cylindrical objects under the wings.

The fresh air feels good as it fills my lungs. Moonlight beats down on us as we walk, and I catch a glimpse of the buds beginning to appear on the few remaining trees. This place looks completely different from the last time I saw it. There are numerous clusters of guards patrolling the area, and I can almost feel the surveillance cameras focusing in on us. We're being watched everywhere.

We'll be lucky if we even make it to the tunnels.

A guard tightens his grip on his gun as we pass by. My heart is pounding. As soon as we get within sight of the terminal, Kace turns off the path and ducks behind the edge of a small potato-skin colored building. The large AirTrans disappear from sight, and Blayze walks up beside me. He leans toward me slightly, so his voice doesn't carry.

"What'd I miss?" he asks, and I shrug.

"Glad you could make it."

"Fell asleep," he mutters. I keep a careful eye on Kace as we walk back out onto the main paths toward the fence.

"Oh," I rub my eyes. "Well, we take the train to the townhous-es, make it to the Slump, warn the rebels, collect our families, and hopefully escape the region before Making Perfect arrives to blow it all up." Even though I've known about Making Perfect's attack plans since the night before, I still can't believe it. They're going to destroy the Slump. My *home*. They've decided to go kill, capture, and destroy the homes of all the innocent people they've banished there. It makes me sick.

He purses his lips as we round the corner. "I'm sorry about Flame. I know you didn't want her to come, but Kace pulled me aside this morning and told me to bring her. Apparently, her older brother Aaron is now in charge of the rebels and would probably want her out."

That's where I recognized the name from. Steele. Of course he'll want Flame out. But it still doesn't stifle my irritation.

"But how can she make it out? What about…you know…"

"Her enhancement?" He shrugs. "Kace drugged her earlier. It'll force her to be compliant, at least until we get her to Aaron. She'll be under constant supervision, but hopefully she won't do any-thing." I glance back at her and notice the faint fogginess in her step. "Then the rebels can figure out what to do with her."

"Okay," I say, looking back at him. "You've cut out your track-er, right?"

He smiles. "Yeah, right before I came. But I decided to bring it with me as a memento." He pats his pocket innocently. "You know, as a memory of all my good times here."

"Shut up." But his joking quells my worry.

Kace comes up behind a small storage building and stops. We're very close to the fence now, and I can hear the faint buzz of electricity pulsing through its wires. He drops onto his knees and digs into the dirt. He feels around for a moment before grabbing ahold of a handle. He yanks it up with all his strength.

A mixture of dirt, sand, grass, and rocks tumbles as he lifts up the narrow trapdoor. A small cloud of dust billows up into my eyes, and I cough softly, squeezing them shut. When I'm able to blink them open, I peer down into the gaping hole in the ground, but it's too dark to see what's inside.

Kace waves us over and urgently ushers us into the hole. Tyler goes first, closely followed by Maggie. When it's my turn, I slowly lower my leg into the gap until it finds the ladder. The rusty metal quivers slightly under my weight. I can feel Tyler's and Maggie's movements as they travel downward.

"Aren't you coming?" I hiss at Kace. He looks like he's about to hit me.

"Yes," he grumbles. "Just wait for me at the bottom; I've got to close up after the others go down."

Okay. I grip the ladder tightly and start down. The darkness intensifies the farther I get from Kace and the others. I try to focus on the ladder and not think about the musty smell wafting up from the tunnels below. There's a thud under me, closely followed by another. Before I know it, the ladder stops and I hesitantly hop to the ground. I underestimate the drop slightly and my stomach leaps up into my throat, but I right myself and manage to land on my feet.

It's dark and muggy, and I can't see the ground. Kace must've closed the trapdoor. I can hear Tyler's and Maggie's breathing, but I can't make out their faces. There's another thud behind me, and I spin around.

There's a long moment of silence before something clicks to my right and a beam of yellow light appears.

Blayze adjusts the settings on the left forearm of his uniform, where the light is coming from. We have flashlights? I didn't know we had those. I feel around on my uniform before pressing one of the knobs. The flashlight jumps to life, shining a circle of light on Kace and Flame, who've just dropped from the ladder.

"Everyone, turn on your lights," Kace orders. "I've never traveled this part of the network before, but it's supposed to be fairly easy if we take the right passages. We have to move fast if we're going to get to the Slump before Making Perfect does." He points his light into the mouth of the tunnel in front of us, and my jaw drops.

These aren't just tunnels. This is the old airport's luggage sorting network.

Old, rusty conveyor belts line the floors. The blades are either completely ripped or gone altogether, making the machinery look naked. Cobwebs are everywhere, and the floor and walls look like they've been decaying for hundreds of years. The remains of torn suitcases and various other luggage containers lie off to the side, almost completely covered with rubble.

This whole place looks ready to collapse on our heads.

Everybody turns on their uniform lights and Kace leads us into the tunnels. A spider nearly the size of my palm recedes into the shadows when I point my light at the wall. As we reach the first conveyor belt, we pick up our pace to a jog.

"These tunnels were originally used to sort the baggage coming to and from the airport," Kace explains as we run. "Since the airport was much bigger than the compound is today, the net-work stretches all around it and even goes under the fence. I doubt Making Perfect even knows it exists, and if they do, they don't care. The tunnels are mostly used by the rebels now, but obviously, not often."

I keep my flashlight pointed ahead of me, trying to make sure I don't trip. Kace takes a sharp right that I almost miss but follow at the last second. It's surprisingly cold down here, given the weather outside. The slight slope of the tracks reveals that we're traveling downward, and it gets a little bit chillier with every turn we make.

I hope Kace knows where we're going. It would be way too easy to get lost in here. I leap over a protruding metal rod and land in a wide puddle, spraying the legs of my tracksuit with mud. A fat, gray rat scampers from under my feet. A shiver runs down my spine. I cringe to think of the other critters lurking in the darkness, and I try to keep my light only where I'm stepping.

As hard as I try to keep quiet, my boots thump loudly on the dirt, and so do everyone else's. We sound like a herd of elephants. I wouldn't be surprised if the guards could hear us through the ground. We need to stop jogging. Kace makes another sharp turn, and a metal crate comes out of nowhere, tripping me. I fall to my knees and curse under my breath. I rub the palms of my hands on my tracksuit pants to rid them of the embedded gravel. When I stand up, Tyler is there, breathing heavily.

"Do you think he knows where he's going?" he asks. He glances at Kace, who's moving ahead, almost out of range of our flashlights. The others are right behind him. We start running again so as not to be left behind. Tyler adds, "This place is kind of freaking me out."

I purse my lips. "He'd better. Hold on."

I quicken my jog to catch up with Kace. This armor feels so much heavier than I expected it to. It's like I'm running through tar. The others don't seem to be doing much better, though. Sterling and Maggie are so red they look like they're about to pass out. My legs feel ready to fall off by the time I reach Kace. His face is knit together, focusing intensely on the path ahead. I dodge another bent rod of metal. My breaths start getting heavier, and I have to work to get my words out.

"Can we cool it with the running? A bunch of us look ready to pass out."

He doesn't slow down. "Do you want to get out of here on time or not?" I purse my lips.

"Are you sure you know where you're going?" I ask him. He lets out an annoyed sigh and doesn't look at me.

"Pretty sure," he grumbles. "I know the tunnels well. We're right on schedule." I scoff.

"I thought you'd never been in them," I say, remembering what he said earlier.

"I've discussed them a lot. Plus, I studied the map."

"That's not enough."

"Yes, it is."

"No, it's not."

He stops abruptly, turning on me. "Listen, if you want to get out of here, this is your best shot. So get back in line and let me focus."

He starts running again, and I do what he says. My legs are screaming at me to stop, but I force myself to keep going. When I reach Tyler again, I rub my eyes.

"What did he say?" he asks, eagerly.

"He read the map."

"That's it?" he looks shocked. "That's not enough."

"That's what I told him."

Tyler falls quiet as Kace rounds a bend. Finally, after an excruciating eternity, he slows our pace to a fast walk. Blayze is now helping Sterling along. His thin, frail body gave out a while ago. I'm surprised he's made it this far. He's lived in a cage his whole life. As we continue to meander along, my mind begins to wander. It feels like we've been in here for hours, though my watch reveals that it's only been twenty minutes.

I wonder how long it's going to take for the officials to realize that we're gone.

I shine my light onto the wall. Practically all of it has been eroded, although its basic structure is still there. The tunnel gets noticeably narrower, and the path gets more uneven. I have to make an effort not to trip on the rocks. Long, glistening oil puddles start dotting the ground, and the gravel-ridden dirt turns to mud. I look up at the rest of the group and realize that I'm now bringing up the rear. I roll my eyes and start jogging faster to catch up. As I run, I keep my light on the wall. I notice another ladder, like the others earlier in the tunnels, leading up to a sealed trapdoor above.

I stop in my tracks, narrowing my eyes. This ladder looks different from the others. Its rungs are thicker, and the metal is a slightly darker shade. My light reflects off it. I squint and take a step closer to it, reaching out to run my fingers over the metal. It's glossy. Rust-free. New.

My stomach clenches.

"Blayze!" I call out. "Get over here."

Thankfully, he hears me. I can hear the crunching of his boots against the gravel as he runs over.

"What?" he asks, his cheeks flushed. I nod at the ladder.

"I don't think we're alone in here."

He rubs his eyes. "I really hope you're kidding."

I shake my head, looking up at the trapdoor. Kace was wrong. Making Perfect must know about the tunnels. I can't believe the rebels haven't noticed this before.

Or what if Making Perfect is allowing them to get out?

I shake my head. I'm not thinking straight. Of course Making Perfect wouldn't let them get away. They must've found another way out.

Something moves right in front of my nose, and I flinch back. When I lean in closer, I find myself staring into a little black lens.

A camera.

39

My heart races.

I grab Blayze's arm. "Run."

"Wait, what's going on?"

I start running. I need to tell Kace. "Just trust me."

With Blayze by my side, I catch up with Kace. He notices the panicked look in my eyes, but doesn't acknowledge it.

"What now? Are you tired of walking?"

"Making Perfect knows we're here," I say, wishing he would move faster. "We need to get out right now."

He scoffs. I want to scream. "There's no way Making Perfect knows we're here. The rebels have used these tunnels for—"

A blaring alarm cuts him off. The sound pierces my ears so painfully that I cup my hands over them. Lights flash, intermittently illuminating the tunnels. Kace looks around as the realization crosses his face. Sterling and Maggie are huddled together against the wall, hiding from the sound. Tyler, knowing exactly what's going on, is desperately trying to coax them up. Flame looks ready to sink into the floor.

Kace tries to regain his composure. "We have to run. Follow me!"

We start to sprint down the tunnels. With my help, Tyler manages to get Sterling and Maggie upright and moving after Kace. He hoists a shaking Maggie onto his shoulders, and I urge Sterling to run in front of me. I keep glancing behind us, waiting for a troop of officials to suddenly appear out of the darkness and shoot us down. All the ladders down this tunnel are the same glossy metal as the last. I hope they didn't see who it was in that camera. If they did, they're going to shut the entire region down to ensure we don't get to the Slump.

The tunnel takes an unexpected drop, though I don't notice it until I'm falling through the air. I come down hard onto the ground, a dull ache reverberating through my bones. The flashing lights are brighter down here. As I take a step forward, water splashes up, hitting my face. I look down. The water is slowly rising above my ankles.

"Um…Kace?" I shout over the sound of the deafening alarm. "What's happening?"

"The tunnels are flooding. They're trying to flush us out."

Great. The water is rising faster now. It's at my knees. Maggie is sobbing on Tyler's back. I lock eyes with Blayze, who's on the other side of Kace. There's a spark of genuine panic in his eyes. I start toward him, but I'm paralyzed by a shrill howl from the tunnel behind us. Not a shout. A howl. Shivers run up my spine. How are we supposed to run through the water? The howls are getting closer now, but there's something off about them. They sound almost… human.

"Summer!" Kace snaps me out of my daze. "*Let's go!*"

I wade through the water as fast as I can, but it's no good. I'm going to have to swim.

Luckily, swimming isn't new to me. Tyler and I used to go to the river in the summer after our food runs. As most of the river in the Slump is polluted, you have to be careful where you go in, and you can't swallow any water. But we found one place near a dock that was safe to go in.

Since I was terrified of drowning, I would scramble to get back to the dock after jumping off, and I never stayed in the water for very long. But now, I have no choice. I push off from the tunnel floor and paddle forward as fast as I can.

If I thought running in the armor was hard, swimming in it is ten times worse. By the time I reach Blayze, I feel like I've already used up all my energy.

Blayze has stopped. He looks completely freaked out. Joining him, I have to stand on my tiptoes to touch the floor. "What are you doing?" I ask.

Another howl sounds. It's really close now. My survival instincts kick in. The others are already ahead of us. I tug him forward. "Blayze, move!"

"I...I..." he stammers. He looks just past me and turns white. His mouth opens slightly. I look over my shoulder.

It takes all of my self-control not to scream. The creature stands above us, right on the edge of the drop. It's completely bent over, like a human running on their hands and feet. I can see the curved spine rippling at a very sharp angle. Long metal talons have been inserted where fingers used to be. Although it's partially hidden by the flashing lights, I can see it well enough to know it's got scales covering the left side of its face and body.

This must've been an experiment gone very, *very* wrong.

What are these things?

The creature raises his head and howls again. Without thinking twice, Blayze and I dive into the water, taking off after the others. I hear a splash and know that it's jumped in after us. A few more splashes follow—there must be a pack of them. I try to focus on swimming and on fighting the resistance of the armor. It's weighing me down so much that I'm winded only after a few paddles. Blayze cuts through the water effortlessly, his armor not seeming to bother him. The adrenaline pumping through my veins forces me to keep going, and I get a sudden burst of energy, but just as I'm about to catch up with him I feel a sharp talon rip into my calf and pull me backward.

I scream. My voice is cut off when the creature pulls me under the surface. As soon as I'm underwater, all the noise stops. I can hardly hear the alarm anymore. It's almost peaceful. I don't have time to enjoy it, however, because the second I force my eyes open I find myself face-to-face with the creature. Up close, it looks strangely human. Though its body has been mutated beyond recognition, its eyes are still those of a person—bright green and narrowed with fury.

What did Making Perfect do to these people?

It is growling at me as it swiftly rakes its sharp metal over my shoulder, ripping through the armor. I cry out in pain and kick out with my boot. The kick lands on its torso but only succeeds in angering it further. Its gills are flaring. It slams me against the wall of the tunnel, my head hitting the post of a ladder. Black spots pepper my vision. Blood is coloring the water around me. I try to fight my way to the surface for air, but I can't. Two more mutants almost identical to the first whip past me, trying to catch the others.

My lungs are burning, and the creature takes a swipe at my throat. I manage to dodge it but before it can try again, it stops. Its grip loosens. It falls limply off me and floats to the surface of the water.

Someone grabs my armor and pulls me to the surface. I gasp for air. Blayze, treading water in front of me, pulls his knife out of the dead mutant.

"Thanks," I say, trying to calm my rapidly beating heart. He mumbles something in return, but I can't make it out. There's a guttural scream from up ahead, and we exchange a quick glance before taking off toward the others.

The water level is still rising and doesn't show any sign of stopping. I swim faster than ever, my head pounding. As most of us are unarmed, it's hard to fend off the agile mutants. Blayze and I throw ourselves into the mess. I push myself off the bottom and pull one of the creatures off Sterling, who's hacking at it with a metal pole and holding on to a ladder for dear life. It spins around quickly, snapping at my head. This one has teeth just as sharp as its claws. I duck down, water splashing in my eyes. I reach over, gathering all my strength, and rip off a rung of the ladder as adrenaline surges through my body. I guess this ability can come in handy. When it tries to bite me again, I shove the sharp end of the pole into its throat. It lets out a shrill scream, and I thrust the pole forward, pushing the creature underwater. It doesn't resurface.

"You good?" I ask Sterling, whose sole good eye is as big as a moon. He nods silently and looks back up at the trapdoor. Even on the top rung, his entire body is submerged below the shoulders. We only have a few minutes until we're going to be completely underwater. I hear someone scream my name, and I spin around, barely missing a pair of razor-sharp claws swinging at my head.

"Summer!" Kace shouts. I rip off another rung of the ladder, thrusting it at the mutant. I miss, and it dives underwater. Kace says something else, but I don't catch it over the alarm. I call out to him, but he is pushed underwater.

What did he say?

"The ladders…of course," Sterling mutters above me, and I glance up at him.

Of course? It doesn't seem very obvious to me.

Sterling doesn't skip a beat. "Summer, can you dive to the bottom and tell me if you see any numbers on the wall?"

"Numbers on the wall?" I say. "Be more specific?"

Sterling sucks in a breath. The water is rising really fast. We only have about a foot of air left. To my left, Blayze slashes another mutant across the face with his dagger. As fast as we keep killing these things, they just keep coming. There's blood all around us now, like we're swimming in a huge pool of ketchup.

"Think. If Making Perfect set this up as a security system, they'd want a way to get out of here from both the inside and the outside. But that system couldn't be accessed by everybody, or it would defeat the purpose. They need a way to lock it. But everything that's locked must be opened. We're looking for a control box. Keep your eye out for numbers. You'll need a code to open it, but come up if you see anything," he orders frantically. "And give me your pole," he quickly adds.

I nod, handing it over. He hits a mutant over the head as it leaps out of the water. He looks like he's playing a messed-up game of whack-a-mole. I look down at the water below, take a deep breath, and dive under.

I can barely see anything as I pull myself down the ladder. The armor must have some sort of flotation built into it, because it keeps trying to lift me up. My lungs start to clench. I reach the bottom of the ladder, looking and feeling around for the numbers. I can't find anything. My hand just finds metal.

If I could scoff underwater, I would. There's nothing here. I'm about to push back up when something catches me eye. A glint of metal. I rub my hand against it to wipe the clay off. As soon as it's clean enough to look at, a weight is lifted from my shoulders. Sterling was right.

This control box is the size of a microwave, with the numbers *4778* branded on boldly. I swim up to it, running my fingers along the sides. It's fused so tightly that I can't even wedge a fingernail in the gap. A small touchpad lies in the front. A number keypad.

My lungs on fire, I push off the floor and propel myself toward the top.

When I break the surface, there are only a few inches of air left. Everybody's completely underwater, only briefly coming up for air. I can't even see most of them.

"Did you find it?" Sterling asks, and I nod. His face lights up. "What were the numbers on the front?"

I try to remember. "Four-seven-seven..." What was the last one? "Eight, I think."

He submerges again for a second. "Go! Hurry! We only have a minute. The code should be seven-four-seven-eight. When you get—"

"No!" I scream as a mutant pulls him under. I shout in frustration. What do I do once I open it? Sterling, come back! But he doesn't. I'm alone.

Taking the biggest breath I can, I dive back down to the bottom. I find the panel and tap it frantically with my finger. It illuminates. I try to ignore the pressure building in my lungs. I can't get sloppy. I type in the code, and the screen flashes green. I pry the door open, revealing another control panel filled with little buttons and switches. The labels are illegible. I hear a muffled scream above me and know there are only a few seconds left. Something cuts through my calf, and I scream. I dodge the creature's next swipe and try to kick it away. Searing pain shoots through my leg, and I chomp down on my tongue. I pull myself back toward the control panel and try to read the labels. They seem to be organized into some sort of chart. Not a chart—a map. A map of the whole tunnel network. Little green dots mark where all the other control panels are located—there's one every four ladders or so. But there are only buttons in one section of the map, not everywhere else. That's where we must be. Each box must only control the doors in its general vicinity. Colors start to dot my vision, and I feel light-headed. My lungs are so tight that my chest is about to implode. Trying to ignore the pain, I press all the buttons with my palm.

Suddenly, everything is silent. I'm afraid I pushed the wrong thing. The alarm stops ringing, and the mutants retreat to the other side of the tunnel. Weakly, I push off and let my armor carry me to the surface.

But there is no surface. My head bangs against metal. I start to panic. I can't breathe. I can't breathe! I look around, but I can't see anything other than the red-stained water. Where's the ladder? Did it work? Did everyone else get out? I try to swim, but I collide into the wall. My hand feels around but everything is smooth. Nothing.

I give up. I can't hold my breath any longer. It comes out of me in a long stream of bubbles. I squeeze my eyes shut. But just as the darkness is about to pull me under, someone roughly yanks me upward.

The second my head breaks the surface, my lungs desperately fill up. Rough hands pull me out of the water, and I collapse on a crinkling pile of leaves. My body shivers uncontrollably, and I suck in deep breaths. I tuck my knees to my chest. I don't remember it being so cold. My hair sticks to my face and to the dead leaves around it.

My body is beyond exhausted. I could lie here forever.

"Yeah, Summer!" I hear Sterling exclaim. "That was *epic*!"

Even after all the weird things that just happened, hearing Sterling use the word "epic" is probably the weirdest.

I use all of my remaining energy to prop myself in a sitting position. I tuck the wet strands of hair behind my ears, trying to wring some of the water out. Thankfully, everybody else got out, though they look just as tired and banged up as I do. Even Flame, who never seems to get injured, sports a long gash down her thigh. The trapdoor leading down to the tunnels has already closed, leaving the seven of us collapsed in the middle of the woods. I can't even see the fence.

My body screams in agony, and I suddenly become very aware of the pain. And the smell. I smell gross.

My calf and shoulder got the worst of it. I pull off one of my boots, wriggling out of my sock. It makes a loud squishing sound when it comes off my foot, and I squeeze all the water out of it. I rip it down the side and tie it tightly around my leg. It doesn't make it feel much better, but there isn't much else I can do.

I look over at Blayze and Tyler. Blayze has a scratch on his cheek, just below his eye. He's dabbing it with his sleeve to stop the bleeding, but other than that, he only looks tired. Tyler is wrapping his left forearm in a ripped piece of cloth, but he also seems okay. Kace pulls out his pack, rummaging through its contents before pulling out a device the size of my palm.

"We can't stick around here," he tells us. "Making Perfect will be able to track where we exited. That doesn't give us long. We need to get to the train." He types something into the device. "It isn't far from here—the flooding just pushed us off course."

I swallow. When I try to talk, my voice is raspy. "What were those things? I thought the tunnels were abandoned."

Kace nods, tiredly. "I did, too. But we were wrong. Making Perfect must've recently rigged them with a security system to fight off the rebels." He runs his hand over his hair. His amber eyes are dull. "On the bright side, they obviously didn't know who we were. There's no way they would've sent those things at us if they knew how many of you were test kids. But that doesn't mean they won't come after us." He turns to the rest of the group. "We have to move. You can rest on the train."

I groan but get up anyway. I hurt everywhere. All I want to do is lie down and close my eyes. I don't remember ever being this tired. We follow the path of trapdoors on the ground until we reach the storage facility. It's one of the smaller ones in the region, but they have a delivery to make to the townhouses tonight, so there's a little more activity. A large cargo train is being loaded with boxes. Kace sneaks us around the back so we won't be spotted. When he hoists himself through an open door and disappears inside, we follow him.

The small, tightly packed space is filled with large wooden crates and cardboard boxes. We crawl all the way to the back and nestle ourselves among them. Tyler slumps down against one of the crates, leaning his head down on his knees. Flame disappears behind a pile of boxes. I suppress a yawn and collapse down into the corner, sliding my legs out in front of me.

After a few minutes, the door slides shut. Darkness envelops us. Blayze sits down on the other side of the cargo container. I feel the train come alive under me. It slowly picks up speed. I manage a smile. We're actually on our way. I'm going home.

Kace is standing by the door. "I'll take first watch. Try to get some rest. We're not in the clear yet."

I lean my head against the wall. Shivers run through me, and I cross my arms tightly over my chest to trap in the heat. I would give anything for a blanket right now. My armor is beginning to dry, but it provides nowhere close to enough insulation. I probably also need to treat my cuts. My teeth begin to chatter, and I bite my lip.

What if we don't get to the Slump in time? What if Making Perfect is already there? Kace assured me that the attack wouldn't happen until later tonight, but what if he was wrong? He was wrong about the tunnel. Everybody could be dead by the time we get there.

I wish there was a way I could warn Lily and Tory about the attack. Just sitting here knowing it's out of my control is killing me.

I try to sleep, but the pain and cold won't let me. But I am so tired that staying awake is almost painful. I grit my teeth and try not to cry from frustration. I hurt so much.

I curl up on the floor, desperately trying to get warm. The faces of those mutant creatures won't leave my head. They were so scary looking, but human at the same time. And they weren't all the same. Could they really be experiments gone wrong? Making Perfect must've just changed something in their brains, put talons on them, and thrown them in there when they set up the security system. The thought makes me sick. Those...*monsters* used to be people. Just like us.

I block out the throbbing of my leg and shoulder. There is nothing I can do about it anyway. After about half an hour, I hear a faint rustle by my head.

"Couldn't sleep either?" I look up and see Blayze sit down against the wall beside me. I shake my head, sitting up again.

"No way." I hang my head down and listen to the rumble of the train. The blood on his face has dried, and so has his hair, but his uniform is just as wet as mine. Are these things designed to hold in water?

"Have you been thinking about the mutants?" he asks. I twirl my bootlace around my finger.

"I guess...I mean, a little," I admit. "How did you know?"

"Because I know you," he says. "I didn't realize what they were until I looked into their eyes. It makes me sick."

I nod. "And to think of all the new ones they're going to have to make to replace the ones we killed..." I shudder. "I'm just glad we're out of there."

"Yeah," he sighs. I notice the creases in his forehead and wonder what he's been thinking about. Blayze hasn't mentioned anything about having remaining family in the Slump. His mom passed away about four years ago, and his dad left without word when he was seven, taking his older sister with him. Who knows where they went, but chances are it isn't the Slump. Although he hardly ever talks about it, I know that having been abandoned hit him hard. I glance over at him. His only family is Flame and her brother, Aaron.

I swallow and pull the little washer out of my pocket, turning it around in my fingers. I'm surprised I didn't lose it in the tunnels. I don't know why, but the little silver disk is comforting. I rub the metal surface with my wet finger. Blayze notices and raises his eyebrows at me.

"What?"

He smirks slightly. "You brought that from your bunk?" he asks.

"Yeah. What's so funny?"

"I bet the rebels have washers, too. You can add to your collection."

I shake my head, melting under his warm eyes. "You're weird."

"That's funny, coming from you."

I shove him with my good shoulder, but it hardly has any strength behind it. The train goes around a sharp bend, and I lurch forward. A loud bang rings through the car and I jump, looking around to find that one of the crates has fallen over. Maggie is laughing so hard that she's curled up in fetal position, and Kace is cursing loud enough for all of us to hear.

I look back over at Blayze to find that he's asleep. I envy his ability to nod off so quickly. He hardly looks peaceful, but he is already deeply asleep.

Seeing him sleeping brings an unintentional yawn to my lips. I rest my forehead on my knees, willing myself to get some sleep. It doesn't work, and I sit back up. I'm too nervous to sleep.

After a few minutes, I feel a weight fall down onto my shoulder and glance over. Blayze has slumped over from his place on the wall, his head leaning heavily against my shoulder. He's still sleeping. He starts to slip, and I shrug him off so he's lying with his head on my leg. He stirs, a sigh slipping through his lips.

I can't help but smile.

I'm going home.

40

I wake up to a hand over my mouth.

My eyes shoot open, and I start to scream, but then I see Blayze crouching down in front of me with his finger pressed to his lips. I nod, and he removes his hand. I look around, all the exhaustion leaving my body in one fell swoop. Tyler seems to have fallen asleep as well and is only just stirring. Kace, Flame, Sterling, and Maggie are all crowded by the open door of the car and staring out at the darkness. I grab Blayze's hand, and he pulls me up. A dull ache shoots up my leg, but it's not nearly as bad as it was earlier. Even my armor is drier. I can feel the train slowing down under me—we must be in the townhouses.

Kace silently gestures for us to come over. Without even looking, I know exactly where we are. The biggest train station in the townhouses—Thompson—is right past the trees outside. All the trains from Making Perfect arrive here. There are two train lines that branch off it to take commuters to more specific destinations, but they both stem from Thompson. My mom used to bring me, Lily, and Tory here to meet Dad straight off the train on holidays. After he passed through screening, he'd come bounding up to us, pick us up one by one, and spin us around before taking us out for treats. Most other days he'd catch one of the other lines that stopped in our district.

Supplies are also delivered there before being distributed to the different communities. Since Thomson is one of the most heavily guarded areas in the region, we have to try and jump out now. We'll be caught otherwise. However, since the track is elevated and the train is still moving at a remarkable speed, jumping out would be suicide. We will have to leap off right before the station and take our chances or somehow make it through Thomson without being spotted. Both sound highly improbable. I hope Kace has a plan.

Tyler walks up to the group, rubbing his eyes free of sleep. I lean out of the door slightly, just enough to see the light of the station approaching. I still can't see the ground through the darkness. But as we get closer to Thomson, I begin to see it more clearly. It's not as far as I thought. I look at Kace, who still has his eyes fixated on Thomson, and grit my teeth.

The ground is close enough to jump…Why aren't we jumping? If we don't, we'll be caught. It doesn't matter that we're in soldier uniforms. They're now on the lookout for us.

"Come on, we have to jump," I say. Kace ignores me. "The ground is close enough now! We have to go!"

"It's too far; we have to wait," he snaps back, and I glance at the approaching lights. Soon it will be too late. Fear blazes through me.

Just as we're about to break out of the woods, I can't take it anymore and launch myself out of the train. There's a weightless moment, and I suck in a breath, fearing that I misjudged the height. I start to fall, and my stomach flies up to my throat. I bend my knees, trying to ready myself for the impact, but I hit the ground before I can even raise my hands to protect my head. The wet, dead leaves coating the forest floor help break my fall, but I still land on my side, my shoulder hitting something hard. I hear a thud to my right and look over to see Blayze collapsed to his hands and knees, recovering from the fall. Flame lands a few seconds later, right on Blayze's tail. There are a few more thuds as the rest of our group follows my example. The woods conceal us pretty well, although I can see Thomson clearly from where I am. The guards pace up and down the border like lions, ready to thoroughly check the train when it arrives. I can see the car we were in, still wide open and completely exposed. There's no way we would've been able to get out if we had stayed on the train. We would've been—

I feel like I'm hit by a bulldozer as a force lifts me up and slams my body into the nearest tree. Kace's hands dig into my shoulders, and I let out a cry.

"What the hell was that?" he hisses at me, his voice full of venom. Despite his rage, he's careful to stay quiet. "You could've gotten us all killed."

"So could you if we'd stayed on that train!" I hiss back. "If we hadn't jumped out, we'd have been caught by now."

"I don't care! It was my call to make." I don't think I've ever seen him so angry before. His face is cold as stone.

"But your call was stupid!"

"You directly disobeyed an order. I am the one who is getting you out of here. I am the one in charge!"

Suddenly, he is pulled off me, and Blayze shoves him backward. Kace falls down, gritting his teeth.

"Leave her alone," Blayze snarls. "Do you hear yourself? She saved us. We would all be caught right now if we hadn't jumped. You're going to get us all killed if you don't shut up." He glances over his shoulder at the station. "Now let's get through the fence and get out of here before this whole mission falls apart."

Kace looks at him for a minute before finally nodding, walking away from us and deeper into the woods. Tyler raises his eyebrows as if to ask, *Are you okay?* Sterling and Maggie take off after Kace like ducklings. Flame looks at us for a minute before running off herself. I look at Blayze with wide eyes. He takes a deep breath to compose himself before turning back to me.

"We should probably follow him," he says, and I nod. I push off from the tree and walk with him away from the train tracks. Kace is just close enough to be seen as he leads us deeper into the woods and toward the fence. I hope he knows what he's doing this time. I always pictured the fence to be impenetrable, but it'd better not be.

"Thanks," I say to Blayze after a few minutes of walking.

He winks at me and smiles. "Anytime. You were right—if we'd waited until the station, we'd have all been caught."

"Yeah." I shrug. "Well, thanks."

Kace's way through the fence turns out to be no more than a shallow ditch. I am skeptical at first, but when he drops to his stomach and slides under, I am quick to follow. This part of the Slump is unfamiliar to me. I normally tried to stay away from the border. We make our way toward the buildings through a drying marsh with tall grasses. I am relieved at how easy it is to stay hidden.

The Slump is dead silent when we enter it. Normally, there's quite a bit of activity here at night, typically involving the Black Spiders, but tonight everything's quiet.

Good. Making Perfect isn't here yet.

The level of anticipation is building in my body. As we near the center of the city, I can't suppress a smile. This is the Slump. I'm actually here, and it's not a dream.

We pass the market, and my heart pounds. It's taking all the self-control I have not to break from the group and make a beeline back to the hotel. I glance down at my watch. It's a little past four.

Please, Lil and Tor, be okay.

Kace stops us just past the market, at the golden DNA statue where Tyler and I used to meet.

"We have about an hour before the scheduled attack," Kace says. "This will give us plenty of time to gather everyone and escape before they arrive, if we move fast. I'm going to gather Troop Five. Flame, Sterling, and Maggie, come with me. Flame, your brother will be happy to see you." He looks at me and Tyler. "I assume you won't leave without your families, so you are free to go get them and meet us all back here." He doesn't even acknowledge Blayze. "TERC's fence has a weak link only five minutes that way." He nods in the direction of the market. "It's bigger than the last one, so it'll be easier for us all to get through. They're expecting us. We'll take refuge there until we can formulate a plan for further action."

TERC? We're escaping to TERC? That's the big plan? What happens if TERC kicks us out? I don't ask, as Kace seems pretty certain about this part of his plan and nothing I could say would add anything. Besides, his idea sounds better than staying here, so I don't overthink it.

"Blayze, where are you going?" Kace asks, swallowing back his hostility.

"I'll go with Summer." He looks at me with a glance that seems to say, *Is that okay?* I nod.

Kace turns to go. "Back here in an hour. We can't wait for you," he says before running off with Sterling and Maggie on his tail.

"You good?" Tyler touches my shoulder and I nod.

"Let's go." I affirm and glance at Blayze. "Follow me, we've got to move fast."

And we're off. I have traveled this route so many times in my life that I could do it blindfolded. The cracked asphalt is familiar under my feet. I anticipate every pothole, every turn. I feel so free. I never thought I'd be so relieved to be back in this dirty, horrific, putrid city that I'd wanted to escape for years.

Blayze and I don't say a word to each other. Tyler breaks off from us about two streets before mine to go find Michael and Riley. I hope for his sake that they're okay and that Lily has been keeping an eye on them. By the time we reach my street, my legs are shaking violently and my lungs are burning, but I don't care. Even in the darkness, I can make out the old hotel's sign clearly. Some of the electricity seems to have returned to it—the red lights are flickering in the night. I stand there for a second, trying to contain my excitement. I'm about to see Lily and Tory again. And Theo. Oh my God, Theo!

I start forward when Blayze grabs my arm. I almost forgot he was there. His face is flushed from running.

"Summer," he says between breaths. He looks worried. "What if they're not there?"

"What?" I chuckle. It takes a minute for me to realize he's serious. "They're going to be there." He opens his mouth to say something, but I grab his shoulders. "Don't worry. They're going to be there."

Before he can stop me, I am running down the street and pushing into the lobby of the hotel.

I don't skip a beat, running into the emergency stairs and taking two at a time. We have to move really fast if we're going to be back at the market in time. I reach the fourth floor and push the doors open, running over to our threshold. I pause, my hand hovering over the handle while I try to steady my breaths.

What if they don't want to see me?

I shake my head. Of course they'll want to see me. They're my sisters.

I open the door to our room and walk in. I look around, my eyes widening.

My stomach tightens.

My jaw drops.

Blayze was right.

There's nobody here.

41

I t feels like I've just been thrown out the window. I'm in free fall.
The entire room is barren. All of our possessions, including the
mattresses and the supplies stowed away in the cabinets, are gone. I
rush to the middle of the room, looking around frantically.

"Lily!" I shout. "Tory? Where are you?"

Do I have the right room? I hope I don't, but with one glance
down at the etchings next to where my bed used to be, I know I do.

I push aside our old dresser, revealing the passage into the wall.
Empty. I check the cabinet I stowed Theo in the night I got taken.
Empty.

Panic overwhelms me.

"Where did you go?" my voice rises. Did Making Perfect take
them? They could've. Other people in the building could've stolen
the furniture, and Theo could've run away.

No. They have to be here. Maybe they're in a different room.

I run to the hallway to check, but before I can get there, Blayze
appears in the threshold. His expression changes instantly as he sees
the look of terror on my face.

"They're not here," I say, pushing past him to get out in the
hallway. Ignoring his attempts to calm me, I run from door to door,
barging into the rooms and finding them all empty. Frustration
overwhelming me, I slam my hands against the wall, pounding it
as hard as I can. My fists break through the plaster.

Stupid, *stupid*! They're not here! I'm too late!

Closing my eyes, I lean my forehead against the wall. Blayze rushes up behind me and pulls me back, away from the hole I created. My fists are trembling.

"Hey," he turns me around to face him, and I sniffle back tears, "stop it. You're—"

"What if Making Perfect took them?" I cut him off. "I wasn't here for them. Tory was sick when I left, and Lily is only thirteen. No—fourteen by now. How long do you think they could've lasted with no reliable source of food? If Making Perfect came, they'd have no way to defend themselves."

"Your sisters are smart," he assures me. I shake my head, cursing under my breath. "They were fine. If they're not here, where do you think they could've gone?"

I try to straighten my thoughts. Where would I have gone? After finding one test kid in this building, Making Perfect must've come back to try and find more. If it became unsafe, of course my sisters would want to leave.

But where did they go? There isn't any other place. The only place we've ever lived is the hotel. Where else could they have gone?

I stare into Blayze's hopeful eyes, searching desperately for the answer.

Then, I think of it.

Tyler's.

Lily and Tory went to Tyler's.

Of course they did. As soon as they realized Michael and Riley were alone, they moved in to make sure they were safe. Besides, even though Tyler's apartment is smaller than ours, it's better insulated. A perfect hideaway for the winter.

"Oh my God," I laugh, tears of relief streaming down my face. "Oh my God, Blayze, they went to Tyler's! We have to go!" I dash down the hallway, not even bothering to check if he's following me. They're not in Making Perfect. They're okay!

Blayze runs beside me, and we dart down the stairs and back out onto the street. But just as we cut into the alley leading to the building, there's a loud roar from the sky and I stop. I glance up, craning my neck, and suck in a breath. Huge, black AirTrans are flying over the city, teeming with Making Perfect soldiers ready to drop down like spiders. I can see two enormous firebombs strapped to each side.

No. Not yet. This can't be happening. They're early!

I stare at them until they disappear from sight. Hope ignites inside me. Maybe they're targeting a different area. That'll give us a little more time. But just as that thought forms in my head, I see one of the transports circle back into view.

I grab Blayze's wrist and take off as fast as I can toward Tyler's building. Our thick boots pound the pavement as we run. The first bomb hits the second we reach his entrance.

The ground shakes violently under my feet. I grab a pole for support. I can see the ball of fire only a street away. The screams start, piercing the night as soldiers drop out of the AirTran. I watch them lower into the city on thin black cables, their guns swinging menacingly by their sides. The fire is moving quickly toward us. It must be a Spark weapon—no normal fire moves that quickly. The AirTran flies over to our left, preparing to drop another bomb.

Fighting to keep my balance, I dart into the building, Blayze right on my tail. We probably have about five minutes until this whole area is completely engulfed by the fire.

"We have to hurry," I say to him, dashing toward the stairs. Tyler's apartment is on the eighth floor. I glance out the front window. The soldiers have already started to move down the street toward the building. They're almost here. They look like lizards, the way their armor layers onto their bodies like scales. Their faces are covered by thick gas masks. It's hard to see them—their black gear blends right into the night. I wonder how many of them I know.

Trying not to panic, I start up the stairs. But Blayze grabs my arm, stopping me.

"Wait," he says. "We don't have time. Go upstairs and find them. I'll buy you some time. Meet me in the alley." I stand there frozen, and the urgency grows in his eyes. "Hurry!"

"What? Don't be stupid." I shake my head, tugging on his arm and turning back to the stairs. But he doesn't budge. He's serious. My insides twist. "We're not splitting up!"

Blayze shakes his head, grabbing my shoulders. "Summer listen to me. We won't make it. They'll corner us upstairs." He glances over his shoulder. "Leave out the back entrance, and I'll meet you there. I promise."

My stomach jumps to my throat. *I promise.* My dad's face pops into my mind—he also made me a promise one night. A promise that he never kept. I won't let it happen again.

"No! Please just come!" I protest desperately. I see a group of black-clad soldiers approaching the door, guns pointed. We only have seconds. My entire body is screaming at me to run. "Blayze just come with me!"

"I can't. Now go quickly, or neither of us is getting out."

Torn nearly apart, I shove my hands in my pockets. I know he's right. Unless one of us stays to hold them off, we won't even make it upstairs. But the way he's looking at me right now, his big, brown puppy-dog eyes stretched wide, makes me want to knock him out and drag him with me.

But I don't. Instead, I grab his shirt, lean up on my toes, and kiss him. My breath is caught in my throat. Forget butterflies. No.

I have a herd of elephants stampeding through my stomach. His body stiffens for a second, his eyes growing even wider.

Taking a deep breath, I pull away from him. "I'll see you soon, okay, moron? Be there," I say. Without waiting for an answer, I turn and run up the stairs, taking two at a time, the giddiness spreading in my chest quickly replaced by a bitter dread.

I can feel the fire approaching by the time I reach Tyler's room. A hint of smoke is already floating through the air. When I push through the door, Lily is sitting on the bed.

When she sees me, her face lights up. A wave of relief falls over me. She's alive. I run to her and scoop her up in my arms, squeezing her so hard she groans.

"God, Lil, I've missed you so much," I say.

"Me too, Sum," she replies. "But you reek." I laugh. She looks different. Older. Her hair is shorter, her glasses are gone, and she's dressed in black instead of her usual bright colors. When she lets go of me, her face is set with determination. I guess Tyler has already filled her in.

"Tyler and Tory left with Michael about five minutes ago," she explains. "I stayed here to make sure you didn't freak out when you couldn't find us." She knows I totally would've. "I'm sorry if we gave you a scare by moving our stuff here. Once we found out Tyler was taken, we moved to make sure Michael and Riley were okay. Riley didn't make it through the winter—Red Pox took her pretty quickly. But Tory toughed it out. She's not doing great, but hopefully once we get to the rebels, she'll be okay." Lily is remarkably calm, given she's only known about the escape for ten minutes. Much calmer than I would've been.

There is a loud crash downstairs, and I instinctively crouch. The fire must be here already. At this rate, it won't take long to destroy the whole city. Without a word, I grab Lily's hand and pull her out into the hallway. There's more smoke coming into the building now, and I have to cup my sleeve over my mouth to try and filter it out. Lily does the same.

"Where's Theo?" My voice strains to be heard as we run. Blayze said he'd meet us at the back entrance. How does he even know where that is? Tyler's building doesn't have any fire escapes—otherwise, it would be easy to get out quick. We have to take the back staircase out into the alley. I open the door and usher Lily through.

"Tory has him," she says as it closes behind us. Hoping that the fire hasn't cut off this exit yet, Lily and I tear down the stairs. There's a loud noise through the wall, and I'm suddenly scared for Blayze. I don't know what I'll do if he gets taken again.

There's so much smoke in the hallway that I can barely breathe. My eyes tear up, and I squint to try and see the steps in front of me. Gusts of heat are bouncing off the walls, searing everything in their path. I practically trip over Lily as we exit the building. The air is thick with the smoke and heat from other burning buildings, but it's breathable. It feels like I'm coughing my lungs out. I look up at the building, and a pang of regret hits my chest. It is completely engulfed in flames. If we had stayed upstairs for much longer, we wouldn't have been able to get out.

I duck behind the closest Dumpster as a squad of soldiers walks by, pulling Lily down with me. She is completely silent as I watch them. As soon as they're out of sight, she turns to me.

"What are you waiting for? Let's go. We have to meet Tyler at the statue." She stands up, and I pull her back down, looking around. Where is Blayze?

I hear someone coughing in the staircase and my heart leaps. But when they emerge onto the street, I bite my lip. It's not Blayze. A boy in a black jacket and a backward baseball cap comes running out, dragging a small boy by the hand who appears to be his little brother. I vaguely recognize them—they live two floors down from Tyler, and the little boy used to come up to play with Michael. As soon as they get outside, the boy with the baseball cap picks up his brother, who is coughing so hard you'd think he's screaming, and looks around for any soldiers. Seeing none, they take off toward the opening of the alley. I hear the roar of a van approaching and tighten my fists.

Don't go out there—turn around and take cover before they see you! I want to scream out at them, but I hold my tongue. If I make any noise, they'll catch us too.

Just as the soldiers come into view, I cup my hand over Lily's mouth. I feel her gasp. She looks at me with pleading eyes, and I wish more than anything that she didn't have to see this.

The soldiers corner the two boys. The taller one clutches his little brother tightly to his chest. The van drives up, stopping next to the entrance. I crouch down lower and press my body against the Dumpster. There's nothing I can do to help them. As the soldiers raise their guns, I look away. The shots are fired. First one, then more. When I finally glance up, the two unconscious boys are being hauled into the van.

That little boy isn't a test kid. Why are they capturing all the little ones, too? The horrors they have in store for these two makes my skin crawl. I try not to think about it as the van rolls away.

Damn it. I should've done something.

Guilt claws away at my chest, but I ignore it. I have to stay focused.

I take my hand off Lily's mouth as the van rumbles out of sight and the soldiers clear out. She stares at the opening of the alley for a long moment before looking at me. Her face has hardened. It looks like mine.

"We have to move. We're not going to get there otherwise," she says to me, standing up. I hear another crashing sound from Tyler's building. She's right. If we stay much longer, we're never going to make it to the statue.

Come on, Blayze. Hurry.

Lily pulls me up and starts running down the alley. I look up the staircase. It's smoking so badly now that I can't see into it at all. But Blayze is still in there. If he was okay, he would've been outside by now.

"Summer!"

I can't go in. I've got to stay with Lily.

But he would do it for me.

Wow, I'm such an idiot.

"Wait here; I'll be right back," I say to Lily.

"What are you talking about? Summer, get back—"

I leap out from behind the Dumpster, throw myself into the building and run up the stairs. The smoke is so thick, it sears my lungs. I can barely breathe through the sleeve of my tracksuit, but I still plow up the stairs. My eyes squint around, and I try to concentrate on taking small breaths. Every piece of exposed skin is starting to sting.

Where would he be? I left him in the lobby, but if he was still there the soldiers would've taken care of him. He said he would distract them…Damn it, he could be anywhere.

"Blayze!" I shout, trying to make my voice heard over the crackle of the flames. I reach the sixth floor, but when I try to open the door, I jerk my hand away from the red-hot metal. When I try to go up the stairs again, I'm met by a wall of fire. One of the flames licks my shin, and I jump back in pain. "Blayze!" I call his name, louder this time. "Where are you?" My voice feels raw.

He must be near the lobby. I run back down the steps to the first floor, tripping over the last one and landing on my knees. I try to hold my breath, taking in as little smoke as possible. But before I can get to the main landing, I'm stopped by more fire.

The lobby is right through this wall. I feel energy surging through me as I back up to escape the flames and throw my body into the plaster. The wall dents, and I do it again, channeling all of my remaining energy. With a cry, I break through and stumble into the lobby. The whole room has been transformed by flame and smoke—it's completely unrecognizable. There's a loud crack above me, and I look up just in time to get out of the way as a flaming rafter crashes down in a shower of sparks. The side of it hits my arm, and I cry out, covering the burn with my other hand.

My throat and nose are burning so much that they feel as if they themselves are on fire.

Where is he?

I don't have much time. The entrance is blocked by a wall of fire that looks impenetrable. If we're going to get out of here, I only have minutes.

"Blayze?" My voice is raspier. My breaths have now become painful. I'm almost at the point of losing hope when I hear it.

"Summer!" Blayze's voice is weak and barely audible above the roar of the fire. I turn around, trying to catch where the sound is coming from. Another rafter falls, crashing to the floor. He calls out again. I turn to the side, starting toward his voice.

I don't make it two steps before something rams into my side and knocks me off my feet. It feels like I was just hit by a train. A cry escapes my lips as I stumble over, fighting hard to stay upright and not fall into the flames. I look around in a frenzied panic and see Blayze standing only a few feet away from me, almost fully surrounded by fire. He looks terrible. There is a thick gash on his cheek, and it's oozing blood down his face and neck. Soot covers every square inch of his body, rendering him almost unrecognizable. I run over to him, dodging a falling rafter.

"Blayze! We have to go!" I snap at him, but he doesn't budge. Anger bubbles up in my chest, but quickly vanishes as he falls to his knees. I drop down, grabbing his face in my hands. His forehead falls limply against my chest. "Blayze." He moans softly but stays still. Every fiber of my being is telling me to run, but my body won't budge.

The fire is creeping closer to us, and I can feel the heat searing my bare skin. My chest tightening, I slip my arm around Blayze's waist. I pull the neck of his shirt up over his mouth and make him hold it, careful not to press too hard into the cut. He is so weak that I am practically the only thing holding him up. I try to cover my own mouth at the same time.

The flames are nearly on top of us now. We have only seconds left. But when we start forward, back the way I came, another piece of the building falls down in front of us, blocking our path.

I grit my teeth and help him over the flaming piece of debris. He is coughing hard. I'm afraid he'll pass out completely. There's no way we can go out the way I came—every path is probably blocked by now. We go back into the lobby, and I look around. Every entrance is concealed by fire. There's no way we can get out without going through it.

Through the fire.

Blayze starts to fall, and I tighten my grip on him. It takes all of my strength to keep him standing.

"Hold on to me," I call loudly. If he hears me, he doesn't show it. Squeezing my eyes shut and balling my hands into fists, I run forward into the fire, pulling a stumbling Blayze with me.

I resist the urge to cry out as the flames lap my body. It only takes seconds but feels like minutes. We're through. The second we exit the building into clean air, the burning quells. My breaths are quick and rapid as I cough uncontrollably, overcome by the smoke.

My arms tremble as I set Blayze down against the nearest wall. There are no soldiers on this street—they must've assumed everyone has either left or is dead by now.

I shake Blayze's shoulders, ripping off a piece of my tracksuit and pressing it against the gash. "Come on, wake up," I say, checking his pulse. It's there, but it's weak. He finally stirs and his eyes blink open. A series of deep coughs rip through him as he fights for air. My head spins, and I want to collapse on the ground. But one glance down the street at the approaching fire tells me that I can't. Blayze looks up at me. My face is scrunched up in anger.

"I'm never letting you make the plans again! You almost got us both killed."

When he opens his cracked lips to speak, his voice comes out raspy. "I didn't know the fire could travel that fast." His eyes are twinkling. In any normal circumstance, my anger would be genuine, but I'm just so relieved he's okay that it doesn't matter.

I lean my head against his shoulder, sighing deeply. I'm so tired. He pulls me closer to him, gently brushing the loose strands of hair out of my face.

We can't rest long. The fire is spreading through the Slump. Slipping my arm around Blayze's waist, I help him up with a heave. We start to make our way to the alley when I hear a scream.

"Summer!" My stomach tightens as I hear Lily's voice. I let go of Blayze and run back around the building to find her shouting profanities into the entrance of the staircase, her face puffy. The fire is leaping to the next building over her head in huge swirls. She turns around and sees me, her face twisted with rage.

"What the *hell*." she exclaims, storming up to me. "Why did you do that to me? Just leaving me here with nothing more than 'I'll be right back.' Are you *kidding* me?" Blayze limps up beside me. She stops and takes a step back, looking at him with a confused expression. "Who's he?"

Before I can respond, I hear an AirTran pass over our heads. I know they are strategically placing the bombs to round us all together for one mass capture, so we have to go in the other direction.

I watch the AirTran hover a few streets over. Another firebomb drops from the wing, plummeting down to the ground. But before it hits, Lily, Blayze, and I are already running toward the statue as fast as we can.

42

A voiding the soldiers in the maze of fire proves easier than I thought. They want to stay away from the flames, too. Blayze and I are too beaten up to run very fast, so we take a few breaks. The fire seems to be pushing us in the direction of the market, which serves our purposes well. The fire in Tyler's building put us behind schedule. We reach the statue just after five thirty. By the time we get there, my head is pounding.

There are soldiers in this area, although thankfully not on this street. When we reach the statue, my stomach sinks. No one is here. Kace probably left with Tyler, Tory, and Michael and didn't wait for us.

What do we do now?

I look past the statue. Kace said the opening in the fence was five minutes from here. If we move fast enough, we can get to the fence before the fire cuts us off. It'll hopefully be easy to find.

I glance at Blayze and Lily, who are looking at me questioningly.

"What do you want to do?" Blayze asks me, and I shrug, rubbing my eyes. They sting from soot.

"Maybe we try to find them at the fence? I'm sure if we go..." My voice trails off as I catch movement out of the corner of my eye.

Two figures dressed in black slink out of the alley. I stiffen. They don't look like Making Perfect soldiers. Their armor is much thinner. I push Lily behind me as they get closer, and I am just getting ready to bolt when they step into the light and I see their faces. I heave a sigh of relief. It's Kace, followed closely by Aaron.

Thank *God.*

"You're late," Kace growls.

"You waited." I brush aside his comment. He looks at the three of us for a second, his eyes lingering on the dried blood and soot in Blayze's gash. His brow knits together, but his expression softens slightly when he sees Lily.

"Is this the other one?" he asks, gesturing at Lily. Obviously, the others have already made it through safely. I nod, and Lily crosses her arms.

"Um, excuse me, *the other one* has a name. *The other one* is right *here*—" Lily snaps.

Kace sniggers at me. "Wow, it's another you. Exactly what we need." I purse my lips. Aaron looks at us with a faintly amused smile on his face. He opens his mouth to say something when a dart whizzes by my head. I duck. A squad of soldiers have come into view, their guns pointed at us as they run across the street. Springing into action, Aaron fires at them. Unlike the soldiers' guns, his has real bullets.

"Go!" Aaron shouts. His bullet hits one in the chest, but it just bounces off. Their armor seems impervious. "Kace, take them to the others." Kace yanks me forward, and we all dash past the statue and in the direction of the market. After a few more failed shots, Aaron takes off after us.

The buildings on this street are on fire and will probably be engulfed within minutes.

"Go, go!" Aaron shouts after us, and we quicken our pace, bolting down the sidewalk as fast as we can. I reach back to grab Lily's arm but find that she's right beside me. I have no idea where I'm going, so I just follow Kace as he leads us through the streets. The soldiers stay on our tails. Darts whiz by our heads. I push my legs to move even faster. We *have* to make it.

A couple more streets, and my legs are about to give out. I grab Blayze's hand.

Then it happens.

The firebomb.

I didn't see it coming—I don't think any of us did. This one hit too close.

Everything explodes at once. The concussion lifts us off our feet, sending us flying in different directions. Blayze's hand rips out of mine, and I'm flung back into the side of the nearest building. All the air is knocked out of me, and a searing pain rips through my head as I collapse to the pavement.

Blackness spots my vision, and searing heat flushes over me like a blanket. I try to refill my lungs, but the smoke is thick and I immediately begin coughing. I force my eyes open. My ears are ringing so loudly that I can't even hear the fire. Everything is completely muffled. The flames are now so close that I feel as if I can reach out and touch them. They're everywhere, pinning me to the wall and traveling down the street. I try to summon the energy to get up, but my body doesn't budge. The fire creeps closer.

Where's Lily?

I scream and throw myself upward, staggering forward out of reach of the flames. I barely make it two steps before I'm back on the ground, a searing pain shooting through my leg. I look down and see a piece of shrapnel sticking out of my thigh. I pull it out and gasp at the sight of my hands. They're completely pink. Patches of skin are turning black, and blisters are popping up all over. My brain seems to just now register the pain, and I cry out, stumbling backward and almost falling right back into the fire when someone catches me. It's Aaron.

He spins me around to face him, holding me upright by my shoulders. I can tell he's talking to me, but I can't hear him. My ears don't seem to be working.

The fire shoots out and brushes the sleeve of Aaron's jacket. He grabs my upper arm, pulling me forward. I try to regain my senses as we run out of the flames. I am staggering, half-carried by Aaron.

We reach the DNA statue again. The fire is closing in. There are no soldiers in sight. I'm breathing heavily, struggling to catch my breath.

"Where's Lily? Where's Blayze?" I wheeze, the ringing in my ears slowly receding. He looks over his shoulder, back to where we came from.

"Kace has them. I lost them after the explosion. He will make sure they get out." The confidence in his eyes is convincing. "We'll meet them on the other side of the fence."

"But aren't we going the wrong way?" I say, my voice too loud. It's so raspy that it's painful to talk. "We have to go back in that direction if we're going to make it out." Aaron nods.

"We'll have to go around it. It'll be pushing us closer to where they want us to be, but we'll stay as close to the border as possible and move fast."

"Okay."

He looks down at my hands and grimaces but doesn't say anything. There's nothing he can do for them anyway.

He takes off down the street toward the market, and I follow. I grit my teeth so tightly that my jaw hurts.

Only a little bit longer.

We cut straight down to the market, trying to outmaneuver the fast-moving fire. I start to smell the trash from a couple streets away—it's much worse than I remember, if such a thing is possible.

I don't know if it's the burning or the accumulation. Aaron doesn't seem to notice.

Just before we hit the market, Aaron and I turn back in the direction of the fence. It's only a few blocks away. I trip on a pothole, stumble forward, and almost fall into him. He barely glances back to make sure I'm okay. As he moves, I can't help but notice how dignified he is. Even in this situation, surrounded by panic, he somehow manages to keep his senses about him. I admire him. It's so hard to believe that he's only a few years older than I am—I could never have the guts to do what he does.

The fence comes into view. We're going to make it. Just then, my stomach lurches as a squad of soldiers appears in front of us, blocking our path. I look around for any possible way to evade them. There's none. Aaron spins on a dime, grabbing my arm and pulling me along with him as he darts into the side street leading to the market. We get a head start, but the soldiers are fast. A dart hits my back, and I wince but keep running. My head spins slightly.

We turn the corner but are met by another group of soldiers. Aaron doesn't even bother raising his gun, knowing it wouldn't make a difference. I look around for possible escape routes, my eyes resting on a narrow pathway cutting deeper into the city. I recognize it immediately. We are at the market.

Going in there makes me nervous. It's too open and has few hiding places, but we have no choice. Before any more darts can be fired our way, we quickly dash into the alley and into the market. Running out into the open space, I glance back to make sure Aaron is still with me and find him standing completely still. What's he doing? We're almost at the fence!

But he just stands there, looking around at the market with a confused expression.

I tug his arm.

"Aaron, what's going on?" I plead. "We've got to move; we're almost at the fence. Why did you stop?"

He doesn't look at me. Fear grows in my chest. "We didn't lose them. Look around; this is exactly where they want us to be."

I look around. Around the clearing, huddled in clumps and in the shadows, are over a thousand people. They're not running. Why aren't they running? I study the entrances. Nothing seems out of place until I catch the flickers of movement. Soldiers are everywhere. It takes me a minute to understand what Aaron is saying, but then it sinks in. My breathing quickens.

This is Making Perfect's capture ground.

It makes sense. This is really the only place big enough to fit this many bodies. They were luring us here to take us all at once.

My heart is pounding so hard it hurts.

I take off as fast as I can toward the nearest exit. I need to get out of here. I can't stay and wait for them to come and take me back. I *can't*.

I jump over the pile of rubble and plow forward to the street. There is no other way to get out—the area around the market is now completely engulfed in flames. I get to one of the openings but soldiers are there, firing darts at me as I run. Another dart hits my shoulder, and the second I get back onto the street, the fire is there to meet me. I stop. The fire roars as it approaches, and I just stare up at it. What I wouldn't give to be able to run through it. Blayze and Lily are somewhere on the other side.

I can't go back in there. I can't go back to Making Perfect. The soldiers come up behind me, and I stand my ground.

Maybe this isn't the only way out. Maybe I can go through the buildings. If we go forward, maybe we can find a way to the fence. I don't care if I have to climb that fence with my bare hands.

One of the lizard-like soldiers makes a swipe for me, and I spin around, throwing my leg out and kicking the soldier right in the knee. He doesn't make a sound, but his knee buckles inward and he collapses.

Wiggling between them, I dash back into the market, pushing past people to get to the other side. As I pass Aaron I grab his arm, pulling him along with me and ignoring the pain shooting up from my hands. I catch him off guard, and he staggers forward.

"We have to get out this way," I urge as I drag him. "We can shoot our way out, get to the fence, and head back to the opening. I'm sure the fire hasn't stretched all the way there yet."

He stops, yanking me back. There is genuine fear in his eyes.

"Summer, stop. It won't work," he tells me. "I've already tried. There are just as many soldiers waiting for us on that side."

I can't believe it. We walked *right into* their trap!

"But there has to be another way. There *has to* be!" I look at the garbage pile and try to think of an effective way to hide in there. Just then, one of the bags on the side of the pile catches on fire. The flame travels until the entire pile is burning, casting a rancid smell over the whole square. I can't take it anymore. My hands hurt so badly that I can't move them. The serum is beginning to take effect, and my body begins to shake. I'm going back to Making Perfect. Back to the place that has caused me so much pain and suffering. The place that, ultimately, wants me dead.

I can't go back there, I think. *Who knows what they're going to do with me once they find out I escaped?*

I wrap my arms around my chest and squeeze my eyes shut, rocking back and forth slightly. I bite the end of my sleeve, clamping my teeth around it and sending a stabbing pain through my head.

This isn't happening. Please, let me be dreaming. It must've been the smoke. I passed out because of the bomb, and Ian now seeing things. I am safe with the others in TERC. Lily, Tory, and Tyler are safe. Blayze is right beside me with his signature trouble-maker smile on his face.

More people are piling into the clearing. I want to scream at them to turn around while they still can, but I know it's pointless. We don't have anywhere to go. If I try to run now, the soldiers will just push me right back in. The fire has trapped us from all sides. There's nowhere to hide. Soldiers patrol the perimeter, tracking our every move.

Suddenly, a bright white light is cast down on us and I look up. Three monstrous AirTrans are hovering overhead, coming down slowly until they're about twenty feet off the ground. Their doors open, revealing large, empty Dumpster-like canisters that they will use to take our unconscious bodies back to their facilities. I feel like I'm in a slaughterhouse. The light from the AirTrans burns my eyes. I squint, seeing soldiers close in around us like lions around their prey. The fire closes in around the market, trapping us in completely.

A soldier comes a little too close for comfort, and I slam my elbow into his chest. I try to slip around toward the rubble, but he slams the butt of his gun into my shoulder, and I back up into Aaron. It's pointless. I'm never going to get out of here.

Aaron and I weave through the tightly packed people away from the soldiers. We reach the garbage, and I try to slow my breathing. My nose seems to have gotten used to the stench, so I don't even smell the burning trash. The pile has gotten bigger since I was last here…it's even more disgusting than I remember. I look over at Aaron, who hasn't said a word this whole time. He's got a small square device in his hand, identical to Kace's, and is typing what I assume is a message to the rebels. His expression is tight, but he doesn't let the panic overcome him. He slips his gun back into his belt, giving up.

This must be just as hard for Aaron as it is for me. Taking a deep breath, he pulls something else out of a pocket on his wrist. I squint at it. It's a white pill about the size of my fingernail. I stare at it for a minute as he turns it over in his fingers until I realize what it is. It's his "kill pill."

I've heard of these but have never seen one before. Of course Aaron would have one. When Making Perfect realizes who he is…I shudder to think of the horrors he'd be put through.

The soldiers close in tighter, and I swallow hard, trying to retain my composure. I glance over at Aaron's pill and want more than anything to snatch it from his fingers and swallow it myself. I look up at him. He meets my gaze. I think I see sadness in his eyes.

"Make them pay for it, okay?" His voice is soft, but his eyes are full of fire. I nod, looking out at the soldiers surrounding us. They raise their guns. Aaron pops his pill into his mouth. I squeeze my eyes shut, tears streaming down my face.

Please, let the others get out okay.

Darts fall from the sky like rain, coming from both the soldiers and the AirTrans. The pain is immediate but nonexistent at the same time. Darts sink into me. People are falling and collapsing all over me, screams muffled by the whir of the AirTrans. So much serum is coursing through my veins that I drop to the ground, all of my energy drained away. Aaron collapses beside me, his body twitching for mere seconds before he falls still, eyes rolling back into his head. I don't even have to check his breathing to know he's dead. I look away.

The lights from the AirTrans get brighter as they descend so close to the ground that they're almost touching the top of the garbage pile. The heat from the fire must be dying down. I can't feel it at all anymore. I gag. The acid burns the inside of my mouth, but I grit my teeth, rolling around to try and stop the pain.

Then my world is swept out from under me, throwing me into a pit of endless darkness.

43

KACE

I haven't slept for days. Since arriving here, actually. I don't think anyone has.

I wring my hands together nervously as I listen to Ridge talk. He had us brought into this conference room first thing this morning. It's been twelve hours, and he still hasn't released us. A yawn stretches over my lips, and I force my eyes to stay open.

Next to me, even Callie seems close to losing it. Her fingers tap nervously on the tabletop, her hair pulled back carelessly into a ponytail. Although her gaze is dutifully trained on Ridge, the heavy bags under her eyes betray her exhaustion. Of course, she refuses to show it.

Sterling, Maggie, and Tyler sit on the other side of the table. Sterling's energy seems bottomless. He continues to drink in every single one of Ridge's words. Tyler is obviously trying to keep up, but since he was just released from the medical wing this morning and called straight in here, he's fading quickly. The two of them were lucky that they got out before the fire had time to spread. It's even luckier that I was able to get out with Blayze and Lily. We barely made it through the fence before the fire closed off the street entirely. Lily sustained minimal burns. Blayze wasn't so lucky. He has been in intensive care since our arrival. The few times he's regained consciousness, he's been in a state of delirium. His burns were severe, along with his levels of smoke inhalation and scorching from the bomb. He's in stable condition, but the TERC medics have him on so many drugs that he can't form any coherent thoughts. He exists in such a state of panic that anytime he wakes up, they end up having to put him under again. He doesn't know about Summer yet, and I don't want to be the one to tell him. It's been hard enough on Tyler, Lily, and Tory.

Flame has also been in intensive care. She wasn't hurt, as she was able to escape with most of the other rebels, but the medics are trying to undo what Making Perfect did to her brain. It's a slow process, and I don't know much about her prognosis.

"Kace?" Ridge addresses me, and I snap my head up. "What's your input?"

I shake my head to clear it. I don't even know what we're talking about. This isn't like me. "It sounds good." Ridge narrows his eyes at me, knowing I'm clueless, and moves on to his next point. I am worried about him. Ever since he took control of the group after hearing about Aaron, he's been acting strange. He's working himself sick, staying up all hours of the night: making plans, talking with the TERC officials, or simply sitting. I think Aaron's death has been much harder on him than he would like to admit.

Tex grumbles something under his breath, and I glance at him. Tex Warren is one of the TERC representatives assigned to oversee our meetings. He is probably around forty, with coal-black hair and beady eyes. He hasn't been a fan of ours since day one. Since Aaron was the one who made the deal with TERC about letting us temporarily stay in their region, they weren't happy when we arrived without him. We were brought to the center of the city instead of the border facility we originally planned on staying at. We're being kept here until further notice. We're not technically prisoners, but it feels like we are. We're under constant supervision, and TERC appears to be deciding what to do with us. Now that the Slump has burned down, we have nowhere to go. Thankfully, they're taking a while to make up their minds.

Ridge seems to realize he's losing our attention and sighs, minimizing the screen and slipping the tablet pen behind his ear. He waves his hand in the air, adjourning the meeting without a word. Callie stops to tell him a few things on her way out, giving his arm a squeeze. I walk out hesitantly, glancing back at him through the thick glass wall. He collapses in a chair, hiding his face in his hands.

The news that TERC has agreed to let us stay comes early the next morning. So early, in fact, that Ridge calls a select handful of us to join him and a slew of TERC executives, including the CEO, Patina Carter, into the conference room to deliver the news. I am so relieved that I want to jump for joy.

But there are things we must do. TERC has a long list of requirements that have to be met if we are to reside in this region. Also, because we're from Making Perfect, we will all be required to go through interrogation and quarantine. We will all become legal citizens of TERC, and those of us that are of eligible age will be required to either become soldiers or work in another capacity. Our families will be cared for through TERC, and we will be treated as full-fledged members of the society.

"The horrors that Making Perfect has been carrying out are unacceptable. No region should have that kind of power over its people or over any other region," Patina Carter explains in a sharp tone. She looks tough. Her dark skin is in sharp contrast to her pale-blue eyes. Her voice commands attention. "TERC must take a stand. We will unite the regions and put a stop to Making Perfect's barbaric practices. We've grown apart for too long. This nation needs to band together to ensure this never happens again." I lean forward in my seat. Callie sucks in a breath. Patina smiles and says the words I've been hoping for since we arrived.

"We're ready to fight. Be ready to join us."

44

Making Perfect saved you.
If it weren't for Making Perfect, you'd be dead.
Making Perfect wants to protect you.
It's because of Making Perfect that you're still alive.

A chill runs through my body, and I tug against my thick leather restraints. The electrodes on my head and chest feel like they're burning through my skin. I try to push the words out of my head, but they are rooted there. When I try to scream, no sound comes out.

Making Perfect is always there for you.
You must protect it like it protects you.
Making Perfect is your home.

My body goes slack. There's an incessant beeping sound.

The resistance betrayed you.
If it weren't for them, your sisters would be here too.
Your sisters would be safe.
It's your fault.
You should've never trusted them.

I suck in a breath.

Everything will be all right.
Making Perfect is your family now.

And I open my eyes.

Acknowledgements

Turning this story into the book you hold in your hands has been a long, but remarkable adventure. It is the product of many (really) late nights, five full rewrites, and the relentless support and help of some truly amazing people. No words can express how extraordinarily grateful I am to everyone who has been a part of this journey and even if you don't find yourself in these pages, here's a resounding THANK YOU! I couldn't have done it without you.

A few people deserve special mention.

My dear friend Marlin Cosar whose honest feedback, from the earliest stages of developing this story, always kept me on the right track. You have been there from the start. Thank you for the hours of laughter, conversation, and most of all, thank you for our long friendship. This book is so much better because of you.

Léna Roy, for teaching me how to edit. You created a monster, and it's a wonder I'm finally letting this story go.

My wonderful teacher and mentor, Casey Erin Clark. Thank you for helping me find my voice and the fearlessness to pursue my other passion, musical theatre. You made me believe that I could.

My grandparents, Mormor, Morfar, Glen and Grandad. Thank you for always reading my stories (even the ones nobody should've been subjected to). You are the best grandparents ever and I'm so grateful for your unwavering faith in me.

My little brother, Tristan, for being the world's goofiest best friend I could hope for. I love you bud.

Thanks to Destination Imagination for teaching me "if it doesn't say you can't, you can!", Starbucks for being the perfect sustenance for long writing days, my best friends (you know who you are) who are always there for me, and Jo March for inspiring me to be brave enough to share this story with the world.

But most of all, I want to thank the two amazing people that I'm lucky enough to call my parents. Mum and Papa, you fill my life with love, fun, adventure and laughter, always encouraging me to follow my passions and never setting limits on what I can accomplish. You taught me to take risks, to own being different and to make my life instead of simply living it. Papa, thank you so much for the hours you spent listening to me talk about this story—I am BEYOND grateful. Mummy, thank you for always hearing me, loving me, and putting up with my constant antics. You two are the best support system a girl could ask for. Thank you for guiding me through these incredible sixteen years and always having my back. I love you so much.

Claire Fraise began writing *Imperfect* as a high school freshman. She lives in Connecticut with her parents and younger brother.

In addition to writing, Fraise is passionate about musical theater, is an obsessive reader, loves playing the piano and guitar and cuddling her two rescue dogs. *Imperfect* is her debut novel.

Made in the USA
Middletown, DE
16 October 2015